The Nothing Girl

by

Patricia Grigg

Grigg Publishing, LLC ~ Arizona ~ USA

Grigg Publishing, LLC
P.O. Box 6154
Peoria, AZ 85381

ISBN-13: 978-1-62555-001-9

This story is a work of fiction. Names, characters, places, and incidents are either a product of the author's imagination, or used fictitiously. Any resemblance to actual persons, living or dead, events, or places is entirely coincidental.

Printed in the United States of America

First Edition, 2017
Edited by Dianna Grigg
www.griggpublishing.com

This book is dedicated to my children.

To John Grigg, Theresa McClure and Joseph Grigg, who have been so supportive and encouraging.

They are the joy of my life.

Acknowledgements

There are many people to whom I just want to hug and say Thank You.

Foremost are my children John, Theresa and Joseph who have pushed me into finally submitting one of my manuscripts. John on the business end always there for me. Theresa who was perhaps my first reader, always showing such joy at every word. Joseph, quietly being there for me all the way.

My sister, Priscilla, who sat and listened to my stories, and brought me laughter. Robert, my brother, has always been in my corner no matter what life threw at us. Jo Carole for just being herself.

A very special thanks to Ray Bilcliff and his wonderful talent for photography. From day one his photos have inspired me. Thank you Ray. You can find out more about Ray at his site. www.trueportraits.com

Finally, my dear friend Les. You told me not to mention you, but you always have been encouraging and supportive. I know you didn't want it, but you get it anyway. Thank you Les.

Over the years people have read parts of books and been encouraging, you know who you are.

To all of you many thanks.

Chapter One

HAVEN

Policewoman Raglan parked in front of the wooden building. She looked in the rearview mirror at the young girl in the back seat of her squad car. Her lips became thin lines as she thought of what this fifteen or sixteen year old girl had been subject to in her short life. If they ever found the men who had brutalized the child she hoped she was there. Then Raglan shook her head at the thoughts she was having. No, shooting was too good for them.

"This is it, Sweetie," Raglan said as she unbuckled her seatbelt and opened the car door. "It is called Haven. The nice people inside will take care of you, see to it you get to school safely and back. There is nothing to fear ever again."

Raglan sighed within as the girl didn't bother to look at her, merely nodded as if accepting the situation. "Come on, Honey," Raglan said, opening the back door of the squad car, and offering her hand to help the girl out.

Felith scrambled from the police car to avoid being touched. She kept her eyes half hooded, non-threatening, non-existing. Her whole manner saying don't notice me, I'm not here. Obediently she walked beside the policewoman up the steps of the front porch to the house. The door to the house swung open with a bang. Felith made her mind go gray as she watched the tall thin man standing in the doorway.

"Officer," Mr. Shadman said, nodding to Policewoman Raglan. He looked at the girl who stood slightly behind Officer Raglan up and down, a frown on his face as if he disapproved of her already. "Is she going to give us trouble here?" he asked Raglan.

"No, I don't think so. She hasn't spoken to us. But all the trauma…," she broke off, her face reddening with fury deep inside at the men who had raped Felith. She had been one of the officers who responded to the call of an explosion where the girl had been found. Clearly she had been gang raped. From what the doctors had told her this wasn't the first time it had happened to the child. The stepfather was gone. Nobody in the neighborhood knew of any relatives. In fact the neighbors claimed to not have known the child was living in the house. The mother had either run off, or just disappeared, leaving the girl with that perverted thing she had married. What mother did that to their child, just go off and leave a little kid like that? And the scars on this child both physically and mentally…. Raglan broke off thinking about it. "She has been through enough. Keep her safe," Raglan barked in her most official manner.

Shadman's frown deepened. "You do know she is too old for it to be likely she will be adopted? Schooling is another problem. From what you said in your call to me, she may not have any book learning at all. She is small for her age, so we might get away with placing her in a lower grade. But, I doubt she'll be adopted, or make much of herself."

Eyes half hooded, Felith stood as if they weren't talking about her right in front of her. She didn't speak, didn't offer facial expression, but she did listen. They thought she was stupid. It was that plain and simple. Just because she was small and dirtied, that made her stupid to them. Then the policewoman made an angry gesture. Fel drew on the strength of will and blocked them out. The gray settled her so she didn't appear afraid, didn't flinch.

"Don't treat her as if she is some dummy. If I find out you aren't giving her every opportunity to advance I'll return," Raglan's eyes narrowed. "You won't be happy if I return. Do you understand?" she said resting her hand briefly on her gun, then she glanced at Felith. "Go on inside, honey. I'm sure they have a hot meal for you," she told Felith gently, watching as she went up the steps and through the doorway. "If she needs anything you call me first," Officer Raglan said as Felith entered the house.

Stepping inside the house Felith froze for a moment. It looked as if kids were everywhere. The kids were clean too. Well, except for a small girl with something smeared all over her face. The child looked the image of mischief as she licked a big spoon covered in the same dark mess that was on her face.

"Middy!" a female voice bellowed out from what Felith took as the kitchen. The little imp twisted her arm behind her trying to hide the spoon. Of course the spoon was sticking up behind her in plain sight. "Middy, bring me that spoon right now, or there will be no cake for you, young lady." Middy rolled her eyes, then stomped her way back into the kitchen.

Over in a corner a boy, not much older than Felith, was entertaining two small children. Felith stood just inside the doorway watching as the boy waved his hands in a weird pattern in the air. Flowers suddenly seemed to appear from nowhere in his hand. The children applauded with glee. Magic, thought Felith. She had read of it, read books of great Magi who did marvelous things with their minds and a few waves of their hands or magic wands. So this boy was a Magi. Someone powerful, someone to stay away from.

Two teenage girls were looking at Felith as she looked around the room. When Fel felt their gaze she went back to not looking, not being. It was the way you survived.

The door shutting behind her made the shutters in Felith's mind snap tightly shut. The frowning man-monster took hold of Felith's upper arm and moved her more into the house. "Listen up," he said, and waited for the room to quiet down before continuing. "This is our newest addition. Welcome her to our home."

"Welcome," rang out from the children around

the room.

"Robert, will you show her to a bed? Then all of you wash up for dinner," Shadman said, walking away. He didn't look back to see if the Robert person was taking over care of Felith or not.

The Magi boy shrugged his shoulders at the two youngster who were watching him. Freeing his leg from one of them, who had come to cling to his leg, he walked over to Felith. "Boys have the right side of the house, girls the left side. This room," he waved his arm making a sweeping motion over all that was around them, "is common ground, as are the kitchen and dining room. Only, don't go into the kitchen unless told to help out. Miss Olivia is very strict on that rule," he smiled at her as if the whole thing was a joke before walking to the left side of the house.

They passed a bathroom with several sinks and shower stalls. The next room was filled with beds. Only three of the beds were made up. Two with flowery spreads, while one had just a plain blanket. Between each bed was a cabinet. The doors on one of the cabinets stood open and Fel saw drawers lined one side of the cabinet interior while the other side had a rod on which to hang things. The top section of the cabinet had two shelves. It was at the open cabinet that the Magi boy stopped. "This will be your space. We keep our personal items in our storage area. In the bottom drawer are the basics for making up the bed. We all clean our space ourselves," Robert said, grimacing as he looked to the bed next to the new girl's bed, which was full of wrinkles. "Some better than others," he said picking up a ragged doll from the floor. For a moment he busied himself straightening up the bed, smoothing the blanket, placing the rag doll on the pillow, which he took the time to center. It was almost as if he had forgotten Felith. Then he turned to her with a bit of a blush on his face. "Sorry. Middy is such a mess. Now, we are about to have dinner. They require we all wash our hands before each meal. So feel free to do that, then join us back in the main room. I'll take you into the dining room when you are done," he said walking back out of the room.

When Felith entered the bathroom to wash her hands there were several girls already there. One was primping in front of the mirror checking herself to be sure that not a hair was out of place. Another was wiping chocolate off Middy's face roughly. The child twisted and turned giving her poor helper a hard time. The primping girl, gave a sideways glance at Felith and poked the other girl in the ribs, then inclined her head in Felith's direction. Both were lovely girls. Both grimaced and left the bathroom. Felith didn't react, didn't show that she knew this was intended as a snub. What could they do that was worse than the monster? Obediently she went to a sink and began to wash her hands, then saw her grimy face in the mirror, and proceeded to scrub it too. All the while Middy watched her as if fascinated, then the child handed Felith a towel, and turned to run out of the bathroom. The kindness had Felith freezing for a moment in confusion. She noticed her reflection in the mirror and came back into the real world, where kindness was a trick to have an excuse to hurt you. She saw the tangled mess that was her hair. There wasn't much she could do about that, so she didn't even try. Once certain that her hands and face were clean, Felith carefully dried her hands on the towel, then hung it up with care. They seemed to place value on neatness here. Stay a non-being, don't make waves, be the nothing she was.

Eyes hooded, Felith went back into the common room. Robert, the Magi boy, was talking to the primping girl, but he broke off when he saw Felith entering from the girl's side of the building. He gave a small nod of approval and came to where Felith stood. Reaching out, the Magi boy went to take hold of Felith's arm. She quickly avoided the touch moving just out of reach. Her shoulders were hunched and her eyes were like those of a doe on the edge of a clearing in the forest, alert, but not showing it, a study in stillness. Robert's mouth became a thin line. Alright, no touching. He got that. A few of the younger children were like that, not Middy, but some of the shy ones who had found homes had been like that. Besides this one was sort of dirty and stunk. Mr. Shadman hadn't given a name, so Robert didn't know what to call her. "Just follow the hungry masses into the dining room," he said, a bit gruffer than he had intended.

Felith saw the others heading to a door in the back of the room just off the kitchen. She headed that way, making certain she was far enough from everyone that passed so no one could grab her arm like that man had earlier. The dining room was a maze of tables. Big tables, small tables, tables where two adults and the teenagers stood. And, short legged tables where two of the small children sat. Then one off to the side where the Middy child sat alone. Most of the tables had the chairs turned over on top of them. Evidently at one time this place had fed a larger number of people.

A grimace kept Roberts lips thinned out as he looked around the dining room. Nobody had made room for the new girl. Usually the girls would all pitch in welcoming a newcomer. It was fairly clear that this girl had already managed to get on the bad side of most of the girls. The only open space was beside Middy, who had her own table. That was because Middy tended to share food. Well, throw other people's food at anyone who even looked at her plate. Robert had heard Middy had been starving when she was found in her mother's apartment. He didn't know if that was true or not, but the girl had an appetite. Reluctantly he took the new girl over to where Middy was standing. Robert motioned for the girl to stand by the chair next to Middy. Satisfied that she was going to do what she was told, he turned and went to his own chair to stand.

The cook, Olivia, stood at the center of the occupied tables. She looked around at the children and seemed to take in each and every one of them in her sweeping gaze. If her eyes rested a bit longer on the new girl it was hardly noticeable, yet it was on the girl her mind was fixated upon. The fax from the emergency room hadn't been clear on the details of the child being orphaned. Well Middy smearing the page with cake batter hadn't helped in the reading of it. She could only guess from the words covered in cake batter that the girl was named Ollie. Olivia's voice was totally business when she spoke to the room of children, "It is our tradition to have any newcomer give the blessing. That would be you, Ollie. Please say the grace so everyone may be seated." She gave the new girl a stern look, then bowed her head waiting.

Felith didn't look at Olivia, she didn't look anywhere but straight ahead. This was one of those tricks, you spoke and got a bloodied lip for doing it. And her name wasn't Ollie. The peaceful gray took over Felith's mind.

The room was completely silent as everyone waited for the blessing. From where she stood Felith could see most of the room. Everyone was standing, waiting, some had their heads bowed, others were looking at her, the primping girl was glaring at Felith as if she was a demon. Suddenly the silence was broken as a small voice beside Felith piped up. "Bless this dinner, and give us lots and lots of cake. Ahem," said Middy. Felith saw Olivia stare at her for a moment, but she didn't come hit Fel, or Middy. And it seemed it was now safe to sit down. As everyone sat down the room filled up with the buzz of conversation. Several glances were sent Felith's way. She heard someone say that maybe she wasn't a believer in God. Felith didn't believe in anyone.

Middy stuck her tongue out at Felith. "You kept us from eating. This time, cause you're new, you can give me your cake." It was more a command than anything else. As she talked Middy tucked a huge napkin into the top of her dress, her little hand smoothing it out. Felith thought it looked much smoother than the bed Robert had indicated was Middy's. Fel shook her head. She didn't remember ever tasting cake, but if she got any she was eating it. No little imp was taking her cake. Where the defiance came from Felith didn't know, but it was rock solid in her mind that she was eating her cake, that is, if she got any.

A boy and a girl started bringing plates from the kitchen They placed each plate on the table in front of a person starting with Shadman and Olivia. It seemed the oldest children were served first on down to the table where Middy and Felith sat. Felith was served last.

To Felith it was a wonder just to be served her food. She had read about people having meals like this where there were people sitting around a table, but in her memory there was not such an event. She looked down at the plate, what was she suppose to do? There was a piece of chicken meat she recognized, and some white fluffy looking stuff, then some green vegetable. Without appearing to, Felith watched Middy.

Middy picked up a spoon and began to shovel the mashed potatoes in her mouth. She liked them well enough, but it was the cake she wanted. You didn't get cake if you left stuff on your plate. The chicken she picked up with her fingers to eat. And, because the new girl didn't seem all there, Middy picked up her broccoli and put it on the new girls plate.

It was something Felith had never expected, Middy was giving her some of her own food. Felith tried not to think of that, to let it affect her, as she picked up her own spoon and took a bite of the white fluffy stuff. The small bite she took melted in her mouth. It was so good she wanted more, and it took great effort not to shovel the food into her mouth the way Middy had. But she knew there was such a thing as manners, although what they were she didn't know. Still, she had read about people being polite and minding their manners in company. The room had grown quiet. As Felith ate, she was copying Middy using her hands to eat the meat. Then she tried to eat the green stuff with her spoon, but it wasn't willing to stay on the spoon. Finally she bit her lip, and reached down with her fingers to pick up a bit of it. It was so good. She had downed all of her own, and all but one bite of Middy's before she noticed the silence. She raised her head just enough so she could see the other tables. Everyone was staring at her. She noticed they were using the fork for eating, not the spoon. Even bits of green were being held in mid-air on forks as everyone stared at her. Felith's expression didn't change, she picked up the fork spearing the last bite of green with it. The room began to buzz again with conversation.

A few moments passed as the others tables finished up the main part of the meal. The two helpers from earlier stood and went into the kitchen. When they returned they carried trays with small plates on which was something dark. This must be the cake Middy wanted, Fel thought. When Middy's was set in front of her the little girl gave it a big sniff as if inhaling the very essence of the cake. Fel took a small sniff of her own. It smelled wonderful! She wanted to gobble it down, but Middy had given her some of her own food. With great reluctance Felith slid her cake over in front of Middy. Middy's eyes opened extra wide and she hugged both saucers to her. "Mine," she said before devouring both slices of cake.

Someone was watching her as the meal ended. Fel could feel the eyes on her, studying her. She raised her head just a tiny bit so she could see the room, and there was the Magi boy watching. Quickly she shuttered herself inside her mind. Be nothing.

Olivia stood up and clapped her hands for attention. "Everyone take your plates to the kitchen window. Today's kitchen help go start running the wash-up water. The rest of you have free time until lights out. Be sure to get your showers during that time," Olivia announced. Then added, "Ollie, you will come with me now."

Ollie, again with Ollie, her name was not Ollie. So Felith stood and followed the others carrying her plates. She didn't look at Olivia, just raised her plates, and placed them where the others were placing their plates. When she turned away from the kitchen window Olivia was standing in front of her with her arms crossed over her ample breasts. "In this house, we listen to what others tell us to do. Now, Ollie, you will come with me, do you understand?"

Felith let herself look at Olivia. "Who is Ollie?" she asked.

Olivia blinked, her brows knitted together. "That's your name," she hesitated, "isn't it?"

"No," Felith said.

The cook's mouth gaped open for a moment. Her face turned red. For all her bluster she was a kindly woman. The thought that she had messed up on this girl's name upset her, for she was always so certain in everything she did. "Well no matter, you can tell me your name as we walk. Come along."

Falling into step with Olivia, Fel waited to be asked her name. Olivia led Fel down a long hallway to a storage closet. Stopping in front of the closet Olivia turned to Felith. "What is your name, dear?" Olivia asked.

"I think it is Felith," she said.

"Then I'll call you Fel. Is that alright with you?" Olivia asked. She started to touch Felith, but Fel pulled back and Olivia let her hand drop. Olivia sighed. "Okay, this is where we store clothes that have been outgrown, or the children have found parents and have all new clothes, so they left them here. Miss Raglan didn't bring you any clothes, so we are going to sort some out for you to wear."

There were plastic bags of clothing stacked on shelves in the huge closet that Olivia opened. The woman looked at Felith then rummaged around in a couple of the bags. She began to stack clothes in Fel's arms. Blouses of soft material, and worn jeans which though faded had plenty of use left in them. It took great will power for Felith not to let her eyes widen in wonder. Such beautiful things were being placed in her arms. And the jeans, to Felith those were like suits of armor. It would be difficult for anyone to get to her through the jeans. Soft material with butterflies and flowers on a blouse had Fel's insides trembling. She didn't know if she could bare it if Olivia snatched it back. The jeans she wanted so much. Armor, armor against the monsters.

Armed with her new, to her, clothing Fel hurried back to the girl's side of the house. She secreted the new underwear, the beautiful blouses, and the jeans away in the storage space Robert had said was for her. The other girls were trailing in from the bathroom freshly showered and dressed for bed. Some wore plush robes, others were in just nightshirts. Felith remembered she was to take a shower before bed. Olivia had given her a couple of nightshirts, but it was the jeans that Fel wanted to wear. She would wear them all the time if they let her. Finally she decided to wear a nightshirt, but put on the jeans under it.

After she made the bed up, Felith took a nightshirt and the softest of the jeans with her to the bathroom area. Seeing the bathroom was empty, Fel relaxed. Carefully she hid the jeans and the nightshirt between the towels stacked on a shelf near the shower. She wanted everything within grasping reach. Getting undressed would be scary enough without having the assurance of the clothes within reach. When she was certain she had everything needed to shower quickly, and get out fast, she stepped into the shower, and stripped. Quickly she turned the water on and soaped up with a washing cloth. It felt so good to wash the grime off her body. She couldn't remember the last time she had chanced taking a shower. There was shampoo on a shelf in the shower. Felith took the bottle of shampoo and squirted some in her hand. The warm water sprayed down on her head feeling like a warm caress. It took three washings before Felith's hair felt clean to her. Her body was pink from the heat of the water beating down on her. Finally, satisfied she was clean, Fel stepped out of the shower and reached for a towel. A gasped "oh" caused Fel to freeze for a moment. Fear raced through her body until Felith realized it was Middy standing in the bathroom doorway. The little girl's eyes were huge saucers, then the child stepped out the door again.

Trying not to let her hands shake Fel dried herself off. She knew Middy had seen her back, but that was not something that could be helped, or mattered to her. More than anything Felith wanted to get the jeans on to protect her. As fast as she could Fel dried her body, not getting it completely dry before putting on the new underwear and the nightshirt. Outside the bathroom door she could hear Julian and Middy fussing.

"I didn't take your stupid doll. Shut up and leave me alone, you little brat," Julian shouted, as Fel open the bathroom door and stepped out. Middy shot a quick look Fel's way then ran off. Perhaps Fel had scared her. If so, she hoped the child would forgive her. For now, Felith was too tired. All she wanted to do was sleep, and have her jeans protect her.

The bed was so soft when Fel laid down, that soon the stress of the day, all the strangeness of being at the hospital, this place where people ate together at a table, all that just drifted off into sweet darkness. She didn't wake when a tiny shadow passed over her sleeping form, or when Miss Olivia came to check on this new troubled youth in her care. For the first time since the monster, Felith slept soundly.

Chapter Two

BUTTERFLIES

The attic was dim and dusty with spider webs hanging in the air. Between two stacks of boxes Felith leaned against the wall. She had found this place when Mr. Shadman had her bring a box of old records up to be stored. Since then this spot had become her hideaway. Clad in her armor jeans and the lovely butterfly blouse, Felith thought of the Magi boy Robert. Were you born a Magi? Or, was it something you could learn? The way he moved his hands must have something to do with producing the flowers out of midair. Felith closed her eyes and moved her hands, weaving intricate patterns in the air. She thought of butterflies flitting about in a rainbow of colors. She could see them in her mind, beautiful butterflies dancing in front of her face. A smile bloomed on her face as the soft breeze from their wings caressed her face causing her to open her eyes. They danced in front of her, beautiful, beautiful butterflies. It worked. She had managed to copy the Magi boy's hand movements and make butterflies. A small sense of joy crept into her.

Where had the girl gotten off to, Robert wondered. It was then he saw the stairs to the attic had been pulled down. Oh, great. Just what he needed, a visit to spider town. He hated going up to the attic. The door was open a crack so he pushed it open a bit more and looked in. At first he didn't see Felith, then the air seemed to stir. Butterflies danced in the air, and he saw her. She was sitting with her knees drawn up, her face lifted as if sitting in a meadow filled with flowers enjoying the day. Robert smiled to himself as that image flashed in his mind. Then there were the butterflies. They danced and wove about her face as she waved her hands as if conjuring them. The door creaked, and Felith froze. Just like that, the butterflies were gone.

Walking over, Robert looked down on Felith. She opened her eyes a fraction wider when she saw him standing over her, his face puzzled. He had caught her trying to imitate him. She wiped all emotion from her face, and looked up at him. "You are a powerful Magi. Please don't hurt me," Fel whispered, fearing he would turn her into a box, or put a curse on her.

Hurt her? Anger stumble through his mind. She pulls off this fabulous trick, and then says something like that. Didn't she know how much it hurt him to know he was nothing compared to her expert trick? Suddenly his anger with this weird girl boiled to the surface. "You mock me," he

said, turning away from her he walked to the door.
"Olivia wants to see you in the kitchen," Robert
called back over his shoulder as he walked down the
attic steps trying to convince himself he hadn't seen
those butterflies. Maybe he hadn't, maybe it had
been a trick of the light, a reflection. Yes, that was it,
a reflection of some sort. Finding an explanation he
could live with, he felt relieved. No skinny, weird girl
was better than he was at magic tricks.

For a long moment Felith sat trembling inside.
She refused to let the fear show on her face, but for
a while there she had thought the Magi boy would
hit her. Just when she had started to relax her vigil
slightly, all the beatings came crashing through her
mind like a run away flood of memories trying to
crush her. She would have to be careful and not let
that Robert monster boy catch her trying to copy
him. It was dangerous letting the monsters see her
do anything.

A man Felith hadn't seen before sat at the
kitchen table with an open briefcase in front of
him. Felith shielded herself, surrounding her mind
in soft gray mist. Olivia looked up, and motioned
Felith to sit down at the table too. Warily she sat as
far away from the man as possible. He struck her as
bad. There was a shadow on him that stank, stank
of monster. The man leaned forward as if trying to
get closer to Felith. She felt like drawing back from
him, but the thing to do with bad was to face it, get it
over with. So Felith sat as if she had not noticed the
attempt to invade her space. Bad she knew.

"What we're going to do is to go through a

series of questions. You will write down the answers, or where it is appropriate, answer verbally. First fill out this form with your name, age, and place of birth. This will be used to register you in school," as he talked Mr. Taylor removed several sheets of paper from the briefcase. Placing one of the paper sheets in front of Felith, he put a pen on top of it.

Felith looked at Taylor, then down at the sheet of paper in front of her. She rested her hands on the table, folding them together. Felith saw Olivia grimace, as if she knew this was another of those times someone assumed something about Felith that was wrong. Not showing the slightest hint of embarrassment, Felith said, "I don't know how to write."

Both Olivia and Mr. Taylor looked confused. But it was Olivia who spoke first. "Didn't they teach you anything, Dear?" she asked.

"Once, long ago, a lady showed me how to read the alphabet. That was the last time I was out of the house," Felith said, defending the teacher who in kindergarten had shown an eager little girl what the letters of the alphabet were. "She couldn't teach me to write." What she didn't explain was that little Felith's arm was in a cast, and when the other arm was broken, the monster pulled her from school keeping her locked away in the house. But she had learned to read, teaching herself based on that one teacher having shown Felith the alphabet.

Mr. Taylor's face turned red as he turned to Olivia. "If she can't read and write you will have to get a tutor. Or," he paused as if considering the wisdom of what he was about to say. "You can home school her. Don't get me wrong. She will have to pass regular tests to see how she is progressing. And it won't be easy. Teaching basic reading at this age is more difficult than with a youngster."

Why did they all think she was stupid? Felith wondered. She could read perfectly well. The cooks face reddened some too. She looked over at Felith and seemed to make up her mind. "Felith, we can ill afford a private tutor for you, but if that is what you would prefer then we will find the funds somewhere. As for home schooling, that means you will be taught by one of us here. This is your choice to make, Dear," Olivia said, making it clear Felith was part of the conversation.

Her choice. It was a moment before that thought could sink into Felith's mind. Her choice, she had a say in what would happen. Olivia was giving her a choice. For a moment butterflies swarmed in Felith's mind, beautiful butterflies. When Felith could think again there was a blue butterfly flitting around over Olivia's head, and Felith knew what she wanted. "Here, teach me here," she said. It was the first time she had a voice in her life. With that choice Felith began to realize she didn't have to take what others did to her. Felith watched the blue butterfly dance and simmer in the air over Olivia. She was the one in charge of her life, and her guide was a butterfly.

Olivia nodded and stood. "It is decided then. We will teach Felith here. If you will leave the papers with me I'll see that all the information needed is filled out," she told Mr. Taylor.

The man pursed his lips at her. "It isn't a

simple thing to do. You will need to give periodic tests, which will have to be turned in to the Educational Department. Because Felith is a charge of the state, any irregularities will be investigated. After all, the local officials are still investigating the disappearance of the man who was holding her captive. So believe me, all must be above board here," he said.

It was amazing, Felith thought, the way short plump Olivia puffed up, and got in Mr. Taylor's face. "If you think for one moment that we are going to let bureaucrats bully Felith, then you best think again. Just give me the paper work and shoo," she told him.

Taylor's face seemed to be having a very hard time not breaking into laughter at the sight of Miss Olivia. "Yes, ma'am, Miss Olivia," he said, his mouth twitching in his effort not to laugh. He ducked his head and began rummaging in his briefcase. Finally Mr. Taylor pulled a sheaf of papers out from his case and handed them to Miss Olivia. "Might I suggest that a computer will come in handy for downloading the needed lesson material. There is a website listed on one of the sheets I gave you which has all the information you will need," he nodded to Felith, packed up his briefcase, and left.

Some of the bluster left Olivia when Taylor walked out. She sat down and patted her face with a tissue. It wasn't reasonable that the bureaucrats could decide a young girl's life. That was one of the reasons she had helped set up Haven, to protect the children who didn't have anyone to fight for them. "I suppose the first thing we need to do is to teach you to read and write. Robert could tutor you in the first learners books to read and how to write. He is so patient with the young ones," Olivia said, looking at Felith. "I don't think you are near as dumb as you let on with that man."

"I can read," Felith said before she could stop herself. Something about Olivia caused that lapse. Maybe she didn't want to appear so dumb to the one person here who had shown some faith in her, who seemed to see her as a person instead of a nothing girl. "But I never learned how to write."

"Who teaches a child to read, but not how to write?" Olivia asked, her face a mass of confusion.

"I had a broken arm when my mother put me in kindergarten. The lady there showed me how to read letters before I was kept in the house," Felith said refusing to let the teacher who had given her the tools to teach herself to read be belittled.

"But who taught you to read, dear?" Olivia asked, wanting to reach out and hug the little girl who had her arm broken, and was denied education.

"The books. In the basement of the house there were boxes and boxes of books. They had the letters of the alphabet," Felith said, suddenly wondering if she just thought she could read. "Am I wrong? Doesn't that mean I can read?"

Not wanting to discourage Felith, Olivia stood. "Why don't we find out? I'll be right back," so saying Olivia scurried out of the kitchen.

Felith sat totally void of any sign of emotion, inside she worried that she had only fooled herself into thinking she could read books. Was she as dumb as everyone seemed to think? The thought depressed Felith, for the only thing she had ever had, that was her own, was her mind. She didn't think she had a better mind than anyone else, but it was hers, something she had control over. The only part of her body that monsters couldn't get to. Hers, she thought, good or bad, even if it turned out she was dumb, her mind was hers.

The books Olivia returned with were a basic beginner reader, and a thick book of fiction. Olivia tried to keep books on hand that would interest all the different age groups in the home, but the thickest of the two books was her own. Now as she approached Felith, Olivia was having second thoughts. What if the child was just too embarrassed to admit she couldn't read? Wouldn't asking her to prove it just embarrass the girl even more? She pulled her chair close to Felith, and sat down. "Now, Dear, if these are too hard for you to read just say so. We will work on the reading while teaching you to write."

Again, was it just that she looks stupid to everyone? Olivia was trying to make her feel relaxed, Felith knew that. The woman was so easy to read. Felith took the thicker book from Olivia. She had never read aloud before. Always, always she read in the near dark of the cellar where the books were stored in half haphazard stacks of boxes. Locked down there for hours on end, learning to read. And, reading kept her sane, and gave a little girl a world to live in, even if it was only fiction, that didn't have the monster in it. Felith looked at the book, and ran her fingers over the cover. This one she knew. She open to the first page. "It was three days hard travel from Thunder Keep through the dense forest which marked the edge of civilized man, and the beginnings of the unknown. Cala traveled over the Mountains of Dreams, and into a second forest before he heard the faintest of booming. Even then the source was too distant to be certain of identification. He could only hope that the end of his quest was now at least within hearing".

"For yet another day he traveled toward that sound until the ground and brush shook. The very air vibrated with the ceaseless noise. Just when he thought his head would explode from the never ending Boom!, Boom!, he broke free of the grasping brush to stand upon a vast plain of lush grasses. Green stretched to the horizon. Upon that green sea was a distant white blob, the source of the relentless sound, of Cala's quest, his dreams," Felith stopped reading and looked up at Olivia. "I don't know if I can read the whole chapter out loud, it makes me so sad when mother dies," she said.

The cook reached over and patted Felith's hand before she remember the girl didn't want to be touched. "Me too," she said, tears already threatening to redden her eyes knowing what was to come in the story. She cleared her throat. "I'll arrange for Robert to show you how to make your letters," Olivia said. Her lip quivered just a little as she stood. She was caught up in the memories of the story Felith had been reading and wanting so much to hug this child who had gone through so much in her short life. But she just shooed Felith away.

Later, as she took her shower, Felith pondered

the wisdom of letting people know she could read. There was an advantage to seeming dumb, a nothing. Worried about the twists and turns her life was taking Felith almost stepped on Middy when she left the bathroom. The girl was setting in front of the bathroom door her face screwed up in a glare at Rosemary, who was pacing back and forth in front of the little imp. Rosemary threw a glance at Middy and rushed past her to the bathroom. "Call your frigging watchdog off so a girl can pee," she snarled as she passed Felith. Watchdog? Middy looked up at Felith, the little girl's eyes filled with tears. With the speed of the young she jumped up and rushed off, leaving Felith to wonder just what had happened.

Felith found Middy huddled under the covers of her bed weeping. This was a totally new experience for Felith. Never had she wanted or needed to give comfort to any one. Sitting down on Middy's bed Felith pulled the little girl into her lap. She rubbed the weeping child between the shoulder blades, and just held her. Finally Middy pulled back and looked up at Felith. "Some…" She hiccuped and started again, "Someone hurt you so bad."

My scars, Felith thought, she saw my scars. Felith tipped Middy's head up so the little girl was face to face with her. "I survived. No matter how bad things are if you use the will power of your mind you can survive."

"I didn't want the others to see," Middy said, her face a study in concern. "They would be so nasty to you."

Smiling down at the little girl Felith shook her head. "Don't worry, there is nothing they can do to me that will hurt. Remember use your will power when things are bad for you. Don't let anyone take that from you," she tapped Middy on the nose with a finger. "Now go wash your face. You are a big girl and can do that on your own. You can do so much on your own. Go on, shoo, then get some sleep." She watched the little girl dash off for the bathroom. A warmth centered in her that this little girl had tried to protect her from gossiping girls. I'll protect you, Middy, she vowed.

Chapter Three

THE GIFT

The room was filled with watchers. The younger children watched Robert as he set up to perform his magic tricks. Deep in a corner of the room, Felith also watched Robert as he waved his hands about talking to the children of magical things. Off to the side Julian and Rosemary stood watching Robert do his little tricks. Julian pursed her lips as she watched, convinced that Robert was wasting his time entertaining the younger orphans. Yet it was his way with those around him that had first made her decide he was hers.

Robert fluttered his hands in the air preparing to pull the flowers out of his sleeve. A smile pasted on his face, he talked to the children. "I see a lovely lady here in the room. A beautiful girl always deserves flowers. Oh my, what can I do? I don't have any flowers. But wait, perhaps I can solve the problem with a little magic." Robert hesitated and

threw a quick glance to the still figure in the back
corner of the room to see if she was watching him.
She, that quiet girl, was so much more a magician
than he could ever dream of becoming. Robert was
actually embarrassed at his amateur act. Then he saw
Middy's face staring up at him in utter fascination.
He knew that this was why he did what he did, to
make the younger children laugh and to give them
some wonder in their lives. Still, that girl made
him nervous. Waving his hands Robert made the
flowers appear in his hands. Again he glanced at
Felith trying to determine her reaction. But as usual
she was stony faced with only her eyes betraying her
intense interest.

Julian's watchful eyes picked up on Robert
glancing continually at the new girl, and Julian
was not happy. Robert was hers and only hers. All
the girls knew to keep their hands off him. It was
another reason to dislike the filthy creature. But that
one, that one didn't respect her betters. Julian was
here only because her family had died in an auto
accident and there had been no relatives to take her.
But she got an allowance from the trust fund her
parents set up for her. She, Rosemary, and Robert
were all just here until they came of age, then they
would be set for life on the funds left to them. But
that one, she was just a dirty creature from the slums,
not worth even spitting on. A nothing. Still, Robert
kept looking at her as if for approval. Was he stupid?

Setting in the shadows of her corner Felith
watched Robert cut a rope into two sections. This
was a new trick of his, and it totally held her
attention. She watched as he took the two cut ends

and put them together in his hand. He waved his wand over his hand with a little flourish, then he held on to one end of the two cut sections, and opened his hand. Healed, the rope was healed. How could he heal the rope, she wondered. To be able to heal, how wonderful that must be. He was a powerful, powerful Magi. She watched each wave of his magic wand. Up, down, three times around. How did she get a wand? Could she make one from a tree branch. She knew, from the books she had read, they were made from wood. And the type of wood could make a difference in the power of the wand. Some were supposed to be infused with part of a wild creature. What would it take? How could she create a wand like that? The problems stewed around in her mind, sliding over many possible methods. Then Robert was done, ending his little act with a bow, and a kiss to Middy's hand. Felith's eyes shuttered. Such a liar. She would have to be sure Middy was safe from the liars of the world. The monsters.

With a final glance in Felith's direction Robert went to stand with Julian and Rosemary. A hand caressed his arm as Julian threw a glare towards Felith. There is nothing she could do to Felith that could be worse than the monster had done. So Felith ignored Julian and pondered how to keep Middy safe, and make a wand. Wood, she needed wood from a living tree she instinctively thought. And something willingly given by a powerful creature. Binding the two to form a wand was something which eluded Felith's mind. How did one instill magic into wood?

Sitting at the table, that was Middy's and hers for meals, Felith practiced her letters. It was getting easier to wield the pencil. Her fingers were learning the shape and how to hold the pencil. She wondered if that was the key to making a wand, learning the feel and the inner shape of a branch. Visualizing the backyard she thought of the trees there and bushes, thinking if she had ever just touched and felt them as living things. A chair scraped the floor and the insides of Felith shivered, but outwardly she didn't show a thing.

Robert sat down next to her and waited for her to complete her letters. "I have a list of words that I want you to write, putting the letters together like I showed you last time. Just make them cursive and continual. Put a space between the words. If you have the time, look up the meaning of each word. Now let me see what you have done since yesterday," Robert said, his tone of voice patient with all the overtones of being displeased.

For a moment Felith didn't want to hand over the letters she had worked on copying over and over. He had seemed so displeased with her when he sat down, that she didn't want him to say bad things about her work. Silly, she told herself, and handed over the pad of paper she had been working upon.

The script was so precise that Robert had at first thought it was printed by a machine. Each letter evidently written with such care to be perfect. Frowning to himself, Robert wondered why he had so wanted to find fault with her letters. Was it petty revenge for her being better at magic tricks, or did he just want her to be flawed in some way, to make her more human, instead of the withdrawn little robot she seemed to be? So petty of him to want her to fail. Robert didn't want to be that sort of person. He looked up at Felith and smiled. "This is perfect. You have beautiful handwriting," he said, watching her reaction, as relief flashed briefly in her eyes, but was quickly followed by wary distrust. As if she was relieved that he was pleased, but didn't trust him, he thought, and that confused him all the more for he had been truthful in his dealings with her.

Felith nodded in acknowledgment of Robert having spoken. She didn't believe liars. They beat you and raped you and…. Liar. Taking up her pencil Felith began to write the words on the list Robert put on the table, painstakingly she formed each letter of a word.

Sighing to himself, Robert left Felith to work on the word list he had given her. He was afraid Mr. Shadman had his hands full with that girl. So afraid to show emotion. Locked up inside herself as if to smile or say thank you to anyone would be a flaw. Did she think she was so much better than everyone else? That didn't make sense either, she wasn't like Julian who was so proud of her bloodline and flaunted it. It seemed more that she didn't trust him. He remembered how she had drew back away from him, from contact with anyone. Trust. Someone had broken her ability to trust. When Robert had first come to Haven he had some trust issues of his own. He hadn't trusted that the police were telling him everything. And then someone turned up claiming to be his aunt. He didn't have an aunt. Fortunately the policewoman handling the case had believed

him and investigated this so called aunt. It was
something Robert would have to deal with all his life,
people after his trust fund. So he could understand
someone having trust issues. The question was how
did someone overcome that distrust? For starters,
not resenting Felith being better at magic tricks. He
smiled to himself as an idea formed in his mind. He
just might be on to something, he thought. Yes, it
might work.

      Her hands cramping from writing out Robert's
list of words, Felith stepped into the back yard of
Haven. Here someone had attempted to keep a
garden, but the flowers were drooping, and the few
trees in the yard had dropped most of their leaves.
A faucet with a water hose attached was off to the
side of the steps. Felith turned the water on and
gave the thirsty flowers a long drink. It wasn't long
before their heads began to raise up and the leaves
strengthen. A small smile spread over Felith's face.
The flowers were so beautiful, they only needed a
little care. Thinking of how she would have to come
take care of the garden, Felith walked to the trees.
She looked up at them wondering if one of them was
willing to give her a wand. Gingerly she touched
each tree, silently asking if it would give her a wand.
Trees were living things and needed respect, she
thought. Going to the water hose she thought that
maybe the trees would like a drink too, but as she
turned something happened. A large blue butterfly
flew over the high wooden fence around the yard.
Fascinated, Felith watched as it dipped down and
up over the flowers, then flew in a circle around one

of the trees. From the tree a small branch fell. It was on that branch the butterfly lit. It's beautiful wings opened and closed several times. Slowly Felith approached as she didn't want to frighten the butterfly. Once near enough Felith laid down on her belly and watched the butterfly. The wings seemed to shimmer in the waning sunlight. Iridescent powder sprinkled over the branch only to disappear into the wood. Once done, the butterfly flew up and back over the wooden fence. Felith looked up at the tree which had gifted her with a wand. Picking up the wand, Felith placed her hands on the bark of the tree. "Thank you," she said. Carefully she watered each tree before going back inside to get ready for dinner.

Having secreted the wand away in her cabinet, Felith washed her hands, and went to the dining room. Everyone was already standing, waiting for her. Middy gave Felith a glare for delaying the meal, but it was not Middy that had made a slight flush spread over Felith's face. Robert, the boy Magi, had placed a chair on the other side of where Felith's chair sat at the table. All Felith's mental shields went up, her mind became filled with gray mist. Not changing expression, or indicating in anyway that Robert had upset her, Felith took her place standing, waiting for the blessing. Dread filled her as much as the mist did. A baby monster was at her table.

The plates were brought out by Julian and Rosemary today. Felith had yet to pull kitchen duty. The thought of it had made her nervous, but at the moment all thoughts of kitchen duty or eating were held at bay by one thought, a monster was at her table. She had to protect Middy.

Robert glanced at Middy, then at Felith. He had the feeling he had made a grave mistake sitting at Felith's table. All he wanted to do was put his plan in action and talk to her to explain his idea. It was amazing, Robert could see Felith's body trembling. Tiny ripples passed over her skin, and there was nothing he could do but leave to make it stop. Yet he stayed. "Middy," he said, as they sat down after grace had been said. "I hope you don't mind me sitting with you and Felith."

Middy's eyes were wary as if she carried a dark secret, and he was messing with that secret. She said, "She will hurt Felith."

It was something Robert hadn't thought about when he came to Middy's table. Of course Julian would be upset. He was supposed to sit with her, the girl had made that clear. Still, she didn't own him. He was his own person and had the right to sit with anyone he wanted to sit with. Did he have the right to cause Felith trouble? The answer was no. "Okay, Middy, I'll go back to my usual spot. You are a brave little girl to protect your friend," Robert nodded to Felith, and walked back to his old table. The shame of all this was that he had only wanted Felith to teach him how she did her tricks. Nobody need be jealous of that.

In the kitchen Julian fumed, how dare Robert go sit with that little tramp. Feeling spiteful, she took most of the food off Felith's plate, giving her the worst piece of meat that she could find. That would teach the little tramp to leave her man alone. As Julian carried the plates out and set Felith's plate in front of her, she felt a moment of remorse. Only it wasn't her fault that the girl was so thin. Her conscience soothed Julian took her own plate, and went and sat by Robert. She smiled sweetly at Robert, she had her way of getting back at those that did her wrong.

Over the next couple of days Felith watched over Middy, making certain she was never left alone with any of the boys, or the few men who work in and around Haven. Between keeping Middy safe, doing her given chores for the day, and practicing writing her letters and words, Felith had little time to take care of the neglected garden. Each day, however, she somehow managed to go out and commune with the plants and the trees in the garden, if only for a few moments. She would touch the plants and give them water to freshen their roots. In time she noticed that birds and insects were beginning to frequent the garden more. Only when she was alone did she practiced making things appear like the flowers Robert often made appear for the kids. She would sit in the most remote corner of the garden and think of butterflies. Beautiful butterflies would fly in circles in her mind. Sometimes when she opened her eyes she would see the iridescent wings of the butterflies flitting about happily touching the plants. Several times she tried to heal some of the plants. But that was much harder, requiring her to send energy into the plant. Even then, she didn't know if she had healed it, or if it had just taken a deep drink of the water she had given the plants. Still, she practiced whenever she had a chance.

Felith looked forward to each day when she was able to go and commune with the garden and relax. It was almost dark before Felith was able to go one day and commune with the garden after a particularly trying day. It seemed that Shadman had been unable to do anything all day without yelling for Felith to come help with everything from sorting out old files to cleaning the bookshelves in the small library. Felith went about touching the plants, and then the trees. Each one she spoke to mentally. She had her face lifted up to the tree which had given her the wand, when something fell out of the sky and landed at her feet. Startled, Felith stepped back as a bird, a tiny bird no bigger than a Wren, flopped about with one of its wings sticking out at an odd angle. Felith knelt down and cupped the small bird in her hands. The bird's heart was beating so fast and hard that it sent shock waves of its pain through her body. There was little anyone could do for the bird, for it would surely die from fright before the wing could be repaired. That didn't stop Felith though. She had seen Robert heal a rope. If a rope could be healed then a tiny bird's wing could be healed. There was no doubt in Felith's mind that the bird could be healed. Sitting down on the ground, Felith, place the little bird in her lap. It struggled for a moment then seemed to just give up and laid still. As gently as she could Felith aligned the fracture bones in the birds wing. Solemnly she pulled her wand out, and waved it over the bird. Were there words she should say? Nothing came to mind, and she rue not having sat closer to Robert listening to what he had to say when he waved his wand over the rope. Regardless

of the need or no need for words, Felith concentrated
on the small life in her lap. With a fragile grace she
waved the wand over the bird, closing her eyes as she
thought of the bones knitting together and the flesh
healing. There was a flutter in her lap. Felith's eyes
opened to find the little bird had left her. Silently she
hoped it would heal and live on.

As if drawn to the garden, Robert approached
the door leading outside. He paused as he saw the
girl, Felith, kneel down and picked up a bird. Robert
was torn between going out to comfort Felith in what
had to be a sad moment, knowing the bird was dead
or dying, or staying away from her. Julian had made
it clear she was not pleased with him just looking
over at Felith during his magic show for the kids. To
keep the peace it may be best if he just stayed inside.
Yet something had drawn him here. He watched as
Felith sat down and placed the bird on her lap. Now
it comes, he thought, the tears, the weeping. Could
he just stand here and watch that. The answer was
of course no, for he was cursed with a soft heart
which didn't serve him well, not well at all. Gingerly
he turned the door knob as he watched Felith
pull a stick out and start waving it over the bird.
Wondering what he could say that would ease her
pain, he paused. Between one thought and the next
Robert stopped moving as the little bird fluttered
its wings and took off. He blinked, then blinked
again, so sure that what he had just seen couldn't
have happened. Now he was the one disturbed,
unsure and needing to think. Perhaps the bird had
only been stunned. That was it, the bird had been
stunned, and then revived. Still, Robert didn't go out

to where Felith was sitting. He was troubled by what he had seen today, and the butterflies that had been in the attic still disturbed his thoughts.

Chapter Four

FEELING PROTECTIVE

All day the anger had been building inside of Julian. Robert had been catering to that girl, despite her telling him to leave the girl alone. That wretched girl was trying to steal Robert away. Julian thought, I'll have to teach her that she is nothing, to keep away from my kind. She glanced to where Robert had gathered the youngsters and was preparing to read them a story. He'd make a good father, too bad, Julian thought, since she had no intentions of having children. But with his money they could afford to adopt maybe one kid, and have a nanny for it too. Anything to keep Robert in line. The anger built inside of Julian as she thought of Robert having gone to sit with that filthy girl the other night. She would take care of that girl right now. Nobody took what was hers, including that butterfly blouse Felith seemed to favor. Smiling at Rosemary, Julian walked over to Felith. "You really don't do my blouse justice, do you? If I'd known some filthy creature like you would get their hands on my blouse I would have kept it tucked away. It really is a shame you don't know how to keep your hands off other people's property," Julian said, much as if she was giving advice to a friend.

It was a moment before Felith responded. Certainly half the room had heard Julian refer to the blouse as belonging to her. Felith loved this butterfly blouse, but if it was Julian's blouse then she wanted nothing more to do with it. The room had grown quiet as the others paused in their conversations to see what was going to happen between Julian and Felith. Each of them had been at some time or another on the receiving end of Julian's sharp tongue. Slowly Felith raised her head so she could see Robert, where he sat with the story book in his hand. Despite the fact he was a baby monster she did enjoy listening to him read the stories to the other children. Then Felith looked at Julian. If Julian wanted her blouse then she could have it. Slowly Felith unbuttoned the blouse and slipped it off. She draped the blouse over Julian's shoulder, and turning Felith walked out of the room to the girls side of the building. There was an old shirt she was certain Julian wouldn't have worn.

Middy ran over and kicked Julian in the leg before going after Felith. The little girl never saw the shock on Julian's face, or the horror on Robert's face as they all watched Felith walk away, her shoulder blades still sticking out from the thinness of her back, and the scars marring Felith's back. The common room was silent. Each child taking the proof of so much abuse in, and trying to deal with what it might mean. Julian turned around to find everyone looking at her. For the first time in her life she felt shame. But it was too late now to take her words back, or put the blouse back on that thin, scarred body. She looked at Robert and saw his mouth in a thin line. Crap, she thought, he'll never forgive me for this.

In the bedroom Middy went to where Felith was sorting through her cabinet drawers. There was a stack of clothing she had set upon her bed. All were the pretty blouses, the ones Felith figured were things Julian had worn. The more ragged tee shirts she kept. Those Felith didn't think Julian would ever have worn, they weren't pretty enough. Carefully she picked up the stack of clothing and carried it to Julian's bed placing the stack on the nice spread covering Julian's bed. Middy followed in Felith's wake. The little girl's face was as set in stone as Felith's own face. Felith looked down at Middy. "You are missing story time. Let's go listen to Robert read. He tells the best stories, don't you think?" she asked Middy, taking Middy's hand and smiling down at her.

The little girl looked up at Felith not understanding how she could be so calm. "But they all know now. Don't you care?" Middy asked, her chin trembling, betraying the turmoil all inside the child.

Kneeling down Felith spoke so softly that Middy had to lean forward to hear her, "If I don't accept who I am, then I am a sad person. What others think of me does not mean anything. Only what I think of me counts, and as long as I know I am the person I want to be, then I am happy. Always be the person you want to be, not something others want." Standing Felith led Middy through the door to the common room. Middy nodded, her chin came up a notch as they enter the common room.

As if waiting for Middy to return, Robert settled down and opened the book he was holding. The room was silent, none of the usual chatter going on. When Middy had taken her seat, and Felith settled on the floor beside her instead of retreating to her usual lonely corner, Robert began to read, "Once upon a time, in a far away land…." Felith listened her mind wrapped in soft gray as the story ran its course, and the Prince saved the Princess to live happy ever after. Only she knew there were no happily ever afters. Just today, this moment, and what you did in it.

After story time was over and the youngsters all went outside to play before dinner, Julian approached Robert. She knew he had a soft spot for the unfortunate kids living at Haven. Even when he had first arrived it was as if he felt the little kids pain and was always trying to ease it in some way. Julian had never understood why, she still couldn't see a reason to walk among the poor. Another year and she would be able to draw from the money her parents had left for her. A huge house with servants was where she deserved to live, not this hovel. She stroked Robert's arm. "That poor child, I had no idea she was so scarred," she said.

Robert stopped Julian's hand from moving on his arm. "The problem is Julian, you don't care. The only person you think of is yourself. These kids never had the life we had. They have always lived in a world of harsh realities. You throw a fit if you break a nail. It was very brave of Felith to bare her back to us. I think she has had more than a nail broken."

Once dinner was over the girls went to collect their night gowns and take their showers. Everyone saw the stack of blouses on Julian's bed. They knew Felith had put the blouses there. They also knew that the girl with the scarred back had loved wearing those blouses. So it was a subdued group of girls that bathed and dressed for bed. Nobody tried to go into the bathroom when Felith went in and took her shower. For once Middy didn't guard the door. It was as if Middy had decided the worst was over and Felith didn't need her protection from the rest of them. Now they understood why Middy had kept them all out of the bathroom while Felith was bathing. Shame laid like a blanket over the bedroom. Still not one girl approached Felith to say how sorry they were feeling. Shame is something you hide away, and try to forget.

The shower shut off making the rest the girls speed up their bedtime preparations. When Felith came out of the bathroom dressed in her nightshirt and jeans nobody looked at her, not even to smirk at the way she was dressing for bed. Felith went to her bed and sat down on the covers. Taking the hair brush from the shelf in her cabinet, she began to brush her hair. It was beginning to grow out, the once filthy matted mess was now softly shining, curling around her face with tiny wisps of reddish Brown. She was not a pretty girl, but the soft halo of her hair gave her a look of both innocence and

vulnerability. She knew that she was no longer
innocent, as to the other matter, only if she let herself
be so.

The morning came with no change as far as
could be seen in the dynamics of the world. The
stack of blouses had disappeared. What Julian had
done with them was of no concern to Felith. That
part, the pretty part, was gone from her life. It had
been foolish of her to let herself care about the
blouses to begin with. She had no memory of pretty
ever being hers, or anything being hers. So she
would wear the jeans armor, until someone claimed
them too.

Upon entering the common room Felith saw
Olivia motioning her to come to her. Shielding
herself, Felith approached Olivia. "You have some
visitors, dear," Olivia told Felith, "Mr. Shadman
has offered his office for your visit. Come along."
A smile curled within Felith's gray misted mind,
although her face never showed the slightest hint of
that smile. Olivia was not one to waste words. Yet a
worry slowly twirled in that same mist. Who would
be visiting her?

Upon entering Mr. Shadman's office Felith saw
Officer Raglan and a stranger standing by Shadman's
desk. Officer Raglan had been the one who brought
Felith to Haven. It was so nice here, Felith wished
she could thank the officer. Only that would mean
showing emotion. Letting someone know she could
feel pain. Felith knew better than to let that happen.
Others enjoyed inflicting pain. Even Julian, a person
she had never even talk to, had enjoyed taking the

butterfly blouses from Felith. Felith looked over at the other person. It was a grown monster. Unlike with Mr. Shadman, who was cross and demanded obedience, this monster seemed to be projecting calm and no threat. A lie no doubt. Monsters liked to lie. It was Officer Raglan who spoke. She smiled at Felith first. "I hardly knew it was you. You must have grown an inch already," she said with a little laugh of relief, as if she had expected to see the same dirty girl she had delivered to Haven. She looked over at the man beside her. "This is a friend of mine. Felith this is Sidney Asters. He is going to ask you a few questions about the night you were attacked. We are trying to find out what happened. The men who attacked you haven't been found yet, and we are determined to see that they are punished. Will you sit down and talk to Sidney? I'll stay right here in the room with you. You need not be afraid."

With a glance at this Sidney monster Felith went and sat down in the chair she took when called into the office by Shadman. The Sidney monster didn't pull a chair close to her. Instead, he placed it a distance that was neither too far away for them to talk to each other, or so close as to be within reach of Felith. Still Felith did not relax her vigilance. You had to be nothing to a monster, they lied, they hit, and burned and....

Studying the girl's body language Sidney wondered what the best method would be to set her at ease. She was closed off to him, but watchful, as if she expected him to attack her right there where she sat. He glanced at Rags, and smiled to himself. His friend would smack him if he called her Rags in front of anyone. Looking back at Felith he gave a slight smile, a smile too big and flashy would only get the girl's walls up higher than they were now. He began, "From what we know, you were held prisoner from kindergarten age until Officer Raglan found you. In life there are men who are bad and men who are good. Your only experience has been from the bad sort. I know you won't believe me, but please don't judge all men as evil. Some of us do care, and do try to make this world safe from the evil.

"Now that I've probably set you against me, let us begin. Would you please tell us what you are willing to talk about. If something is too hard for you to talk about, or you feel embarrassed, then just leave that for some other time when you feel able to handle talking about it. Okay?" Sidney said sitting back so as to not present a threat.

For a long moment Felith was silent. Then she looked down at her hands and told them. She told them of her mother's body buried in the basement, of how the ground rose up over the grave and she had thought her mother was alive and trying to get out of the ground. The smell that came up out of the earth. The broken arms, the burning of the flesh, the beatings, the fucking parties when the monster brought men to use her. She told it all. And when she was done Felith finally looked at the monster across from her… and he was crying. It shook Felith. She didn't know what to think. So she sat with her mind in her gray place waiting to be hit, or locked away.

Finally getting his emotions under control, Sidney glanced over at Rags. Her face was white, but she wasn't crying like him. He was going to need her tonight, maybe every night for a long while. She knew how these abuse stories affected him. He reached out for Rags and she came to stand behind him, her hand on his shoulder. It was enough, for now. For now they had a child who had every reason to hate all men and all grown-ups. For certainly everyone who had visited that house, and had seen her, had a responsibility to get her out of there. Sidney knew he had to stay calm and present the child with the first threads of trust. So he wiped the tears from his eyes, pulled himself together, and gave that slight smile that said I understand and believe you. "Thank you, Felith," he said, then cleared his throat, which was still tight with the fury and pain he felt at what she had gone through. "It may be of some help to you to talk to a counselor. People of all ages find that very helpful. Would you consent to a few sessions with someone. It could be me or a woman if you would like. It is up to you, you have this right to have sessions with a counselor if you want. We merely provide the service."

A small frown line appeared on Felith's forehead. So much was happening that she felt overwhelmed. She didn't want to talk anymore. The truth was, she had said all she ever wanted to talk about regarding the monster and his friends. Now, now if she was truly in charge of her life she wanted to be left alone to make her way in this world, where people lived a great deal as people in the books she had read in that dark basement. "I would rather not. You have been told all there was, let it be enough," Felith said in a soft voice.

Sidney stood slowly so as not to startle the girl, "Of course. Thank you for talking with us." He made as if to turn away and leave, then turned back. "Oh, Rags and I have lunch here from time to time. Would you have time for a little lunch with us once in a while? Believe me someone has to be there to keep Rags from eating everything," he said.

Immediately Middy flashed in Felith's mind and she was so grateful to have been distracted from the many contradictions swirling in her mind that she seized on Middy. There was no way she would leave Middy alone, unprotected. "If Middy can come too," she said.

A hand slipped into Sidney's hand, and he clutched that lifeline for a moment. "Any friend you want to bring is fine," he said, leaving the room before he grabbed the girl and hugged the life out of her. His head tilted to Olivia who was watching them both as they left. For her he gave a real smile, his face lighting up with relief. Olivia nodded back, as if approving. Rags punched him in the ribs as they walked to the car, and he bent over kissing her cheek. "My place or yours later?" he whispered in her ear.

"Behave are I will have you in handcuffs, Mr. Asters," Raglan said in her officer's voice, then ruined it all by smiling. Inside she was pounding with fury, shooting was too good for the creeps who had harmed Felith.

The dining room was quieter than usual. They hadn't waited for her to come to breakfast. Or, maybe it was just guilt from the previous day that kept them quiet. Everyone acted as if they didn't notice Felith as she entered the dining room. The others were almost finished eating, but as Felith sat down Robert got up and went to the kitchen, soon returning with a plate of hot food. Sitting the plate in front of Felith, Robert stood beside her chair for a moment. When Felith started eating her food as she would have done on any other day, Robert walked back to his seat next to Julian. He had wanted to do something, Robert just was not sure what it was he wanted to do. Comfort Felith? He had heard part of what she told Officer Raglan when he had gone to ask Olivia if they should wait to say grace, or just eat. Now he understood why she didn't want to be touched. There was a knot in his stomach and such anger inside him at men he didn't even know. He shook inside. That girl, that weird, scarred girl. How could she have bore up under all the torture? He didn't know if he could have had the strength to endure it and come out whole. And then there were the marvelous things she could do. How? She was a puzzle. A weird, scarred puzzle.

It was four days before Officer Raglan called to ask Felith and Middy to go to lunch with her and Sidney. At first Felith wanted to refuse to go. Then she saw Middy, a vision of the little girl's eyes when she saw food made her answer yes. For that tough little girl was finding a way into Felith's heart.

It was Raglan that came and picked up Felith and Middy from Haven. Middy had put on her cutest dress for the lunch date. Felith wore the old T-shirts and jeans that were all she would wear any more. Pretty was for somebody else. Raglan looked the two girls up and down as she pulled the car to the

curb to pick them up. A frown line appeared on her
forehead as she took in Felith's ratty clothing. The
frown was not for Felith, but for the idea that she was
not being treated like some of the paying children.
Haven was a place that took in needy children. Some
of the ones who had trust funds ended up here with
their trust fund paying a small fee until the child
reached an age when they could decide to live on
their own, or if very young, were adopted. Those
children also received an allowance to spend on
clothing, or on their needs. But Felith had nothing.
She had no clothing of her own, nothing to call her
own. Now that they had found her mother's body, as
far as Raglan knew, she had no family. It just wasn't
right for a child to have gone through everything
Felith had gone through, then to also be treated as
dirt by those around her. Rags found herself wanting
to buy anything the child wanted. To give her a
happy life. A happy ever after.

The girls slid into the back seat and put on
their seat belts. They sat in silence as Rags pulled out
into traffic. "You shoot a gun," Felith said, suddenly.
Rags almost swerved into the oncoming lane of
traffic, the question took her by such surprise. This
girl who hadn't said a word when Rags had taken
her to Haven asking something like that. "Yes," she
answered, for she believed that only the truth should
be told to kids.

Using the rearview mirror Rags watched as
Felith battled with herself. Hardly a muscle moved
on the girls face, her eyes alone betrayed the conflict
she was feeling. "Would you teach me how to
shoot?" Felith asked.

"Honey, guns are not something you want to have around. They are a tool I use in my job. Why would you want to know how to shoot?" Rags asked, although she had an idea what the answer would be.

"I need to protect Middy from the monsters, if they try anything," the girl said, so serious, so totally convinced that she was the only thing standing between monsters and the little girl. Rags heart ached. A child protecting a child. The thought that Felith even thought this was necessary was heartbreaking.

It was because she knew Felith was serious that Rags answered the question seriously. "The things I tell single women to do to protect themselves vary as to the woman's situation. There are basic things that you and all women should try to follow. Like don't go anywhere after dark alone. Always carry your car keys in your hand. Get a dog if they fit into your lifestyle. You need to take care of the dog and love it. So don't get one just to have a dog. And their upkeep costs. Have locks on all your doors and windows, and lock them. Set up a security system which covers not only break-ins, but fire and health alarms. Always carry a cell phone with GPS active on it.

"There are so many things that you and anyone else can do to protect yourselves like take self-defense classes. There is just too much to tell you now, but if you want we can work on some things for you today. Like the cell phone, we can get that today. Would you like that?" Rags asked, afraid to push Felith too far.

Middy squirmed in the car seat she was in. In a quivering voice she said. "I don't want monsters to get me."

"Oh, Sweetie, Felith and I will always protect you. For you we can get a pager, so you can page me any time you are feeling scared. Would you like that?" Rags soothed realizing that they shouldn't talk of monsters in front of the child. "Now no more scary talk. We're going to have a fun time. We will have pancakes and eggs and ice cream. Then go shopping for your new phone Felith and Middy's new pager."

"And cake?" Middy asked, thoughts of monster, stripping away by the thought of food.

Even the worry in Felith's eyes seemed to soften at Middy's voice. She turned to the little girl. "You may have my cake too," she said. Rags thought for a moment that mask of stillness would crack into a smile when Middy bounced in her seat and clapped her hands in glee. "Cake must be wonderful," Felith said to herself, so softly that Rags knew Felith had not intended the words to be heard. That put another crack in Rags' already fractured heart. A girl that had never tasted cake. She would bet that Felith always gave Middy her cake.

Sidney and Rags had discussed where to take the girls for lunch. In the end they decided on a family restaurant for the first time. This was the place Sidney had picked. Practical Rags had suggested a fast food place more suited to today's teens. Sidney had pointed out how crowded these places were going to be, and the fact that Felith had been isolated most of her life. It was a delight watching Middy running to the nearest booth and jumping up and down on the soft seat. With Felith, however, the experience seemed totally different. She first carefully looked over the restaurant, then selected a straight-backed chair pulled up at the same booth as Middy had chosen. Sidney watched the choices of the two girls carefully without appearing to. Later he would explain to Rags why Felith had picked the straight-backed chair. The chair was easy to get up out of to runaway if needed, whereas the soft booth seat would be more difficult to get out of to escape.

Watching the children looking over the menu had Rags smiling. Felith read so carefully over the menu, not taking anything but looking at everything. While Middy punched her finger at pictures of food saying, "That and that and that and that too." The pair of them were so precious. When it finally came time to order Felith listened quietly to what each of the others ordered before giving her order. Even then, she hesitated until Rags said, "Well, we can't eat until you select something." Meantime Sidney managed to cancel most of what Middy had ordered.

Sidney was at his best, making Middy and Rags laugh, being his most nonthreatening with Felith. "And then I tried to climb up the rope," Sidney was saying. "With Jim and Johnnie watching. I thought if I could just make it to the top of that rope they would both like me, and we'd be buds for the rest of our life. Now remember I was this scraggly boy with glasses and not one muscle that could claim to be a real muscle, as of yet. So I huffed and puffed and worked on climbing that rope making it all of maybe two feet up. My arms gave out on me and down I slid, landing on my behind on the gym floor. Jim looks at me, a frown upon his face, and I thought, oh heck I'm sunk now. Johnnie is trying so hard not to belly laugh that his body is shaking. Jim says, 'Okay, your nickname is Scrags, come with us now.' And that is how I got my best buds."

Middy's eyes were wide in wonder. She sat open mouthed. Then, being Middy, she couldn't help herself. "For life?" she asked.

"Yeah, for life. We went through high school together. Then Johnnie and Jim wanted to join the Marines. I was pretty doubtful that I could get in to any branch of service, since I was so scrawny. But, Jim and Johnnie were there doing their best to put weight on me and muscle me up some. I think we all saved each other at one time or another while in the Marines."

"Me and Felith are best buds. Tell them Felith. You are my best bud for life," Middy announced looking up at Felith.

For a couple of seconds Felith didn't say anything. She just looked at Middy, then she looked at Sidney, her face so stony and serious. "Yes, we are. And nobody better ever hurt Middy."

Sidney nodded in agreement. "I think we are all best buds here at this table. If anyone tries to hurt any of you the other three will be there. Right?" Sidney said, placing his hand on the table closer to Middy, so she could reach it, then the others. "One for all!" he said, and smiled at Rags when she slapped her hand down on top of his hand. Middy was quick to follow with her tiny hand on top of Rags.

Usually when a group of people proclaimed

the one for all bit everyone just jumped in, but not Felith. She looked at the stack of hands then back up at each of them. Middy her face flushed with excitement was the turning point for Felith. Lightly she placed her hand on top of the other hands. Her face was wary as if this was something she couldn't quite let herself believe, as Rags said, "and all for one." It was too much like a fairytale. There are no happy ever afters.

Still the fairy tale seemed to continue. Twice a week Rags would pick up the girls and take them to where Sidney was waiting for them. It took a while, but gradually Felith began to relax enough to begin to look forward to the outings. The cell phone Felith treasured, being careful not to display it, or to let others know she had a cell phone. She had it set to only vibrate, so on the times Rags called Felith, she would sneak off to answer it in private. Often she would go to the attic and sit among the spider webs to play with the phone. Searching the Internet gave her such a feeling of freedom. Anything she had questions about could be found on the internet. One of the first things Felith did was look up butterflies. She learned how they changed from caterpillars to butterflies. This, she thought, is why it is my guide. I'm changing too. Only, not into a butterfly.

The cell phone vibrated in Felith's pocket. She glanced around, there was nobody around. Still Felith did not want to take a chance on someone seeing her talking on the cell phone. Picking up a stack of books Felith went casually to the attic. She was fast yet didn't appear to hurry. "Hello," she said answering the phone.

"Felith? This is Sidney, I… uh… need your advice," Sidney said.

For a long moment Felith didn't reply. She weighed the dangers of such a call. At last she found her voice. "What is it you want?" Felith asked.

"Well… uh… I am going to ask Rags to marry me," Sidney said. "I would like you to help me pick out a ring for her. Okay?"

In all her life nothing had shocked Felith as much as Sidney's words. "You want Middy, and me, to help you?" she managed to get out.

"Oh, would you? I'm just at my wits end on how to go about this. Me!" He stopped talking and Felith could hear him fumbling with his phone. "Hold on. Something is going on." In the back ground it sounded like a television or something was giving an announcement. Suddenly Sidney was back, he sounded different, all business now. "Felith, I need to go now. Thank you." And just like that he was gone.

It was Rags who showed up later. But this was not a social visit. Rags brought a teenage boy. The boy was blond headed, with eyes that seemed to sparkle blue, his face was set in an angry scowl. There was nothing about him that spoke friendly. In Mr. Shadman's office Raglan was speaking softly to Mr. Shadman. From the look on Shadman's face, he was not happy taking in this angry boy. Finally Raglan won out. She smiled at the angry boy, and handed him a bag of belongings.

As Rags was leaving she came over to Felith. She looked worried and sad. "Help him if you can.

He needs somebody who will understand, and not be judging." With that Raglan patted Felith's arm and hurried out. Felith looked doubtfully at the boy. Help him? He was one of them, the monsters. There was something about him that reminded her of herself. She watched him glare at everyone around him, as if daring anyone to approach him. It was then she realized what Raglan had meant. They hurt boys too.

No one saw him. They looked at him. What they thought they saw, he didn't know. But no one saw him. Except the one girl. She only glanced at him, but there was knowing in her eyes. She will tell them, Fred thought. So he stared at her until she glanced up again at him, Fred did his best to look threatening. Let her think on that, he thought.

It was the pretty girl in the larger group that came over to him. She smiled at him and placed her hand on his arm. "You can come sit at our table when we dine tonight," she said. Fred tried to smile back at her. It took an effort, but he thought he had succeeded.

Dinner was when Fred learned all about the knowing girl. The other girls talked about her as if she was a bit of trash under their feet. She was said to be a whore, a common thief among other things. All this according to Rosemary and Julian, although they talked in whispers when mentioning her, as if some shame was attached to what they were saying. Fred was amply warned to stay away from her. Julian flirted with him often trying, so it seemed, to get a rise out of the Robert guy. Off to the side at another table the knowing girl sat with the little girl. Fred tried to be sociable, he was just so angry. It was like steam was building up inside him, boiling his brain. He wanted to scream at everyone to shut up and get away from him. Only it was easier to just play along. So he was the new guy that they confided in, or tried to charm. All of them made his skin crawl, he just wanted to be away from everyone. Deep down, he had to admit to himself that that girl, that strange girl, was the only one who respected his personal space.

By the time it was bedtime, Fred thought he had an idea of how the dynamics of this little group worked out. Julian was the queen bee while Rosemary was her sidekick. Robert was like the boyfriend to either Julian or Rosemary. And the rest of the children were just orphans. They didn't really count as far as Julian's little group was concern. Then there was the weird girl and her short companion. How they fit into everything he wasn't quite certain. Of them all, the weird girl was the one who worried him most. She somehow knew what he had been through recently. Only she didn't seem of a mind to gossip with the other girls about it, or with Robert. But, could he trust her to keep quiet?

Chapter Five

TRAUMA AND REVENGE

Over the next few days several of the children found homes. Only Julian, Rosemary, Robert, and Fred remained of the older children, besides Felith. Of the youngsters there was just Middy left. Still, Sidney hadn't come to go shopping with Middy and Felith. While on the one hand it was a relief to Felith, there was part of her that felt let down. She had been unaware of the bit of belief and trust that had started to creep upon her where Rags and Sidney were concerned. As far back as that tiny spark of belief was shoved, it had been there despite the knowledge that there were no happy endings, ever. People didn't care, it was as simple as that. Felith looked over to where Middy was doing her homework, and knew that she cared about Middy. So, maybe it was a decision as to whether a person cared, or didn't. Of the people left in Haven, it wasn't hard to see where the lines were drawn. Middy and Felith were on one side of that invisible line, and all the rest on the other side. Although Robert had continued to tutor Felith, she didn't need much in the way of tutoring now, and that was finally coming to an end. As for her lessons, Olivia had managed to purchase a computer for Felith to work her lessons upon. The few written tests she had to turn in to advance through the grade levels had prove little challenge. Writing itself had at first been the real challenge.

The musings which had been running through Felith's mind were abruptly interrupted with a knock on the door. Mr. Shadman came out of his office and went to the door. From the expression on his face, he was anything but pleased at whatever he knew to be on the other side of the door. As the door swung open Felith saw Sidney standing in the opening. He spoke softly to Mr. Shadman, glancing into the interior once to send a little smile to Middy and Felith. There was such a seriousness about the conversation between Sidney and Mr. Shadman that Felith's cool mask slipped a bit into a line of worry. She quickly recovered as Mr. Shadman turned around. "Go to your rooms. Remain there until we have settled our newest member in," Mr. Shadman said.

Curious looks flickered to the doorway as everyone obeyed. Felith took Middy's hand as they walked to the girls side of the room. She looked once more towards the door thinking to see Sidney again, but he had left. From outside a scream of terror erupted, followed by weeping. Shooing Middy into the bedroom, Felith turned to see who was in such pain.

Mr. Shadman opened the door wide for a blue uniformed officer to enter the common room. The officer had a screaming boy in his arms. The child screamed and kicked, his face a mass of pure terror. At that moment one thought flashed through Felith's mind and she reacted. Going up to the officer Felith used one of Middy's favorite actions, she kicked the officer in the shins. Like a scared monkey the boy sprang free of the officer and leaped to Felith. He hid behind her peeping around her to scream. Not once did he stop weeping.

The officer, Mr. Shadman, and Sidney all stood staring at Felith and the crying boy. Sidney squatted making himself smaller, at Eric's level. The boy had had his entire family ripped into bits. Any movement set him off into hysterical screams and weeping. Mr. Shadman was shaking his head. "We aren't equipped to handle this level of mental trauma. You will have to get him committed at a hospital," he was saying over the noise Eric was making.

Staying in his squat, Sidney shook his head. "Everything has filled up. We have more cases than space. You are the last resort. I can't even tell you when I'll be be able to come back. Let's get him settled and see if he can find some sort of security in the routine," he said, then looked up at Felith. "Do you think you can calm Eric down? Right now he sees every movement as a threat. This is the first time he has responded to anyone."

Another baby monster. This time Sidney wanted her to help the baby monster, Felith thought. Still she found herself nodding. Turning she motioned the boy Eric to follow her. He came with her in a jerky manner, constantly looking back and around at the men and every shadow. Instead of going to one of the other rooms, Felith took Eric to the little sitting area where Robert used to read stories to the little ones. She sat down on a low child chair. Eric scooted behind her. Even though the little boy wasn't touching her, Felith could feel the trembling of his body. Not looking at him she opened a book and began to read aloud a story. It was a book that had frogs and princesses, mushrooms that danced about, and wishes that came true. Moments passed until the sobbing ceased and eased to hiccups. There was a rustle as Eric moved. At the first touch of the boy, Felith wanted to get away from him, but it was such a tentative touch, as if the child was afraid of being rejected, and that kept Felith still. Slowly Eric climbed into Felith's lap. His arms went around Felith's bony body, and he snuggled against her. She continued to read, her voice soft and even. Moments passed with Eric crying softly against her. Her shirt became wet. Soft hiccups between tears slowly died away. Reaching the end of the book, Felith realized Eric was asleep. He looked so vulnerable, not like a monster at all.

Mr. Shadman walked past Felith into the boys' bedrooms. Soon Robert and Fred appeared in the entrance to the bedrooms. Both teens looked at Felith holding Eric. They had heard the screams and the wild crying. Seeing Felith holding the sleeping boy was as much a shock as the screams had been. Felith, who everyone thought so cold, without emotion, she was the one holding the little boy. Not Rosemary, who often wiped Middy's face, or Julian

who tried to appear to be the best of the whole group
of them, or at least claimed to be the best. Behind
them, Mr. Shadman came up and motioned for Felith
to bring Eric into the room. Robert started forward
to help, but Felith shook her head at him. Fred just
stood and watched, as if trying to figure out the why
of everything.

A bed had been turned down waiting for
Eric. Felith struggled to carry the child, stepping
carefully so as not to wake him. This was another
new experience for her, to feel something for a
monster. It both surprised and terrified her that she
felt anything for a monster, even if he was still a baby.
Aware that both Fred and Robert were tagging along
behind her, Felith smoothed her face, and tried to
walk as if the child wasn't heavy to carry. Placing the
boy upon the bed, Felith stood a moment looking
down at the sleeping child. Carefully she placed the
top sheet and blanket over Eric. As Felith tucked
the blanket around Eric's sleeping form, it occurred
to her that this was what storybook mothers did,
tucked their children into bed. How ironic that
Felith should be tucking in a monster child, when
she had never experienced being tucked in herself.
Not looking at Robert or Fred, Felith went back to
the girls' side of the building.

It was the middle of the night and a screech of
pure terror had Fred leaping out of bed. Robert was
not far behind him. The new boy Eric was running
like mad for an open cabinet. Once he reached the
cabinet he climbed in and slammed the door shut.
Unfortunately, he had picked the one cabinet in
the room that would not remain closed. The door

swung open. By then Robert was one bed away from the cabinet Eric was hiding in. It was Fred's hand that stopped Robert from getting any closer. "Stop, damn it! You can't just go up to him like that," Fred whispered. "Get that girl. Go. Go now, I'll watch the kid."

Seeing the sense in Fred's order, Robert went quickly out of the room. Only to find Felith already crossing the common room. He waved his hand in a hurry up motion. She hesitated, then heard Eric's sobbing and rushed on past Robert. Fred was sitting very still two beds away from where Eric was hiding. As Felith came closer she could hear Fred talking in a soft monotone. "This is a safe place. The girl is coming to hold you safe in her arms again. Just try to relax. You can see me, I'm not going to approach you, not going to hurt you. This is a safe place."

It was then that Eric saw Felith. He was out of the cabinet as if shot from a cannon, and wrapped around her bony figure before anyone could stop him. Felith knelt down and held him to her. She didn't say anything, as she shifted them both to the nearest bare mattress. Laying down Felith held Eric cuddled up against her. There was a movement by the door. A short shadow was followed by Middy. She looked around at Robert and Fred in their boxer shorts, and continued on until she spotted Felith laying with Eric. The little girl's chin went up. She went to one of the beds and pulled a blanket off of it. Middy struggled with the blanket but finally got it free of the bed. Then promptly tripped over it. Eric let out a little scream. Then Fred began to talk all over again, the same thing over and over, "This is a safe place. The girl is holding you safely in her arms. You are safe." While Fred helped Middy up, taking the blanket from her, he watched as Middy climbed on the bed and wrapped her arms around Felith from the opposite side of where Eric was laying. Carefully, Fred placed the blanket over the three of them in the bed. Shaking his head as he walked away, Robert looked at Fred. It had been a good move on Fred's part, for all the anger the boy displayed, he had shown good sense in talking to Eric. Robert motioned to Fred to come and get back in bed. The look on Fred's face surprised Robert. There was something close to longing in the final look he gave the three damaged kids cuddled all together in one bed. None of them saw Mr. Shadman standing just outside the doorway. He wasn't stupid, the problem had been solved on what to do with Eric, only, how to do it was another matter.

Mr. Shadman paced his office, his face tight with worry. Olivia had gone out to buy milk last night just before Sidney had brought Eric. She hadn't returned. How did she expect him to feed the children? That was her job. And what, what if something had happened to her? It was that worry which sent him finally to the phone. As Mr. Shadman's hand touched the phone it rang. He jumped, then chided himself, that old fear of his that a ringing phone was bad news wasn't true. He had often answered the phone to have pleasing conversations. Picking up the receiver he said, "Haven" into the phone.

There was soft weeping on the otherside of

the line, then Olivia's voice, ragged, broken, hardly recognizable, "Th… They(gasp) hurt me. Hospital… I'm at the hospital." Soft weeping followed.

"I'm coming, Olivia. Don't you worry one bit, I'm on the way," Mr. Shadman said, his voice more assuring than he felt. Hanging up he felt in turmoil. Olivia hurt and in the hospital? It was something his mind just wouldn't wrap around. The children, he couldn't just leave the children here alone. But Olivia needed him. He bounced back and forth between worry about leaving the children alone and helping Olivia even as he picked up his car keys. Only then did he know what he would do.

"Robert. Felith," he called out as he left his office. Both Robert and Felith appeared from the boys' side of the building. Shadman stopped short. This was something he would have to deal with when he came back, Shadman thought. Then, he realized Felith had two satellites clutching her legs. Of course he had forgotten about Eric, and Felith going to him when he woke screaming. It was a relief he didn't have to deal with some sort of budding romance. Still he couldn't help but give Robert a stern look. "You two will be in charge while I'm gone. Olivia has been hurt and is in the hospital. That means the chores around here fall on all of you for now. Felith, set Rosemary and Julian to making breakfast. Robert, you need to keep everyone behaving. Get them to cleaning, or whatever it takes. Nobody is to leave today. Got it?" Shadman said, looking sternly, first at Felith then Robert.

Felith and Robert nodded as one. It was Middy who spoke though. "Can she come home and make us cake?" she asked, with all the innocence of someone who had no idea of serious illness.

Felith and Robert both knelt down to Middy's level. "We don't want to bother Miss Olivia with making a cake while she is sick. If you are very, very good today, we will all make cupcakes together. But only for dinner," Robert said, hoping he could manage cupcakes. Yet it was Felith that Middy looked towards, while on the other side of Felith, Eric began to cry. Shadman turned away and started to the door. When he did Eric screamed and clutched Felith so tightly she could barely take a breath.

It was Fred who saved Felith from Eric's grip. "Eric, you have to let the girl take a breath. You don't want to hurt her do you?" he said from behind them. The little boy's head whipped around to Fred then back to Felith, and suddenly Felith could draw air into her lungs. She glanced at Fred giving him a small nod of her head in approval. He, in turn, scowled as if he had been insulted.

It was Robert who smiled at Felith, and offered his hand to help her stand. By then Felith was her old self, the mask of indifference back in place. With a bit of effort she manage to stand up without help from Robert, with Eric in her arms. She glanced over to Fred again. Then looked down on Eric. "You need to take a shower. I'm not allowed to go into the boys' bathroom, so would you go with Fred and let him guard you so no one enters while you shower? Robert here will get you something to wear. Is that okay?"

Eric's eyes widen in fear for a moment. He shook his head, but a look at Fred's scowling face seemed to change his mind. Slowly he loosened his grip on Felith and slid down her body to the floor. When he just stood there Middy's mouth scrunched up to the side. She stepped slowly up to Eric. "I'll guard Felith. She will be safe with me," she said in a very serious voice, as she poked herself in the chest with her thumb. As ridiculous as that sounded, it worked. Eric skittered over to Fred and followed him to the boy's bathroom.

Now for the hard part, Felith thought. Face set in stony indifference, Felith went into the girls' bedroom. Rosemary and Julian were dressed sitting on their beds talking. Felith had orders, and they would be carried out. Stepping in and over to her own cabinet to get a clean shirt, Felith spoke as if this was something she did everyday. "Rosemary, you and Julian will cook breakfast, and serve it. I will do the dishes after breakfast. If this emergency should carry through lunch, Robert and Fred will cook the meal, and you two will do the cleanup. Miss Olivia is in the hospital and we have orders to do these things. You had best get started."

"You can't order me around. You are nothing. A smear upon the dirt of the world," Julian spat out just as Robert poked his head in the door.

"Yes she can. Mr. Shadman left her in charge of things. So lets get to it, Jules. I do want to see if you can cook," he teased

Sending a dirty look in Felith's direction, Julian went up to Robert and tapped him under the chin. "Oh, I can cook. Well eggs anyway," she said. Then, she ruined it all. "But I'm no servant to be ordered around."

"Well until Mr. Shadman says different we are following Felith's lead. And I know I'm pretty hungry so best make a lot of eggs," Robert said. He left then as if that was the end of the conversation.

"It might be fun cooking for Robert," Rosemary said.

Julian gave a little laugh, then turned her back on Felith. "If Robert says to do that. I guess I will. But once we are married he's not going to boss me around," she said. Then she laughed and grabbed Rosemary's arm dragging her off chattering about what sort of wedding she was planning.

Picking up a clean shirt and another pair of jeans, Felith went to the showers. Things had changed since the first time she had taken a shower in this room. She no longer hid clothing under the towels. She was soaping up in the shower when that revelation hit her. So many things changing, not only the shower, but there was a baby monster, who she felt sorry for. Was this the sort of agony a caterpillar went through when it changed into a butterfly. Only she wasn't a butterfly. After showering Felith towel dried her hair and left it alone. She knew she was delaying going out to the common room. Middy, Felith's shadow, had been guarding the doorway. She looked out and then ran to Felith. "He is out," she announced. "Eric." Inside Felith sighed, called on her willpower, and went out to face being touched by a baby monster.

It was strange, after spending the night being clutched tightly by Eric, to see the child following

Fred along obediently. When Eric saw Felith from across the common room he started to rush over to her. She braced herself for being clutched in the child's hands and arms. Suddenly he stopped and looked up at Fred. It was amazing how Eric went back to a walk, slowly approaching Felith. He tucked himself up next to her, a slight tremble running through his little body. Felith gave him, and Fred, an approving nod.

Felith settled the two little ones at the reading area. A glance at Fred seemed to assure Eric it was okay to sit in a chair instead of crowding Felith. She breathed a breath of relief at not being sat on, yet at the same time, she sort of missed holding Eric. She wondered about that missing bit. The why of it. Having not come to any reasoning for the missing, she tucked it away to look at another time. For now she pulled out the coloring books for Eric and Middy.

Looking at Eric from the corner of her eye, Middy twitched her little mouth, then she plopped down closer to Eric prepared to give him a lesson in coloring. The reaction was immediate. Eric let out a screech of pure terror, and ran. He was so fast, so fast, that nobody was able to catch him. He was into the boy's room and shut inside the closest cabinet before anyone but Fred and Felith could react. Middy looked up at Felith, her eyes filled with tears. Without even thinking about it, Felith picked Middy up and headed into the boy's room.

Fred was already there, near but not close to the cabinet, keeping a distance, yet there. His voice was soft and even, as if he had done this 1 million times, "The girl is coming with the little one. The little one is crying because she scared you. The girl will hold you when you are ready. She is here, for you."

Slowly the cabinet opened up. Middy slid down Felith and stood back, being very still, her tears covered her face, which was scrunched up in intense concentration. The boy's head came out far enough from the cabinet that he could look around. His face was tear streaked, and it was as if a constant flow of tears leaked from his eyes. First he looked to Fred, who sat at a distance, but close enough to be a comfort. Then, his face fearful, he tracked his looking over to Middy and Felith. Carefully, pausing at every other step, Felith came closer to Eric. Middy followed in her wake copying Felith's every move. Felith looked over at Fred, giving a slight nod. Then she looked over at Middy and back to Eric, she spoke. "We are all for one. Each prepared to come to the aid of the other. Remember that."

Felith could feel Fred staring at her when she spoke to Eric. She had not known what else to say. Maybe it sounded stupid. Whatever truth there was to those words could only be felt inside the person. To deceive herself into thinking that others truly would be there for her was not something she would do. Only what she did herself could she know for true. Eric pointed to her, then at Middy, and finally at Fred and himself. And there it was, the moment when Felith was being asked to include two more into her circle. She faced it, the truth of it, and gave a little nod.

Slowly Eric came out of the cabinet. He

looked at Fred, who stood up just as slowly. The four of them walked back into the common room to wait for breakfast. Robert was there, his face holding worry. Before he could come over to the four, Fred held up his hand in a stopping motion. In contrast to Robert's worried expression, Fred's was one of anger. "Breakfast is ready. I thought it better not to ring the bell," Robert said. Felith gave a slight tilt of her head in approval. That simple tilt of the head had a warmth spreading inside of Robert. Slowly Robert turned and went into the dining room. It looked as if he had talked to Julian and Rosemary, as both stood quietly at the kitchen door. Walking over to his usual spot Robert waited for Fred to join him.

For a moment Eric paused when Fred walked over to stand by Robert. He looked up at Felith, then over to where Fred stood. Biting his bottom lip, trying to hold back the tears brimming in his eyes, Eric went over to stand next to Fred. Fred was the protector, his protector. Fear sprang inside of him when Felith and Middy didn't join him. Then Fred slowly placed his hand on Eric's head, and Eric knew he had made the right choice. They weren't going to rip him to pieces. Tears began to roll down his cheeks, but he stood fast as Rosemary sat a plate of food in front of him. He was so hungry.

An awkward moment passed before Robert said the grace. They were all so used to Olivia appointing someone to say the grace. There was little in the way of conversation as they ate eggs and toast. Julian brought everyone a glass of orange juice, but there was no milk. It had been milk that Olivia had left to buy when she was hurt. Felith ate her food quickly. She had assigned herself as the person to do clean up after breakfast, and wanted to start the water filling the sink as soon as possible. Slowly she stood up and collected her own plate. Looking over to where Eric sat with the others, Felith gave a tiny nod of approval, then walked into the kitchen.

The kitchen was a mess. It looked as if eggs had been transferred from plate to plate. Most of the dishes were left dirty, as were the pots and pans. Felith knew this was Julian's attempt to hurt her in some way. She resented Felith telling her to do things. Just like that Julian was off the work list Felith had formed in her mind, as she ran hot water into the sink Felith reset her mental list. There was nothing on it now that included Julian. Behind her she could hear plates and glasses being stacked on the bar that separated the kitchen and the dining room. Everyone could see the mess made in the kitchen. But nobody said anything.

Robert was so angry at Julian. Her childish attempts to sabotage Felith made him realize he didn't want to be with her. And that alone was upsetting. From the moment he had met Julian she had always assumed that the two of them would be married. There had never seemed to be any reason to disagree with that assumption. Julian was beautiful, sexy, and knew the same set of friends as he did. Now he wondered if she was going to be a vindictive woman as a wife. Looking at the mess Julian had made for Felith to clean up, Robert was about to go in and help, when Felith spoke up. "Robert, please entertain the little ones. You and

Rosemary will have clean up after lunch. Fred and I will do the cooking," she said, as she rinsed another dish and set it in the draining board to dry. She was right, of course, the little ones need not be subjected to any argument between them. Although Middy would have figured it out by now.

Julian heard Felith giving Robert the lunch orders. I suppose, she thought, that I'll have laundry duty now. Dealing with dirty clothes might be easier than the dirty looks Middy was giving her. The little brat had put a bruise on her leg last time Middy kicked her. And Robert, Robert was irritated with her again. Why did she do these things? She had been so mad at that dirty girl telling her what to do, and wanted her to pay for presuming to be better than she and Rosemary. The nerve of the girl giving her orders. Should she be sorry for teaching the idiot a lesson? Not hardly. It was that dirty girls fault, all of it. She stewed, brewing up her anger as she waited for the orders to be given to do the laundry.

In the kitchen Felith scrubbed the last of the pots and pans. That chore done she wiped down all the surfaces as she had seen Olivia do after every meal. It was time to put Eric and Middy to work. Felith watched as Robert read a book to Eric and Middy. The little boy's face was looking up at Robert, intent on the story, still now and then he looked around until he saw Fred over in a corner, silently doing push-ups. Felith waited until the end of whatever page Robert was on in the storybook before breaking into the little group. "I think it is time that Middy and Eric do their part of the chores. We want everything to be done when Olivia gets back from the hospital," she said, knowing that Middy wanted Olivia's cakes more than anything else.

For a moment it looked as if Middy was going to jump up and clap her hands in joy at the thought of Olivia coming back. Then she glanced at Eric. "Olivia makes the best chocolate cake ever. Lets make it clean for her, so she can make cake," she said. Eric nodded, his lips trembling, as though he barely suppressed crying. He stood up and reached out for Felith's hand.

Fortunately Felith was becoming accustom to being touched by the boy. She allowed the touch without flinching away. "What I have for you two is the laundry. Middy, you have helped me with the laundry when I've had laundry duty, so you know about the gathering and sorting. We will all do the sorting together," Felith continued to explain things to the youngsters as they walked first to the boys' side, and then to the girls' side of the building gathering up the bedding and clothing that nobody wanted to wash on their own. She tried to make it a fun thing to do for Eric's sake. In the back of her mind was constant worry about Olivia, and the fact that Shadman hadn't come back yet. It was then that Felith's phone vibrated.

Glancing around first before she answered the phone. Felith made certain that nobody was nearby, except Middy and Eric. Middy knew about the phone. So there was no sense hiding it from her, and Eric, Eric, she thought was in her circle and she didn't want to have to hide anything from him. "Hello," she said into the phone.

"I'm on the way home with Olivia. Have her a bed set up in the common room, near the bathroom. The hospital has kicked anyone who can be cared for at home out, and some that can't," Shadman seemed to take a breath, "We will be there shortly," Shadman's voice said over her cell phone.

"Middy and Eric, look here. This is how much you put in each of the loads of laundry. Wash them in the piles as we have separated them. Use this setting for all of them," Felith said, showing the two youngsters how to set the dial. "I need to set up a bed for Olivia. Will you be okay doing the laundry?" Felith asked.

Immediately Middy's head nodded, though she threw a glance at Eric as if in doubt. "One for all," Middy said. "This is our part. I'll guard Eric too," she added in that determined tone of hers. It was then that Eric nodded too. As ridiculous as that seemed, little Middy guarding Eric, it was enough to reassure the little boy that he was safe.

The bed was ready for Olivia, and they had placed a string of curtains tacked up all in a line, to give Olivia some privacy going to the bathroom. Everyone scattered to clean up their own sleeping areas, even Julian. A sense of anticipation hung in the air as time passed. Then Robert began to pace, shortly Middy was squirming when she sat down between laundry loads. Even Eric kept throwing quick worried looks at the door. And still it didn't open.

An hour passed, then two hours. "Traffic," Robert said. "It has to be the traffic."

Then, Felith's cell phone vibrated in her

pocket, and she knew. For a moment she thought about answering it in the open, in front of all the others. But this was her only possession, and she was not quite ready to have it taken away from her. She went out into the garden area, as she did most days to answer a call. Between two of the trees Fred was doing push-ups, hard and fast, as if punishing his body. His face was hard and angry, with sweat dripping off of his skin. If not for the urgency Felith felt she would have gone back in and sought out the attic to answer the phone call. But not this call, it needed answered now, she could feel it and knew, just knew.

Fred watched the girl, knowing she had seen him. There was worry in her eyes. When she pulled a cell phone out of her pocket and answered it, he was surprised. Not once had he seen her with a cell phone. The girls face was blanched as she answered the phone, and set as if of stone. She has braced herself for bad news, soon she will clutch her stomach as women do, Fred thought. He waited for Felith's arm to grasp her stomach as if to hold everything inside and ward away blows however invisible. The grasping never came. It was as if instead quiet resolve swept over the girl. She beckoned to Fred to follow her. As she went back inside.

The others were in the common room, Robert was still roaming around the room, now and then straightening something that didn't need to be straightened. When he saw Fred and Felith enter the room he called out to the others, "Gather round." His eyes stayed focused on Felith. She was so hard to read. Robert glanced at Fred, his scowl if anything darker than usual. For once he had no words. No matter how hard he tried to make himself asked what news Felith had, he couldn't. The little ones gathered close to Felith and Fred. Rosemary and Julian stood off to one side, their reluctance to appear part of the group that Felith was in, was very clear. Finally Robert managed to get out a word. "Felith?"

She nodded to Robert. It was up to her to tell them. Her mind went to the gray place seeking butterflies. "Mr. Shadman and Olivia were killed in a vehicle accident. The details are too gruesome to tell. It seems the world has gone crazy."

Chapter Six

SAVING RAGS

The world had gone crazy. Olivia and Mr. Shadman were dead. There was some virus driving the people of the world inside their homes like scared rabbits in a burrow. Grocery shelves were empty as people hoarded food, afraid to go out and eat in restaurants, or even attend work. It was not safe to walk the streets. People were taking advantage of the empty streets to commit crimes, and unthinkable things were happening to good people. At Haven it was a waiting game. They were waiting to see what would happen to them, now that Olivia and Mr. Shadman weren't in charge of their care.

The little ones had been quiet. Even Eric had stopped screaming when someone around him moved. Now he just sobbed for the most part. Felith and Robert were still in charge, for now. Sidney came by and brought a huge load of food once. Rags came on another day and brought even more, mostly canned goods. She warned them to stay inside as much as possible, and to practice emergency safety. Felith started the training immediately. Middy and Eric were shown how to stay hidden, and if needed, to clamp their hands over their mouths to keep quiet. She tried to impress upon Rosemary and Julian the importance of staying back when the doors were opened. They strung empty cans on strings across the windows and placed them at the doors at night. Everything that Rags had recommended they set up, except for a dog.

Julian thought the whole thing was stupid. "It is only an outbreak of flu," she said. "Soon, social services would send someone to take care of us." But nobody came.

Each day the news on Felith's phone seem more dire. People were beginning to riot demanding medications. Others were just taking advantage of the chaos to strip stores of their goods. The police and the hospitals had their hands full. It was dangerous to be out even in the daytime. The president had announced a national emergency. People were to remain in their homes, going out only if it was absolutely necessary. The National Guard was activated and sent into the larger cities to try and control the riots. In the little town in which Haven was located, it was a matter of too few to take care of too many. And the numbers were decreasing by the day. This virus was extremely deadly. It had spread through mosquitoes who had evidently sucked the blood of infected birds then bit people. Once among the populous it spread like wild fire. There was a 99% fatality rate. The one percent who survived the flu, more often than not, died of secondary infections. The worry load on Felith increased with each day that passed.

One morning they woke up to find a teenage girl huddled outside the door. She looked in good health and clean, her clothing of middle class quality. She wouldn't speak, just shook her head yes or no when asked a question. Her face was framed by soft blond hair, her skin pale and fair. There didn't seem to be anything wrong with her other than she wouldn't talk.

Fred watched as Robert tried to get the girl to tell her name. Finally he could take the badgering no more and went into Shadman's office where he picked up a pen and tablet. Walking over to the girl he offered the tablet to her. Her eyes grew round with surprise, but she took the tablet and wrote 'Emily'. So it was that Emily became part of their little group of people.

After Emily came to them, nobody came to Haven. Not Sidney or Rags with food, nor any of the rowdy people that seemed determined to tear the neighborhood to apart. The little group of survivors were starting to run out of food. It became clear that someone would have to venture out to find food of some sort for the them all. One morning as the group waited for Felith to issue the work orders for that day, Fred stepped forward wearing a long-sleeved black turtlenecks shirt and jeans. "I'm going out and hunt up some groceries. All we have left is some oatmeal and a few things in the freezer. So take me off the morning work list," he told Felith.

"I'll go with you, two can carry more than one

person," Robert said.

"No, you have to be here to protect the girls and Eric," Fred said, holding up his hand in a halting motion. Eric looked up with fear in his eye at the thought of his protector leaving. "It is okay, Eric. The girls and him," he motioned with his thumb towards Robert, "will be here. I'll be as fast as I can be. Okay?"

The fact that Fred had asked Eric if it was okay seemed to calm the child. He went over to Middy and stood by her. Something, maybe a smile, played with Fred's lips at the thought that Eric thought Middy a better protector than Robert. It was then Fred glanced at Felith. She had been silently watching him. There was a worry line on her forehead. When had that appeared on that face so devoid of expression, Fred wondered. For a long moment she just stood looking at him, as if trying to read his purpose in going. I'm not leaving you, he thought to her. At last she gave one of those brief nods that meant she approved, and that nod seemed to sweep over him with this sense of well-being. For once he felt he belonged here, with her and this motley bunch of misfits.

Robert laid on the floor, if not for the rise and fall of his chest Felith would have thought him dead. Her mind still shook with the shock of Robert trying to fight the group of boys who had broken into the house. Behind the sofa Middy was huddled where Felith had shoved her out of sight. Julian and Rosemary were crouching behind the large potted plants Felith had nursed back to life before the world seemed to shatter for everyone. One of the boys could see them and laughing he told the leader he could use a good banging. The girls gasped as Felith watched. Julian's face turned white as if the blood had drained out of it. Felith knew there was a danger that Fred would walk in on the gang of boys from grocery gathering. The boys would rape them all if something didn't happen soon to distract them. She took a step forward eyes never straying to betray the whereabouts of anyone hiding in the house. "Its a deal then. I'll go with you. You can use me. There is nothing here but a few starving kids. The rest of them would be more trouble than you need. Let them be and I'll let you use me all night."

The apparent leader looked at Eric, and Eric, as if on cue, started to bawl loudly. The leader of the gang twisted his mouth in disgust. "Okay, all night, all of us, anyway we want."

Felith nodded. How she managed to walk out of the house she didn't know. Julian's pale face kept flashing in Felith's mind, and Middy hiding behind the sofa holding her hands over her mouth so as not to make a sound. This is one of the things she had tried to drill into Middy and the others, if hidden don't make a sound, or move until someone they knew came.

It was slow and painful trying to wake up. Robert could hear Eric bawling from the other room. The light seemed to want to pierce his brain through his eyelids, so he kept them closed. That is until he heard Middy sobbing over and over. "They took her! They took her!" He wanted to ask who, but someone was beating him inside his head. All he managed was a groan.

"Shut up, you stupid child. He's waking up," that was Julian's voice.

"Robby, they took Felith," Middy screeched, and with that it all flooded back to Robert. The boys breaking into the house. Him stupidly trying to push them back out and being hit.

"Shut up," Julian screeched right back. "They didn't take her, you bothersome brat. She went on her own."

Robert fought through the pounding in his skull and sat up. For a moment the room seemed to tilt dangerously, then it all straightened. The broken door had a chair shoved under the doorknob to hold it closed, and there was a pounding. Only it wasn't in his head.

"Let me in," Fred yelled, "I've got the frigging groceries." Rosemary removed the chair propped under the door's knob. Fred entered, looked around, and took command of their ragtag group. Soon Eric and Middy were in the kitchen sipping juice. Julian looked more angry than upset by everything that had happened. Fred took Robert, Rosemary and Julian aside once the kids and Emily were more settled. "Okay, what happened after I left?"

Julian pinched her lips together, never a good sign. Most often it meant she was hiding something, or thinking of hiding something. It was Rosemary who finally told Fred about the boys threatening to rape them and Felith's deal with them. All Fred could think was that stupid, stupid girl she sacrificed herself, and for who? Them? It was that which had Fred pacing the floor all night, and the thoughts that kept creeping into his mind. Those boys hurting Felith. And her words to Eric, 'All for one,' what she really meant was, one giving for all. It played on his mind that he wasn't there to stop the boys. It was his fault. He should have stayed here and sent that wimp Robert out for groceries.

Dawn came, and still there was no Felith. The shadows lengthen, and grew longer as the day began to fade. Middy refused to give up her place on the sofa, where she watched the door for some sign of Felith returning. Robert too kept watch. He and Fred had kept everyone inside during the day, feeling it wasn't safe to search for food with that gang of boys roaming around. Each hour that passed Robert grew more fearful of Felith having been killed. The world had gone crazy, none of them were safe.

Near midnight Middy fell asleep. Fred covered the child, then turned the lights off, leaving only a small lamp glowing in the kitchen window. It wasn't left for Felith to find her way home, not really. No, not really. Placing a chair in a darkened corner Fred sat down to watch over Middy and wait. He must've dozed. The sound of water running woke him up.

Robert came out of the boys' room then, wondering who was wasting water in the middle of the night. Then Robert saw the clothing thrown in the trash can. They were filthy and bloody, and belonged to Felith. Nausea threatened his stomach. As silently as possible he went to the boys' room and laid down. It seemed like hours passed while Robert laid there pretending to be asleep, listening to the shower running, and running. When it finally turned off he thought about getting up and seeing if Felith was okay, but images of her with those boys flashed in his head, and he couldn't get up, couldn't even go look at her. He didn't think of himself to be a coward, yet at that moment he felt like one.

Fred had heard it all, the bit about the boys breaking in, Felith leaving with them. It had taken all his will power not to hit Robert for letting this happen, but he knew it wasn't Robert's fault. One for all. Those words burned inside him since the day Felith had spoken them to Eric. She had proved that. One for all. The shower running alerted Fred to Felith being in the house. She would want to wash them off of her and wear something loose and heavy to sleep in, something soft and thick to hold her as she shivered. Fred thought of all that, and went and found a thick winter set of sweats in the closet where Olivia kept the used clothes. Quietly he slipped into the bathroom and placed the sweats where Felith would see them. If this was the only thing he could do for her he would.

The sweats top was difficult to put on, it was the bottoms that took the last of Felith's strength. She had to sit down and slip her legs in one at a time. The material was well worn and soft against her skin, so warm. Yet nothing in her felt warmed. It was as if her very heart had been pierced by a sword of ice, freezing her from the inside out. No warmth. No warmth ever. Crawling into her bed she curled beneath the covers shivering as constantly shadowed figures grabbed and mauled her, until the blackness of exhaustion finally gave her sweet sleep.

Something was laying on top of Felith. Her nose smelled chocolate, chocolate meant Middy. Slowly Felith opened her eyes. Middy, her face scrunched up in what passed for concern for her, sat on top of Felith. "Hi, midget," Felith said, reaching up to wipe the tears off the little girl's face. She watched Middy struggle to get the crying under control.

Sliding off of Felith, the child stood by the bed. When she spoke there was only the slightest tremble to her words, "You are making us late for breakfast." Those words placed one tiny spark of warmth inside of Felith. With effort she struggled to her feet and started the painful shuffle to the bathroom to wash up for breakfast. After all she couldn't keep Middy from food.

They were all sitting around one table, those of them that were left. Rosemary, Julian, the boy Eric, silent Emily, and angry Fred. Lastly there was Robert. Robert who had tried to protect them all. Robert who couldn't, or wouldn't, even look at Felith. She didn't care. Slowly, painfully she made her way to the small side table with Middy.

It was Fred that came and sat with Middy and Felith. He sat his plate down and ate for a while in silence. Felith concentrated on trying to eat her food. Middy kept placing spoonfuls of her own food on Felith's plate. But soon it was obvious that Felith had no appetite. It was then that Fred spoke up. It was the first time he had initiated a conversation of his own with her. "You can have my shower time. We need today's schedule," he said. He got up then, and took his plate to be washed. It was if he knew how unclean Felith felt, and that she needed that nudge to duty. Slowly she stood up. "Today we will go over the openings in the house. String extra lines of cans on all openings. Every door will have a chair placed under the doorknob. We will rig some sort of bar to fit across doorways too. From now on nobody will leave to hunt for supplies alone. Rosemary and Emily will have kitchen duty all day to free the guys up for securing the house. Although I will do the evening wash up, while the chores are being done I'll be in the office going over what we will need in the near future. Any ideas?" Felith asked. She had taken to asking for input. Some of the ideas she used, others she tucked away in case they might be of a practical application later.

It didn't surprise her that nobody spoke up. She was a nothing to them. They only took orders because there was still the feeling that Mr. Shadman had left her and Robert in charge. When that wore off then she would have no voice again. For now she had the duty of keeping them all safe. Today though she was so tired and sore that it took great effort just to stand, the office chore was more an excuse to be doing some things while sitting down. Eric and Fred had cleared dishes from the tables as Felith had been giving the run down of what needed to be done that day. Of course they were part of the circle that she protected. The others had not made it into that circle, still she protected them. It was her duty.

It was getting dark outside by the time the evening meal was finished and wash-up done. Felith was inspecting the improvised drop bars that Fred and Robert had rigged across the doorways when a lightening of the sky caught her notice. She stood watching that glow as it seemed to spread and grow redder and brighter. When an explosion rocketed a shower of flames and sparks into the sky Felith realized what was happening. The town was being burned. "Fred, Robert, come here," she called out. Soon the window on the door was crowded with faces looking out at the bright flames eating the town block by block.

"What does it mean?" Rosemary asked, her voice small as if she was afraid to even ask about it.

Nobody answered, each of them staring at the redness of the sky. "The garden hose," Felith said finally. "Robert, Fred, wet the house down. Rosemary, Emily gather some portable food and a change of clothing for everyone, just in case we have to leave."

Julian puckered her lips and glared as the others jumped to obey Felith. This was getting old, being left out of all the chores. Sure, at first, she had felt she had won a point. The little whore hadn't ordered her to do anything since that first breakfast. Now though, now she felt left out. Wasn't she living here too? It wasn't as if they had all gone and started talking to the little whore, or sat with that girl. It was more… She wasn't sure what. Maybe that they listened to the little witch, showing her respect, where as they didn't seem to respect Julian any more. It struck her then why she was so upset. She, Julian the Jewel, had become the outsider. Oh, they were all friendly enough, but still nobody asked her to help out, or included her in the daily work. Who knew that not lowering yourself to servant level was wrong socially?

It had been a long night. The fires had come close enough that ash, which had sparks mixed in, had fallen on the house. Keeping the roof and the sides of the house hosed down had kept any of those sparks from taking root and causing the house to burn. Still, hosing the house had been almost a constant through the night. The bed they had set up for Olivia in the common room was littered with sleeping bodies. Robert, Eric, Middy and even Silent Emily were sleeping there stretched out in a long line across the bed. On the floor lay Fred. There was room on the bed, still Fred had curled up on the floor rather than sleep with the others. Rosemary and Julian had retreated to the girls' bedroom rather than sleep with Eric and Middy. Felith looked at the sleepers. She didn't want to wake them up. Already most of the morning was gone, and she needed to think on things. It was one thing to hunker down inside the house. Another to keep them supplied with food and other needs. When the monsters had taken her back to where they were staying Felith had seen what was becoming of the town, store windows were broken, the stores looted. All this chaos had passed by Haven, with it's stores of food, until the boys had broken in. That had brought the truth of what was going on home.

There was a knock at the door. Everyone except Middy woke up immediately. Fred was on his feet holding his hand out in a wait motion. He waved at Robert to pick up Middy and take everyone into the girls' room. When he looked at Felith, his expression was so stern and hard, that for one moment, she was afraid he meant to hit her. Instead he motioned towards the bedroom, and then pointed in a go now manner. Felith shook her head and walked to the door. It was her responsibility to take care of them all. She was reaching out for the door, just intending to put her hand on the door itself, to ward off any intruder, when Fred grabbed her from behind and swung her aside. The glare he gave her could have burned her had it been fire. Putting a finger to his lips with one hand, he pointed at the spot she was standing with the other. The meaning was clear, be quiet and stay here. So she did.

"Who's there?" Fred called out.

"Robert? I've come to be with Felith and Middy. Rags...," the voice broke off followed by soft sobbing.

"Sidney?" Felith asked. The voice was so broken Felith couldn't be certain it was him. Still, it did sound like him. "Open the door," she told Fred, not even realizing how commanding she sounded. Fred looked at her, for just a fraction of a second something flashed in his eyes, whatever it was he opened the door, catching Sidney as he fell into the entrance. Felith and Fred helped Sidney to the bed intended for Olivia. Fred quickly laid Sidney down, then ran back to lock the door, shoving a chair under the doorknob with more force than needed.

"The town is lost. Rags... Oh God, they're killing Rags. Gave her the virus," Sidney broke off and covered his face with his hands, "They wouldn't let me hold her. She sent a text telling me to come take you and Middy out of town, to my family's farm." As Sidney was talking Middy came out of the bedroom and climbed up on the bed. She patted his shoulder, like a mother soothing a child. A cabinet door slammed shut in the bedroom, Felith knew Eric was hiding again. The other girls and Robert came out of the bedroom, to stand listening.

"Is it that bad out there?" Robert asked. "I don't see how we can move, nor if it is even legal for us to move."

"Legal has gone out the window," Sidney said. "They won't take in patients at the hospitals any more. We were barricaded inside the station, until Rags and two of the officers that are left got ill," he sobbed. "They locked them up in a warehouse. Someone wanted to shoot them all. I fought, begged, tried to reason with them, but fear is a powerful force. Rags is the practical one. She sent me here. I have to get you all out of town."

"He should be thrown out of here. We'll get sick too," Julian said. Rosemary nodded her head in agreement. Emily and Robert looked uncertain as to what was to be done.

Only Fred and Middy looked at Felith for the answer. They were all her responsibility, she thought. "No. We will all go together. And Rags, nobody gets left behind," she said, looking first at Fred, then Robert. Both nodded. "First we free Rags."

"Are you crazy? We're all going to die!" Julian shouted.

Very slowly Felith looked over to where Julian stood. It was Emily, however, she addressed though. "Emily, you and Robert will stay here with Middy, Eric and Sidney. Both of you will start gathering food stuff and clothing. It may be a while before we find food or can grow it, or whatever it takes. Also you and Robert will make a hot meal for when we return with Rags. Middy, you guard Eric."

Sidney started struggling to his feet. "I'm going. Rags will need me." He swayed a bit, then straightened. "And I can show you how to get in," he said, just to be sure they took him. For a long moment Felith seemed to study Sidney, finally she nodded.

"So I'm tossed out too with Julian?" Rosemary said. "Are you just going to act as if we aren't a part of the group? I could understand you ignoring Julian, she has been pretty nasty to you, but me? What have I done?"

There was a gasp from Emily as Felith looked to where Julian and Rosemary stood again. "Trust is the issue," Felith said and motioned for Fred and Sidney to follow her. As she walked by Julian and Rosemary, their expressions were one of shock. It could not be helped. Julian had not shown the least desired to be part of the whole. Rosemary was a victim of her own desire to follow Julian, to be in the upper class. Classes were nothing to Felith, yet she understood that for some, most, there were lines, even walls, placed between what they thought were a different class of people from themselves. I am a nothing, Felith thought, I do not threaten you girls in any manner. I do not desire anything you have. Still you will want to rid the world of me and others you feel do not deserve to live in your world. She could not understand the reasoning.

A hand grasped Felith's arm, stopping her.

She turned expecting to find Rosemary wanting to express some grievance she felt Felith was causing. But it was Julian who had her by the arm. Julian's mouth was scrunched up as if she was tasting something sour. "You are right I haven't trusted you," she said. "But you have flirted with Robert when you knew he was with me."

Standing frozen for a moment, Felith at first could not believe she was hearing right. Flirting with Robert? Why would anyone think that? "First, it has never entered my mind to flirt with anyone. Second, it is a matter of me being able to trust you to be there for the rest. Now, let go. We have somebody to rescue," Felith said, twisting her arm out of Julian's hand. Julian's face turn bright red as Felith and the others left.

It took over two hours to get to where Rags and the others suspected of being infected were being held. It was a huge warehouse with windows boarded up and bars placed over the boards. It was more a prison than anything else. The smell of the place was horrible. The three were in a battered van. The wonder was the van was still running. Sidney had insisted on driving, telling them that he knew what roads were passable. And passable was a word that had been used loosely, as everywhere vehicles were wrecked, abandon, or beat into shapeless mounds. It was eerily quiet. Not even a breeze stirred to indicate life. Sidney stopped twice on the trip over to the warehouse. Once he ran into a ravaged hardware store. The second stop was at a pharmacy which had been gutted. When he came out of each he had bags in his hand.

By the time they had surveyed the warehouse and formed a plan of action, Felith was feeling the results of her previous injuries. Life had taught her to live with pain and move when her body was telling her to lay down. Only, the paleness around her lips showed the pain. Fred's part of the plan was the dangerous end of it. Fred and Sidney hooked chains through two windows on one side of the warehouse and connected the chain to a truck from the parking lot. It was the only vehicle that would run, and was a vital part of the plan. Inside the warehouse were desperate people. Some most surely were infected with the flu virus. Others, those suspected of being infected, had to be scared at being locked up with those that were ill. Either bunch were dangerous. The plan hinged on the fact those inside wanted out, and their reaction to being freed.

While Fred sat at the ready inside the truck on one side of the warehouse, on the opposite side of the warehouse Sidney and Felith set up to pull out yet another window. Timing was important. Fred had to open the front so the masses would run out. Then make his way around to where Sidney and Felith would be hopefully pulling Rags out. They had positioned themselves where Sidney had last seen Rags. Sidney had sent her a text to explain the plan. Hopefully she was lucid enough to understand.

As with all plans things happen. There was the sound of the building groaning, and Felith knew Fred had opened the front of the building. They waited a couple of minutes for Fred. But Fred didn't come. Grim faced Felith nodded for Sidney to yank out the window. It was a terrible sound, the window being retched from the building, shattering the sides of the surrounding structure. Felith ran to the van and released the chains tying it to the shattered window, while Sidney bound inside the building. A long moment passed, screams from the front of the building echoed through the building and out to where Felith stood. Sidney staggered out of the hole they had made in the building with Rags in his arms. He was pale, and sweat dripped off his face. His eyes were half closed as if he wanted to just shut it all out of his mind. At that moment they heard Fred. "Fuck off!" he yelled, then fell silent.

Helping Sidney sit Rags limp body inside the van, Felith looked at Sidney and he nodded. He knew that Fred was in trouble. "You drive around so you are ready to leave the area. I'll get Fred," Felith said. There was no arguing, to Sidney it was Rags he was here for, but he wouldn't leave Felith either. And Felith wouldn't leave Fred.

Going as fast as she could, which wasn't all that fast, Felith headed to where she thought they had heard Fred's voice, and was immediately in the middle of madness. There were at least 10 of them around Fred. Kicking him, punching him, ripping at his clothing. It was like a mob gone crazy to kill. Already Fred's face was swollen in lumpy bumps. His eye on the left was near swollen shut, but he saw her. With a flick of his head he said no in silent appeal.

That was when the dog appeared. It was a huge brute, with ugly folds of skin hanging loosely on it's frame. It was on the mob in two bounds, a ferocious growl rumbling like thunder from it. It's mouth opened and grasped one person by an arm. The huge beast gave a shake of it's head and tossed the person away. Next it grabbed a police officer, shaking him vigorously before slinging him off into the air. A long moment passed, with nothing but growls and thuds, then, as if it had taken that much destruction for things to penetrate the mobs collective minds, the mob ran. Like so many rats they scurried away. And Felith was at Fred's side.

"You stupid girl," he said, "they might have killed you." A long wet tongue licked him over his face, then licked over Felith's face.

"I remembered Rags saying get a dog," Felith said. "Come on, Sidney and Rags are in the van." It took all of her strength to get Fred up. They just leaned on each other, Fred hobbling, Felith slowly waning, yet stumbling on with the huge dog trailing along beside them. The last few yards were difficult to maneuver. So much debris was scattered about from the rioting that the trio had to twist and turn through the wreckage. Fortunately, Sidney saw them coming, and got out of the van to assist.

He stopped when he saw the huge dog and gave Felith a questioning look. She shrugged. "It's my dog," she said, her chin came up as if ready to fight for the dog. Sidney looked a bit strange, but nodded. Together they managed to get everyone in the van, including the dog. Twice on the journey back to Haven, they had to detour to avoid people acting crazy, tearing things up, or scavenging for food in the wreckage of stores. Those that appeared to have escaped the mob insanity and were only out for food took one look at the dog's huge head poking out the passenger window and let them be. Once the dog bound out of the van's open passenger side window and sent a small group of teenage boys running. Sidney's mouth tightened at that, still, with a glance back at Rags and Felith, he stopped and let the huge dog back into the van. Then they were back at Haven and the slow painful chore of transferring everyone inside began.

Rosemary ran forward to help Fred hobble in. Sidney carried Rags to the bed in the common room. Lastly Felith and the dog made their way into the common room. The huge dog was leaning into Felith, taking as much of her weight as she would let him. Robert saw her then and waved to a chair, he wasn't quite brave enough to go over and chance the dog. Although Felith could feel the last of her strength seeping away, there was one thing left for her to do. She sat down on the bed beside Rags and placed a hand on Rags sweaty forehead. For her, the rest of the world went away. All that existed was Rags. She sent the gray of her mind out seeking, seeking the bad inside Rags. It was there, billions and billions of it all through Rags body. This would take more than the mending of a bird had taken out of her. Perhaps she would die. With a soft sigh Felith let the healing force flow as she had seen Robert heal the ends of the rope during his show for the youngsters.

Robert was talking to Sidney, as Sidney stacked the bags he had carried in from the van. "Julian has left. She just up and left with out a word to any of us. She left about an hour after you did and hasn't returned. I'm worried about her."

"Shit!" Fred exclaimed. He had been watching Felith as she touched the woman on the bed, Rags, yes, they called her Rags. Suddenly Felith had seemed to die. She collapsed on top of Rags in a limp piled, and slid off the bed into puddle on the floor. In one bound the dog was standing over Felith. Everything about him said I'm protecting her, keep away. Rosemary screamed, and suddenly Rags, who had been unconscious seconds ago, was sitting up with her hand whipping down to her hip as if trying to draw a gun. Then she fell back onto the bed and seemed to fall into a deep sleep.

The problem was the girl laying as if dead on the floor. The boy Robert found a broom and rushed at the dog foolishly. The man Sidney was trying to creep passed the dog to get to the girl. Everything was happening at once. Fred saw it all from his swollen eyes, as he tried to get up. His injured leg wouldn't work. He kept collapsing, but he did manage to stand finally, if only on one leg. "Leave the dog alone," he said, his voice more calm than he felt. From one of the bedroom cabinets Eric let out a steady screaming adding to all the confusion. A small being, the little girl, zoomed pass Fred at that moment. She stood beside the dog putting her small clenched fists up, as if to fight anyone attempting to get to the girl on the floor.

By then, Fred had managed to hop on his good leg over to where the dog and little girl stood over Felith. He patted the dog on the head, then did the same to the little girl. "I have her now," he said. The two protectors looked at him, dog and girl.

The dog gave his face a big sloppy lick and lay down next to Felith. Middy promptly sat down beside the dog. Fred just let himself lean against the bed and slide down until he too sat on the floor beside Felith, so he could touch the thin figure of Felith. She was alive. Her body felt cold to the touch, but her heart beat. Fred looked over at Middy. "Blankets," he said, and the girl was off in a flash. She must have pulled half the blankets off the beds in the girls' room. Middy was dragging them over the floor to Fred. Something inside him felt like a smile.

Soon Felith was wrapped tight in blankets. Fred pulled her to him, half holding her, half using her to hold himself up. They were a pair, two broken people, thought Fred. Gradually he felt the warmth returned to Felith's body. He began to relax as her breathing became more natural.

Sidney worked over Rags, now and then asking Fred to count Felith's pulse and breathing rate. He had no idea why Felith had collapsed. Finally he felt Rags was settled enough to focus more on Felith. "Has she suffered any trauma lately?" he asked. Rosemary bit her lip and looked away. Even Robert seemed uncomfortable with the question. There was a long silence.

"Those men took her. They hurt her," Middy said, giving the room of people a glare.

"From what I understand, when some thugs broke in here, and threatened to rape the girls, Felith made a deal with them. If they left the others alone she would sacrifice herself to them. One of them, or maybe all of them, hit her while they had her," Fred said. Robert nodded at the words.

"All for one," Sidney muttered. Giving the dog a quick glance, Sidney bent down and kissed Felith on the head.

The words rocked through Fred, leaving him weak and unsure as to what he felt. Then, like Felith, he gave into his battered body and fell to sleep, holding her in his arms. All for one echoed in his head, all for one, he thought, as blissful darkness claimed him.

Chapter Seven

FAREWELL HAVEN

Felith woke more hungry than she had felt since starving as a six year old girl, and warm. For a long moment Felith considered just letting her mind slip back into the midst of sleep, but the hunger won out. She opened her eyes and froze. Her head lay on a chest, which was rising and falling slowly. Ever so slowly she looked at the arms that wrapped around her. The arms were bruised, and in spots bloody. Fred, she thought. The last thing she remembered was sending her healing into Rags. After that there was nothing but blankness. Thoughts of Rags caused Felith to stir enough that Fred woke up.

Confusion clouded Fred's mind. Had he been attacked again? There was a body laying on him! The reaction was instant, over before his mind woke up enough to be reasoning. "Get the hell off me, you filthy bastard," Fred growled, shoving the body off him. He tried to get up to be ready for fighting, but his body betrayed him. In the background he heard a soft swoosh of breath from the person he had thrown off him. It all came back to him then, him holding broken Felith. And now, now he had broke her more. He looked to where the girl was getting off the floor. She turned, looked over at him and gave a little nod of her head in understanding. There it was, the common ground between them, she knew, he knew. Fred gave her a wary smile, shaking his head. "I can't get up by myself," he said.

The dog licked Fred's face just as Middy came flying across the room and wrapped her arms around Felith. A second small body zoomed out of the boys' bedroom, and then stopped short. Eric looked back and forth between Felith and Fred as if trying to decide who to attach himself to before kneeling down next to Fred. Sidney's head came over the side of the bed where he and Rags were sleeping, "Looks like it's time for breakfast, Rags. The kids are up." Just like that all seemed right in the world. Except, of course, it wasn't.

Reaching down Felith offered her hand to Fred. There was such a wariness in his eyes as he took her hand and let her help him up that, for a moment, Felith felt her heart go out to him and try to heal him. Even that light touch made her dizzy. She swayed. Instantly Middy was leaning into Felith's side, propping her up. She couldn't give into the weakness, there were too many things to be done.

A door opened, fresh air rushed into the house, along with Julian. She didn't look into Felith's eyes as she walked over to where Felith was standing with the others. Stopping in front of Felith, Julian cleared her throat. "If you haven't assigned anyone to do clean up after breakfast I'll do it," she hesitated, then continued, "And any other chores you wish to assign." Having finished speaking Julian stood waiting. Everything inside her said that now Felith would berate her in some manner for revenge. She finally looked up at Felith.

Felith nodded at Julian in acceptance. The trust was not there yet. Trust had to be earned. Still she accepted that this was an attempt by Julian to fit in with the others. Then Robert was beside Julian hugging her.

"Are you all right? Where were you? What happened?" His questions came out in one long breath. Julian leaned into him, then they were holding each other, and Julian was sobbing. Looking helpless, Robert held Julian and patted her back. "It's going to be okay, you are here now, safe," he kept saying over and over again. By then Emily and Rosemary were around Julian too, patting her back, giving her hugs.

Felith waited until the others had reached the point when they had gotten over the initial excitement of Julian's return before issuing the day's orders, "Rosemary and Emily will cook breakfast. Robert and Julian, you are on clean up. The rest of us will do laundry, and go over the plans to leave Haven. Anything you want to take with you when we are all up to leaving, be sure to pack." As she talked Felith made her way to the door to let the dog out, he had gone to the door behind Julian, and was looking expectantly over his shoulder. Julian hadn't seen the dog, yet.

On the bed Rags sat up. You couldn't tell
that the night before she had been so ill. Unless you
looked closely at her face. There was a look about
her that spoke of her will having been beaten down.
Her voice was scratchy when she spoke, "We need
to keep a watch set too," she said, "I'll take morning
watch, I'm not much good at anything else." Felith
nodded.

Sidney spoke up then. "I can do laundry. That
will free you up to pack things. And I can cook some
too. What if I volunteer for cooking lunch?" he said,
looking to Felith. Again Felith nodded, and smiled
inside as Middy stepped up to Sidney. "Don't worry,
I'll show you how," she said, her little chin out and
mouth set in a line that spoke of command. Middy
was Felith's reason for continuing. Her and the baby
monster, Eric. They needed her. Fred gave a hop on
his good leg, towards the laundry room. Felith had
to admit then, to herself, that Fred needed her too.

"Fred, you can come help me make a list of
things we need to take for certain. Then, if you will
help me pack, I'll help you too," Felith said, heading
Fred off from laundry duty. For a long moment he
looked at her as if trying to see inside her mind. The
nod was slow in coming. Hopefully he could see that
she too was weak and was needing to rest. The two
made their way to Shadman's office. Neither of them
thought it strange they hadn't included the two adults
in the planning stage of this exodus from Haven.
Clearly Fred's leg was giving him a lot of pain. The
urge to reach out and heal him was strong in Felith,
yet she was so depleted from healing Rags that to

do another healing might be beyond her. Food, she needed food first, she thought as she pulled out a couple of tablets and pens for them to make lists on. "Sidney said this is a farm we are heading to. I'm thinking that along the way we should look for seeds and plant a vegetable garden. What you think?" she asked Fred.

The affect on Fred was instant, the wary look left his face, and for once he didn't look angry. He nodded. "Yes. I don't know anything about growing things, but from the look of things in the town, I doubt supplies are moving through the country. Growing our own food never occurred to me. We certainly should start a garden as soon as we get there, just in case.

"Stuff like milk, won't that all be spoiled by now in the stores?" he asked, an uncertain look on his face.

"Cows? Isn't it from cows and goats? So you are thinking we need to find cows, and maybe chickens for their eggs too?" she responded.

Absently Fred nodded. It was clear the idea of them having to make and grow things had not been on his mind before. When the groceries started running out Felith had wondered what they would do without supply trucks bringing in fresh food to the stores. Sidney's solution of moving them out of town into the country set her mind to thinking of all the stories she had read as a little girl locked in a basement filled with books. The tales of the olden days when families lived off the land had come to mind. The Bell rang to indicate breakfast was ready. Standing, Felith offered her hand to Fred to help him up. With a grimace of pain he let her pull him to his feet. Slowly the two damaged teens made their way across the common room toward the dining room. There was a scratch at the door. Felith left Fred for a moment to let the dog in. He had to be hungry too. Ahead of her and the dog Fred hopped to his usual spot at the table. Eric stood beside Fred as if this was his normal place. Sidney was there too, he had Robert helping him put another table up against the one the others were around. Soon he had it arranged so all of them could sit together. He motioned Felith over, indicating that she should take the head of the table seat, with dog beside her.

Immediately Julian began to protest the dog being there. "Get that beast out of here. It isn't sanitary. He needs to be thrown out of the house," she ranted on for a moment, then Fred slammed his hand down on the table.

"The dog stays. Anyone who has an objection can eat after everyone else has," he said, his voice suggesting that he would not hear any argument on the subject.

"He stays," Echoed Sidney and Middy. That seemed to settle the matter. For the first time they all ate at the same table. As the food was being served, Sidney asked for suggestions on when and how to travel out of the town.

"I'll get us another van, as soon as I can walk that is," Fred said. "We think we should gather any vegetable seeds, and whatever other seeds that may be of help on the way. Felith and I thought of cows and chickens too."

That brought Robert up in his chair. "I never thought of that. Tools too, to use on farming."

Sidney added, "gasoline, and a generator for electricity. Extension cords. Light bulbs, matches."

"And chocolate," Middy tacked on. That caused a laugh from Rosemary and just like that the whole table was involved in the planning of life on a farm. Suddenly the dog growled, the hackles on his back rose up. Robert placed a hand over Eric's mouth, as those at the table fell silent. Rags stood up, her hand going to her hip, but there was no gun for her to draw. The door to the common room broke open with a sound of splintered wood and banged loudly against the wall.

It all happened in what seemed to be a frozen moment in time. The door crashed open, Fred struggling to rise. Rags and Sidney placing themselves between the dining room door and the others. The little ones doing as they had been drilled, hiding in the nearest cover, hands over their mouths so as not to make a sound. Two men came in with axes in their hands. When they saw the people of Haven in the dining room they started forward, axes swinging threateningly. Then the low rumble began from dog. It grew to a snarl and he was on the pair. They didn't stand a chance against the great beast. Screaming in pain as the dog grabbed and shook each of them in turn, in quick snapping bites and shakes of his head, the two men dropped their axes and ran out of the house with the dog snapping at their heels.

There was a moment of stunned silence, then softly Julian said, "The dog stays."

"Dog food," someone said, and they all laughed.

It was Felith who broke the jubilation, "I think this means we need to leave here soon. We are not safe in this town." Reaching out she touched Fred's hand. His face became as stone, and then the anger began to build in waves upon that stone. The stone melted into a dark scowl, still he left his hand there for her to touch. It was a long moment finding the source of Fred's pain, for there was so much of it, both mentally and physically. The leg was her focus though, and finally she wove the healing over the worst of the damage of his leg. Some healing leaked into other parts, and Felith was not sure if she did it deliberately, or if the healing just sought out the worst of things. Then she fainted, plopping face down into her empty plate.

It was the last thing Fred had expected, Felith touching him. He froze and tried to analyze the why of her touch. It occurred to him that she was flirting, brought on, no doubt, by him stupidly holding her all night, and the anger started to build inside him. The why of him leaving his hand under her touch was a puzzle to him. When she fainted, slamming face down into her plate, his mind went blank for a second. Automatically he tried to stand, not even aware that he had, and was lifting Felith up. Her body was limp, and so light. The girl needs to eat more, he thought. Then Sidney and Rags, along with the ever present Middy were surrounding Felith and him. Dog bound into the middle of the group around Felith and Fred. His muzzle bloodied from attacking the intruders. "She has worn herself out, and needs to eat more," Fred said, to the crowd. Carefully he moved through them placing Felith on what he thought of now as the sick bed. Dog was about to climb up on the bed with her when Fred grabbed him by the skin on the back of his neck. "No you don't, not until you have a bath. Middy, Eric take him into the showers and scrub him clean," Fred said stepping aside so Sidney could look Felith over. Only then did Fred realize his leg didn't hurt. He looked down on Felith laying so still and pale upon the bed, his mind a confusion of impossible thoughts. She had touched his hand, just his hand. A vision of her slipping into a limp heap upon the floor after touching Rags crept unbidden, unwanted, into his head. From the dining area he could hear Julian rattling plates, her voice piercing.

"She is probably expecting, from one of those boys she went off with," Julian told Robert. "It was a chancy thing to do, unless she is on the birth control pill, which I doubt she is." She headed into the kitchen with the stack of dishes. Nobody had put their plates on the bar as they should have, but then the little Queen had fainted so it was to be expected.

"You shouldn't say such things, Jules. You know she only went with them to save you from being raped. And if she is expecting, then Fred or I will step up," Robert said

There was silence after that in the kitchen, other than the sound of running water and dishes clanking together. It was the plausible explanation, Fred thought. Relief swelled inside of him, it wasn't the impossible after all. As for stepping up, rather him than Robert, who clearly had a thing for Julian. Better him than me, he thought, a shiver running through him at the thought of Julian's clutching hands. He looked again at Felith laying so very still. She was tiny and thin, how could she bear a child? She'd need someone who understood. He'd have to do it, Robert didn't understand anything. Book smart, yeah, but nothing of the real world penetrated that lofty dreaming head. A flutter wit. The anger was building inside him again. He tried to shrug it off, but it was there, eating at him.

Felith slept until lunch time. She woke with her tummy rumbling and hunger gnawing at her insides. Fortunately, Sidney had been busy in the kitchen. How he managed the rich stew, hot bread, steaming corn on the cob, and chocolate cake was a wonder. Her mouth was watering even before she was fully awake.

"Cake," screeched Middy, rushing up to where Felith was awkwardly trying to stand. "He remembered. Cake, cake, cake!" Middy was literally jumping up and down in her excitement. When Felith swayed, the little girl suddenly sobered. She put an arm around Felith, and together they slowly made their way to the dining area.

The group table was set with napkins and silverware. A huge bowl of hot stew sat in the middle of the table with steaming ears of corn and hot bread at either end of the table. Each place setting had a glass of iced tea. Sidney had indeed been busy. This looked like a huge family table. By the time Felith and Middy had made their way to the table everyone else was ready.

"Sit," Rags said, giving Felith a worried glance. Everyone sat down but uncertainty hung in the air. Up to this point they had always said grace before being seated. A change in routine did not go well in the already uncertain world. "Join hands, and today I'll say grace," Rags said. She looked over at Felith as if judging her approval. Felith nodded. She saw this for what it was, an attempt to bond this ragtag bunch together. Once everyone was linked around the table, their heads bowed, Rags began, "We give thanks for each of our companions. Alone we are easy to defeat, but as a whole we know we can over come so much more than the world has to heap upon us. For each of us, thank you. Amen."

The wonder of the meal was that everyone was at the table, even Sidney. He had each of them pass their plates around and dished up the thick rich stew. Then the corn was passed around, as well as the bread. It was a different experience. Middy dug in with relish, as this was the first full meal they had had in some time. The two adults were sharing a secret smile, as if pleased at the outcome of the meal. Fred ate with an eye on Felith, who was shoveling food in as fast as she could chew and swallow. Her hands had a slight shake to them when they had started eating. As the meal progressed the shaking eased and finally stopped.

Felith was so full by the time Sidney brought the cake to the table that she didn't feel there was room left for even one more bite. Only then did she speak. "Do you think we will be ready to leave in the morning?"

"Will you be rested enough for traveling?" Fred asked before anyone could voice an objection.

For once Felith blushed. She had been such a weakling fainting like that, twice. Weakness was the path to pain. Don't show emotion, don't let on things hurt. Her chin went up slightly. "Yes," she answered. She didn't ask about his leg or other injuries, for she knew they were better. And Rags, Rags would be okay too.

"I think," Sidney said then, "that we need to cook up any perishable food we have. I noticed a few chickens left in the freezer, and was thinking that the roast in there should be cooked up too. The chicken fried up will give us something to eat as we travel in the vans, just in case there is no safe place to stop and eat. The roast cooked in a slow cooker tonight and eaten before we leave tomorrow will give us a good start. Any canned food there is we need to take with us, as well as the pots and pans and dishes. Maybe we could find a trailer to pull for a generator and larger items to go on. What do you think, Felith?"

They discussed plans for leaving and what should be taken. Rags insisted they take lots of toilet tissue, which got a laugh around the table, even Fred gave a snort at that. Bottled water was put on the list along with many other sound ideas. Once they all began to think on what was needed to survive it was as if their mind set shifted. Action was something positive, something that gave them all a sense of control over their shattered world. They had been lucky so far to have not been harmed more. Although Felith and Fred had been the two to receive the physical harm, mentally they had all been harmed.

Fred left after lunch was cleared and the
dishes washed, the dog at his heels. He was glad
for the beast's presence. Now and again the people
surrounding him kicking him near to death flashed
through his mind. There was a moment when he
had been certain he was going to die. When he had
seen Felith, he had only wanted her to run, to get
away before these creatures in human form got to her
too. Then the dog was on the creatures ripping them
apart, scattering them, and they ran. It was as if the
beast had appeared out of thin air. "I remember Rags
saying get a dog," Felith had said. The stupid girl, she
could have been killed. You don't just conjure a dog.
And his leg, he had felt the bone crack, felt it. Yet it
was fine now. The stupid, stupid, girl. "I remember
Rags saying get a dog." A soft tongue licked Fred's
hand. He scratched the huge furry head. Get a dog,
get a dog. At least he was a good dog, Fred thought
and smiled to himself. Maybe he was the stupid one.

Dog growled. Immediately Fred crouched
down among the rubble he had been picking his way
through. "Where?" he whispered to dog. The huge
beast looked to the left, then right. It was to the left
that the dog kept staring, his lips drawn back in a
snarling grin. Hunkering down they waited for what
seemed like an hour, but was more like minutes.
Finally Dog licked Fred's face and stood up, his
lips relaxed. "Good, Dog," Fred said softly, patting
the broad head. More wary now, Fred continued
the search for another van, and maybe a truck.
So much fury had been taken out on the vehicles

parked awkwardly in the middle of the road. Dark blotches on the pavement and sidewalks testified to the violence that had taken place. Fred fought off his reoccurring flashbacks, trying to stay alert, trying to find something, anything they could use for travel. He saw the string of banners proclaiming 'cars, trucks,' before the car lot came into sight. Softly. Fred laughed to himself, unbelievable, just unbelievable. All the chaos around him, and there stood a car lot that hadn't been touched.

The first dusting of dawn was lifting the gloom of night as Felith stood in the garden for the last time. She had come to say farewell to the plants, trees, and creatures. The sun began to peek over the buildings, golden, shrouded in purples, and hues of golden clouds. Closing her eyes Felith breathed in the morning air as she spread her arms in farewell to this bit of peace and nature. Dog padded out and sat beside her. They came then, the butterflies, the birds, the small creatures in the area. For the briefest moment they surrounded Felith bathing her in peace and beauty, and for that moment she was not the skinny girl with the lobbed off hair.

Robert and Fred were both looking for Felith. By chance they ended up at the door to the garden together. Wild things scattered before them when the door opened. Felith, scraggly as ever, turned to face the two. For just a second her hair was a halo of fire from the sun. Robert caught his breath and held it. Fred scowled darkly, his face not betraying anything he might be thinking.

"Julian wants to know if she has kitchen duty," Robert said.

"You should be resting," Fred said at the same time.

The time for farewells was gone, responsibility was the road she must travel now. "I think Sidney is going to finish things up in the kitchen. The rest of us will take turns helping him and load the vans and the truck that you brought, Fred. Felith stroked Dog's head. "Dog guard," she whispered. She felt stronger, as if the creatures and the trees had given her the strength to carry on. It was a bit of a surprise to see everyone up already gathering things to be loaded into the vans and the truck.

Sandwiches and the last of the juice was passed around, as the boys carted things out to the vans to start with, clothing, ice chest with water jugs, and bowls of potato salad to go with the fried chicken they intended to eat on the road. The crock-pot had cooked the roast all night and the aroma filled Haven. When the last item had been loaded, except for their last meal in Haven, they sat for the last time at the tables which Sidney had pushed together to make one table. "We should do something symbolic for this occasion," Sidney said.

"Perhaps each of us should tell how we ended up here," he added. "I'm here for the love of this woman beside me, and all of you. I came because Rags, and all of you, you are my family now. In times of deep trouble it is to family we look, and it is to family we seek to give comfort, to hold tight, and to defend. This was at first a gradual thing, the coming to think of you as family. I found such wisdom and bravery here that I had to be part of it."

Rags stood next and spoke. "I'm here for

much the same reason as Sidney. This man I selected as my life partner. He has made me laugh, given me joy in the darkness of events which threaten to mar my very being. And when I saw the bravery of you." She glanced at Middy and Felith, then the others. "I fell in love with you too. Except for that bravery I would not be alive today. I'm used to telling people to 'spread them' and searching them for weapons or drugs. This is going to be a whole new experience for me, and for you."

Then it was Robert's turn. He looked troubled but stood. "I came here because my parents were killed, and without any other family this is where the overseers to my trust fund placed me. I have been biding my time until I'm of age to live on my own. This… This was never in my plans for life. But it is what it is here and now."

"Same for me," Rosemary said, barely waiting for Robert to sit down. "Just waiting, having fun with my two friends. Waiting to leave, to get married, have kids, or to become a business tycoon."

"Yeah, waiting, but I won't be waiting forever. Robert is going to marry me, and we will live a good life," Julian said, before Rosemary even sat down.

Emily stood. She hadn't said anything since first showing up at Haven. She shrugged, then made a walking motion with the fingers of her right hand. It was enough, she had walked and found Haven.

The next person would have been Fred, but Middy jumped up and put her hands on her hips. That stubborn lip of hers jutted out. "I'm adopted," she declared, and plopped back down into her chair. Suddenly she hopped up again and pointed at Eric.

"And he is too."

For a moment nobody moved. With his face uncharacteristic in its smooth calmness, Fred stood. He looked directly at Felith, and only at her as he began to speak. "My route here has been round about. No one event or happening. My parents didn't die. I'm not waiting for a better life. I'm not biding time to marry someone rich and live a good life. And I didn't walk here." Fred looked at Emily as if apologizing for his last remark. Once more his eyes locked on Felith. "I'm here because of hate. People hate those they do not understand. Anyone who is not of their little group. Hate brought me here, the hate of others," he said, and sat down.

Aware that every head at the table had turned to look at her, Felith stood. "I'm here because there was no other place for them to put me," she said, and sat down. Eric, having been spared from talking by Middy, patted Felith's hand before climbing into her lap.

One by one the others stood and began to clear the table. Each seemed determined to take part in this last chore in Haven. The dishes were washed and packed away. The boys carried out the last load of boxes to the vans. Each person either said their goodbyes to this place which had sheltered them all, or went swiftly out to find a spot in the various vehicles. It was time to go.

Chapter Eight

NEW HOME

Nobody spoke as they hunted a way to the Highway through the destroyed town. For some of them this was the first they had seen of the destruction they lived in. None of the streets were completely free of wreckage and debris. Buildings that had escaped the chaos were few, scattered among either broken shells, or burned out husks. Bodies were occasionally seen in stages of decay. It was as if this crazy virus ran its course and the patient died. I could have saved more, Felith thought, as they passed by a woman crumbled against a car she must of been beating with a baseball bat. The weight of all the deaths and all those that were still sick sat heavy upon her shoulders. Dog barked and started struggling to get out of the van window. "Stop," Felith called out to Rags who was driving the van. The van came to an abrupt stop. Sidney saw them stop and put his own brakes on. He was driving the truck leading the way. Fred almost ran into Rags' van before he came to a jerking stop. By that time Felith had the van door open. The huge dog bound out of the van and stood rock still. Finally his great head swung to the left. His nostrils whiffed the air and off he went. Scrambling over the rubble of what was once a store.

Rags was out of the van with a gun she had found before they left. "Felith, don't," she called as Felith began to follow Dog. She was torn between staying with the little ones and following Felith. It was probably just a pit stop for the dog, still any stop could be dangerous. The girl was stubborn, and changed from the starved tortured girl Rags had first brought to Haven. How Rags' heart had ached when Felith had said she was there because there was no other place to put her. She watched as that once shy 'don't touch me' girl stopped by the huge dog she had somehow found and adopted. When Rags had said get a dog she was thinking some small yapping dog to warn intruders off. Not that huge beast.

Sidney stepped up beside Rags and kissed her cheek. "Pit stop?" he asked, watching Felith, bending down to look at the ground as the dog began to dig at the rubble. Then Felith was helping the dog. Sidney saw her suddenly stop moving rubble and give the dog a hug. Reaching down she picked up a bundle.

Cradling the baby Dog had found to her chest, Felith turned and picked her way carefully back to where Rags and Sidney were standing. Fred walked up just as Felith reached the pair of adults. "It is a baby," Felith said, as the little bundle began to make weak noise. "It was in the mother's arms."

"Did you see any formula or bottles? Diapers? We will need that and more," Rags said, looking at the rubble. "This looks like it was a store. The mother may have been shopping. Perhaps something survived that we can use."

The nod of Felith's head was all Fred needed. He was off before anyone could stop him. Felith handed the baby to Rags and followed Fred, dog at her heels. The mother had died in the baby section of the store. It took a bit of digging before they scrounged up a few boxes of diapers, some baby wipes, canned formula and one, just one, small bottle. In the meantime Sidney and Rags watched over the others and cleaned the baby's bottom, which was raw from being in a soiled diaper. "Diaper cream," Rags called out to the two searching the rubble.

Diaper cream was not among the scattered items Fred and Felith found. Giving the area one last search Fred looked up at Felith and gave what might have been a smile. Reaching down he picked up an item. Felith came over and looked at the item her face for once showing something, puzzlement. Looking up at Fred she could have sworn he had a twinkle in his eye. "It warms bottles," he said. "The little tyke will need a warm bottle for a while."

There wasn't a sound from the infant when Fred and Felith returned to the van with their loot. Rags was fretting, while Sidney held the baby close to him to give the baby his body warmth, even though it was a mild day. In the van Fred set up the bottle warmer, connecting it to the van's lighter socket. The way he managed to open the formula and measure out a feeding spoke of experience. Felith watched the whole procedure fascinated at how this would feed the baby.

Once the bottle was warm, Fred tested the milk in the bottle on his wrist. Satisfied he took the baby from Sidney. It was clear that feeding a baby was not a new experience to Fred. The problem was the baby was too weak to suckle the bottle. Felith reached out a hand to touch the baby's cheek. Fred blocked her hand and shook his head. "Not before you eat something. Eat then you can touch her." The truth was there in his eyes, he knew, or suspected, that it was the healing which caused her to pass out.

Sidney looked at Felith, a strange expression on his face. "I don't think this is a safe place to eat our meal. What if the girls come up here with Rags and Felith goes back with you? She can eat as we travel to a safe spot…. Then… the rest of us will eat while Felith holds the baby."

While the baby things were being transferred to Fred's van, Julian and Rosemary scrambled out of the van. "We are not riding with that black thing," Julian began.

Fred sharply cut her off, "you, Rosemary and Middy will ride with Rags. Emily, Eric and Felith will ride with me, Robert in front with Sidney. It is the only sensible arrangement."

"Not me!" Middy shouted. "I'm not riding with them," she said, pointing at Julian and Rosemary.

"You will. This is for Felith," Fred flatly stated.

Middy blinked back tears, her lip jutted out as

if she was going to argue, then she looked at the baby in Fred's arms and nodded. She was growing up so fast mentally, yet she was still a little girl with all the opinions of a child.

When all the squabbling was done and over with the caravan of vehicles set out again. Fred had Emily hold the baby as they had no child seat for her. With his blackest scowl on his face he pointed at the ice chest that contained the cooked chicken from Haven. He smiled inside himself when Felith closed her eyes as she gave in and opened the ice chest. Their caravan began to move forward, as he weaved in and out following Rags' van through the debris on the road, Fred kept a watch on Felith too. She hadn't eaten enough to satisfy him when she started to put things away, Fred set his mouth in a grim line. "More," he said flatly. Emily's eyes tracked back and forth between him and Felith. What she thought of this he didn't know. Foremost in his mind was the image of Felith sliding to the floor after touching Rags. If making her eat ahead of time helped prevent that reaction happening, he'd hold her down and stuff food in her personally.

Her tummy was feeling as if it were stuffed to the bursting point, Felith again started cleaning up the mess of eating. She cast a wary look at Fred. Looking at her in the rearview mirror, he nodded. "Now?" she asked, and he nodded again. Relief flooded through Felith as she reached her hand out to stroke the baby's cheek. She had been afraid the little one would die before she could heal her. She sought out the weakness in the baby, willing good health into her. The edges of her vision began to turn blurry, darkness threaten to claim her mind, when suddenly the baby let out a lusty wail, shocking her, so she jerked her hand back. Feeling distant mentally from the world around her, she heard Fred instructing Emily to give the baby the bottle. There was the sound of sucking. It worked, Felith thought. Laying back in the seat she drifted off into a peaceful sleep, never feeling Eric curl up against her, nor seeing the relief in Fred's eyes.

The small satisfaction Fred felt at having Felith follow his orders warmed him inside. A sense of rightness filled him, he was her protector. She was so powerful, and who was he to question her? Yet someone had to use common sense when it came to her health. Robert had no clue, and Sidney meant well, but had blinders on, unable to see what was really going on around him, or was so besot by Rags he couldn't see anything else. Adults were like that, one tracked minds, unable to see what was happening right in front of them. Not that he, himself, was so swift on the uptake. Look at how long it had taken him to figure out why Felith was passing out. The amount of energy she must use up, it is a wonder Rags hadn't killed her. And his leg. Thinking of that made him feel weird. It was like his mind wanted to just slide right past it. He had felt so angry when she had touched him, and all she was doing was healing him. Not trying anything. He heard Felith whimper in her sleep. Glancing in the rearview mirror, he saw an expression of such agony scrunch up her features for a moment, then it was gone. Did it hurt her to heal others? Why? Why would she go through that for others? Fred jumped when Dog's tongue slurped over his ear. The beast seemed to like him, as much as everyone else despised him. He smiled inside at that thought, and went back to concentrating on driving.

They cleared the town, and still they drove on. Sidney didn't want to stop too close to the town. Fortunately the road was clearer on the highway letting them leave the town behind. They came upon a wreck of a huge semi truck, which blocked most of the roadway off. A recent rain had made the sides of the roadway soft and mushy, making going off the road to go around, not such a good idea. Rags broke out something to eat while the guys worried over the problem of clearing a way past the huge semi-truck. Emily had taken over the care of the baby ever since Fred had her take the baby while Felith slept. Dog romped around and around the huge truck, across the grassy ditch on one side of the truck, and around again to the other side of the truck, jumping into the ditch splashing in the water. He was like a puppy playing in the water, leaping out and running like crazy around and around. It was the most fun Felith could remember ever having. Then the boys pulled the cab of the truck out of the way. And with the truck moved it was time to go.

Sidney knew the way to the farm. When he pulled off the Highway to a small paved road the others had thought the journey was almost over. The farther they drove, the more open the countryside became. The first small town they came upon was completely deserted. The virus must have swept over the people in this town like a tidal wave. Sidney stopped only long enough to siphon gas from several cars. On the outskirts of the town there was a feed store. It was here they stopped to eat and take bathroom breaks. It was the bags of grain, potatoes, and beans that were the boon though. For a few minutes Sidney became the driving force of their little group. He and Rags marshaled the boys into loading bag after bag of anything that could be planted or eaten. Fred was just as quick to set the girls to bagging up packets of seeds and tools.

About 40 miles from the farm, Sidney pulled the truck he drove over. One-hundred yards down the road sat a small town. The surprise was the pristine condition of the town. Only four or five houses showed signs of being vandalized or burned. Across the road was a barricade of felled trees and a couple of junk looking cars. The cars had been placed and positioned in the middle of the barricade, much like a gate. Armed men were stationed at several spots on the other side of the barricade.

"Turn around," said an amplified voice. "If you advance we will kill you. There is no place here for those who are sick. Turn around."

Rags and Sidney both stepped out of the vehicles they were driving at the same time. Behind them they heard Fred open the door of the van he was driving. Rags motioned behind her back for him to get back in. Her heart sank when she heard another door open and shut behind her. "Get back in the cars," Rags said, without turning her head to see if they were complying or not. Facing armed criminals is what she had been trained for and these people were threatening them. Looking for the person who had spoken over the bullhorn, Rags took one step forward with her hands raised. "We are not a threat to you, or yours. We are only passing on this road to our destination. Allow us to pass and we will not bother you," she said in her negotiators voice.

"How do we know you don't carry the sickness?" A sandy haired man called back.

"The sickness seems to have run its course. Every place we have come across, we've found those that were ill have died. We are traveling to our home, and are no threat to you. Let us pass," Rags said.

Three of the men grouped together and started what looked like an argument between them. From behind the protecting group a woman came out on the porch of one of the standing houses. It wasn't long before she joined the arguing men. Suddenly she sobbed out one word that Rags and the others heard clearly. "Please!" It was a cry of desperation and despair. There was more discussion before the group turned to face Rags and the others. By that time, Julian and Robert had both come up to join Fred and Felith beside the front of the vehicles. Rags gave the four teens a stern look and pointed at the vans.

The sandy haired man stepped in front of the barricade. "We have agreed to negotiate your passing through the town."

"Negotiate? What could you possibly want from us?" Rags asked. She felt, rather than saw or heard, movement behind her. Placing her hand behind her she frantically motioned halt, halt, halt. Then, Felith was beside her. "All for one," the girl said softly.

The sandy haired man spoke again. "Antibiotics. We have a boy with an infected wound. You have antibiotics we'll escort you to the other side of the town."

"May I see him?" Felith asked.

"No." Only it wasn't the man who spat that word out with such force. Fred had his hand on Felith's arm before she could walk forward. "No," he said more softly. "Not until you eat." He noticed the slight change in her face muscles. Was it stubbornness, anger, or something else? Whatever it was, he wasn't about to let her kill herself to heal a boy. "I mean it. You eat, then you can touch him." For a moment he thought Felith was going to argue, but she nodded, and inside Fred breathed a sigh of relief. Who knew he'd feel so protective of a crazy girl who hadn't any sense of self-preservation, and was a frigging scary person with powers to heal, or else he was just crazy himself to think that. Whatever, someone had to protect her, and not Julian's toy Robby boy.

It was Rags who again addressed the man. "We need to eat and look through our supplies. To tell the truth, I'm not sure what we have in the way of medications. Give us about an hour to eat and search out anything we might have that will help your child. No matter what, you are welcome to whatever aid we can offer," she said, with a sidelong look at Sidney, a question in her eyes. Sidney was biting his lip, an indication that he knew, or suspected something she didn't.

In the meantime the man who had been addressing them nodded. "That seems a reasonable request. In one hour give us any antibiotics, and we will let you pass through our town." The 'our' was slightly more pronounced, an indication of possession.

Rags nodded, turning around she gave a shooing motion to the four teens, a scowl upon her face. Once they were all back behind the van which held their medical supplies, Rags faced the four teens. "When I motion for you to get back, you get back no matter what is going on. You realize you put everyone in danger by not staying back? What would happen to Middy, Eric and the baby if you, Sidney and I were all killed? Don't ever do that again. Got it?" she said in a stern voice poking a finger in their direction.

"Dog whined," Felith and Fred said at the same time. "The dog whined?" Rags almost shouted at them, just managing to keep her voice down. It was Sidney who spoke up. "You mean he whined. He didn't growl," he said, nodding to himself as if in understanding. For a moment Rags just looked back and forth between Sidney, Felith and Fred, slowly her face changed. "Dog whined. He didn't sense a threat." Felith nodded.

A scowl was back on Rags face, as she pointed her finger at them again. "Don't go thinking that excuses you getting out of the cars. And you two," she said shifting her attention to Robert and Julian. "You didn't have Dog's smarts to tell you anything, what is your excuse? Well?"

Immediately Julian's temper flared up. "You are going to let that little whiny bitch get away with getting out of the car, and then come down on us? I don't think so. You aren't the boss over me, or Robert. We are not working class trash to be yelled at," she snarled.

"That is enough, Julian," Robert said, his face turning bright red. "Be thankful, Rags and Sidney are here to take care of us. Now shut up, and lets get that food Fred was talking about." With that he took Julian by the arm and pulled her along behind him. As he went back to Rags' van.

It was not a power-play, Rags knew it, and so did Sidney. They were scared, all of them were scared. They had all been yanked from the life they knew, and were comfortable with, into a nightmare. Rags rubbed the back of her neck, her anger gone. She glanced over to where Sidney was looking through the medicines they had taken from different pharmacies along the way. What was he hiding? And Fred, what was that outburst of his about. No? No what? Rags' mind went back to what Fred had said. He had told Felith, "You eat, then you can touch him." Rags looked to where Felith was sitting with two of the peanut butter sandwiches on her plate in front of her, plus a pile of chips, and where those cookies? Beside Felith sat Fred, his own plate holding half as much as Felith's plate held. She is thin, Rags thought, seeing Middy, who sat on the other side of Felith, place one of her cookies on Felith's plate. How odd. Middy had such an obsessive nature when it came to sweets. Was Felith sick? The more she tried to reason out the nagging thought of something being held back from her, the more confusing the whole thing became. Clearly she wasn't herself yet after her own illness.

"I found a couple of things that might help," Sidney said behind Rags. "I don't think we should give it all to them, but I'm thinking we might only need to keep a couple doses for our own people, and they have so many more people who could be in need. What you say, Rags? Shall we save a child?"

Nodding, Rags picked up a couple of sandwiches for Sidney and herself. It didn't pay to not have the energy needed in an emergency. "Sidney," she said, as she handed him a sandwich, "is Felith sick or something? Or, is Fred just infatuated with her, and protective?" She watched him closely and saw a flicker of doubt cross his face.

At last he sighed. "I don't really know, Rags. When you were so ill, dying actually, I did what I could, which wasn't much. Just gave you every medication I could think of giving. But you were so sick, and we know that thing kills when it is done with a person. Then, Felith came over and touched you, just that, a touch. Then, she went as limp as a dead person herself. That huge beast of hers stood over her threatening anyone but Fred. Poor Fred was so beat up himself he had to hop on one leg over to her. He just sank down on the floor and held her. I thought you were both going to die. It was…. It was the closest I came to losing my mind in sheer terror of loss. Then you woke up and started getting better. It was like a miracle had happened. Fred has been protective of her ever since, in his own way. I'm not sure if he feels feeding her will keep her from fainting again, or what. You know it will be hard for that boy to ever…," Sidney's voice trailed off as he relived that

horrific moment when he thought he had lost both
of them.

"Low blood sugar?" Rags asked, her mind
having found a reasonable explanation to Felith's
weakness. "We will have to watch her, be sure
she eats regularly. Fred has the right idea of it
then. Protein, I think she'll need protein. No
sweets though." She looked around at the rest of
her charges, all of them eating. Julian with an air
of distaste, Middy protective of her food almost
to hoarding it. Robert eating with a resigned air
about him as if he felt weighted down. Little Eric's
watchful, careful eyes filled with shadowed fear.
Emily feeding the baby a bottle with one hand, and
feeding herself with the other. Rosemary was the
one that seemed to follow Julian's lead. The pair of
them could team up on the others and needed to be
watched. They were a family now. A mismatched
family, but isn't every family mismatched? Felith,
how odd that she seemed to be the heart of them, the
unspoken leader, with Fred her right hand man.

Felith stood, her tummy was as full as possible.
There was a child needing help, it was time to see to
it. She glanced at Fred and he nodded as if agreeing
with her unspoken thoughts. As they turned united
towards Rags and Sidney, a small shadow came
up beside them. Middy. "Middy, your job is to
protect Eric while we see to the hurt kid. Okay?"
Felith said, looking down at Middy. The little girl's
mouth scrunched sideways, but she nodded and
went over to where Eric stood. The pair were both
just young children, but there was Middy, her most
fierce expression warning the world in general not to

mess with Eric. It was adorable and touched some warm spot inside of Felith. She didn't understand the feeling, yet there was no doubt in her mind that she would protect those two little ones with her life if needed. Protect a baby monster, only Eric wasn't monster, not yet.

Robert stood when he saw the others were preparing to go see to the sick child. He felt he should be part of this, the command group. After all, he was more or less the senior of the orphans and had been left in charge as much as Felith had been left in charge. Julian grabbed his arm to stop him from leaving. She was always trying to keep him from doing what he thought was right. If only she were…. He let that thought trail off and sat back down.

Waiting at the barricade was the sandy haired man. He eyed the four people coming toward him, as if looking for weapons, or signs of illness. "If you will let us see the boy I might be able to recommend which of these antibiotics might work the best for him," Sidney said, as they grouped in front of the barricade.

"I'll have your names first. My name is Harry Barlow, spokesman for this town. We've had raiders come this way before. Nobody will be allowed to raid us again. Are we clear on that?" Harry Barlow said. There was a touch of truth in his eyes for the words he spoke.

"Officer Nancy Raglan. This is my spouse Sidney Asters. Fred and Felith," Rags said, nodding towards Fred and Felith, her look saying little. She was in protective mode, after all, no matter how well intended Barlow's words were, they were a threat.

It was Felith who defused the situation. "I would like to see the child, please," she said ever so softly. Beside her Fred reached out, as if wanting to restrain Felith. Then his hand dropped to his side.

Surprisingly Barlow nodded, the bluster challenge gone from his face. The strain this man was under showed briefly in his features, then he was all business. "I appreciate the antibiotics. You may meet Henry before leaving, but let me be clear there will be no threat to his life or to my wife…. If I feel the least bit of harm will come to them, I'll shoot you myself, got it."

"Me alone," Felith said.

Fred closed his eyes, as if trying hard not to speak out. He shook his head negatively, afraid to say out loud what he was thinking. She could be so stubborn. Not this time, this time he would override her wish to kill herself. Out of the corner of the eye he saw Rags starting to step forward too. He held his hand up in a stopping motion. It might be possible for him to go with Felith, but he knew she would never allow the others to go anywhere they might be in harm's way. With that thought he found his voice. "No, I'll go with her. You need to protect the babies. Go on, go back."

"What if she faints again?" Sidney asked, clearly worried about Felith.

"I'll carry her out. I can and I will if needed. Now go. She needs to be strong," Fred said, his voice level as if discussing the weather.

Sidney looked doubtful. Finally he nodded and motioned to Rags to follow him. It was difficult to get Rags to move away. One of hers had been threatened, and Middy would never forgive them if Felith or Fred were hurt. She had seen the stubborn mask fall over Felith's face though, and if what Sidney suspected was true, then Fred was right. They didn't need to stress Felith out by staying. Reluctantly she nodded and stepped back.

Harry Barlow watched this exchange with confusion. What the hell were they all talking about? He looked at the girl. She did seem pale and bony. Maybe she was just a fragile kid. Question was, why did she want to see Henry? And most importantly would she infect him with something his system couldn't stand right now? "If this gal is sick she isn't going near my son. You can all pile in your cars and get going right now," Harry said, waving his hand towards the vans.

There was only the slightest change in Felith's expression, it was enough to have both Fred and Sidney stepping forward. "She needs to see your son," Fred said.

"Why?" The question was thrown out more as a challenge than something Harry expected to be answered.

"She is…," Sidney started saying, then hesitated glancing over at Felith. Taking a deep breath as if girthing himself for a fight. Sidney continued, "Felith is sort of a faith healer. I don't know what, if anything, she does, but it seems when she touches someone who is sick or hurt they get better. Maybe it is all nonsense. Maybe it is some sort of miracle. Just ask yourself this, what can it hurt? Maybe, just maybe, your boy will get better after her touch, maybe not. What can it hurt?"

Harry looked over at Sidney as if he had lost his mind. He drew his lower lip into his mouth and stared at Felith for a long moment. "She thinks she can heal people?" he asked.

"Yes, but it wears her out. If she passes out, don't worry, it is just that all her strength saps out of her," Fred said. "It is very important nobody touches her. I'll get her if she faints."

"You can't believe in that crap. It sounds like a con to me. Next you'll be wanting me to pay you for doing voodoo," Harry's voice got louder as he spoke.

"Do you believe in God?" Sidney asked.

Harry nodded. "Okay, so you pray when you feel in need. You have no way of knowing if those prayers will help, yet you do them. I'm sure you have prayed for your boy. Now tell me, how do you know Felith isn't the answer to those prayers? Do you want to take a chance? If it doesn't help, at least you tried," Sidney said.

Raising a hand, Harry scrubbed his face with it, as if trying to rub a decision into his very being. He was so sure this was some sort of con game. What if it wasn't? What if he turned away the only chance of saving his little boy? Feeling slightly sick to his stomach, Harry nodded. "Just the girl and the boy. Rest of you get ready to leave," he said, anxious to be rid of these people.

The child laid on single bed, his body exposed from having kicked off the covers. Fred looked down on the sick boy. The wound was angry with red and a line was shooting upward from it. There was little doubt the boy would die if Felith didn't help him. Reaching out, he pressed two cubes of sugar into Felith's hand. "Eat them now," he said, waiting until Felith but the cubes in her mouth before moving over so she could see the boy. Worry sat like a heavy weight on his chest. This might be the one that kills her. Had there been anything else he could have done to prepare her for the ordeal? That thought spun around and around in his mind as Felith went to kneel by the boy's bed.

Lightly she touched the child on the forehead. This was a different hurt, filled with poison which heated her skin and made her blood feel like 1 billion points of fire frying her from the inside. The air in her lungs felt like Frost mingling the fire and burned her insides. She grabbed the poison holding it away from the child as she tried to reach the wounded flesh and start the healing process. Suddenly the world went black and she felt the breath swoosh out of her lungs.

Fred was there before she could slip to the floor, holding her, cherishing her, trying to give her something like she had given the boy on the bed. All he could do was hold her though. He was not able to do whatever Felith did to heal others. Fred kissed Felith on the cheek as he held her to his chest. He looked to where the angry red line had been to see the skin pink and healthy. "Your son should improve rapidly now. Don't let her sacrifice go to waste," Fred told Harry and his wife. Carefully he carried Felith back to the van, worry and fear in every step he took. She couldn't keep doing this. Only, how could he justify stopping her, even to himself? Laying Felith in the back of the van, he covered her and placed a pillow under her head. Middy was at Felith's side immediately. Fred put a finger to his lips in a quiet motion, then placed his hands against his face like a person sleeping. Middy, her lips pressed so tightly together they were white, nodded her head and lay down beside Felith. Eric crept up and lay on the other side.

Starting the van, Fred slipped it into drive, and followed Rags in her van. His mind was so muddled that he didn't know what to do. Never did he think he could trust anyone ever again. Now this strange girl had made him care, made him believe in her. How the hell had that happened? And how the hell was he going to survive another betrayal? I swore, he thought, never, never again. That word kept beating against his mind like a hammer pounding everything into a bloody pulp. For a frantic moment he felt like screaming, but he didn't, not him, he'd fight first, fight anyone. Like a balloon pricked with a pin he deflated. She wouldn't like that, him fighting, and that was the problem, what she thought mattered. The eternal trap, caring.

An hour later the small caravan was on the dirt road to the farm. The place was more run down than Sidney remembered it. The fields had not been turned in months. Out in the small side pasture was one cow in need of feeding up. Bantam chickens ran here and there. Other than that there was no sign of life to be seen. Rags stepped out of the van she was driving and motioning to the others to stay put. She drew her gun and slowly approached the house. The worst sign was the farm door hanging open. The house itself was empty, having been tossed in what looked like a hurricane search. If the layer of dust on the floor was an indication, nobody had been in the house for some time. Still Rags went from room to room, making sure nothing nasty was there for the kids to see, before she called out to Sidney that it was safe. Turning around Rags pursed her mouth, as she saw Sidney, Fred and Robert all standing just inside the doorway. "I told you all to stay in the vans," she sniped out. Sidney waved his hand to include the boys. "All for one. You didn't think I was going to let you out of my sight, did you?" A small curve came to his lips when Rags threw up her hands in defeat.

The rest of the day was spent cleaning the house out, preparing places for them all to sleep and caring for the baby. Through it all Felith slept, as if in the hold of death. Tiny and large shadows fell across that sleeping form, blankets were shifted now and then, even though Felith never moved to shift them. They kept watch even while they cleared the dust away and straightened furniture. Night came and tired bodies fell onto mattresses, all but two.

Sunlight filtering through the curtains woke Felith. She felt weak, her body shaky in its weakness. It took all her willpower to sit up. Hand trembling she swiped her hair back from her face. Something moved at the edge of the bed, followed by a loud shout of, "She's awake!" from Middy. Had the child spent the evening there watching over her? Or was it morning? There was a sound of little feet pounding on a hardwood floor, then Eric launched himself onto the bed and had Felith wrapped in a death grip.

Felith watched the door knowing where Eric was, Fred wouldn't be far away.

Only the next to show up was Rags, a tray of food in her hands. "Get up you lazy bones. Do you want us to do all the work around here?" Rags said in a teasing voice. The stricken look on Felith's face had Rags regretting her choice of words. She placed the tray with breakfast, consisting of scrambled eggs, oatmeal, and what looked like an attempt at making a biscuit on a bedside table. Rags shrugged her shoulders. "Well I don't know how to cook, and Sidney is busy seeing what needs to be done to get the fields planted. Manly work. You know how men like to feel manly."

"They do?" Croaked Felith, her eyes growing just slightly wide. There was so much she didn't know yet, so much to learn.

Rags laughed, "Yes, men have these huge egos that tell them they have to be the best, the most productive, the first in most everything they do. Although," Rags tilted her head in thought, "I don't think Sidney has too huge an ego. He seems rather balanced. Now you eat, or Fred will be all grumpy. Well he is always grumpy, but more grumpy."

There was a difference to Rags. She seemed more relaxed than Felith had ever seen her in the past. "How long?" Felith ask as she began to shovel food into her mouth, sometimes missing as her hand shook so much.

For a moment Rags clamped her mouth shut tight, then sighed. "Since you touched the boy..., a day and a half ago. You can't keep doing whatever it is you do. It takes too much out of you," she said, watching as Felith continued to eat. It was like talking to a brick wall, Rags thought. Shaking her head in defeat, Rags went to check on how the chores she had set the girls to doing were coming along. That was another matter. They just didn't listen to her and Sidney the way they listened when Felith gave an order.

It took an hour before Felith was able to get out of bed and change her clothing. She set about cleaning the room she was in, with Middy and Eric shadowing her ever step. Middy helping to lift anything Felith tried to lift up. Nobody said anything, there was no need for speaking. Once the bedroom was clean Felith went to find the kitchen. Eric and Middy carried the tray with the empty plate and bowl on it between them. When they reached the living room Middy pointed to a door. The three made their way into the kitchen.

It was apparent that Rosemary and Julian had kitchen duty. The problem was that Rosemary was the only person doing any actual work. Julian was sitting on a stool with a dish towel draped over her shoulder, fanning her face with a booklet of some sort. Rosemary, standing at the sink, was half-heartedly scrubbing at a dish. Then, she saw Felith and started scrubbing harder at the plate she was washing.

Walking slowly, for she still didn't have much energy, Felith went to where Julian sat. She reached up and took the dish towel off Julian's shoulder. "You are dismissed from duty for the rest of the day," she said to Julian. Making her way to the sink

Felith started to pick up a dish, dizziness swam like a million bees over her mind. For a moment she felt darkness closing in on her, and sagged against the sink. Then she straighten and picked up a cup. Slowly she dried the cup, handing it to Middy, who was hovering at Felith's side. Middy's mouth was so tightly drawn that she almost looked as if it were glued shut. With a glare in Julian's direction Middy took the cup and carefully carried it to the cup rack.

No one looked at Julian again, not even Rosemary, who was washing dishes with more vigor than she ever had before. Somewhere in the house the baby cried out for attention. It wasn't long before Emily came into the kitchen to make a bottle for the baby. She, of course, still wasn't talking to anyone. Julian continued to sit on the stool looking irritated, but avoiding looking to where Felith, who was obviously weak and shaky, continued to do the job Julian had been assigned. Felith's helpers, Middy and Eric, stayed close to her.

Once the dishes were cleaned and put away. Felith considered what to make for lunch. She had Middy and Eric tell her what supplies were on hand, and was surprised at the amount of frozen meat and vegetables that where in the farmhouse freezer. Quickly she and Emily pulled together a meal for lunch, as well as one for dinner. Emily batted Felith's hands away from the table and put together the makings for fresh bread and a cake. Middy, the little imp, managed to swipe a spoon full of cake batter. The morning passed with Felith managing to stay on her feet and active. By the time the meal was cooked and set up on the table all her energy was gone. She needed food.

The boys started trickling in, sweaty, needing to wash up before eating. Sidney took his place to one side of the head of the table. Robert looked limp when he entered the dining room, as if working in the fields had sapped him dry. Perhaps it had, for he was not used to doing work more than the house chores assigned him. Middy waited to see Felith seated before sitting down, even though she was eager to eat and have the cake served. Eric had left when the boys came in and was most likely with Fred. They were the last to arrive. Only two chairs remained unoccupied by then, the two next to Felith, who sat at the head of the table.

Middy sent a glare at the two boys as they entered. She was not too nice to anyone delaying a meal. Fred laid his hand briefly on Middy's head as he sat down next to her, leaving the chair next to Felith for Eric. Something was different about Fred, Felith noticed it immediately. Still she didn't appear to look at him, she just felt the difference. For one thing he wouldn't look at her, at all. She didn't know what it was, only that it was a feeling she had. Certainly nothing she had ever experienced before. Maybe it was disappointment. Whatever it was, Felith stored it away and tried not to let it show on her face. Instead, she concentrated on shoveling food into her mouth, eating until her tummy was so full there wasn't room for even the cake.

Night came bringing coldness from Fred towards Felith. Julian smiled when she noticed what was going on between Fred and Felith. Felith, in her typical manner, ignored Fred's behavior towards her.

The day had tired her out. Even with the big meals she had eaten for lunch and dinner she felt drained and shaky. Survival meant not showing weakness though, and she refused to give in to that weakness. It was her body that betrayed her. Sometime, before the little ones were sent to bed, Felith fell asleep.

He saw her, even though he wasn't really watching her, not really. He had tried to make it clear he didn't want to have anything to do with Felith. It was called a clean break. It didn't feel clean. In fact, he felt dirty. And there she was asleep in her chair looking so helpless, so peaceful. It took all his will power not to get up and carry her off to her bed, to tuck her in, to watch over her. Fred was telling himself he had passed the first test. Maybe he would survive. Then, Robert got up and looked over at Felith. When he started to walk over to Felith's sleeping form something strange happened. Fred found himself already there scooping Felith up in his arms. He didn't remember moving, or even deciding to get up. But there she was in his arms, safe. Safe from Robert. He wasn't jealous, not really. He just didn't like the idea of Robert touching her. Robert didn't understand how much Felith disliked being touched. If someone had to carry Felith to bed it was just better that he did it himself.

Julian watched as Robert got up to go to that filthy girl. That boy Fred beat him to the whore. What was it that attracted them to a slut like that, she wondered, then gave a snort of a laugh. Of course, because it was free. Men were like that always after a free lay. That whore wasn't getting Robert, Robert was hers. She made her way over to Robert and rubbed his back as if soothing him. Looking up at Robert she parted her lips, then licked them slowly. Julian could see the pulse in his neck jump a little faster beat. Inside she crowed to herself, feeling powerful in the knowledge she could arouse him so easily. When Robert glanced to the doorway Fred had carried that slut through, anger raged through Julian. She traced her fingers down his back and around his hip to his stomach, still playing at soothing him, while watching his pulse rate rise. He'd be all hers tonight, of that she was certain.

In the bedroom Fred placed Felith on the bed and covered her up. He resisted lingering, or touching her cheek. There was no reason she should know he had brought her to bed. He could do this, guard against her or anyone who would…, use him. Inside the anger started to build. He regretted losing that sense of well-being, of the belonging she had given to him, if only for a short time. One for all, the words slipped into his mind, haunting him, as he walked out of the bedroom.

Chapter Nine

DUKE

Over the next few days all of them would gather at the table for breakfast. At times Sidney would cook breakfast, but more often Emily had already started the meal before the others were up and dressed. Emily had taken over care of the baby and the kitchen. She had found her spot in the family. Everyone still left the spot at the head of the table open for Felith. Neither Rags nor Sidney tried to take over that spot. There seemed to be some sort of agreement between the two adults where Felith was concerned. Fred and Eric had taken to sitting farther down the table from Felith. Middy and Emily now had the seats beside Felith on one side while Sidney and Rags were on the other side.

As they ate breakfast the chores for the day would be discussed. Sidney, who had helped his grandfather out on the farm as a child, had charge of the plowing and planting. He had made a chart showing the fields and what they had on hand to plant for this season. Clearly there was a lot of physical work ahead for all of them. Emily and one other person would stay at all times in the farmhouse, doing what needed to be done to maintain a household, such as the laundry. Sometimes, if there were a lot of household chores, or nothing the youngsters could do around the farm, then Middy and Eric would remain to help. Rags acted like a floater and guard. She would check on the house, and the others while doing some of the chores, collecting eggs from the chickens, feeding them and the few animals they had. And watching, always watching. She carried her gun with her everywhere.

As always Felith was fair in handing out the chores. She rotated each person from the fields and outside chores to the house so that each day a different person had a day of house duty. The exception was Julian. Julian was left out of her orders by simply telling the others that if they felt Julian would be of help they could talk to her about helping them. She had washed her hands of the girl who didn't want to help out. In her mind, she had given Julian the only chance she deserved. She would not allow Julian's laziness to affect the others and took it upon herself to work twice as hard. She was the last one to come in to eat. The first to go out to work, always going where the need was greatest. She was ever aware that Fred didn't watch her like before. Considering his wanting to avoid her, which he made clear, she seldom invaded his work area. It was as if this was the unspoken agreement between them.

How she felt was another matter, for never had she been so confused about anyone as she was about Fred.

Middy watched for her chance, striding out with a small bowl of feed for the chickens in her arms, Middy angled just enough to intercept Julian with little thought she slammed into the prissy girl. Julian's shocked body stood firm causing Middy to fall down. Middy screamed at the top of her lungs. Huge tears running down her cheeks.

The reaction was immediate. Little Eric was there first, for once not screaming and running away in fear, the little boy put up his fist, threatening Julian. Felith and Fred arrived at the same moment. The color had drained from Felith's face, and was the only indication of emotion. Fred stopped short taking in the situation, noting Felith was there, seeing the scorn on Julian's face, the huge tears on Middy's face, and little Eric all in protective mode. That last bit sent something like warmth through him. He felt something akin to pride in the boy. Middy however was faking it, this was revenge, more than likely for something Julian had done to Felith.

Fred tensed as Felith reached out to touch the crying Middy. His resolve not to be near Felith still held, but his body readied to catch her should she faint upon touching Middy, as he could be wrong, the child might actually be hurt. He couldn't help his reaction to Felith. No matter how solid his resolve to not be involved with her. Then he found himself wishing Felith had fainted, that Middy really had been hurt by Julian and not just faking for some petty revenge. What he saw on Felith's face was so much worse.

Felith touched Middy, prepared to heal the child from some minor but painful bruising. Felith's eyes closed for the briefest of seconds, then she looked away from Middy. Nothing about her face indicated what she was feeling. Inside she felt betrayed by the one person she had felt she could rely upon. "Middy, you are excused from work for the rest of the day," she said, turning she walked away.

Middy stood up, this time the tears were real. Her rounded little girl face was the picture of being devastated. Head hanging she walked back to the house with Eric following in her footsteps.

Julian's eyes flashed in anger. "I didn't do anything to that brat! She rewards the little snot for assaulting me. I didn't do anything," she ranted.

"Felith knows," Fred said, his tone flat. "It wasn't a reward. She punished Middy, and Middy knew it." He looked at Julian. "It is a shame you don't." With that he went back to work, leaving Julian standing there, alone.

It was as if she was once again locked away in that dark basement. Felith knew it was her fault, she was the one who had let her guard down, allowed herself to feel something. Knowing that it was her own fault didn't ease the awful pain of betrayal she had felt when she had touched Middy and knew the little girl had lied. First Fred's coldness, now Middy. Felith felt cold and alone as she worked at weeding a patch of new growth in the potato field, the sun beating down on her back. The sun couldn't warm her, she wasn't sure anything would ever warm her, at least not inside, where it counted.

The shadows lengthen, and soon it was time to call it a day. Still Felith worked. The potatoes were weeded, and the ground holding the plants loosened around them. There was nothing left to do. Finally she took the tools she had been using to work the potato bed and put them away in the shed. It was time to go in, Middy would be upset if she had to wait to long to eat.

There was one last thing Felith could use as an excuse to prolong going in the house and feeling alone inside. She circled around to the front of the house to check on the flower bed she had started in front of the porch. A lone figure sat upon the steps leading to the porch of the farmhouse. Everyone else had entered by way of the kitchen to wash up and get ready for dinner. Felith stopped when she saw the old woman sitting on the steps. The woman was very elderly, her face showed many years of being in the sun, and was deeply creased. The woman stood slowly, as if the act of rising took great effort. "Are you the girl?" The old woman asks.

"What girl?" Felith asked in return.

"The healer," said the woman her voice snapping, sounding filled with aggravation, as if she had no time for stupid girls.

No one referred to her as a healer. She didn't know how to respond. Finally she nodded. The old woman started forward, then looked at Felith. "Well, what are you standing there for? I got a sick baby that needs you, move it."

A baby? It was the thought of it being a baby that got Felith to moving. She followed the old woman down the road. For someone elderly the woman moved at a clip pace. Felith had been tired and hungry only moments ago, but the urgency of a baby being ill drove all thoughts of rest and food from her mind. She was in accord with the woman, a baby needed healed. Later Rags would find their footprints in the dust of the road and wonder who had stolen Felith away.

It wasn't until they were all seated at the table that anyone noticed Felith was gone. Middy had avoided being near anyone, so seeped in her own guilt at having lied about being hurt, and was just sitting down when Fred and Eric entered to take their own seats. Everyone waited for a couple of minutes, then several became restless wanting to get on with the meal. Finally Middy began to fear that Felith wouldn't even eat with her in the room, blaming herself, as children often do. "I can eat in the bathroom," she said.

"No," Fred said, at the same time as Rags said, "What? Why would you say that?"

"Go get her, Robert," Fred said, not bothering to explain who or why.

Surprised, Robert stood. He gave Fred, then Julian an unarmed certain look, before going off to find Felith. Only he couldn't find her, not in the house, not in the yard, or in the fields. He returned to the dining room expecting Felith to be at her spot at the head of the table. Only she wasn't there.

Rags, Sidney and Fred all left the room looking for Felith. Upon seeing Robert return without her, it was Rags who found the footprints going down the road. Two sets, one most certainly

belonging to Felith. The question was who did
the second set belong to? She immediately found
something to rope off the start of the footprints.
Falling back on her training as an officer of the law,
her first thought had been to not contaminate the
evidence. Then Rags went back and told Sidney and
Fred to come with her, and bring flashlights. She
instructed the rest of the kids to eat, and then to go
to bed. Middy's bottom lip trembling, she refused
and followed Rags and the others outside. "This line
you are not to cross yet," Rags said. "It looks to me
as if Felith walked off with someone. As we were all
at the table, I suspect it was a stranger. In that case,
what we have to determine is if she was being forced,
or went on her own for some reason. We all know
how serious this might be. Let's first look for other
footprints to see if there was more than one person.
Then we will decide on how to go about finding her.
Stay on the porch while we investigate, Middy."

Middy stood still, hardly breathing as the
other three looked carefully in front of the porch,
then walked along the side of the road shining their
flashlights on the road. When they returned, and
Rags checked her gun to be sure it was fully loaded,
the seriousness of what had happened reached pitch
form. Middy's trembles turned to the hard, tightly
controlled look that was always on Felith's face.
Before she could blame herself again, Sidney spoke
up. "We have to believe she left on her own with this
stranger. I can only think of one thing that Felith
would do without having thought to tell us about it."

"Heal a kid," Fred said. Up until then he had
been thinking Felith had gone off in a fit of anger,

only in reality he knew that wasn't like her at all. The stupid girl hadn't thought to eat either. Just like her to risk herself without a thought about how it affected anyone else. Just like that Fred was in charge again. "Middy, go get as much left over chicken from the table that you can carry without making a big mess. Sidney, help her, put it in a bag or pillowcase if you have to." He looked over at Rags. You need to be here, just in case we are wrong. I want you and your gun protecting the rest of them."

Almost smiling at how Fred had leaped to the front where it regarded Felith, she nodded instead. Those two kids needed each other, they were stronger together. "How are you going to find her?" she asked, as Middy and Sidney returned with a bag full of what was to have been their dinner.

Fred spoke softly one word, "Dog." The beast was there before he finished saying its name. The fact Dog hadn't growled a warning when Felith left, more than anything else, convinced all of them that she had left to heal some kid. "Find her for me," Fred told Dog. The huge beast took off down the road at a fast trot his nose skimming over the packed earth of the road following the scent of footprints, that the humans could only see with their eyes. Fred grabbed the bag of food and scrambled to keep up with Dog. Middy would have followed had not Rags and Sidney placed their hands on her shoulders.

Running after Dog, Fred fumed inside. His fault, his damn fault. He should have been keeping watch over her. She was stupid about her own well-being, and he knew that. And stubborn beyond reason. What do you do with somebody like that?

Damn stupid girl, damn stupid girl. If she died it was his fault. He knew she was upset about Middy, and he had just ignored her, knowing how she must be hurting. Reckless. All for one, all for one, all for one. The words beat Fred up inside his mind. Only, the only one who lived up to those words was Felith. What a stupid, stupid girl.

Dog stopped, then turned off the road. It was a path of sorts, so overgrown that there were spots where it disappeared. The huge beast was wind scenting now, no longer with his nose to the ground for her scent was in the air, on the leaves, in pockets of still air up under the brush. It was a feast for Dog's nose. He pushed his way forward, aware of Fred on the fringe of his senses. Once he stopped, turning his head to stare off to one side of the path. A low warning growl rumbled up from Dog's deep chest. He looked back over his shoulder at Fred as if to check on him, then continued forward. Whatever had lurked in the brush to the side of the trail scurried off, crashing through the brush as if in a panic.

Up ahead a light appeared leading Fred and Dog to an old wood framed house. The house was run down with a board missing here and there from the siding. The door hung open, and it was at the door that dog stopped. His whole butt waved in a happy beat as he stood with his head just poking into the house. Suddenly Dog moved back and off to the side. The big dog curled into a circle and appeared to fall asleep. Fred knew immediately that Felith had given the dog some hand signal, sometimes he had seen her do that before, directing the dog to go lay down. So she was okay. Relief flooded over him. He had made it to her in time. Fred knocked on the door while at the same time pushing it the rest of the way open. In all the walk over here following Felith's trail he had not expected what he saw in the house. At a plain wood table was a very old woman and Felith. Before Felith was a plate filled with turnip greens, beans and cornbread. Felith stopped with a fork full of food halfway to her mouth. She blinked once as if Fred's appearance had surprised her.

The old woman stood up, "You must be Fred. Don't worry. We are feeding your gal. She said you'd be mad if she didn't eat first. Come on and have a seat. I'll dish you up a helping too."

Fred felt all his anger at Felith deflate. She had told them she had to eat first. No, she had told them he would be mad if she didn't eat. That meant she had thought of him. A strange feeling came over him both of being sad and elated. The thought that Felith thought about him sent a whole world of fireworks going off inside him, warming him. She wouldn't need him anymore now that she knew how to take care of herself. For some reason that thought depressed Fred. The bag of food seemed to burn in his hand, carefully he let the bag slide down in front of Dog and opened the bag before entering the house.

"Thank you so much for looking after Felith," Fred said, sitting down. He chanced a glance at Felith, noting that she was energetically shoving food into her mouth. She could at least acknowledge me, he thought. Then he noticed how she avoided looking at him. Perhaps she was aware of him after all, it was hard to tell, but part of him believed she was aware of him. It was dangerous to care about her. No way was he going to trust again. He regretted coming, regretted that he had felt anything.

"Mimi, can I come eat too?" A male voice called from the next room.

"You'll watch over your brother, or I'll tan your hide!" the old woman yelled, then she smiled at Fred. "The boys are twins, and twins should take care of each other."

Thing was, they didn't seem to be kids. Fred could see the thought of that enter Felith's mind too. Had the old woman lied to Felith? That would've been a mistake if she had. Felith continued to eat, and anyone looking at her, besides Fred, wouldn't have noticed a difference in her. Almost beneath hearing, he heard her whisper one word, "Dog." Dog entered then, pushing against the door until it came open, he walked over and laid down beside Felith's chair. Shoving the last bite of food into her mouth Felith stood as she chewed. She swallowed and said, "Now."

Fred and the old woman both stood. The old woman gave Dog a nervous glance, but she didn't object to the huge beast. Perhaps her need for Felith's touch was stronger than her fear of Dog. "My baby is in here," the old woman said. "You have to fix him. He is going to die if you don't. These boys are all I have left of my Doris. She died giving them life and I ain't about to let some damn seizures kill one of them. People in town said you can heal, now heal my baby for me."

Felith had her mouth clamped shut. Whoever

was in that room was someone held dear by this forceful old woman. She wasn't about to turn away from such a need, just because it was a grown up monster. Dog rumbled softly, as if picking up Felith's feelings. She felt betrayed by this old woman. The thought entered her mind that, to this woman, the young man in there was a baby. The elderly woman must have raised the boys after the daughter died. The thought eased some of the hurt she was feeling at being betrayed, not all of it, but some of it.

Fred slipped ahead of Felith, through the door to the bedroom, and stopped, blocking the entrance. His jaw clenched at what he saw. Not a baby, he thought, as he saw the boy a bit older than himself lying on a bed jerking and shaking. She can't do this, was Fred's second thought upon seeing the strapping man on the bed twitching and jerking in a seizure. "How long?" Fred asked the brother sponging his twin.

"This time since I asked Mimi if I could eat. It gets longer each time. The medicine is all gone. Town says they are out of everything. Duke's temperature starts going up when he is twitching like this. Thought I could eat, that's all. Just eat," the boy's voice trailed off as if wanting to eat made him feel guilty.

Behind Fred, with Dog at her side, Felith was listening to what the young man was saying. She didn't touch Fred, still he could feel her there. Steeling himself to tell her she couldn't heal this one, he started to turn to face her. He had forgotten how small and thin Felith was built. He had barely turned when Felith slipped by him. Fred reached out to stop her, but it was already too late. One of her hands dropped to the forehead of the twitching boy on the bed. For once Fred wasn't fast enough to catch Felith as her legs gave way beneath her. The boy sponging Duke gave a cry of surprise and caught Felith in his arms. Something inside of Fred seemed to shut down, to freeze as if in shock. He closed his eyes for the briefest of seconds then stepped up to help lay Felith down on the bed beside the deeply sleeping boy who had been a twitching mass only moments before. She wasn't breathing.

The boy started to lift Felith's T-shirt, and the rage took over Fred. "Get your damn filthy hands off her," Fred hissed between clenched teeth. It took everything, every thought of what Felith might think if he beat the boy to a bloody pulp, to stop him from giving in to the rage. Hands trembling, Fred moved Felith's still limp body to the floor, positioned her head, he gave her a breath from his own lungs, then began to do CPR. He could feel Dog's breath on his back. As he pressed Felith's heart to keep the blood circulating to her brain. He was scared, so scared, and so damn angry.

Only when Felith pulled in a gasping breath did the ridged horror begin to leave Fred. When the normal deep sleep of healing took over Felith, Fred stop compressions. Gathering her into his arms he stood. Not one more minute would he stay in this place that had killed her. "Dog," he said, and walked past the old woman, who looked as if she might pass out too. With Felith clutched to his chest, he told himself he didn't care. Let them all faint, they had killed Felith. But he found himself speaking anyway.

"Take care of your grandmother," Fred called out as he and Dog walked out of the house.

All night, through the day, into the next night Felith slept. Most of the first night her body shook as if she were in a frozen wasteland. The others took over her care, wrapping her in soft, warm blankets. Everyone but Julian took turns sitting beside Felith's bed and wiping her face with a cool wet cloth. Middy tight-lipped posting herself as guard over sleeping Felith. Dog climbed up on the bed and refused to leave. Eric tried not to cry, coming in and out of the room with his face screwed up in a mask of fearful worry. Fred stayed out of the room where she slept. The anger inside him still boiled, raging to be let loose. So, he worked hard in the fields to tire himself out, to keep from smashing Robert's face just because he didn't trust the man, to not grab sniping Julian by her throat and shake some sense into her. He didn't want to ever give in to the rage again.

It was the panting in her ear that woke Felith. Dog, the huge beast, had stayed beside her the entire time she was sleeping. Felith petted his head and that seemed to satisfy him. He slurped a wet tongue over her cheek, then made the mattress bounce by leaping off the bed. Middy was the next one to be up against Felith. The little girl squirmed her way up against Felith and put an arm across her waist.

"You are going to make us late for breakfast," Middy said, her voice trembling slightly.

Felith put a hand on the back of Middy's head and smiled at her. "Then you had best let me up as I'm starved."

Breakfast was silent and tense. No one would look at her. It was like she had done something wrong and was being punished. Finally Rags walked into the dining room and smiled at Felith. Strange how she had started to collect the sometime smiles of others. There was little chance any of them cared for her, she was as always nothing. But the once in a while smile had softened her heart, made her have more vulnerability. Even stranger was how she sometimes looked for Fred to help her. That, more than anything, was a worry. He was one of the monsters. Still, today, when she felt so weak, so far from being herself, Fred was acting as if she wasn't there, was he thinking she was a nothing girl, and…, it hurt. Never let them hurt you, the monsters, Felith reminded herself.

The anger Fred felt wouldn't leave him. When Felith died such a rage had taken him over that he had thought for a moment he wouldn't be able to control it, to get back from the urge to harm someone. He had just managed, because of her, because she needed him, even if she would never admit it. That was the trap, being needed. He would not fall for it, not now, not ever. So he was shunning Felith, keeping his distance, and trying to pretend she didn't exist. Hopefully she would use some sense from now on, not kill herself again. Just the thought of her dying like that sent the rage boiling in his blood again. He turned and walked out of the house. Somehow he had to get control again.

Robert watched Fred leaving, and wondered what had happened that had the guy so tense. Maybe he was done with Felith. Maybe, just maybe he could try to get her to like him. Just until…. The thought stopped as Robert saw Julian staring at him, a knowing smile on her lips. Those lips could do wonders. He was getting hard just looking at those lips. With a sigh he went outside to cool down. When Robert saw Fred standing looking out towards the road, he debated going back inside, or if he should speak to Fred. After all, Fred was one of their bunch. He fit in with Julian, Rosemary, and himself. Perhaps if he just asked about Felith, what Fred's intentions were towards her. "You seem to be on the outs with Felith. Do you mind if I talk with her?" he asked in his most persuasive voice.

Fred turned on Robert, the rage inside him so close to being let loose. One more word from this high tone snob and he wouldn't be responsible for his own actions, and that was something he never wanted to feel again. His voice soft, full of restrained threat, he said the only thing he could, "Walk away from me. Now!"

Robert stepped back, as if he had been punched. Cold fingers of fear ran down his back, he almost lost control of his bladder, only barely saving himself that embarrassment. Quickly he went back into the house. His eyes sought out Julian and he nodded his head at her. He needed to feel alive after being the coward once again. Only he didn't want just her mouth he wanted to feel manly, to take her, and not just her lips.

The next few weeks there was a strained air among the teens. Robert was tense when working around Fred, and there was something like guilt in his eyes when he was around Julian. While Fred seemed to be the same, only he didn't seem to care what Felith did, or where she was at any moment of the day. He listened to her daily orders and did his work without contributing to the conversation. Even Middy seemed affected. The little girl kept a close watch on Felith, as if she expected her to faint, or run off again. For that Felith was truly sorry. She didn't know what to do to quiet Middy's fear, except to be there for her, to never leave without telling Middy first. Fred's distance was like a nagging pain in her chest. She felt as if she had done something wrong, only she couldn't see what it could be. Was he upset because she hadn't told him and the others where she was going? This thing, this interacting with others was hard for her to do. She didn't understand why anyone was upset over her leaving to go heal a child. Only it hadn't been a child. Perhaps that is what was wrong with Middy and Fred. Or, was she to be a prisoner here too?

The sun was beating down on Fred's back as he checked the front field to see how close the crop was to being ready to harvest. A movement upon the road had him looking up to see what it was, and he saw a man walking along the road. As the man got closer, Fred realized it was one of the twins that was walking up the road to the house. Immediately Fred's heart started beating faster. He, or the other twin, had killed Fel. What did the creep want now wondered Fred as he finished his inspection of the field, Fred started back to the house. There were other things he could do, things he should do, as to why he wasn't doing those things he wasn't about to debate with himself. At the moment the only thing he was doing was greeting a neighbor, right? Cutting across the field to the road, Fred came out right in front of the man walking up the road.

Stopping, Duke looked Fred up and down as if measuring him up. Duke was muscular certainly, but about 4 inches shorter than Fred. He smiled at Fred. "You must be the boyfriend. I'm Duke. Mimi sent me to pay the healer for her service. We don't have any money, but I'm willing to help with the harvesting. We brought our crops in, as we planted earlier than you all. I'm good and strong," Duke said, flexing the muscles of one arm.

Fred wasn't interested in a pissing contest. "There are rules here that you will have to follow, understand?" Fred said and waited until Duke nodded before continuing. "Felith, is in charge. If she tells you to do something, do it. Rags might shoot you if you do anything to harm anyone, so be on your best behavior. Listen to Rags and Sidney, do as they say, unless Felith has told you differently. Best to voice conflict, than to let it cause trouble later. Treat all the women with respect. Understand?" Fred clenched his teeth as he watched Duke's body shaking with merriment trying not to laugh at him.

"Dude!" Duke said, "I'm just here to work. So take me, as they say, to your leader."

Berating himself, for he had stepped into the pissing contest after all, Fred waved for Duke to follow him. They found Felith coming out of the house. She had her usual jeans on and had added a long-sleeved cotton shirt. Fred figured she was heading out to hoe around some of the vegetables in the garden. "You remember Duke. He has come to help out for a while," Fred said stepping away. He only went a short ways before pretending to check out a fence that looked like it was leaning. He heard Duke exclaim, "I'll have to be sure to keep Kit from seeing you. He always wants the girls I court. You have such lovely eyes." Turning, Fred hurried off, he didn't want to hear Felith flirt with Duke, which was bound to happen, girls went for that sort of bull crap.

Felith stared at Duke for a moment as if trying to figure him out, then glanced towards Fred retreating back. Looking back at Duke she said, "You can go help Robert. He is on the far right field clearing stones so it can be plowed for perhaps some cooler weather crops. Wait here for a moment." Turning she retreated into the house, only to return with a thermos. "You will be needing something to drink. Robert has his own." That done she continued on to the chore she had set for herself, dismissing Duke.

Duke watched Felith, walking away. That hadn't been his best moment with a girl. Not that he wouldn't win her over, after all. She was a potential gold mine. The prices they could charge for her healing someone would make him rich. For now, he had to play it cool, just flirt when he could, wear her down, and keep her away from the boyfriend. The game was on and he was the game master. Left to find his own way to the field in question, Duke detoured to where he knew Fred had been working, at least he thought he was working. It was time to stake a claim on the healer. Only Fred wasn't where Duke thought. Not wanting to make a bad impression on Felith, Duke went on to the area where she had indicated he should meet up with Robert.

"Dude!" Duke called out upon finally seeing Robert tugging at a medium sized rock. "You must be Robert. The healer girl sent me to give you a hand. Don't you know anything about leverage? You need a pry bar here, or a tractor to pull the larger ones out. And why don't you use a trailer to stack them on, then move them all off the field at once. You guys really are new to farming, aren't you?"

Wiping sweat from his neck and face, Robert looked up at the intruder. He was thankful for the interruption. Physical labor was just not something he had ever thought he would be doing in his life. He smiled, "You have some good ideas. Trouble is we are saving fuel on the machines around here just in case we can't get any more for a while. You know the world has gone nuts, right?" he said

"Yeah, so I heard. You know what that means?" Duke went on without waiting for an answer, "Finally something good is coming from living here. We're going to be rich. People have to eat, and we grow the food. They will pay anything for our crops. Just you wait and see. By the way, I'm Duke, and you must be Robert." Duke stuck out his hand.

Carefully wiping his hand first, Robert took Duke's hand and gravely shook it. "Felith sent you to help me?" he asked, as that seemed so out of place. Seeing Duke starting to laugh he went on, "I mean, how do you know Felith? If you don't mind me asking."

Shaking his head in wonder Duke said, "What is with you guys? Her boyfriend almost threatened to beat me up. Now you. She must be some special chick for you all to be that crazy about her."

Now it was Robert's turn to shake his head. "No, you don't understand. Felith doesn't have a boyfriend. Well, I'm not sure what Fred thinks he is to her. But she isn't sweet on anyone as far as I know. She is special. I fancied her myself, still do. Guess Fred does too. She isn't pretty like Julian, but there is just something that seems to attract me. I mean, she is the boss, so we all respect her, a lot."

"Respect her all you want, dude. I'm the one who's going to marry her. I'm staking my claim right now, so if you fancy her, you can stop doing it right now. She is taken." Duke poked his finger at Robert to emphasize his point. "Got it?"

"I think she will have something to say about that," Robert said. "Now, let's get to work." Although Robert was grateful for the help clearing the field, he fumed inside at Duke saying he was going to marry Felith. The guy had just met her, he couldn't be in love with her, and if he wasn't in love with her why would he be determined to marry her? It just wasn't reasonable. If anyone had the right to marry Felith it was himself. He had known her the longest. Granted he hadn't held her, yet. And there was Julian to think of, she could be pretty cruel when she thought someone was getting between them. Thinking of Julian had him getting hard, so he tried to not think, just to work.

For the rest of the day Duke turned on his charm. When lunchtime came he flattered first

Rosemary, then Julian. He tried his charms on everyone, only keeping his distance from Fred. Felith he doted on, offering to carry anything and everything she picked up. Three times she sent him off to help in the fields. Somehow he always ended up back around her. Finally she set him to doing kitchen work and went to the fields herself.

Rags and Sidney shared a worried look as dinner approached. The girls in the kitchen were giggling like school girls. Middy looked pissed off. Eric was pouting, while at the same time trying to appear as stern as Middy looked. Emily was the only one of the girls in the house who hadn't given in to Duke's charms. He had said something about the baby that had her shooting dagger looks at him whenever he came in sight. Felith, having given out the orders for dinner, had been in the pasture tending to the cow, and the slowly growing population of farm animals. Rags had gone out to check on her once and was not encouraged by the way she looked. A storm was brewing on the farm, the emotional people sort of storm.

They gathered, this little group of stragglers and orphans, for the evening meal. It had been part of the day to day life for them to eat as a family. Fred was the last to arrive. As he walked in Duke was seating Julian, then he went to Rosemary and seated her. The guy was working his way around the table. Middy kicked him when he approached her and Eric already sitting at the table was waiting for Fred. Sidney and Rags placed the last of the bowls of rolls and potatoes on the table and took their seats.

It looked as if Duke had placed a chair next to the head of the table where Felith usually sat. Or had she placed it there for her lover boy, Fred wondered. Fred started to his usual seat, then stopped as Felith pointed at the chair beside her. Duke saw the motion and said aloud for Fred to hear, "I'm coming, sugar bun, don't be so impatient." Soft gasps came from those seated around the table, and the non-expression on Felith's face sent a shiver through Fred. He leaned over and spoke softly to Eric. Like a spider monkey turned loose Eric jumped up and ran throwing himself so hard into the chair by Felith the table shook. The look on Duke's face had Fred laughing in his mind.

Walking to where Eric sat, hands clenching the seat of the chair to either side, Duke laughed. "Oh no, little brat, this is my seat. Go on back to your chair," he said tipping the chair as if to dump Eric out. Eric hung on tight-lipped with all the stubbornness a child can display. After all, Fred had given him an assignment.

Around the table everyone was silent. It was clear they were trying not to stare at Duke or even look at Felith, but they were doing both. Slowly Felith stood. Her cold gaze shifted to Duke as she spoke in the hush around the table. "You will sit next to Fred. My children will sit with me from now on." Beside her Middy smiled, her expression was one of worship. Eric blinked rapidly and looked first over at Fred. When Fred nodded his head, Eric looked up at Felith too, his little face confused, searching her face. He found her words a language he couldn't understand. His hand came up, it shook as he pointed first at Fred, next Middy and then at himself and finally at Felith. Felith nodded her head at Eric placing a hand on his head and one on Middy's head.

Duke in the meantime looked as if he had eaten a lemon of the extreme sour type. Then he smiled, and put a hand on Felith's shoulder as if in comfort, "I just love that you are so good with your kids. I hope they take after their mother, only, Darling, you don't look old enough to have two kids. I'll think of some family things we can all do while we eat." Acting as if it was an everyday occurrence to have a teenage girl claim to have two children she would've had to have given birth to at a very young age, Duke went around and sat down in the chair Eric had occupied before. He missed the way Rags looked over at Felith, the pride that was there for a moment on her face.

Fred too was proud of Felith. She had reacted totally different from Julian and Rosemary towards Duke. He winked at Eric equally proud of him. Being a father to kids like Eric and Middy wouldn't be bad at all, that is if he were to ever have kids of his own. Mentally he shook his head at himself. He'd never have kids. What shocked him the most was having let that weird girl get to him, making him think of having kids, of being married, having a life. Never. You just couldn't trust anyone, not enough to love them.

Throughout the meal Duke tried to make small talk with Felith. She would look at him as if he had lost his mind. By the time the table had been cleared for dessert to be served, it was all he could do to keep pretending he even liked her. She was his meal ticket. Somehow he had to get on her good side and make her want him. He had those two giggle twins eating out of his hand already. That girl with the baby was just old maid material. For the life of him he could no longer see what attraction there was to Felith, other than her being a gold mine. Maybe he could foster her off on Kit. Only, Kit was such a bleeding heart, he would let her give the heals away.

"Why did your Mimi send you here to help, Duke?" Sidney asked.

Duke had to pull his thoughts back from the problem of getting Felith to marry him. "Uh, well she said to go pay back that good woman for saving me. So here I am," Duke told Sidney.

Felith looked up from her plate. This was the first time she had heard that he was here because he had been healed. "Then you may return home now. To help another is not something that requires payment of any sort," she said.

Oh shit, Duke thought, then, his face seemed to lighten up with good cheer. "That is the best news you could given me. Now I'm free to court you all day long. Thank you, Darling."

Beside her, Eric kicked out his feet almost hitting Felith's shins. She looked at him, to see if he was okay. He was so much like Fred, and seemed to be trying to make his face hold the fierce angry expression on Fred's face. Some spot inside her warmed. She cut her slice of cake in half and gave half to Middy, the other half she gave to Eric. He looked at her uncertain at first, then he smiled, and began to devour the cake with all the enthusiasm

Middy had for her cake. That warm spot seemed to grow inside her. For some reason she found herself glancing at Fred. For once his face seemed relaxed as he watched Eric digging into the cake. This, Felith thought, is what I read about families being together. Was it true?

A certain contentment settled on Fred for all of the moment. He had kept Duke from bothering Felith, for now, and the big plus was that Eric was happy. This moment was what people called happy. Then Duke leaned close and whispered, "I didn't know she had kids. She must've slept around from a young age." The rage came back in full force, blackening the air in front of Fred. It was all he could do to ignore Duke. To not take Duke by the throat and choke him to death in front of Felith and everyone. Only... SHE would try to heal the creep and probably die trying it. So he forced food down his throat, and gave Eric an approving nod for taking his plate to the kitchen.

His mood dark, feeling dangerously close to breaking his own determination to never go down that tunnel of mindless rage again, Fred sat out on the porch breathing in the cool air of the night. He could hear Duke just inside the house talking to Felith. "Come on, won't you walk me part of the way home? I promise to be good. Please," Duke was saying. Despite his efforts not to listen, Fred found himself straining to hear what Felith would say. Only she didn't say anything. The door opened and she and Duke came out to walk past where Fred sat and off down the Lane. Duke kept leaning in close and whispering to Felith. It made Fred close his eyes, so as not to see the two of them together. Still he couldn't help opening his eyes and watching for Felith to return.

Glad to be rid of Duke, Felith almost skipped as she walked back to the house. He was a problem she had no idea how to handle. If he had done anything to the girls then she would have made certain he went far way, but the truth was he hadn't done more than make a fool of himself. At least that was what he appeared to be to Felith. As she walked across the yard to the house she noticed Fred was still sitting outside. He had been in a particularly bad mood after dinner. Was he hurt? When she reached the top of the steps Felith paused. She reached out her hand and touched Fred on the leg trying to see if he had hurt himself working today. His eyes widened, she closed her eyes and sought out his pain. Anger swept over her like a raging tornado, stripping away, her defensive armor. For a moment she felt raw inside, and so much pain and confusion. Something else surged up to wipe out the rage, then intensified in another direction, it blazed like a flaming Dragon, hot, searing, an aching desire. She staggered, drawing back into herself. Looking down at Fred she saw contempt grow on his face, for her. For the first time since she was a tiny little girl a tear found its way out of her eye. It trickled down her cheek and fell off her chin as she turned away and went inside the house.

Shock zinged through Fred's body. She had cried. The small wet spot on his pant leg was proof. He wanted not to feel anything, but she had cried. What a deep hell he was in. The question was how could he get free? And did he want to?

Duke arrived at lunch time the next day. He remembered when they had eaten the day before and timed it perfect. Rosemary was helping Emily in the kitchen. Her face lit up when she saw Duke walk in and offer to peel potatoes. He smiled at Rosemary, although he only nodded at Emily. "I have a surprise for Felith, you gals will have to pretend you don't know about it. There is a dance tonight in town. They say there will be games for the kids, and each family is to bring a dish of some sort for the feast just before the dancing. I cut a mean rug, my ladies," Duke said, doing a fast few steps in front of them.

"Why can't we all go?" Rosemary asked. "All we've done is work since getting here. I think we deserve a night out. Only, is it safe?"

"Darling, I go into town all the time. It is how we found out about the healer, my future bride. Hey, maybe I can marry her tonight. Or is there a waiting period?" Duke said, laughing and dancing around Rosemary.

Emily pulling a face at Duke's words turned her back. Rosemary was shaking her head. "You'd be wasted on her, she is as cold as the North Pole. She doesn't even have a pretty dress…," her voice trailed off as she remembered the butterfly blouse Felith had loved so much. "Yeah, okay. Maybe you'd be good for her," Rosemary finally said. Guilt still ate at her over what Julian had done to Felith.

"I know she is going to be good for me. I just have to convince her I'm the one for her," Duke said. Rosemary looked doubtful.

Remembering Eric stealing his seat the day before, Duke was already sitting in the chair next to Felith's spot at the head of the table when people began to enter the dining area. Julian smirked upon seeing Duke, swishing her hips back and forth as she went to her seat. She sniffed at the aroma of the various dishes on the table. Meals were always better when Emily was cooking.

The frown line that seemed to be Robert's permanent companion lately, creased to an all new degree upon seeing Duke, and where he sat. Walking around to where Duke sat, Robert said, "Look you are just going to cause trouble sitting there. Felith already told you the kids are to sit by her."

"Yeah, but she isn't going to care once I tell her my surprise. You'll see, women are nuts about going out for a night," Duke said, a satisfied look on his face, as if he had all the world by the tail, and only he knew it.

It was then that the rest of the group arrived. Sidney seeing Duke took charge, fearing a fight might start otherwise. Teens were so quick to feel anger, and he knew Felith had strong feelings about men in general. "Duke, come sit by me so we can talk," he said, patting a chair next to his usual spot.

Sensing he had miscalculated how things would go, Duke changed tactics. That was his strong point, being able to switch to a different approach in the middle of a situation. He had won his way into every local girls heart with ease, and had no doubt that he'd get Felith too. "Don't worry, Sir. I'm not planning on staying to eat. I just came to invite you all to go with me to town for the dance tonight. The town is celebrating the end of the virus plague with a covered dish meal, games for the kids, dancing and hopefully some fireworks later on. You have to admit we could all use a bit of a break from work. Come on, sir, say you'll all go," Duke said, in his most upbeat manner.

Julian and Rosemary added their voices. "We have worked since getting here, please let us go," Rosemary said. Julian on the other hand declared, "I'm going with him. I have a right to a life." She didn't see Robert's jaw clenched when she said she was going with Duke. Jealousy flared to life inside of him. Julian had always been his, or rather he had always been hers, and here she wanted to go with another guy? He cleared his throat. "I'd like to take Julian to the dance and dinner," he said, giving Julian a smile. "How about it, Jules? Could be a fun date." There, he had sort of staked his claim. Although from the look on Julian's face she would rather go with Duke. He automatically glanced at Felith, and wasn't sure what he saw on her face. But he didn't want to be Duke at that moment.

Rags could see this wasn't going well. The girls wanted a break from working everyday. And Robert certainly seemed to want the same. However, there was a baby, and the house to look after. She looked at Emily. The girl had been taking care of the baby sense Felith found it. She certainly deserved a break. They all needed a little down time. Giving Sidney a glance she nodded at him. "Okay, lets see how we can go about this outing. We go as a family if we go at all, agreed?" he said, looking at each person for that nod of agreement. Emily seemed reluctant, but finally nodded her head. Middy and Eric looked to Felith and Fred, both of whom appeared anything but pleased. For once showing something resembling expression, her mouth a thin grim line, Felith nodded. If anything at that nod, Fred seemed to become even angrier than he usually looked, only to grudgingly nod when Eric came over and hugged tight to his leg as if giving comfort.

"I have a condition," stated Felith, the tone of her voice soft, yet they all knew she was serious. "Nobody is to stray off, and if anyone approaches any of you, you will tell Rags or me. Rags, bring your gun."

Duke, who had grinned like a fool at having won the day, sobered at the mention of the gun. Problems, problems, one solved and two more pop up. How did he get rid of the others and get Felith alone, and avoid the pistol packing momma? Mimi had taught him you never raise your hand too ladies, but how did you control them when they were so damn cold hearted? This whole thing was getting to be too much like work.

Chapter Ten

DON'T DIE ON ME

The rest of the day was spent in preparing to go to the dinner and dance. It was to be a 40 minute drive there and back. A lot of preparation went into taking a baby on an outing. Formula, diapers, multiple changes of clothing, an endless list of what might be needed. Finally Sidney called for the vans to be loaded with the food they were bringing and all the baby's traveling bags. The girls came out, each dressed in pretty dresses. Even Emily wore a nice dress for the occasion. Felith was the last to walk out to the vans. She was in her jeans with a clean T-shirt on. In her arms she cuddled the baby, and at her sides were Middy and Eric. She was like a sore thumb on a hand of beautiful fingers. Julian felt the tickle of guilt. That dang butterfly blouse flashed through her mind. It was the girls own fault, trying to steal Robert like that. She had, hadn't she? That bit of doubt caused the feelings of guilt, and Julian didn't like that feeling at all.

They had to pass a checkpoint before being allowed to enter the town, but this time it was a more relaxed group of men barricading the road. Fear of the illness which had swept over the world was fading as the months passed with no new outbreak. There was a difference in the people. They were thinner, with worry lines permanently etched in their foreheads. Their eyes held a haunted look of sadness, for they had seen the dark underside of themselves and their neighbors. This party was about a new beginning for all of them, hope anew.

People were laughing, actually laughing. It was so strange to see people everywhere talking, smiling, and laughing. Rosemary and Julian seemed to fit right in with the crowd. They went from booth to booth looking at the things people brought to trade, and it was a trade. It seemed nobody had faith in money since the plague. If you could make something, grow something, you brought it into town and traded for whatever someone else made or grew. If the rest of the world was in the same condition then perhaps they too had fallen back on this old-time method of trade. The hope was that somewhere out there in the world other people were getting together, learning to live again instead of just surviving. Still it was hard, hard not to worry, to wonder if the next people that came along wouldn't carry the plague or be out to raid the little town that had managed to produce a sense of well-being. Fortunately for this town they were situated in the middle of farming land. People were used to having to pull together and help each other. They hadn't all been like that, of course, greed still had a grip on some, anger on others. For the moment they had agreed to play fair and try to help each other get on their feet.

To Felith it was all confusing. She could not understand why anyone would want to be in a crowd of people. The constant chatter, people yelling across each other to someone else was disturbing to her. She kept close watch on Eric and Middy. Now and then the baby complained because she was holding on so tight. Despite saying they would all stay together, the others kept straying off, teens seeking teens. Trying to keep watch over them all had Felith stretched thin. She hardly noticed the booths of trade items set up. Nothing that could happen to her could scare Felith, but those under her protection, the ones she had come to care about, the thought of something happening to them scared her so much that her insides trembled. There were monsters in the world, horrible filthy monsters, and the thought of one of them touching Middy or someone else made her feel ill. So Felith watched, as the girls and Robert danced. She watched Fred turn Middy in circles as if dancing. She watched Rags dance with Sidney then Eric.

It was while Eric and Rags were pretending to dance that the blue butterfly appeared. It flitted in front of Felith then over the heads of those on the dance floor. Around and around it went as if searching for a spot to land. It is trying to tell me something, Felith thought. For a moment her attention left the dancers as the blue butterfly fluttered over to the nearby booths. She watched the butterfly settle on a necklace with an amulet shaped like a butterfly. Until that moment Felith had not noticed the jewelry for sale at the booth. The butterfly spread its wings and glitters of blue settled on the amulet. Rising again the lovely blue butterfly drifted back across the crowd of partying people. To Felith's surprise it flew to Fred. Once over Fred the blue butterfly fluttered around his head. Eric came running up to Fred just then and looked up, pointing to the butterfly. "Be still, maybe it will let us watch it for a moment," Fred told Eric, extending his hand. Slowly the butterfly drifted down and came to rest upon Fred's hand. An expression of wonder came over the hard frowning features of Fred's face. He smiled as he slowly lowered his hand for Eric and Middy to see the butterfly. It stayed for a moment longer before flying off into the approaching night.

A gift! And far more, approval. Her mentor approved of Fred. The problem of acquiring the amulet would have to wait until the thought of Fred being approved had stopped shocking her system. He was one of them, one of the monsters, how could he be good?

Tired, sweaty, but happy, the crowd of people made their way to where the covered dishes were set out. By lantern light two lines of people made their way slowly down the laden tables. Middy was filling her plate with some of everything. And there was no way the child would be able to eat it all. Eric, on the other hand copied Fred in his selections, taking reasonable amounts and passing up on many of the dishes. Felith, just ahead of Eric and Fred had no appetite. Her belly felt full of nervous knots. She kept seeing the butterfly on Fred's hand. It was so unreal to what she knew to be of the world. Her mind was a jumble of contradictions, nothing made sense. Deep in thought she passed dish after dish up. When they reached the end of the line all she had on her plate was an ear of corn on the cob. Suddenly Fred's hand took hold of Felith's plate. "Sit and take this. I'll go through the line again for me. Eat," his voice was soft yet commanding. Felith looked at him. Of course, she thought, he was watching over her. Taking the heaped up plate Fred handed her, Felith went to sit with the others while Fred went back to the end of the line. Her insides felt warmth seeping into them. The butterfly was right, approval it was.

Duke had been off setting up a booth to place Felith in. He figured they could charge people a small amount this time, for the healing, then gradually go up on the price. The only thing he had to do was convince Felith to sit at the booth and heal. He'd do the rest, see to the fee and collect it. If he could pull this off he'd have his foot in the door, so to speak. He'd be thought of as the person to come to for getting to the healer girl. Once a connection was made it would stand up for the long haul. He'd take part of the loot they made this time. And once they were married he'd get it all. Fred came up getting in line behind Duke. Duke couldn't help himself, he had to rub Fred's nose in the fact that he, Duke, had gotten his way. "Man, the line is long. I can't wait to go sit with my sweetie. I knew she'd love coming to the dance," he smiled and glanced at Fred to see if he was getting to the guy. "Next time I think we'll come without the whole house coming with us too."

Fred put a spoonful of some casserole on his plate. He was not going to let this idiot get to him. The creep knew nothing about Felith, but Fred knew his kind, the sort who always came up smelling of roses even after doing the most despicable things to others. If possible he wouldn't let this sorry excuse for a human get his hands on Felith. He could still feel that wet spot on his leg where her tear had fallen. Why? Why had she cried? That thought worried him more than anything else she had done. So often he thought she would cry over something and she hadn't. All his preconceived ideas of her had been proved false. She touched him, and cried. It haunted him. In his dreams he saw that tear fall. Awake he agonized over it. All his determination not to feel anything was ripped into 1 million shards of glass by that one tiny tear. Duke was still rattling on about how he was going to marry Felith, but Fred didn't hear a word of his yapping. He reached the end of the line and saw Felith, sitting, picking at her food. She had to eat.

Duke took care to be seated directly across from Felith. She had those darn kids to either side of her. If only he could get rid of them for a little while he'd have her swooning over him. Tonight, however, he just had to get her to use the booth he had set up. "I've been thinking," he said, as he sat down and put his plate on the table. "You don't get to town very often, darling. There are so many people here that need someone like you to touch them and make them well. What if we set up a booth and screen a few for you to heal? It won't take long. I just think we owe it to them, darling, for having this little outing. I'd screen some people, to make sure they really needed to be healed. What you say, sweetheart, help them out?" Beside him Duke could feel Fred, the guy had become very still while Duke laid out his plan for having Felith heal people. You'll see, Duke thought, she is mine now, not yours.

He is trying to use me, Felith thought. Still, even knowing that all Duke wanted was to use her for some reason of his own, the thought of someone needing healing touched her inside. She wanted to be able to heal for just that reason, to help those who were hurting. So often she had been hurting, alone, in the dark, and nobody had ever come to heal her. She looked over at Fred, who was stanch, so still he didn't blinked. In her mind she saw the butterfly giving approval of Fred. No matter what else she might think of him, that approval made her trust him. Ignoring Duke, she kept her eyes on Fred while she spoke. "You are the only one I trust to help me when I heal, Fred. Tell me what you think," she said.

If she had stood up and shot him through the heart Fred could not of been more surprised. His jaw clenched, as he thought things over. The problem was anything serious might kill her, especially since she wasn't eating much of her meal. The look in her eyes spoke of her need to help anyone who needed healed. She'd do it too, even if he disapproved. He was certain him vetoing the idea of healing wouldn't mean she'd forget it, not as long as she felt she might help someone. Fred didn't want this responsibility, at the same time he didn't want anyone else to be the one she turned to for help. "You haven't eaten," he said, looking at her plate, which was barely touched. "If you eat all your food and some desert, only then, should you heal anyone. What we have to determine is should it be several small heals or one very ill person. Eat, and then you and I will talk it over. Okay?" For a moment he thought he had over stepped and she would turn to Duke instead, but with barely a second of hesitation she nodded and began to eat her food.

"But it's my idea!" Duke protested. "Darling, please let me do it."

"No," Felith said, with a flat finality.

"How can you do this to me? I put a lot of effort into setting things up so you could heal people, and you just toss me away once you get it. What sort of woman treats her man like that? You are selfish, just a selfish whore. I don't know why I waste my time on you," Duke raged at Felith.

Felith looked at Duke, her eyes not betraying anything she might be feeling. For just a moment he felt a twinge of fear. But he was in the right, he had done all this for her and she was wrong to toss him over. Then she spoke, "I don't trust you. It is best if you leave." This wimpy scraggly girl dared to threaten him. Down the table Rags shifted slightly, and he remembered she had a gun. Okay, he'd leave, he was done with this bitch. Picking up his plate, he smiled at Julian and motioned with his head for her to follow him. Julian laughed and got up. Duke heard that puny Robert say, "Jules, no." Robert couldn't control his woman, but Duke could.

Eric reached over and patted Robert's arm.

He did not understand what was going on, only that the bad guy had left, and Robert was sad. Robert managed a smile for Eric and reached up, appearing to pull a penny out of Eric's ear. The world became normal for at least a little while for Eric.

The world had turned upside down for Fred. There was nothing he could do to set it right side up. He was caught as surely as he had been caught by another girl. It wasn't the same, but how could he be sure this one wasn't out to make a joke of him, hurt him in the most vile way? True, she had been nothing but fair in her dealings with the others. Yet evil hid in many forms, it lurked inside pretty faces with pouting lips, and in guys you had thought of as friends. Julian and Duke could be planning at this very moment to hurt hi... Felith, they would be after Felith, not him. If he took on this job, committed himself to Felith, he'd be given up any chance at becoming his own person. There would be nothing else more important, he'd either do this or not have anything else to do with her. Inside his mind he shouted at the universe (What am I to do!), but it wasn't what he was supposed to do, it was what he could live with doing. First he had to decide what was best for Felith to do tonight, and after that either run like hell from her or decide he cared enough to stay.

Matters were taken out of Fred's hands as he watched Robert get up and go after Julian. Robert was a fool. Still knowing that Julian had left because she wanted to leave didn't prevent Fred getting up and following Robert.

They found Duke and Julian leaning against

a secluded section of the wall around the area set up with tables for people to eat. Julian's skirt was hiked up and Duke was pounding into her. Robert went wild when he saw them. He ran at Duke and started hitting him for all he was worth. All the time sobbing, "Jules, Jules", over and over. The surprise of the attack allowed Robert to land several blows before Duke slammed him in the face. Robert dropped like a sack of potatoes.

Fred stooped to check Robert's pulse, then looked up at Julian. "You have caused enough trouble tonight. Go get some ice for Robert." He whirled in Dukes direction, and started to stand. "Zip up your damn pants and leave," he said, his voice low and dangerous

"Like hell, you interrupt me and tell me to leave?" Duke kicked Fred in the jaw. When Fred fell back Duke went on kicking him, and stomping him. Duke saw a pipe laying on the ground and picked it up striking Fred over and over on the head and body. The bones in Fred's right arm, which he had thrown up to protect his face, shattered. When Fred no longer moved Duke spat on him. "Now lets see you interrupt me." Turning he took Julian again, even though she tried to leave and reach Robert's still body. When he was done, he let her go. "Go on, run back to the city folks, little whore," he said to Julian, zipping up his pants when he walked away.

Duke walking off was the first thing Fred saw when he woke up. The next was Julian crying and running off. He tried to get up then, pushing up with his arm, but his arm wouldn't work, and pain seared through him from it. Over and over he tried to get up, his face bloody, and pain a constant reminder of what had just happened.

"Hurry up, Robert's hurt!" Julian yelled at Rags and Sidney. Everyone at the table got up. They were, after all, a family. They followed Julian to where Robert, a growing bruise on his jaw, and Fred, beaten almost beyond recognition, lay upon the ground. Fred tried to rise again, his face swelling, one eye swollen shut, and that is when he saw Felith and the others. "No," he tried to say no, but it didn't sound right even to his ears. He pleaded with his eyes, saying what his mouth couldn't get out. "Please no, don't die for me, not for me." All he could do was watch her come to him and sit down on the ground beside him. He saw her mouth move as if she was speaking, hardly louder than the breeze passing his ear he heard her words, "I won't let you die. I won't forgive you if you do, so live." Then she closed her eyes and touched him with those delicate hands. He could feel it this time, feel the strength flowing into his body, the soft touches in all the damaged areas of his body. It felt so good. He wanted that feeling so much that for a moment he reached out for it, drew it to him, and then he looked up and saw life begin to leave Felith's body. "No!" He got the word out and managed somehow to push her away from him with his one good arm. Sidney was tending to Robert, but stopped and rushed over to Fred and Felith. "Kee her varm and fu… fuud. She needs fuud," he managed to get out before he too passed out.

It felt like he was buried in a dark hole. There was noise, people talking. He felt touches, but not hers. Tears leaked out of Fred's closed eyes, he had killed her, else she would be there. It was a certainty he felt to his bones. If at all possible Felith would be there for him. A cry of anguish, eerie, a lost soul weeping in hell, sounded in his ears, and he welcomed the darkness as it took him once again into its depths.

When next Fred woke it was light outside, but he didn't care. Nothing mattered. There was only one goodness in the world and he had killed that warm light. He didn't deserve to live. He felt a light touch on his arm, he didn't want to see anyone, talk to anyone, all he wanted to do was to die. But the hand was small and it could only belong to Eric. For Eric he'd have to live another day. Fred turned his head, so he could see Eric. The little boy looked so frightened. We made him a family and now he is afraid he lost us too, like his real family, Fred thought. "It's okay," Fred managed to croak out, and from the direction of the rooms door he heard Middy yell out, "He's awake."

Eric was replaced by Sidney. The look on Sidney's face was one of relief. "You had us worried. I'm not sure what Felith did to you, but whatever it was it kept you alive. Now you have to finish getting well," Sidney said as he checked Fred over. "I don't think you want to disappoint Eric. This little guy has kept vigil over you all night. Between Eric watching over you and Middy standing guard over Felith, well, it has been a tense night."

Suddenly Fred was trying to get up, falling out of the bed he was on, then attempting to get up off the floor. "Whoa there," Sidney said. "Where do you think you are going?"

"Fel. I have to see her," Fred said. The determination on Fred's face had Sidney helping him to his feet.

Nothing mattered but that he see with his own eyes that Fel was alive. Only she was so still, and pale. Sitting down on the side of the bed, Fred used his left hand to smooth Fel's hair back out of her closed eyes. She didn't wake up to the touch, didn't move, barely breathed. "You stupid, stupid girl. Why couldn't you just let me die? I never wanted to hurt you like this. You don't know how hard it is for me to stay away from you. If you did, you'd run from me. I can't... I just can't fight it any more. You stupid, stupid girl, I think I love you," he whispered to her.

Middy came and laid down beside Fel. The cover was wrinkled on that side of the bed where the little girl had been keeping her vigil watching over Felith. Eric crept into the room looking wide-eyed and scared. Fred was scared too. Fel still might not make it. Nothing about her looked as if she was alive except the slight rise and fall of her chest. If you die I'll kill Duke, Fred silently vowed, then his body started to sort of tilt and kept on tilting until his face planted on the bed beside Fel and darkness claimed his mind once more.

It was the whispering which woke Fred. He was surprised to find himself in bed with Felith.

"He's waking up," a child's voice said in an excited whisper.

Middy, Fred thought just as the unmistakable worried sound of Eric whispered back, "Did I hurt him?"

Poor kid, Fred thought, he lost his parents and now Fel and I being both down at the same time has to impact him hard. "No, you didn't wake me, it is just time I get up," Fred assured the kids. Then he found he couldn't sit up on his own. "Well if you both help me maybe I can get up." It was then he saw the needle taped to Fel's arm and the tube running up to a bag of fluid. I did that to her, he thought. Guilt ate at him like a pack of gnawing wolves, but he had no time for guilt, not now anyway. Not with two kids, and Fel looking like death, to care for. Fortunately Sidney showed up at that moment. "How long since the party?" Fred asked.

"About a day and a half. You had said food for Felith so I rigged up this to give her some substance. She hasn't moved, but I think she is stabilizing. Good call you laying down with her, the body heat was a good idea," Sidney said, as if he didn't know Fred had just passed out, no forethought of keeping Fel warm had entered his mind at the time.

"More like I passed out beside her. It was such a relief to see she was alive. I think I just gave in and slept with relief. Why is she so still?" Fred asked

"I'm not sure. I'm hoping it is just that her body needs all her reserves to heal." Sidney looked uncomfortable for a moment then finally spoke, "We have skated around this healing thing she does. I think for me, it was something my mind didn't want to believe. That said, I've seen her in action too often to deny the fact she does something to people when they are in bad shape. Rags…." His voice caught as if it was hard for him to even think about what would have happened if Fel hadn't healed Rags. Sidney cleared his throat and went on. "Rags was going to die for certain if not for whatever Felith did to her. She pays a price though each time she touches someone. I think this time was the worst."

"No, not the worse. Healing Duke killed her. She died, I just managed to get her back," Fred said, reliving that moment when her heart had stopped. "I didn't get her off me soon enough. If only I had acted quicker," Fred stopped speaking, unable to even voice the horror he had felt when he had seen the life starting to leave Felith's body.

"Son, your arm was badly broken, you were beaten so badly you were dying. What you did, pushing her off like that, that was something near impossible for someone else to have done. And don't forget she wanted to heal you, wanted it so much she was willing to give her life. The miracle is you managed to save you both."

"She will kill herself. I can't watch her close enough to prevent it from happening. What am I going to do to protect her? She is so stubborn," Fred said, his voice sinking into a pensive state. He looked up as Sidney laughed.

"You are going to teach her how to heal without dying. Somehow, someway. You'll find a way, I have faith in you, Fred," Sidney said, his tone one of certainty.

How, and why did she heal people? Those questions were a constant in Fred's mind as the next couple of days passed with no change in Felith. She was losing weight, weight she couldn't afford to lose. Fred sat in a chair beside the bed watching over her. She looks so still almost as if dead. Leaning forward, taking care not to start his leg throbbing again, Fred touched a finger to the palm of Fel's hand. "Take strength from me. You can do it, pull it in instead of pushing it out. Either take from me or wake up. Don't make the kids suffer another day of this quiet shell you are now," he whispered

Slowly her hand closed on his finger until she could feel his hand. "I wake," came the soft words from her. Her eyes opened.

It was another two days before Felith could do more than be propped up enough to eat. Rags carried her to and from the bathroom. The kids brought her so many offerings of food that she felt she would burst open with another bite of anything. Their hopeful eyes had her eating their offerings. On the third day she walked to the bathroom leaning on Middy. From then on there was no keeping her in bed. She insisted on helping out doing anything she could while sitting down. Snapping beans, drying dishes, mending clothing, anything that would help relieve some of the burden from the others. The others were acting strange around her when she was up and about. Julian spent all her time with Robert, and Robert was any place that wasn't around Felith or Fred. Fred was always around, not so near as to be hovering, but close enough he could see Fel. He hobbled about in worse shape than she was in, with his face still showing yellowing bruising, his arm in a cast as was one of his legs. That didn't keep him down, at least not that she saw, for he was doing things too, what he could do with only one hand and one leg that worked. After several tries Rags and Sidney left the pair of them to do as they wanted. Felith heard Rags mutter something about stubborn teenagers. It wasn't that they were stubborn, not completely anyway, but more that two little kids needed to see them up and about as much as possible. For Eric and Middy they hobbled about, hurting as Fred was, and weak to the bone as Fel was.

Then one day Fred came hopping into the room, where she was cleaning, and flopped down next to Fel. He had picked a time when everyone else was occupied in other parts of the house or outside. He drew a deep breath as if fortifying himself for what was ahead. "We need to talk," he said, slowly looking up at Fel. Felith sat rock still, her face became an image of a stone statue. This was her facing difficulty, or just her look, Fred wasn't certain which, but he knew he had to approach this subject with great care. "I need to talk to you about your healing. How did you learn to heal like that?" he asked, hoping to ease into talking about her not killing herself.

Fel blinked, this was not what she had thought at all that he would say. She hadn't been sure of the topic, but, she had been certain he was going to try to make her go lay down. She blinked again, sorting her thoughts and thinking back to when she had first healed that little bird. "I watched Robert heal the ropes and copied what he did. After the bird, it became easier to heal. Ask Robert, he knows how it works, I just copied him. He is the real Magi."

For the longest moment Fred sat in silence. She had to be putting him on. Robert couldn't heal anything. He was a joke. What now? Did he push her, tell her she was telling him a lie. Looking at Fel, he knew, just knew she believed what she was telling him. Okay, first he'd talk to Robert.

Cornering Robert alone was the problem. Julian always seemed attached to Robert, wherever he was and no matter what he was doing. It was obvious she was trying to get back into his good graces. Her betrayal, for Robert saw it as a betrayal, had hurt him deeper than he thought it was possible to be hurt. Still, she was winning him over. He had never been able to stand up to her wily ways. He had sent her off to get him a drink, when Fred came into the room where Robert was working on a small heater, and closed the door. Robert had been dreading this moment, for he knew Fred had to be angry for the beating he had taken, and more than that for the state Felith had been left in.

"We need to talk," Fred said, hopping over and sitting down in a chair.

"It was my fault. I shouldn't have gone after Duke like that. But Julian, I was so taken with her. I couldn't think of anything but stopping her from making a mistake. She did it anyway. I should have known you'd try to help, and Felith. I'm so sorry Fred, so very sorry, can you forgive me?" Robert asked.

Fred looked at Robert, his face an angry storm, then he seemed to collect himself. "I didn't come about that. I want you to tell me how to heal."

"How to heal? I don't know how to heal. Why did you think that?" Robert said, his face a mass of confusion.

"Fel said that you heal the ropes. She said

that's how she learned to heal. So tell me what you did," Fred said.

"I didn't heal the ropes. It's a trick that came with my magic set. Just, just a trick. I make like I cut a rope into two pieces. Then I put two ropes into my hand, wave the wand over my hand, and let the longer piece of rope drop-down. It's only a trick," Robert said.

"And you did this trick where Fel could see you?" Fred said, after sitting for a long moment silence.

Robert blinked a couple of times, "Well I performed my little magic show for the kids. She was always watching. I thought she was judging me, because she is so much better than I am. When she made those butterflies appear in the attic I almost crapped myself. It was the most amazing thing I had ever seen," he said.

"What butterflies?" Fred asked.

"One day I went up to the attic to tell her Olivia needed her. She was sitting between some boxes, and I didn't see her at first. Then there was a stir in the air, and these amazing butterflies were circling around and around in front of her face. But I made a noise, and they disappeared," Robert said, his face reflecting the amazement, he had felt at that moment.

For a long while Fred just sat, not moving a muscle, his face reflecting deep concentration. Slowly he raised his eyes to look at Robert. "What else did you do in your magic act?" he asked, and then held his breath waiting to hear what Robert would say.

"Not much, I had only recently started learning how to do the tricks. I had the flowers up the sleeve trick down. You know where you appear to produce some flowers out of thin air, and had just perfected the rope trick. I was going to start working on making something disappear in one cabinet and appear in another when all the trouble started. So, I never did get that down well enough that I could perform it for the kids," Robert said.

"Give me a hand up," Fred said, he had a lot to think on. Foremost he needed information, more than Robert could give him. Once Fred was on his feet, he went to look for Sidney or Rags. They could tell him more about Felith. Unable to find either Sidney or Rags in the house, Fred went about doing what little housework he could do. It irritated him that Felith wouldn't just rest. That was the whole reason he was pushing himself to do housework. Maybe if she saw him hobbling around working she would see how ridiculous it was for her to continue to work when she needed to rest. But, that hadn't happened, and he didn't think it was going to happen. To Fel it was normal to work even when you were hurting.

It wasn't until dinner was on the table that Fred finally was able to approach Sidney and Rags. "I need to talk to both of you when dinner is over," he said. They both gave him a questioning look, but nodded and took their seats.

When the table had been cleared and the dishes washed Sidney and Rags helped Fred out onto the porch. Then, as they sat down on an old wooden bench, Sidney spoke. "What is up?" he asked.

Fred looked around before speaking, as he didn't want anyone listening to what he had to say. "I need to asked you about Fel, what kind of person is she?"

It was Rags who answered him. "I don't know if I have the right to speak about her. She was one of my cases. And I got Sidney involved," Rags said, speaking in short sentences as if trying to figure out just what to say.

"Why were the police involved?" Fred asked.

Rags looked over at Sidney as if asking him silently if she should continue. Sidney nodded, and Rags took a deep breath before speaking again. "We had a call out about some sort of explosion in a residential home. When we got there, there was no obvious damage. But the door of the house was open, and that was suspicious enough for us to check it out. The insides of the house were a mess, beer bottles laying everywhere as if there had been a drunken party going on. And there was Felith battered and bruised, and obviously she had been molested. The worst thing was, nobody even knew she had been living there. The guy that lived there had kept her locked in the basement, bringing her out only when they were going to…," Rags broke off her voice catching as she recalled the state that Felith had been in.

The anger threatened Fred, sweeping over him with such force at what had been done to Felith. Somehow he managed to tap it down, keep it under control, so he could think. Finally, when he had himself under control and felt like he could talk again, he said, "So she grew up with no social experience?"

"Yes, son, pretty much. She is self-taught everything she knows. Did you know she taught herself to read? I don't know how she came out so calm and reasonable as she is," Sidney said.

Fred sat biting his lip for a long moment. What he was thinking seemed so unreasonable like something out of the story you saw on TV. Finally, he looked up at Sidney and Rags. "So is it reasonable to think she may not have any formed idea of what is real and what isn't in the real world?"

Sidney thought for a moment, "I suppose that if all she knew was from fiction. She might not realize what fiction is, and what the real world is about. What are you getting at, son?" he said.

"Well it has to do with her healing. Suppose she didn't know that people aren't supposed to be able to heal other people with their minds. Do you think she could have developed this talent because her mind was open to the possibility?" Fred asked. "I mean Felith isn't like the other girls. Oh heck, I don't know what I mean. But I'm going to find out, and I'm going to help her stop dying when she heals someone."

Rags stood up and hugged Fred. "If anyone can find a way to help Felith it is you," she said. Sidney stood up too and placed a hand on Fred's shoulder giving it a slight squeeze. And so it was settled, Fred would train Felith not to kill herself.

Now, Fred had to convince Felith to let him train her. The only problem was, he didn't have the slightest idea on how he was going to train her. He

needed some way for her to heal someone and yet
be able to pull her away if she went too far. But you
can't just tell someone get sick so she can heal you.
The whole thing seemed more bizarre as he thought
about it. The only person he could trust was himself.
And he didn't know if he had the strength to push
her away when he felt that wonderful warmth of her
healing. But he would have to. It's all there was to it.
He had to do it.

His mind made up. Fred went in to find
Felith, his stomach a mass of nerves, for this scared
the hell out of him, facing her. He looked into her
bedroom and there she was, folding laundry sitting
on the bed. He smiled to himself, wondering if
she would ever stop working. Hopping into the
bedroom, he sat down beside her. "I have something
serious to talk to you about," he told her.

Felith looked at Fred, and wondered what it
was he wanted to talk about. She knew she disgusted
him, so it wouldn't be anything personal. Not that
she would ever accept anything personal. Perhaps it
was about the kids, and if it was about the kids, she
wanted to hear it. "Okay, I'm listening," she said.

It was disconcerting how seriously she sat
there looking at him. There was trust in her eyes,
something he had never expected to see. I can't
let her down, he thought to himself, and hated
thinking it. Still he was the one that had made the
commitment. She had not forced anything on to
him. "I think that you need to be trained. Up till
now you have used your healing force full out. You
need to learn how to heal only as much as needed so
that you will have some reserves in case somebody

else needs healing," he paused for a moment thinking. "Suppose, both Middy and Eric were hurt, and both were very seriously injured. If you healed one of them, like you are healing people now, you would pass out and the other one would be in big trouble. You don't want that, do you?"

Felith stood, she was ready to run out of the room to check on Middy and Eric. Fred reached out his hand, and stopped her. "Sit back down. They haven't been hurt. This was an example of what could happen. What you need to do is learn how to heal the worst part and go on to the next person to heal them. Do you understand what I'm saying?"

Still shaken from the thought of Middy and Eric both being hurt Felith nodded. She understood she needed to learn how to keep from passing out, how to moderate how much healing she gave someone. Fred was right. Right now she was only good for one person, not for many if there were more than one injured.

"Okay, you and I are the only ones that are hurt at the moment. So we are going to use me for you to practice on. What I want is for us to start training after breakfast tomorrow. I've already talked to Sidney and Rags. They agree we need to get you trained. So each day after meals we are going to practice having you heal just a little bit. Just a little bit at a time until you can control how much healing you do. If I feel you starting to heal too much, I'm going to push you away. It is the only way that this is going to work. Either you pull back, or I push you away. Got it?" Fred asked, watching Felith's face the entire time. He wanted to see some emotion. Some indication that she understood, and either hated the idea or thought it was good. Only this was Felith and she didn't show emotion.

The worry had been planted in her mind that something could happen to both the kids. And she needed to be able to heal both of them. Fred was right, and she was going to work her hardest to do what he asked. "Promise you will push me away," she said.

Fred reached out and took her hand in his. "I promise," he whispered softly, then his own emotions started running wild, his heart rate went up, and he pulled his hand away. He had to watch out for the trap, the trap of caring too much.

Chapter Eleven

CHANGING TIMES

The next morning began as usual, with Felith giving the morning orders, and each of them going about their chores until breakfast was served. After breakfast, and because Fred knew that Felith wouldn't be happy until they helped with the wash up of the breakfast dishes, Felith and Fred did the wash up. It was when Felith and Fred went off into her room and closed the door that everyone exchanged glances. This was something new, and they had learned not to trust new. Middy and Eric, however, seemed to understand what was going on in the bedroom, and parked as if guarding the door.

Fred and Felith sat down on the edge of the bed facing each other. Fred was a study of nervousness. For him, the idea of training Felith was both a relief, and a worry. Felith was all seriousness. This was for her kids. She needed to be ready to help them both. If anything ever happened to them together she had to be able to heal them both. The two adult teens faced each other and Fred was the one who spoke.

Fred held up his right hand and pointed at his little finger. The finger had been crushed. The fragile finger bones were broken. "What I want you to do is to try to heal just this finger. If you feel yourself seeking out other parts to heal, stop. And if I feel you going to other parts, I'm going to push you away. I'll try not to hurt you," he said. Then, he held out his hand. He could feel the hand shaking, but there was nothing he could do about that, so he tried to hold it steadfast and held his breath waiting for Felith's touch.

Just the finger, Felith kept saying to herself, as she steeled herself to touch Fred. She blanked out the rest of the world and looked at that one finger, that poor swollen finger, gradually reaching out to touch it. She could feel the bones inside the finger broken apart and began to weave the healing around them. Then just beyond the finger, there was the hand. There was bruising in the hand, pain. Her mind sought out the pain, the bruising, and began to heal them. Connected to the hand there was the arm, the bone shattered her mind sought out the bones.... Wham! She opened her eyes to find herself on the floor. She looked up at Fred. His face was so filled with rage.

When Felith touched his finger Fred had felt the most wonderful warmth. He could feel the healing weaving over and around the bones of his finger, the tissue healing. And it felt so good, that warmth. Then that warmth went up into his hand, circling around the bruising and the pain that robbed him of peace, and he gave into that warmth. But when it spread up his arm, he realized that Felith had lost control. He hadn't meant to hit her so hard, or to knock her to the floor. It was the fear, the fear that she would kill herself again. That fear hit him so hard sending adrenaline flowing through him so fast that he pushed her harder than he had intended. He was instantly angry at her, and at himself. "You lost control. You let yourself sink into total healing. You can't do that," Fred said, reaching down his good hand to help Felith up off the floor. "Did I hurt you?" he asked softly. She shook her head, he wasn't convinced she was being truthful. "This is a learning thing for both of us. I have to try not to react so strongly when I feel you healing too much. And you have to try to control your healing to just the area we have selected. Agreed?" he said, and waited until she nodded before breathing again.

"Try again. I'm going to try saying stop if I feel you going too far. Ready?" Fred asked. Felith nodded and sat down again on the bed. "This time try healing just this cut over my eye. Don't go beyond it, okay?" Felith nodded, her face so serious that Fred wished he could do something to lighten the mood. But this was to save her life and mood lightening wasn't something he did.

Her hand trembled as she reached up to touch the cut over his eye. It had been one of the spots where Duke had hit him so hard with the pipe that it had split the skin. That memory of Fred laying on the ground trying to get up over and over flashed in her mind. There had been a bleed in his brain when she had touched him that night, and a major bleed started in his broken leg. It had taken all of her power to reach those spots and heal them as she went to stop the bleeds, stop him from dying. She closed her eyes while remembering that night.

"Open your damn eyes!" Fred commanded in a rough voice, then softer he said, "Watch what you are healing, it may help you control things."

Felith's hand jerked back, her eyes open. The girl's whole face seemed to turn to marble, unmoving, not giving away even one thought she might be having. Okay, Fred thought, be like that, be stone, so long as you stay in control. Then he felt her touch him and control seemed such a silly thing.

Looking only at the cut over Fred's eye, Felith touched it. She didn't let the healing flow from her for a brief moment, only felt the cut with her mind, as she examined it with her eyes. Holding the image of the cut in her mind she sent out the feelers of her being and touched it with healing, letting it flow out and start the tissue to healing. Beyond the cut there was damage still, worse damage than the cut, the healing part of her wanted to seek it out, heal it, and do whatever was needed, but this time she took control pulling back to herself. She looked at Fred's full face then. He had such a strange look in his eyes. "I did it," she said.

Her words brought Fred back from the brink of losing control. He sat up straighter, the dark scowl safely back in place on his face. "That is enough for today," he said, his voice gruff sounding. He pushed himself up onto his good leg and hopped to the door. Opening it, he was out before he could do something stupid, real stupid.

The next morning Felith woke with a sense of anticipation. Seldom had she felt any excitement at starting a day as she did this day. She was learning to control her power, and she was all about control. She went out into the living room and gave the days orders, taking care to be certain almost everyone would be out of the house after breakfast. She had again put herself and Fred at doing breakfast cleanup. Butterflies seemed to flutter in her stomach, and it was hard for her to settle down and eat her food. Dutifully, she forked fluffy eggs and slices of bacon into her mouth. She knew Fred would not let her heal unless she ate all her food. Finally, breakfast was over.

Eric and Middy seemed to pick up on some of the excitement that Felith was feeling. They hopped about like little bunnies collecting plates and carrying them, in the clumsy way that children do, to the kitchen. Fred hopped in and sat on the stool in front of the sink. It was better if he washed the dishes, and Felith and the kids put them away. That way he wouldn't have to move about and take a chance of causing his leg injury.

Fred washed the dishes with vigor, trying not to think of why he was eager to start the training session. He ruffled Eric's hair when they were finished with the cleanup. The little boy seemed to beam with joy. But Fred had eyes only for Felith. He watched how she made Middy want to stand up taller. And, inside, he smiled.

Curious eyes were on Fred and Felith as they

went to her bedroom again. Julian giggled and whispered something to Rosemary. Robert was looking daggers at Fred. Sidney and Rags, however, both nodded and motioned the rest of the group to go outside and attend to chores. "Well we will know who the daddy is when she comes up pregnant," Julian said as she walked out the door.

Healing was the farthest thing from Fred's mind, all he really was thinking of was getting Felith alone. Some switch had flipped over inside of him, and he was as eager as a little boy with his first crush. Once they were in the room and the door was closed, he had Felith sit down on the bed. "Lay down," he told her. She gave him a wary look, but laid down upon the bed. "Now close your eyes, and relax," Fred said, and smiled when she did just that. He leaned over her and brushed a strand of hair from in front of her eyes. His body seemed to go into overdrive when he touched her.

Then her face changed. Right before his eyes the change took place. Everything that he thought of as being Felith disappeared. It was as if she was now a vacant shell, with nothing inside of her. "Felith?" he said softly. "Felith open your eyes." Nothing happened, that blank expression stayed on her face. "Felith," Fred said louder. "Felith open your eyes." Nothing, nothing happened. Panic started creeping into Fred, what the hell was going on? What had happened? He had been about to kiss her, and was being as gentle as he could be. But she wasn't there, she had gone away somewhere in her mind. "Felith, come on, honey. Come on. Wake up. You're scaring me," he whispered. When she still didn't react, the panic inside of him peaked to terror. Fred pushed himself up off the bed and began to hop as fast as he could for the door. He opened the door and started calling out, "Sidney, Sidney." All the while he was hopping as fast as he could on his one good leg looking for Sidney.

Fortunately, Sidney was out on the porch talking to Rags. They were both reluctant to leave the two teens in a bedroom for very long. Upon hearing Fred calling out they both rushed to him. "What's wrong, Fred?" Sidney asked. From the state Fred was in he knew it had to be something bad.

"I don't know. I told her to close her eyes, she did, and she will not wake up," Fred said, as he turned and started hopping back to the bedroom. Hopping into the bedroom, the first thing he did was look at where Felith lay still upon the bed. She was just the same, a blank shell of herself laying there limp. "Felith, this isn't funny. Come on now wake up," he said. Looking over at Sidney, he just shook his head.

Sidney was all business. He went to where Felith was laying on the bed, and checked her pulse. Next he looked into her eyes, lifting each eyelid and peering into each eye. Finally, he looked up at Fred and motioned for Fred and Rags to follow him out into the living room. He closed the bedroom door behind him. "Tell me exactly what happened," he said

Fred ran a hand through his blond hair, his eyes looking far away, as he relived the moment they had come into the bedroom. "We came into the bedroom, and I told her to lay down on the bed.

Then I told her to close her eyes and relax. That's about all."

"Are you sure? Did you touch her in any way?" Sidney asked.

"I brushed a strand of hair off her forehead. I didn't touch her any other place. Just that strand of hair off her forehead," Fred said.

"Fred, do you remember how Rags said Felith was found?" he waited for Fred to nod before continuing. "All her life she had been molested and brutalized by men. When you told her to lay down on that bed think what must've passed through her mind. Every time she was in that position someone would molest her. How do you think she lived through that?" Sidney asked.

Fred's face had gone pale as Sidney was talking to him. The thought that Felith had thought he was going to molest her made him sick to his stomach. "She went away inside her mind, right?" Fred asked.

Sidney nodded. "It was the only way she could survive all those years of the brutality and sickness of the person who was keeping her isolated in a dark basement," Sidney said. "What you need to do is talk to her, the way you did yesterday. Keep talking her through the exercise so she clicks back into a safe zone in her mind. Don't, whatever you do, touch her. Rags and I will go back out on the porch, I think we can hear you from there if you call out." Sidney hesitated a moment, as if he had more to say, then he turned, and taking Rags by the hand, walked out on the porch.

Fred took a deep breath, before opening the door and hopping back into the bedroom. He left the bedroom door open to be sure Sidney and Rags could hear him if he called for help. Then he pulled the bedroom chair over close to the bed and sat in it. He felt he shouldn't even be on the bed, as that might seem as a threat to Felith. Gathering his thoughts, he started to speak. "Now that you are relaxed, I want you to think back over how you managed to stop yourself from healing yesterday. Hold that image in your mind. Think over the mechanism you used to make yourself stop. I want you to have that image firmly in your mind, and only then, open your eyes and sit up. Then we will try working on my leg." Fred stopped talking, and watch Felith's still form for some sign of life. Her eyelids fluttered and she opened them. Then she sat up, and it was all he could do not to grab her and hug the life out of her. But he had to stay in control now, he couldn't give in to his lust. For that was all it could be, just lust, not love.

He nodded at Felith, as if nothing had happened. "Now when you start touching my leg, I want you to concentrate on one spot. Heal just that spot and stop. Remember, if you don't stop and I feel you healing more than that one spot, I'm going to say, "Stop." If you don't stop. I will push you away. Understand?" he said.

Felith nodded. She sat, for a long moment, just thinking about what to heal in his leg. The bone she hadn't been able to make knit when she first healed him came to mind. Slowly, she reached out her hand and placed one finger against his leg. She sought that bone out, the two ends, matching them up in her mind and started weaving the healing.

When she felt the bone started to knit together her mind wanted to reach out and heal the next area, the bruised and damaged muscle and tissue. Then she remembered she wasn't supposed to heal more than that one spot, and reluctantly drew back. She looked up at Fred and caught that strange look on his face again. "I did it," she said softly.

Fred nodded. "Okay, I think you have that down pretty well now. Any time you start to heal someone, heal only a part at a time. If you heal them a little bit at a time, I think you'll be able to stop before you pass out. Will you do that for me?"

She nodded her head, but seemed troubled. Finally she spoke, "Let me heal your leg. It won't take much. And I will stop before I pass out."

"Okay," he said, he wanted her to be touching him, but not to heal, yet he wouldn't risk sending her off to wherever she went when he had moved the hair off of her face. Bracing himself, he waited for her touch, eager to feel her fingers on his skin, but dreading it just the same. This was what you call hell. Wanting somebody that you couldn't have. He laughed inside at himself. It hadn't been that long ago when he had thought she was the one after him. Now he was the one wanting her. Then, she was touching him, sending that warmth through his muscles, making him long for more.

True to her word, Felith stopped once the tissue and muscle were healed in Fred's leg. She heard the breath swish out of his lungs when she stopped touching him. "Thank you," he said. "Sidney," he called out.

Sidney was there almost immediately,

surprising Felith. He smiled at Felith and looked over at Fred. "What do you need, son?" he asked.

"I think we can remove this bothersome cast from my leg," Fred said, relief in his eyes.

"But…," Sidney started to say, but stopped. He looked over at Felith and smiled. "You healed his entire leg?" she nodded. "Well, let's get this bothersome thing off of your leg, Fred."

Over the next few weeks Felith managed to heal Fred's arm. The various bruises had disappeared and he looked as whole is he ever had looked. There wasn't even a scar from the cut that Felith had healed. Felith had noticed a change, however, in Fred. She wasn't sure exactly what was going on, but he was sort of attentive. He would bring her a drink of cold water when she was out working in the fields, or point out how one of her flowers was blooming in the little flower bed she had placed in the front. The flowers themselves were slowly dying as the seasons changed and cooler weather approached. Julian often laughed at Fred when he sought out some little thing to please Felith, and that puzzled Felith all the more. None of it made any sense. Perhaps he was making fun of her, but then she would remember the butterfly giving approval of Fred.

The work in the fields had all but stopped as Fall began to end. They had planted only two fields of things that were suppose to grow during colder weather. The work load had eased enough that each of the teens had time to themselves. Felith took her time to relax and conjure butterflies.

Fred had noticed those times when she was

absent. He took to trying to follow her at a distance to see where she was going. He was careful not to let Felith see him following, being always wary of making her go off to that distant place in her mind. Today was the first time he had succeeded in following Fel to an old tree trunk where she stopped to sit in the woods and produce her rainbow of butterflies. He stopped when he saw her sit down on the old tree trunk. Feeling foolish Fred watched as Felith became a study of beauty. Her face took on a serenity he had never seen before as she closed her eyes and lifted her face up. There was a blurring of the air over her up lifted face. Butterflies of every color danced over Felith, dipping down to touch her face, flying high to twine around in spirals of colored rainbows. It was beautiful.

A loud rumbling from the highway caused Felith's butterflies to disappear. Looking toward the road that led to the highway, Felith could see a cloud of dust rising up as two trucks came up the road toward the farmhouse. They were military trucks. As to what their intentions were, Felith was not sure. Her first thought was to protect the others. Rising she headed toward the farmhouse, just missing seeing Fred head off through the trees to get there on his own.

Rosemary and Julian were the two that were closest to the front of the house. They stood from where they were sitting sunning, and waved at the men in the trucks. Felith arrived at the same time the trucks arrived. She looked with wary eyes at the men climbing out of the trucks. There were two men in each of the trucks dressed in camouflage, carrying guns.

The front door of the farmhouse opened, and Rags and Sidney came out. The pair had volunteered to do the cooking today to give Emily a break. Rags, as usual, had her gun strapped on. Ever since Duke had proved a menace, and Fred and Felith had almost died, Rags had been armed. She did that little motion she always did when she felt that they were being threatened, waving her hands in a shooing motion to the girls to get into the house. Rosemary was shamelessly flirting with one of the men from the truck. And Julian, it seemed, was well on her way to seducing another of the men.

"Officer Raglan?" one of the men said stepping forward, a look of surprise upon his face. "I can't believe my eyes. Last time I saw you you were being taken to the... warehouse. How did you survive?" the man asked.

Rags glanced over to where Felith was standing before answering. "I must not have had the virus. Sidney came and got me out of the warehouse, which was really a madhouse. And I recovered a couple of days later.

"It is good to see you up and kicking, Jesse. But tell me what's been going on. Have they reestablished order in the city? And what are you doing in the Guards?" she said.

The man looked around at the teens standing here and there before answering. "Well the police force was pretty much wiped out, as you know. There was this one guy from the National Guard, he isn't much to look at, but man he knows his business. So he goes around recruiting anyone that was standing and not sick. And then he starts organizing us to put out the fires, get help for everyone. And next thing we know, here comes a group of fellows from the other town. We managed to get them to join forces with us, and before you knew it, it looked like we were a real National Guard group. So Lieut. Randolph decided we better go around and start seeing how many people have survived and what supplies everyone had," he said. Then he looked around and saw Fred with his arm in a sling. "Some fellas in town said that one of your guys had been beaten up pretty badly and they thought the girl had too. So we came out here to see if we could help," he said

Fred stepped up, and took the measure of the man who had been talking. "I was the one beat on, but as you can see, I've pretty much healed up," Fred said. "You might want to keep an eye out for the guy that did this. His name is Duke and he lives up the road a bit sort of back in the woods. He seems to be a troublemaker of some sort."

"Will do," Jesse said. "In the meantime I see you have a little bit of a farm here. What we'd like is for you to plant a little bit extra so that we can distribute it to the folks that are needy."

Sidney stepped up beside Rags. "We are doing that on a small scale here. This was our first time to try our hand at farming. So our crops are not quite as great as they should be. Anything we have extra we have been taking into town to help out," Sidney said.

"Great, that is just what we need. What I'm going to ask you to do is to call me, or our supply officer, and give us a list of what you have available. It will help a lot with the distribution of supplies to have a central organization of everything on hand," Jesse said.

Felith had been quiet up to then. She stepped forward and before anyone could stop her started speaking. "I'd like to know who determines who gets the food," she said.

"Well you see, the idea is to have a list of everyone who is in need. From that list we will have an idea of how many are in each household, what sort of needs they have, and if any are specialized needs, like a person being diabetic. Then the quartermaster will know about how much to send to each location. We want to be sure that everyone gets a fair shake," Jesse said, giving the standard answer that had been prepared by Lieut. Randolph.

"So you don't know," Felith said.

Jesse blushed, "All I know is that we are trying. That's better than anyone else is."

Sidney put a hand on Felith's arm, and looked at her with appeal in his eyes. She didn't like it, still she stepped back as Jesse continued to speak. "We'd like to look around and see what resources you have on hand. I don't want to take anything. We just need to know where to reach out for the resources needed to take care of the people," he said.

"I'll show you around" Rags said, taking Jesse by the arm and leading him off.

Felith did not like these grown-up monsters exploring the farm. She kept an eye on all the girls and especially on the two kids, which she kept next to her as much as possible. Only when the men had gotten back into their trucks and left did Felith breathe a sigh of relief. She would have to be on guard now, the monsters knew where she lived.

In the meantime, Fred was having a fit over what he had seen Felith do in the woods. She had created butterflies out of thin air. Dog came up and nudged Fred's hand to be petted. A memory flashed through his mind of Felith saying she remembered Rags saying to get a dog. Before that, the huge brute hadn't been around. Was Dog created? He felt real, and certainly drooled real. No, Dog had to be real. To think otherwise was just too mind-boggling. Fred scratched Dog's head, "You are a good dog. And you're real," he said. Yet in the back of his mind was that little nagging voice of doubt.

Julian took everyone's minds off the men who had come in the trucks. They had all sat down to lunch when Julian suddenly jumped up and ran for the bathroom. Everyone could hear her in the bathroom evidently throwing up. Worry hit them all, as memories of everybody who had been ill with the virus came into their minds. Robert got up and went to the bathroom, knocking gently on the door. "Jules? Jules are you all right?" he could hear the water running in the sink and then the door open, and Julian came out.

"Of course I'm not all right, you fool," Julian said. "My stomach's upset. But I feel better now."

Later that evening Julian threw up again. Robert sought Felith out, finding her sitting out on the porch watching the road. "We haven't talked, not for a while now. I'm worried, Julian's been sick to her stomach twice now, and that virus stuff is scary. Would you touch her," he said softly, almost apologetic.

Felith turned her head and looked at him, as if trying to figure out what it was exactly he wanted. Then she spoke, "If that is what she wants."

"I want it, won't you do it for me," Robert asked.

"Julian has to want it too," Felith said, and went back to watching the road.

Robert's face burned with embarrassment, for he knew how much Julian disliked Felith, and convincing her to let Felith touch her was going to be hard. He would just have to wait and see if this was only a temporary stomach virus.

The next morning, Julian was in the bathroom again throwing up. Off and on through the day she would run to the bathroom and throw up. Finally Sidney took her aside. "We need to have you checked out. I'm going to have Felith come in here and touch you. I know you don't like her, but that is beside the point. The point being, you are sick and it might be possible that you will infect the others. Now, whatever complaint you have against Felith, you are just going to have to forget about and let her touch you, understand?" Sidney said.

Julian stood up as if about to argue with him, then made a mad dash to the bathroom where sounds of retching could be heard through the closed door. Finally, her face pale, Julian came out of the bathroom and nodded. Her face was set as if she was so angry she couldn't even talk. Perhaps she was. Still Sidney had the whole group of them to worry about, not just her. Her petty argument with Felith would just have to be shelved for now. "Stay here and I'll get Felith. You don't need to talk to her, you don't need to do anything, just sit here and let her touch you. Understand?" Sidney said, and waited until Julian nodded before leaving.

Sidney found Felith out on a small side garden where they were trying to grow some cabbage. He hesitated before approaching her, for this quarrel between the two girls was something he felt was entirely on Julian's side and not Felith's doing at all. There is nothing to it, but to ask her to heal Julian. Walking up to Felith, Sidney smiled. "I don't know what it is, but any of the plants that you tend to seem to do better than if anyone else tends to them," he said, waiting to see how she would react. He didn't have long to wait, for immediately that look of suspicion passed over her face. He couldn't blame her for not trusting any man, but somehow he was hoping by now she would trust him a little bit. "I want you to check Julian out. She has agreed to let you touch her. Will you do it?" he asked.

The last thing that Felith had expected was Sidney asking her to heal Julian. She would never refuse to heal someone no matter who that person was, or what they had done to her. So she nodded. Dusting her hands off, Felith stood and walked with Sidney back to the house. Julian was where Sidney had left her, her face pale with a look of scorn upon it. Felith didn't say anything. She walked up, extended one finger, and touched Julian's hand. Her eyes closed and she stood for merely a moment before removing her finger from Julian. Turning she spoke to Sidney "She is with child," she said, and walked away.

It explained the vomiting, Sidney thought. But, who was the father? From the look on Julian's face being pregnant was the last thing she wanted to be. She shot a dirty look at Felith's back as the girl walked away. "I can't be," she said. It didn't occur to her until later that she no longer felt nauseated. She didn't credit Felith with that miracle though, she had nothing in her heart but anger where that one was concerned.

Sidney and Rags gathered the teens into the living room, and set Middy and Eric to watch the baby. It was time for a serious talk, actually it was past time as Julian was now pregnant, and there was no telling what the other girls had been up to. "Sit down," Sidney said, pointing to the sofa. Julian looked like a thunderstorm about to exude lightning, but she sat on the sofa, folded her hands on her lap as if she was a meek little kid. The others looked confused, except for Felith. Felith was the same as she always was, cool and calm in appearance.

Sidney took a deep breath, and looked over at Rags. "This is a talk about something serious that has been going on. We all have seen firsthand what Duke is capable of doing. We have to be certain that someone like that doesn't insert themselves in our lives again. You girl's must guard against the flattery that this type of person deals out. In the studies that have been done on this type of personality, the subject usually has a winning personality. I'm not telling you to turn away from anyone who seems to be interested in you, but use common sense and take it slow. Let us all get to know what sort of person we are dealing with, agreed?" Sidney said.

Julian seemed to relax some after hearing what Sidney had to say. She nodded along with the others. But Sidney wasn't done.

Taking a breath Sidney started talking again. "Now we get down to what all parents dread, the sex talk," Sidney said with a bit of a laugh. "First I want you all to know that I'm not judging you, nor am I telling you how to live your life. You are all almost what is considered an adult. Being an adult means taking responsibility for yourself and consideration for others. Safe sex is accepting that responsibility when it comes to someone you love. You are all at the age when passions flare, and all you can think of is easing that flame that burns inside you. But there are consequences, one of them is producing a child. So I'm telling all of you, think about that before you experiment with the gratification of sex.

"Precaution is not one hundred percent a guarantee that a baby won't be produced from having sex. As Julian has discovered. Julian has some serious decisions to make now. I want to impress on everyone that these are her decisions, not yours, and not mine. Her and the father of her baby need to decide how the child will be raised," Sidney said

Robert stood up almost immediately, he looked first to Julian, then at Sidney, avoiding looking at Felith. "Julian and I will get married. The baby will be ours. This way, they can't say that you haven't been taking care of us. Julian and I have always been going to get married, now would be a good time," he said, then looked over at Julian. "That is, if you'll have me, Jules?" he said with a smile.

It almost looked as if Julian had teared up during Robert's talk. She didn't smile back at Robert, but her answer was positive. "Course I'll marry you," she said. Robert went over and kissed her, took her hand and sat down beside her on the sofa.

Sidney, however, wasn't done with his serious talk. "Today we saw the first sign that the world is beginning to recover. In that world there will be rules and laws that we all must follow. One of the things we must think of is how to safeguard our little family from being ripped apart by bureaucrats. It is possible, and this is only a guess, that once they find out we are from Haven, they will split us up and send you all to different orphanages. Rags and I may be pressured into service. I don't want that, Rags doesn't want that. The question is how do we prevent this from happening? The worst-case scenario is that they send each of you to a different orphanage, and that Middy and Eric are adopted out. This is of course, if they decide to go by the laws that used to be."

Felith stood up, her eyes had turned so determined that they knew anything she said she meant totally. "Nobody is taking Middy and Eric. I won't let that happen."

Sidney looked at her with sympathy. "If Rags and I had been able to get married, and put in for adopting all of you, we wouldn't have this worry," he said.

Fred stood up, his face a mask of anger. "What if, Felith and I get married and take Middy, Eric and the baby as our kids? Wouldn't that solve the problems? You and Rags could take in Emily and Felith and Robert. By marriage, the rest of us would all be related to them."

Sidney looked over at Felith. "Would you do that? Would you marry Fred?" he expected her to give an emphatic no.

For the longest moment Felith didn't say anything. "Marriage is a piece of paper correct? And adoptions are pieces of paper correct?" she asked.

"Yes, but it will bind the two of you legally together. It means you live in the same house and are considered a couple. It means the kids will be considered Fred's and yours. It is not something to take on lightly. You will be responsible for seeing to all the children's needs, sending them to school, clothing and feeding them, and all their medical bills. Before they will let you adopt, you must have an established marriage and established home. You must also prove that you are financially able to take care of the children. That is, according to the old laws. I'm not sure if we establish that now if it will carry over to whatever the new laws are," Sidney said.

"I will not let anyone harm the children. Fred has been chosen, and he too will protect the children. If that means we must have a piece of paper saying we are married, then we will do it," Felith said. And the fact that she had said it warmed Fred more than anything else.

"Okay, I can see that both of you couples have some serious talking to do. Why don't we break for now so that you can all discuss everything and get back to it later on this week," Sidney said. He didn't want them to make a rash decision. If they thought it over and then decided whatever action they wanted to take, he would back them, as Julian being pregnant was bringing everything to a head. They had to take action now, before the world did it for them.

Fred was so angry with himself, he had to stand up and practically rope Felith into accepting him as a paper husband. He watched Emily get up and go to relieve Eric and Middy of baby-sitting, and knew the kids would be here shortly. What he needed to do was talk to Felith alone, not with those two pair of eyes watching their every move and listening to what they were talking about. Robert and Julian were snuggling in the corner of the couch. This was certainly not the place to talk with Felith. He walked up to Fel and said, "We should discuss things and make decisions. Walk with me." There was such a wary look on her face that for a moment he thought she gave him one of her emphatic no answers. It was a relief when Felith nodded. As much as he wanted to take her hand and lead her down the path to the nearby woods, he couldn't. For even worse were the flashbacks to another girl, and how he had taken that girl's hand for a walk into the park. He had to get over that betrayal before taking Felith by the hand. And he had to remember that touching her could send her off into that coma like state she had been in over just a brush back of her hair from her face. So he walked in the direction of the woodland path, mad at himself, mad at Felith, mad at the world and wanting, always wanting.

When they reached a fallen tree Fred sat down

on the trunk of the tree. "I was sort of winging it in there, you know. I didn't mean to broadside you with that whole marriage bit, but it does make sense as a way to protect the kids. And… we sort of told them we are a family. I don't think we can let them down now. What do you think?" he asked.

"This is binding? Like we have to live together?" she countered.

"I think it will be. We'd have to establish that we are a family. It will mean sleeping in the same bedroom, but don't worry, I can sleep on the floor, or anywhere you want. The kids are the important ones. Eric needs a stable life, and Middy… who can resist her impish ways. She is so much like you," Fred said, growing more use to the idea of raising the little ones with Felith. This might be the answer for the two of them, broken yet able to function as a family.

He looked at Felith waiting for her to say something. Her eyes had a far-away look to them as if she was thinking backward or forward. "The butterfly gave approval of you. If this is what we must do to save the kids then we will do it," she said.

"The butterfly? Tell me what you mean," Fred said, wondering if he was committing himself to a crazy person.

"When we were in town, the butterfly danced over your head and gave approval. It went and blessed that butterfly amulet too, sprinkling the essence of itself on it as it did my wand, but I never got to try to bargain for the amulet." She paused and looked at Fred as if seeing him for the first time with his blond hair and sparkling blue eyes. Those eyes sparkled now, as if realizing some point that had been hidden from him had opened up at the sight of her. It was an uncomfortable feeling.

"Like the butterflies you make in the woods?" Fred asked.

He had seen her attempts to produce the butterflies, she thought, then realized that he hadn't fussed at her for what she had done, merely asked if they were the same as the butterfly which had approved of him. "No. The big blue one is real," she said.

"The one that landed on me?" he asked trying to understand what she was talking about. "And that was real? Yes, I remember it. And you think it gave approval of some sort to me?"

Felith looked at him for a long moment. The suspicion was back. She had never talked to anyone about the butterfly, or about anything. Why had she let her guard down? Because the butterfly had given approval is why. She reverted back to the one answer person she had always been. "Yes."

The slight shuttering of the eyes, the clip one word answer were clearly signs that she was pulling away from him. What did you do with such a woman? You can't touch her, can't disagree with her, can't let your frigging own guard down, so what do you do? "I believe you. So we are meant to work together as a family then," he said and watched as there was a slight relaxing of the muscles of Felith's body. It was hard for him to wrap his mind around all this butterfly stuff, yet he had seen her project that mass of butterflies earlier. What you do, is believe in the person you are going to marry he decided. But that was so hard for him to do, that believing in someone bit. They lie, they hurt you in the worst way. What do you do?

Chapter Twelve

MAKING IT LEGAL

Two days later the family of orphans and strays traveled into town once more. Julian insisted on buying a wedding dress after the arrangements were made for the weddings. She was milking the day for all she could get out of it. For her the day was all about herself. Julian insisted that the weddings be separate not a group wedding as the minister had suggested. There was no argument from Felith on this arrangement, for she wanted nothing to do with something that belonged to Julian. After having made Robert promise an elaborate wedding later when he came into his inheritance, Julian settled for the dress and the traditional bits of a wedding, the something borrowed, something blue, and so on. She insisted on picking out her own ring, going for a gaudy showy ring.

Sidney, true to his word, took Felith and Middy to pick out the ring for Rags. Their opinions varied greatly, Middy was all excited and looking at everything and anything, and saying this one, or that one. While Felith quietly studied the ring selections, and zeroed in on one that seemed to say, "Rags". Sidney agreed. The ring was totally Rags. The thing that struck Sidney the most was that Felith never looked at a ring for herself, and that was so sad.

It took a while for Fred to track down the vendor who had been selling trinkets and amulets at the dinner the night he was beaten. While Felith was off advising Sidney on a ring for Rags, Fred spent his time looking for that vendor. She had mentioned a butterfly amulet and he felt that more than a ring that amulet should represent their marriage. After all, if not for that butterfly settling on his hand she would have never agreed to the marriage. How odd, that someone would agree to marry him over a butterfly. Women had thrown themselves at him from the time he had became a teen, that is until they realized he was different. Until Dorthea had betrayed him and ruined his youth, branded him so that even his own family had agreed with her opinions. He would never forgive them for that, not Dorthea, or his family.

Julian's wedding was first. They had decided to have the weddings in a small park. Julian had selected an archway with ivy growing up it to frame her as she and Robert were married. Once she learned the banks were up and running, she had Robert buy her the most expensive wedding dress in the shop. It was beautiful, one of the most beautiful dresses that Felith had ever seen. She watch the pair as a local child skipped in front of them and spread rose petals. They thought of many of the things that would make it a beautiful wedding, and Robert spared no expense to see that Julian was happy.

Next to be married were Sidney and Rags. Rags had selected a simpler wedding dress, still it was lovely. She had Felith come and stand with her, and Middy and Eric took part in the wedding as well. Middy scattered flower petals down the path to where Sidney stood with Fred by his side as best man. Eric came behind Middy with a pillow on which was the ring they had selected for Rags. Rags and Sidney were obviously so in love that the glow of their love was a thing of beauty. They spoke loving, binding words to each other and kissed.

Felith became concerned after watching Julian and Robert's marriage. She hadn't realized that she would need to speak vows to Fred. She was not about to say anything she didn't mean and she didn't expect Fred to either. The concern deepened as Rags and Sidney said their vows, each had made such loving and devoted remarks that the thought of having to say something now to Fred was eating at Felith and becoming a pit of fear in her stomach. Then the dresses, she didn't want a dress, a dress left her open to the monsters, to Fred. Even though he didn't act like a monster, still the worry was there. She had been worried when Fred was almost late for Julian's wedding. And as the sun began to dip down in the sky, her insides began to quiver. This looked like more than something on paper to her. That thought had Felith's insides tied in knots.

Having seen the beautiful dresses Julian and Rags wore, Fred felt that Felith should have something beautiful to wear too. He had never seen her wear a dress and didn't believe she would appreciate having a dress forced on her, still there had to be something that she wouldn't object to. Finally he chanced upon something he felt would be acceptable by his temperamental bride to be. He had it gift wrapped with lovely paper and beautiful ribbons along with two other gifts for the little ones. They were, after all, to be his children.

It wasn't until Sidney and Rags had run back down the path having birdseed tossed at them that Fred became nervous. Up until then he had been too busy arranging things for the wedding to have to think about the actual fact he was getting married. He waited until the others began to group back around for Felith and his wedding before giving Fel and the kids their gifts. The look Felith gave him was priceless, he hoped the photographer who had volunteered to take pictures at this unprecedented bunch of weddings caught the look on Felith's face. "For you to wear for the wedding and keep after the wedding," he said, quickly adding, "Not a dress."

It was the first gift anyone had ever given her, besides the cell phone Rags had bought her. Her mind just went blank when Fred handed the beautifully wrapped package to her. Middy squealed in delight when Fred handed her and Eric each a similar wrapped gift. He had even thought of the baby, and gave Emily a gift for her, and one for baby Susan. A look of bewilderment came to Felith's face as she and Middy along with Emily and baby Susan headed to a place to change their clothing. Fred and Eric went to another area to change, while Rags was changing out of her wedding dress.

Her hands were trembling, actually trembling in fear, as Felith opened the gift Fred had given her. Middy was ripping the paper off her gift and little Eric was picking at the bow, trying to slide it off one corner of the box his gift was in. Middy was squealing again, jumping up and down in glee, but Felith didn't hear her, didn't see or hear anything, just the gift. Slowly she unwrapped the present, taking care not to undo the bow or tear the paper. It was something pretty, and pretty was not a part of her life.

Carefully Felith lifted the tissue paper folded over the content of what was inside. On top was a pair of new jeans. A sigh of relief escaped Felith as she took the jeans out and set them aside. When she lifted up the tissue dividing the jeans from the material under them her breath caught in her throat. A blouse, at least she thought it was a blouse. The sleeves seemed to be a finely woven bunch of long white feathers created of lacy material, like the wings of some white bird they were folded over the bodice, but the bodice…. On the bodice was a scene of butterflies swirling in a beam of sunlight, as if ascending into the sky.

"Look, look!" Middy demanded, spinning around and around in front of Felith in a powder blue dress which swirled about the child. On the shoulder was a white butterfly broach. Behind Middy stood Emily in a dress of the same color. Her dress too had a butterfly broach pinned to it. Emily held little Susan, the baby was waving her chocolate arms zipped in a powder blue jumpsuit. They were all perfect.

Rags came rushing into the room, her face still glowing from her own wedding. She saw the girls all in blue and Felith standing there still not dressed. "Okay this won't do, get yourself dressed and I'm going to start on your hair," Rags said, whipping a bag out from behind her which looked as if it held the tools of a hair-dresser.

Fred's palms were sweating as he stood waiting for Sidney to bring Felith down the path of flowers Middy had laid down. He wasn't sure about this marriage bit, he wasn't sure about how Felith would take the gifts he had sent her, he just wasn't sure about anything at the moment. Eric squirmed beside him and Fred settled the child by placing his hand on Eric's head. Robert was standing in as one of the groom's men, but it was Eric Fred had next to him, entrusting the child to follow directions to the letter. On the opposite side Emily and Middy stood, well, Emily stood holding baby Susan, and Middy, unable to stand still, kept twirling around ever so often.

Then, Felith was there. She and Sidney paused at the start of the short path to where a small bridge went over a stream. It was on this bridge that Fred and the others stood. Fred's breath went out of him when he saw Felith take the first step. Robert whispered something about her being beautiful. Eric stood up straighter. Fred, Fred just filled his eyes with the sight of her. Then he saw the butterflies beginning to drift down and around everyone. Butterflies of ever color flew in lazy sweeps over the heads of people walking in the park. They swirled and dipped around and behind Felith as if petals from flowers raining down, only to rise again and sweep down again, a flowing cape of butterflies. And then, she was there in front of the minister at last. The butterflies settled as the minister began to speak. Through it all Fred only saw her. Then it was time for the vows and he forgot all the prepared things the minister had told him to say.

"I pledge to you, Felith, the rest of my life. I will cling only unto you and these our children. I vow that only death will part me from this bind between us. All that is mine is now yours. For now until the end of our lives I shall be yours," he swore meaning every word.

Then it was time for Felith to give her vows, "We are bound by more than vows can bestow upon us. I too pledge to you, Fred, the rest of my life. I will hold you and our children, and this vow for now and forever." She couldn't quite say she would be his, for she didn't know if she was capable of being any monster's.

The minister was saying you may place the ring upon her finger when Fred motioned for Eric to step forward. The child held his hands together as if he had a frog inside them. Slowly he opened his hands and Fred picked up the butterfly amulet. He held it up so everyone could see it. Suddenly there was the sound of hundreds of wings fluttering in the air as the butterflies took to the air, swirling down as if to touch the amulet, their iridescent wings sprinkling dust of ever color onto the amulet. They continued to circle the couple as Fred placed the amulet around Felith's neck and it settled between her breasts.

"You may kiss your bride," the minister said in a strained voice.

Felith, having seen this bit of the ritual preformed by Robert and Julian, then by Sidney and Rags, braced herself.

"Is it okay with you?" Fred whispered to Felith. Her eyes were wide like a frighten doe caught in the headlights of a car on the highway. She looked so scared. But she nodded. My brave girl, Fred thought, as he leaned forward and gave her as gentle a kiss as he could. He took her hand and faced the crowd which had gathered because of the butterflies as the minister said, "I introduce to you for the first time Mr. and Mrs. Fredrick Whiting.

Julian was fuming the next morning. The local paper, now back in print, had covered the three weddings. Only it wasn't her own wedding that was splashed all over the front page. There, for all the world to see, was huge headlines about 'The Butterfly Wedding', and a picture of the trashy girl with Fred. It was the first thing Julian had seen when she and Robert exited the small hotel in town. All the town people were yakking about how lovely the wedding had been, as if her own wasn't the best. Why that bit of trash hadn't even worn a wedding dress. How trashy was that? She hadn't stayed for that trash's wedding, but had gone to the room and ordered room service, enjoying the freedom from the others. She expected to take up residence in town now that she and Robert were married. Finally she had him, and his money. She wouldn't have to take any crap off of anyone once they were able to draw the inheritance. For now she would play the good wife, even if it meant going back to where she had to put up with that trashy girl.

Sidney had worried, all night. It'd been on his mind that perhaps Fred didn't understand that he couldn't force Felith into a physical relationship. He thought Fred understood, and at the time it had seemed that these two people who had endured so much, belonged together. Yet now there was that nagging doubt that gnawed at him, that protective surge that a father felt when his daughter went off with her new husband. He pulled the van up in front of the hotel to pick up Julian and Robert. Julian was dragging her feet as usual. Her expression was anything but one of bliss. But she finally entered the van and they were on the way back home.

At the farm the morning started with Middy jumping into the bed where Fred and Felith laid. Fred was on top of the covers while Felith was tucked under them. She had on an old tee shirt and her jeans. Fred had slept in jeans too, out of concern for Felith. He had been true to his word and had started to make a pallet on the floor. It had been Felith who told him to lay on top of the blankets. She had understood that they must appear to be a married couple in order to protect and adopt the kids. That she was willing to put herself through what had to be terrifying to her, for the sake of the kids, made Fred determined to make this work. He could feel his body wanting her, but his mind knew better than to want anyone. Still the night was torture for him with his body hard and his mind looping through a constant rant about how stupid he had been, how much he wanted this, how much he didn't want this, and the big kicker of all those butterflies at the wedding, over and over until he thought he finally fell asleep about the moment Middy jumped on the bed.

Middy pointed at Fred, her face filled with joy, "You are the daddy, and she is the mommy," she said pointing over at Felith. She gave an impish laugh, "And we get cake!" she caroled.

Felith sat up then, and shook her finger at Middy, "Only if you let us get up. Now scoot and take care of Eric." Middy bounced on the bed all the way to the edge and then slid off. Carefully Felith raised the covers to check and be sure her armor was firmly in place. Only then did she look over at Fred. He looked worn out, and concern took over Felith. "What is wrong? Are you hurt?" she blurted out.

A sort of snorted laugh erupted from Fred as he got off the bed. "In more ways than you know, but no, nothing you are able to fix today," he said in a cryptic manner. "We need to look into making the kids ours next. I think Sidney can help us with that," Fred went on, trying not to look at her, because his body was hot and hard enough already to send him up in flames. One night, one night and he was so lost, how could he continue for a lifetime? He had to endure, had to continue, because she needed him even if she didn't know it. And worse than that, he needed her. What a pile of crap he had gotten himself in this time.

Felith busied herself changing Susan and preparing the soft food for the babies breakfast. It was as she worked the blender making mush for the

baby to eat that Felith realized Emily was not happy.
It dawned on Felith that she had taken over the care
that Emily always gave to Susan. "Do you want to
feed Susan, Emily?" Felith asked, watching as Emily's
face brightened. "I understand. You are wondering
where you fit in with the changes that we have made,
right?"

Emily nodded. She had been so certain that
she had found a place in the family life of this group
of people, and had been happy. Now everything was
changing. The baby would belong to Felith. What
was there for her to do? Where did she belong?

"What if you live with Fred and I? We are
going to need somebody to look after Susan, Middy
and Eric when we are off doing things. You would
be part of our family. Or if you'd rather, we could
consider it a job, although I don't know how we
would pay you," Felith said.

Emily thought for a long moment, then she
nodded her head yes. As to which she was agreeing
to she didn't know. But baby Susan had become part
of her life, and she didn't want to give the baby up.

Adopting the kids had turned out to be a
matter of paperwork. In the aftermath of the virus
which had wiped out so many people there were
an abundance of orphans. The laws governing
adopting had been temporarily restructured. Sidney
and Rags put in to adopt Felith, Emily, Rosemary,
and after some discussion, Robert. Julian was of
course against the adoption of Robert. He, however,
argued that until he was of legal age to acquire his
inheritance, they needed a stable household. In the

end, Julian decided it was better to bide her time before separating Robert from the others.

In the meantime Felith and Fred put in the paperwork to adopt Middy, Eric, and baby Susan. The paperwork went through very quickly, and the kids where theirs finally. On that day there was jubilation in the household. Emily baked a huge cake, chocolate, as that was Middy's favorite. Sidney played music on the radio, and they all danced and feasted until near midnight. There was such joy filling Felith's heart, now she could legally protect the kids. Fred too breathed a sigh of relief, knowing they would be together and the children couldn't be taken away to be put in separate orphanages. Now they were truly a family.

Two months passed with each family grouping settling in and becoming a true family. Felith, Emily, Rosemary and Robert were now adopted siblings. Felith told Emily that this made it easier for them to form a family unit with the kids. Everyone seemed happy except for Julian, who was biding her time until she could get Robert to herself. The children were already calling Felith and Fred as Mom and Dad. So much had happened since Felith had first come to Haven. If on that first day you had told her that one day she would have a baby monster as a child and a monster husband she would have said you were crazy. But now those two, the boy child and the man husband, did not seem to be monsters. What they were Felith didn't know, but she couldn't characterize them as monsters in her mind.

Felith watched Fred out in the yard as he

played catch with Middy and Eric. The children were laughing and having a grand time chasing each other and catching the ball, which Fred was careful to throw just right so it would land in their hands. He seemed to be made to take care of children. The way he was able to change baby Susan's diaper, and knew what a bottle warmer was, spoke of experience. She wondered what his story was, how he came to be a person who cared for children. But she wouldn't ask.

Taking careful aim Fred tossed the soft sponge ball to Eric, making sure it landed directly in his cupped hands. The little boy caught it, and a smile blossomed on his face as he tossed it back. Dust was rising from the dirt road that led up to the farm. Keeping a close eye on the children, Fred stopped tossing the ball to watch the road. Two black cars were coming up the drive, and they looked official, and one of the cars was a staff car. Fred handed Eric the ball and said, "Take your sister into the house." He waited until the children were safely in the house before calling out to Sidney and Rags to come see. If this was someone coming to take the kids away from them then they were in for a fight. Neither Fred nor Felith would give up the children to anyone.

Two men in suits climbed out of the front car, and a man wearing a uniform stepped out of the rear car. Fred knew of such men from the dealings his father had had with the government. He stepped forward and greeted the men. "Looks like you had a dusty ride. Aren't you a little off the official track?"

The two suits flanked the man in uniform, and it was pretty clear that they were Secret Service. Fred couldn't believe that this was some attempt by his family to get him back, after all they were the ones who had tossed him out. Still, with all that had been going on in the world, anything was possible.

Then the General spoke. "I'm looking for an Officer Nancy Raglan, would she happen to reside here?"

The screen door opened and closed as the General was speaking. Rags stepped forward and extended her hand to the general. "I'm Nancy Raglan, now Nancy Asters, what can I do for you, General?" she asked.

"I'm very pleased to meet you, Nancy. I am General Avery Richards. Your country has need of you, Officer Raglan. It is my understanding that you contracted this virus and survived. We have been searching for you, or someone like you, for some time now. You have been drafted into the service of your country. We are here to escort you to Washington DC."

Sidney came forward then and put his arm around Rags' waist. He looked the General up and down as if measuring him and his intentions. "Just what is it you intend to do with my wife?" he asked. Behind him, Fred breathed a silent sigh of relief, they weren't here for him after all.

"I don't have to tell you how serious this virus is, or how desperate is the need for a vaccine. Your wife is perhaps the only person who has survived an infection. That means there are antibodies in her blood. We have initiated the draft, and have drafted Raglan here to help us in creating that vaccine," the General said.

"So what you're saying is, you made it legal to

kidnap her and take her blood. Why didn't you just come and ask? Rags would have been happy to help. What you're doing here is something neither of us will forget or forgive. I suggest you rephrase your quoted request," Sidney said.

Felith stepped forward. When she had come out of the house, Fred didn't know. The expression on her face was anything but welcoming. He knew he had to do something to defuse the situation, before Felith decided to take matters into her own hands. He was, however, a second too late.

"You will leave now. My family will discuss the situation. When we have reached an agreement, then we will contact you," Felith said.

The two Secret Service men step forward flanking the General. It would have been comical if it wasn't such a serious situation. Three men feeling threatened by a thin little girl, a woman, in fact, now. Fred noticed that dog had not come to face down the General. So that must mean that the General and his two Secret Service buddies were not a real threat. Still, Fred could not let them get away without letting them know there were big guns behind them. "I believe that is the best thing. Listen to my wife and go to the town. We will contact you there when anything is decided," Fred said.

"And what is your name?" The General growled, his look saying he felt Fred had no right to speak in this situation.

Fred took Felith's hand before answering. "I am Frederick Whiting, and this is my wife Felith."

The General looked confused, but recovered quickly. "Any relations to Stanley Whiting?"

"He is my father," Fred said.

The General looked as if he was going to choke. He stepped forward and extended his hand. "I'm sorry to have inconvenienced your family, Mr. Whiting. We will take up residence in the town and wait for your call," he said, motioning for the two men to follow him. He went back to the car that he had arrived in, got in and slammed the door.

Through the tinted window of the black car, Fred could see the General already on the phone. Let them stew on that fact, this was his family now. And they were legal.

As arguments went it would be considered a mild one, the family talk they had after the black cars had left. Sidney was against Rags going with the General. This was, after all someone they didn't know, and from the way he made it sound, Rags would be like some experiment subject. What, and above all, Sidney objected to was the fact they had supposedly drafted Rags, which would mean she was in the service, and not her own agent, but under orders.

For once Julian agreed with Sidney as did everyone else. The sticky point came in what to do. Did they blatantly refuse to let Rags go, or what? And if they did refuse, would they come and just take Rags?

"If we go on the run, they will find us. It will be a near impossible thing to hide our family from them," Rags said.

Julian immediately jumped up and objected. "We aren't going if you leave. Robert and I have a future ahead of us. We will be somebody. I'm not going to leave all that behind me to run off with you," she said.

For once Rosemary didn't side with Julian. Her thoughts were split between not wanting to go on the run and giving up the security of having a family again. Emily went over and stood with Rags as a way of saying she'd go if they needed to run. That left Fred and Felith to decide what to do. Felith stood up, she looked around at everyone. "What we do we do together," she said, "these people will hurt us, if they can. I will not let Rags go with them alone." From her point of view, it was a statement of fact.

Fred stood up as Felith was talking, and began to pace. He looked like a caged animal trapped between two thoughts, which indeed he was. On the one hand was his desire not to be put back into the world which he had escaped. But the other part of him didn't want to let Felith down. She was his wife, and despite what she thought of him, he would give his life for her. Suddenly he stopped pacing, and looked up at Rags. "I want to make it a condition of you going with them that I come along. I know these people. They are ruthless, and have little regard for who you are as a person. Their focus is on their own stature, and how they are seen by others," he said.

"Fred, you don't have to do this," Rags said. There was pain in her voice as if she felt his distress.

"I do," Fred said, "It's time I face them."

Felith had watched the interaction between Fred and Rags. As usual she took control, "Then it is agreed. Fred and I will go with Rags. Sidney, you will look after the kids along with Emily. Middy, you will protect Eric. Rosemary, you will help anyone and everyone." She didn't mention Julian and Robert. When Robert stepped forward as if to protest, Felith held up her hand in a halting motion. "Robert, you have a wife and baby to look after. That above all is your job," she said, and they all knew that this was the final word. They would go the next morning to see the General and set the terms of Rags helping the government.

Felith awoke in the middle of the night feeling Fred thrashing about on his side of the bed. So far he had kept true to his word and never touched her. This thrashing about was new though. His legs kicked out and she had to dodge a punch in her direction. "How could you?" he cried out. Then the angry scowl that was so much a part of him took over his sleeping face. Pain radiated from him in shocking waves that nearly caused Felith to lay down and weep. Only, she didn't cry, instead she reached out her hand and touched Fred on the cheek. She sent comfort, and understanding. A great gasping sob was wrenched from Fred, then he grabbed her and hung on as if his life depended upon it. For a moment everything went blank in Felith's mind. Her whole being threatened to shut down, then, she felt him. He was so shattered inside. Whoever had hurt him had taken away his trust and left him broken inside. Felith could not stand to have him hurt so much. She wrapped him in her arms and held him as she had held Eric and Middy. Finally Fred's body relaxed and he slept, clutching to Felith as she held him tight comforting him keeping him safe from the torments inside him.

Fred dreamed that Felith was in his arms, willingly. He could feel her soft skin, smell that scent that was only hers. He tightened his arms and felt her against him. His heart beat spiked and his eyes flew open. She was there for real, in his arms. It wasn't a dream at all, she was there laying against his tormented body, and he was so hard that it was all he could do not to take her as she slept. But he wasn't an animal like others were, and he would never do such things to her without her being a partner to his loving. He remembered how she had gone away in her mind at his slightest touch once, and that alone was enough for him to loosen his hold on her body. She woke then, awareness coming into her face first, then her eyes opening. Fred waited for her to go away, for that dreaded blankness to come over her features.

It was the warmth Felith felt first, then the awareness of where she was seeped into her mind. This time she had been the one who had taken the contact, and that made all the difference. She released her hold on Fred and scooted off the bed. "We must get ready," she said, as if she hadn't been in his arms only a moment before.

He wanted to laugh, but seeing the serious expression on her face, he didn't. Trouble was he didn't know if he could even stand at the moment, his traitor body wanted her so much. "Give me a moment please," he said, his voice sort of croaky. He saw her give him a quick sharp glance, then turn away and sorted out clothing for the trip into town. He had to get her to dress up as much as possible, maybe buy some new clothes for her in town for the trip to Washington DC. "Wear your wedding outfit. I'll wear mine too. These people are all about appearance. We must be ready to face them in their world," he said.

Felith nodded. "As a family," she said, and went off to shower and dress.

Sidney watched the van throwing up a trail of dust as Rags drove off with Fred and Felith. It should be him with her he thought. A lump had formed in his stomach when Rags had placed her gun in his hands. She had kissed him after handing him the gun with such love that he had felt dread fill him. "Take care of the kids until I get back," she had said, and walked to the van. It was like so many times when she had left his bed to go to work as a cop. Only, this time, she had left her gun. "You better call me every two hours, or I'm going to come there and shrink some DC heads," he had called out as Rags scooted into the driver's seat of the van. It was a joke between them that she would shoot them and he'd do his shrink thing on their heads.

There was no mistaking where the General had taken up residence in town, the black staff car gave it away as well as two military jeeps. First thing Fred thought was they meant business, but then, so did he. He had tried to wipe this part of his previous life out of his mind. After all, they, his parents, had been the ones to turn their backs on him when he was hurt and in need of their help. Still it seemed you couldn't go far enough to leave the past behind.

Two uniformed men were guarding the door

when the three civilians approached the General's room. One blocked the way while the other knocked and opened the door only to announce that Rags was there to the occupant, with friends. The guard blocking the door pulled out a hand held scanner and ran it over Rags, then Fred. He frowned when he turned to Felith as the end of her wand was sticking out of the top of her jean pocket. "Cover her, while I pat her down," he told his buddy.

"Touch my wife and it will be the last thing you ever do," Fred said, his voice soft and low full of deadly intent, but the look on the face of the guard hardened.

"She has a weapon on her, I can see the hilt. I will protect the General with my life. So step back, sir," the guard said.

"Stand down, soldier," barked the General stepping out into the hallway. He turned a wary eye in the direction of Fred. "Sorry about that, Mr. Whiting. He is a good soldier just doing his duty," he said, then turned his attention to Felith. "Now what is this weapon you have on you, young lady?" he asked her.

Felith looked over at Fred, when he had told that guard not to touch her something inside her felt strange, there was a question in her eyes that she didn't voice. Instead, she reached down and pulled her wand out of her pants pocket. "This is mine and you may not have it," she said in that way of hers when stating a fact.

The General blinked at the small stick she held in her hand, then he threw back his head and gave a belly laugh. He laughed so hard that tears trickled down his cheeks. Finally he stopped laughing and wiped the tears off his face. "I have to admit my reaction may seem odd to you. You see we've encountered a few touchy situations, and all of us have been on edge for so long that it was just good to have a laugh. Come on in and have a seat, little lady," General Richards said, motioning the three inside.

His face flushed with embarrassment the guard stepped aside. Felith entered, wondering what was so funny about her wand. Her hand went up and touched the amulet hanging around her neck. Having sensed the tension inside of Fred, Felith had come prepared with all her protection. The wand and amulet had both been blessed by the butterfly. The amulet had the colors of all the butterflies in the world sprinkled on and inside it, so it must be powerful. As to how she was to use it she didn't have any idea.

The General went and sat down in a huge armchair which had been placed in the room, it was a commanding chair which said the occupant was in charge. Felith and Rags went to the sofa. Fred, however, didn't go sit down. Two flags were positioned on one side of the room, signifying that this was an office of power representing the government. It was there Fred went to stand, so that he was framed by the two flags. He knew this gave him a certain appearance and would do more than standing over the General could ever accomplish. "There are conditions to our letting you have any of Mrs. Asters blood to use," Fred said, his voice all business, with a strong indication that he would not budge from what they had decided.

General Richards scratched his nose and heaved a sigh before answering. "Let's hear what you have to say and I'll determine if we can live with your terms," he said.

Fred glanced over at Felith and Rags as if telling them not to interrupt. "First, you will cancel the draft you say has been placed on Mrs. Asters. She will not be beholding to the armed service, or any other organization. Second, my wife and I will accompany Mrs. Asters and remain with her. These two points will not be argued, understand?"

As Fred had been talking the expression on General Richards' face had stayed frozen in that command mode. He had thought he could deal with anything the boy could throw at him, this however was not his call. The President had thought drafting subjects into the service would make things so much simpler. They would then have an obligation to their country and be considered a traitor should they decline. Only this was Whiting's own son making these demands. What the hell should he do? Things had been so much simpler when he had been a grunt. "When we get to DC we will see what can be done," he finally said, then saw Fredrick's face, damn his old man had that same look when he wasn't about to listen to reason. The General held up his hand in surrender, he knew when to attack and when to pull his forces back. "Okay, let me make some calls."

"We will wait," Fred said, not backing down even a fraction. He was more concerned about Felith, she had a strange look in her eyes. If that creep saying he would touch her had caused her distress he'd see him sent to the coldest place on

Earth. He scowled at the thought of the guard even thinking of putting his hands on Felith. His thoughts had to be pushed back as General Richards came into the room, although the scowl remained on his face.

"Arrangements had been made, we will drive from here to the airport. A puddle-hopper will take us to the city where a private jet will be waiting. We'll be in DC before you know it," the General said, his eyes never leaving Fred's face.

"Only if our conditions have been met," Fred said.

"They have," Richards said, not adding that legally he could have Miss Raglan seized and haul her in, that is he could have if he hadn't jumped through hoops getting her off the draft list.

Fred nodded. "Good we have some shopping to do either here or when we reach the city where we transfer. I assume you will provide us with guards to make certain nobody approaches us. I think three will be enough, as I don't intend to let the ladies out of my sight. One should be a woman to accompany my ladies into the restrooms, else I'll go in with them myself. Understood?" Fred said, as if he were the one who was in charge instead of the General. He surprised himself with how easy it was to remember all the ins and outs of traveling with a guard.

Chapter Thirteen

VIALS OF BLOOD

The airport and plane were the first stumbling blocks for Felith. She just stopped walking when they started out to board the first small plane. The look on her face was so different from her usual set in stone appearance that at first Fred thought she was passing out. Then Rags whispered in his ear that she had never seen a plane before. Who hadn't seen planes fly over before, even if they had never rode on one? It just showed how little he knew about Felith's life before he first met her in Haven. Okay, they would deal with this and worry about the past later. Carefully he took her hand so as not to set her off into that coma state of hers. "I know it is small, honey, but it will be safe. I'm going to be with you all the way, you just hold on to me," he said in his most reasonable voice. Slowly he saw her turn her gaze to look at him. "I'm here, my love, I'm right here with you. One for all. Let me be your one, hold on to me," he whispered for her ears only. Felith blinked, and her head went up a fraction. Fred could see the determination come back into her, his brave girl would face this now. Hand in hand they walked to the plane and boarded it. Anyone watching wouldn't have been able to tell this was Felith's first experience with planes and flying.

Rags had voted for them buying clothing at the lay-over for the jet which was to take them to DC. Fred bought them each a small set of luggage on his long neglected account. Then he shopped for suits which would exude power. The big problem was Felith. She behaved as if anything that would look beautiful on her was wrong. Fred racked his brain trying to find something that would convince her to accept the dresses he had picked out, but she was stubborn, so stubborn. What the hell was wrong with her? All girls like pretty clothing, didn't they? It hit him like an axe lodged in the top of his head, not if they had never had the option to wear pretty clothing. For some reason Felith behaved as if she didn't deserve nice things. Fred had never seen her in anything but the jeans and a tee shirt, except for the wedding blouse he had bought her. He wanted her to wow everyone the way she wowed him ever single day. In the end he appealed to Rags to talk to Felith about wearing a dress.

Rags took Felith aside, away from the guards and Fred. She saw Fred hold up his hand to stop the guards from getting closer to her and Felith. "Sweetie, why won't you wear a dress? We are going to have to look our best in DC. So tell me why you won't wear a dress so I can understand," Rags said, figuring the best approach was the direct one when it came to talking to Felith.

Taking a deep breath as if girthing herself Felith answered. "I need my armor. It makes it harder for the monsters to get to me," she said, her face and voice not betraying the little girl inside her who had been brutalized.

Rags almost grabbed Felith to hug her. She stopped herself just in time, and instead went to report to Fred.

He listened as Rags told him about Felith's reasons for always wearing jeans. He listened to her saying how Fel had been molested while locked up from the time she was a small child. As he listened, his hands clutched the metal rod holding a row of dresses, slowly the rod began to bend. It wasn't until one of the guards came up to him that he realized what he was doing. "Sir," the guard said to Fred, "let go of the clothing rod."

Looking at the guard for a moment Fred prepared to hit him, then it sank in what the man was saying and he motioned the guard to step back. Jeans it was then, the best damn jeans in the world would be hers, and pretty blouses, anything in the world she wanted he'd get for her. "We are in the wrong section," he said flatly. "Come on, honey," he said beckoning to Felith.

Floating, that is what Felith felt like she was doing, simply floating, and so nervous. She had two suitcases filled with jeans of ever shade and color, and blouses which took her breath away. Then there was the underwear. Fred had insisted on every beautiful color in the world for her, and her alone to know what she had on beneath her clothing. He said.... Her mind didn't know if she should believe him or not, but he said all these things were hers and only hers. New, and never having belonged to anyone before, only hers. He had stressed that over and over. Felith wanted to believe him, only experience had taught her that monsters lied. Oh, how much she wanted all he said to be true. She floated for the moment. Floated all the way to the next plane. Floated to the seat and sat down not even aware that her face glowed with a look called happy.

The plane landed at a darkened airstrip instead of the lighted airport which Fred had expected. He was immediately suspicious. "Where have you taken us?" he asked the General, his voice soft, yet deadly.

The General frowned at Fred's tone of voice. "We are going directly to the medical facility. I thought it best, considering the urgent need of a vaccine to let the geeks get started."

"Then lets get started," Felith said.

The General looked surprised, but stood up and motioned them to exit the plane. He had expected some sort of temper flare at the rush to get the Raglan woman's blood. The fact that they were willing to submit right off made things simpler. Still, the girl wasn't in charge, it was Whiting, and the General knew how difficult a Whiting could become when he thought someone was trying to take charge of anything.

The lab they took Rags and the others to was so bright inside that it made Felith's eyes hurt. She had spent so long in that dark basement that the brightness still hurt her eyes now and then. She was worried too, because Fred didn't seem the same as before, he acted more like the monsters, and that was a big concern. Still she wanted to believe the butterfly wouldn't have approved of him if he wasn't to be trusted. That and him telling her to let him be her one kept her warm inside, but watchful.

"I hate needles," Rags whispered as the General rushed them through the halls to where a man stood by a chair with a tray of empty collection vials. It looked like a lot of vials. How much blood did they plan to take from her?

That same question crossed Felith's mind too. She held her hand up before Rags could sit in the chair and Rags stopped. She had learned to listen to Felith's instincts. Felith turned to the man with the vials. "Tell me why you need her blood," she said.

The doctor looked at Felith as if she was the most stupid person on the earth. Then he saw the General gesture for him to tell her. He sighed, the dumb-ass people they brought here to be tested were unbelievable. "We know she actually had the virus from the test run on her blood where she was living. We will check to be sure the antibodies will prevent a person from catching the virus. We take her blood to make the vaccine and develop it so we can mass produce the vaccine, and inoculate everyone so they won't catch this virus in the future." He waited for the usual reaction of awe that came next, and instead saw the girl just nod. Perhaps she was too dumb to even understand that simple explanation.

"You may take one vial to test," she said, as if dismissing him.

What an arrogant bitch, the doctor thought, yet when the subject didn't sit down he finally nodded. They could start with one vial, but if she was the one lone survivor, he was going to get his blood one way or another. Smiling he drew the one vial of blood, knowing he had the upper hand, and there was no way the little bitch could keep him from accessing the subject if she proved to be the right donor.

Felith watched closely as the doctor drew the blood from Rags. As soon as the band-aid was put on Rags' arm Felith reached out and touched her with a finger. She was careful, the way Fred had taught her to be, and sought out only the hurt from the blood being drawn. She encouraged Rags body to produce more blood to make up for the lost blood and carefully withdrew.

"Thank you," Rags said, smiling up at Felith. Rags believed in Felith now, she had no doubts any longer that Felith could and did heal with her mind. Her worry at the moment was that this bunch of bureaucrats would take advantage of Felith, or decide to take her apart to see how she worked should they find out her secret.

It did not take long for the test results to come back. Rags had none of the antibodies they were looking for in her blood. "We are running a comparison of the blood that was taken when you were diagnosed to what we now find in your blood. It shouldn't take long," the man who had taken Rags blood said. "I just don't understand, she was positive. But there are no antibodies," he mumbled to himself as he started walking away.

Concern flickered in Felith's eyes, and she turned to Rags. "Did I mess up? I should have left you antibodies right?" she asked Rags.

The doctor stopped and turned around, staring at Felith. "What did you say?" he asked, rushing back to where Felith stood. "You should have left her antibodies? What do you mean?" he demanded.

There was a movement so fast the doctor hadn't even seen Fred coming, but there he was between him and Felith. "Step back from my wife," Fred said softly. Felith reached out and touched Fred's hand, as if to soothe him. He looked down at her hand, then back up at her. She didn't touch him often, so when she did he treasured it. His eyes looked warmly at her, and a slight smile crept onto his face.

"We are having a conversation here, sir. I want to know what your wife meant by she should have left some antibodies. What did she do to Mrs. Raglan? This is a matter of national security. You know how serious national security is?" The doctor said, trying to stare Fred down. But that was a battle he knew he couldn't win.

Before Fred could stop her Felith stepped in, the way she always did when one of hers was threatened. "I only healed her. I didn't know about the antibodies," she said.

The doctor sputtered and choked, as if he was having a heart attack. "That's ridiculous, you have a cure for the virus and you haven't come forward?"

"I don't think it is a cure. I just made her get well is all," Felith said, suddenly aware that Rags was shaking her head at her, and Fred had a tight grip on her arms. They didn't want these men to know she could heal, that much was obvious in their behavior. Felith could not understand what the problem was, she was only being honest.

"You'll have to remain with us, young lady. We need to get to the bottom of what you did to cure the virus. Come this way," the doctor said.

"Like hell," Fred said stepping forward to stand between Felith and the doctor. "You're not taking my wife anywhere."

Because he was tired of dealing with stupid people, the doctor did something he never should have done. "Guards restrain this man. Young woman you are coming with me," he said taking Felith by the arm, and trying to lead her away. The dumb girl wouldn't budge, so he started dragging her.

Behind the doctor Fred exploded. "Get your fucking hands off my wife!" he snarled. Two guards came up and grabbed him one on each side, and Fred turned into a wild man. He hit and kicked, head butted, and even bit the men hanging onto his arms. He saw Felith fighting with the doctor, to get to him. And the sneaky doctor giving her some sort of shot which seemed to put her out. That was when Fred turned into a maniac. In the end it took eight men to take him down, and most of them paid a small price. Rags had not been standing passively during all this. She managed to punch two of the men in the nose before they restrained her.

Gen. Richards thought he was having a heart attack, as he watched Homeland Security beat the crap out of Stanley Whiting's son. How in the hell was he supposed to tell Whiting that his son had been beat up again, and was arrested by Homeland Security? He could see his career going down the drain before his eyes. It was best to take the bull by the horns he decided, and opened his phone to make the call that would end his career. "Sir, they've arrested your son and beat him up a bit. We are no closer to finding a cure for the virus," he said, then listened to the silence on the other end of the line, and finally a click. Whiting had hung up on him.

Fred woke gradually, first hearing a rumbling sound like metal moving along a metal track, then voices approaching as if from a distance. "I'm sorry, sir. He attacked the men because of that girl. We can't have a civilian hitting our men. You understand, don't you, sir? He just went nuts…er…sort of wild. The girl too, but the doc, knocked her out."

"He do that to you?" Fred moaned inside, that was his father's voice.

"No, Sir. That would be the woman with them. She has quite a punch, for a woman."

Fred didn't want to open his eyes and have to face his father. The man had never been on his side. He'd probably have Fred sent to prison, just out of spite. Only he didn't give a crap what his father wanted to do to him. Fel was the only one that mattered, and those evil bastards had been touching her. So he opened his eyes and managed to stand up. Damned if he'd let the old man see him laying down and weak. Straightening his clothing Fred was ready when his father walked into sight. "Mr. Whiting," he said in way of greeting, not calling him father, the man had lost the right to be called that.

"Fredrick, you look a bit worn. I hear you put up a fuss at the medical center. You do know that this is a matter of great urgency, our finding a vaccine?" he said, then went on without waiting for Fred to answer. "There has already been a secondary out-break in Japan. We can not risk being unprepared here."

"Then you have a problem. I won't risk my wife," Fred said, in a low voice that played softly on the ear.

"Your wife? You are too young to get married, so the marriage isn't valid," countered his father.

"I came of age one week before our marriage and I am emancipated in case you forgot. We also have three children, not that that matters to you. My wife is not to be touched by anyone. Anyone who puts hands on her, I'll track down and destroy. Be sure you let them all know that I mean every word, Mr. Whiting," Fred said, his voice still soft and low.

Stanley Whiting stared at the boy he raised having had such hopes that he would grow up to be at least half the man he, Stanley, wanted him to become. But this boy, this man in front of him couldn't be his son, not the wimpy boy that baby-sat little kids and wiped their snotty noses instead of playing football. The boy who had limped off after he had called him a fag, and told him he was no son of his. Looking at this man, Stanley regretted those words. It wasn't until after his son had declared independence that Stanley had found out the truth, how that girl had lured him into an ambush and the other students had beat Fred saying he was gay, then…. Stanley didn't want to think of the then. He wanted forgiveness, but he was never a man to ask for forgiveness, or one who backed down. So how did he get his son back, or this version of his son?

"Tell us how you cured Raglan, girl," the man said again. He had been badgering Felith for several hours after having her waken. He was getting to the point where he felt they should consider other options, torture came to mind. Maybe they could get away with it, just maybe.

"No. You will let me see my husband and Rags now," Felith said, she too was getting tired. Fred had been hurt, she saw them beating him, and they had to let her heal him.

"You are dumb as a dirt, girl. You will never see your boyfriend again unless you tell us what we want to know. I have the power to see you locked away in the darkest hole you have ever seen. Now tell me how you cured Raglan," he said, waiting for the inevitable paling and flinching to happen. Only it didn't happen.

"I have lived in the darkest hole. The answer is no. You will take me to my husband, now," Felith said, her mouth set.

The man rubbed his forehead as if he was getting a headache, and indeed he was, he knew when he was beat. Perhaps if she saw the boy she'd talk. What other choice besides torture did they have? "Okay, come with me."

The twist and turns of the hallways seemed endless to Felith. The man, the doctor, was taking her to Fred, and that was all that mattered at the moment. They made one more turn and ahead was a cage. In it stood Fred and another man. The door to the cage was open, but there were armed men standing close enough to catch Fred if he tried to escape. They parted enough that the man and Felith could walk forward to Fred. Felith's steps picked up speed then.

The light in the cell was dimmer than the hall leading to the outside. It was that dimness that allowed Fred to see the two people walking towards him so clearly. She was here, his Fel. He started to step out of the cell's open door, but two men pulled their guns on him, so he stopped. He watched her, his eyes burning with the warmth he felt building inside him. Then she was in front of him. "Did they hurt you?" he said at the same moment that she spoke to him.

"They hurt you," she stated simply, and he knew she came to heal him.

Fred took a step back, shaking his head. "Promise, only the worst," he said, then pointed to his stomach. "I think it is here, my belly is feeling tight. But you have to do as you have learned, control. Understood?"

Felith nodded, reaching out to touch his face. There was bruising there, on his face, still she ignored the bruising, searched for the worst of what had been done to him. There, bleeding, bad bleeding. She worked in silence, knitting the pathways for blood-flow back together, forcing the tissue to unite, to heal. One last spot, she thought, just let me do a little more, but the weakness was seeping into her and she pulled herself back. Felith swayed, her legs threatened to collapse on her.

Fred was ready, he had felt the warmth spreading. He knew the damage was bad from the blood draining from her face. He had her in his arms the moment he felt her withdrawing. He held her with all the tender love inside him, and couldn't help but kiss her on the cheek.

Stanley Whiting watched his son and the woman he had married. He listened openly to what they said to each other, some sort of couples understanding passed between them. Something about his belly and the worst? Stanley looked at his son's belly. It was popped out some as if over full. The bastards! They had beat his son. It isn't the first time, he reminded himself feeling the guilt rush into him. You didn't do anything that time, did you? No, he admitted to himself. That wasn't now, now he would. "Who the hell hit my boy!" he roared.

Startled the two guards jerked up their guns not sure who was the threat to their leader. His words finally registered and the two men lowered their weapons. One stepped up even though he feared he was ending his career, maybe even his freedom. "We used necessary force only, Sir. It took eight of us to get him under control. We stepped on him a bit. He freaked out over her," he said, motioning towards Felith.

"Eight? Eight of you hit on him? It took eight of you to take him down? What are you, girls?" Stanley stared at the guard.

"Felt like it, sir. He was a madman. Tough lad you have there," the guard said.

Tough? Fredrick tough? Stanley looked over to where Fredrick was lowering his wife to the sparse bunk in the cell. Fredrick married and with kids, he was still wrapping his head around that too. What else had he thought of his own kid that was wrong?

Taking off his suit jacket Fred wrapped it around Felith, "Hang on, dearest, I'll get some food for you." He kissed her on the forehead and whirled around prepared to do battle if needed to get Felith something to eat. Striding over to where his father was yakking with the guards Fred scowled at them. "I want a full meal brought here right now. Make sure it is healthy with lots of protein. And none of your prison swill. Get it fast, move, move," he said.

"He is going nuts again. Get some more men up here," one of the guard said. "Get out of here, Sir," he told Stanley, as his gun came up to point at Fred.

Fred glanced at the gun pointed at him, "Shoot me if it will make you feel safe, but get some food for my wife. If you don't you best kill me, even then I'll get up off the floor and kill you if my wife isn't taken care of. You understand?"

The guard paled, then nodded. There was so much conviction in the perps eyes that he believed the guy would get up, even if dead, and kill him. "All you want is a meal for your wife, right?"

Fred nodded.

"I can get that. First get back in the cell," The guard said.

Fred looked over at Stanley, then turned and walked back into the cell pulling the door shut behind him. Stanley pulled out his phone, a goal he could take care of immediately was before him.

Fred went and sat down by Felith, then wrapped his arms around her to give her extra warmth. "Hang on, Honey. They are bringing some food." It was sad that he felt so pleased she didn't push him away from her. Gradually he was getting her used to his touch, to him. He could hear the rattling of a cart being pushed down the hallway and knew the food had arrived. "It is here, dearest. You need to eat it all, understand?" he told her.

Off to the side Stanley stood watching, trying to figure out what was up with the son he didn't know. Earlier, when it hit him that his son was willing to die to protect his wife, he felt such pride in the boy. He always knew his son would fight for what he wanted. He had wanted to take care of children, and that seemed so wrong, so weird for a young teen to want to do. Stanley had agonized over what he thought Fredrick was becoming, the softness, the lack of interest in sports, all of it seemed to indicate he was becoming gay. That embarrassed him so much, the way people snicker when they mentioned Fredrick in his circle of friends. And then Fredrick told him about what Dorthea and those boys had done to him. God help him, he believed his son had asked for it. That night he was so upset at himself over what this would do to his reputation that he told Fredrick he was no son of his. Ever since, he had been ashamed of himself. He'd tried to live better, not be so judgmental. But it was too late, Fredrick quietly filed with the courts for emancipation from his parents, and Stanley had let it go uncontested. Even set up a fund that would provide for the boy's independence of himself, so the boy had income. To everyone else in the world Fredrick was off exploring the world. So now he watched and wondered what influence this woman had over his only child.

They had brought two full helpings of chicken and red beans and rice, but Fred was not interested in anything but getting food inside of Felith. He watched her as she dug into the food as if she was starving until she noticed he wasn't eating. She pointed at the plate made up for him and at him. Her look stern, and that made him smile at her. Always bossing him and the others around, what a gal he had married.

When Felith spooned the last bite of food into her mouth they came for her, the doctor and ten guards. Fred looked them over, then looked to Felith, she nodded that it was okay, except she reached out her hand to touch him once more as if afraid she wouldn't get to do it later. "Please," he said softly, "save your strength, do it for me, honey, please."

"I won't go until you let me get that last spot I saw. It won't take much. I'll be careful," she said, and he knew she had to do it. It was what she did, so he nodded. She place her hand on his face and sought out that last bleeder, it wasn't hard to locate, or to heal. When she was done she looked at Fred, her one. What possessed her she didn't know, but she did as he had been doing, she kissed his cheek, then turned to face the waiting men outside the cell.

"Tell everyone that if anyone touches her,

even casually, I'll break out of here and break their frigging arms. Make sure they know," Fred said to the group of men waiting on Felith, so softly they had to listen intently to hear him, but they did hear him. Several raised their guns to point at him. Fred sneered at them, kissed his wife on the cheek, then sat down motioning them to unlock the cell. He laughed to himself as he watched the space the guards left around Felith. Yeah, they got his message. And she had kissed him, he thought, reaching up to touch his cheek where her lips had caressed him.

"Okay, you've seen your husband and have had a meal. I've lived up to my end of the deal, it is time you start telling me what I need to know," the doctor said, sitting at a table across from the girl. Her husband was one scary bastard and he wasn't about to take any chances after seeing what he did to the guards. Just to be safe he held his cell phone in one hand and a pen in the other, no casual touching, not him. "What did you mean when you were talking to the Raglan woman?"

"That I must have healed her wrong. I should have made the antibodies, like you said. I didn't know they were needed," Felith said in her truthful direct manner.

The doctor sputtered out a curse. "What sort of game are you playing here? You think you are some sort of faith healer? Or are you just making shit up? Tell me what you gave the Raglan woman that cured her, or I'll see your husband hanged until he is dead for treason."

Felith looked at the man before her, to her he

was a vile monster. He was trying to use her in some way. How, or why, she didn't know, but he was trying to use her, and threatening Fred had just assured him he wouldn't get what he wanted. Rags had made her believe she was in charge of her own life, not some slave to the monsters.

"You will now take me to see my mother," she stated.

He looked at Felith as if she was really stupid. "You must think you are really something to keep trying to order me around. I'm the one in charge here. You are nothing in this world."

"I know," Felith said calmly. "Now take me to see my mother."

Getting up, the doctor walked to the door. When Felith got up to follow he shook his head at her. "You can just stay here and think about how much trouble you are in here," he said and walked out closing the door behind him. She heard the lock snicker into place, then the light was turned off, and there she was in darkness again, locked up. Darkness she knew, monsters she knew, what she didn't know was what was happening to Fred and Rags. That was the only thing that worried her. Well, and rats in the dark, so she climbed up on table and laid down, curling up to keep warm in this dark, cold place.

Rags paced the room they had locked her up inside. She knew it had been well over the time she was suppose to call Sidney. He'd be on his way by now, she knew him well enough to know that he'd come ready to take on the whole world if needed. Thing is, what would he do with the kids? The thought of Felith being dragged off drugged like that spiked sharply in her mind. We have to get her out of here, Rags thought, before they do something that kills her.

Locked in the cell, Fred too was trying to think of a way to protect Felith. He had let the beast in him come out more out of panic than anything else when they had first taken Felith. He regretted that madness now, but at the time all he could think of was they were about to hurt Felith. And he had fed that beastly side of him to the guards and that dick of a doctor to warn them off of harming Felith. Still they had her, doing something to her. If only he had kept his head, not gone to that dark insane place where rage tore him up. If only he had swallowed his pride and gone to his father. If onlys were not things that would free Felith. Action of some sort was required. But what the hell did he do? The anger was starting to build up again, and it took all of Fred's will to beat it down, to keep from trying to break the bars on his cell and go to Felith. He had to be smart and think.

The hours seemed to drag on, and Fred was at the point of letting loose the rage inside him when he heard footsteps coming down that long hallway. His heartbeat spiked into a pounding throb of anticipation, then stopped and stuttered down to a thrum of anger when he didn't see the frail form of Felith. It wasn't until he saw Sidney that hope crawled into him. It wasn't a solid hope, but the trickle was there tickling his mind, Sidney would do something. "They touched her. I know they don't know what that does to her, but the filthy beast touched her. We have to get her out of there," he spilled out the moment Sidney was close enough to hear without him raising his voice.

"Take a breath, son. I'm getting you out of here," Sidney said, his face held a certain grim look mixed with determination. "Whatever you do don't hit anyone. I've convinced them that you were off your medication. Here, take this now so they all see you take it," he said handing Fred a large pill.

Fred grabbed the pill and dry swallowed it. He opened his mouth wide and flipped his tongue around to show everyone he had swallowed the pill. Fred didn't even question Sidney as to what the pill would do to him. He'd swallow poison if needed to save Felith and Rags. "Where are the kids? Are they safe?" Fred asked.

"Robert and Emily are watching them. Emily has turned into a tiger where the kids are concerned," Sidney paused. "Now I'm going to give you a shot, which is to sedate you," Sidney said as he pulled a filled syringe out of a pocket and a cotton swab.

With quick swipes Fred pulled up his shirt sleeve to expose his arm. He didn't flinch when Sidney plunged the needle into his upper arm. He faked a little sway as if the shot was affecting him. There was no way to know what Sidney had shot him up with, but Fred was certain it wasn't anything that would sedate him. "Okay, that should keep him calm, boys. Now we need to get Officer Raglan to take charge of him. That woman is a force of nature. Believe me, she can lay him out flat if he gets out of hand again," Sidney said to the men behind him. "And, as agreed, this will all be wiped from the records. You boys never saw any of us. The

President appreciates your cooperation," Sidney went on as he led what appeared to be a woozy Fred out of the cell and down the hallway.

Moments later they were at a door that was locked. When it was opened for them Fred saw Rags pacing back and forth. She saw the two of them and walked calmly to where they stood. Sidney again took over. "I sedated him, Officer. He shouldn't give you any trouble now. We just need to collect my other patient and we will be good to go," he said, acting as if he barely knew Rags.

She took her cue and grabbed Fred roughly as if aggravated at the trouble he had caused her. "I hope you used a rusty needle on him, sucker getting me into a fight," she turned to Fred. "Your little outing has been cancelled. Now walk," she barked at him. The guards snickered at seeing Fred being bossed around by a woman. He let his head droop as if the drug he'd been given was knocking him nearly out, and shuffled along beside her as the guards took them over to another locked room.

When they unlocked the door to the room Felith was being held in, it took all the strength in Fred not to raise his head and run into that room. The darkness of the room hit him like a fist to the gut. What the hell? A guard reached over to a switch outside the room and flipped it up, flooding the room with light. He felt Rags grab his arm and grind his teeth as tight as he could to force himself to play the part Sidney had given him. Fred slumped against the door jamb preventing anyone from going in while he looked his fill of Felith's body curled in a tight ball on top of a table. His body actually trembled with the effort of assuming the pose of a drugged out guy. His eyes drank in that pitiful figure on the table and only when he saw her take a breath did he allow Sidney to enter the room.

"Who the hell locked my patient in a dark room?" Sidney demanded. His face was a mask of anger, as he bent over Felith and took her pulse. She was so damn cold.

"The doc put her in here," one of the guards said. "We had orders not to touch her." There was a defensive air to the man, as if he felt it unfair to have to take the blame for something he hadn't done. He also glanced quickly at Fred as if assuring himself Fred was under control. He watch Fred's mouth move and thought he said 'I'll kill him', but he couldn't be certain. It was a relief when the Raglan woman took Fred into the room and told him to carry the girl out. He watched Fred kiss the girl's cheek and wondered what he would do if anyone mistreated his own wife. He'd kill them. So he caught Fred's eye and nodded at him. His way of saying I understand.

Chapter Fouteen

THOSE SHE LOVES

A black car with tinted windows was waiting at the exit to the building as Sidney led his charges outside. Sidney motioned Rags to get in the front passengers seat, while he and Fred scooted into the back seat with Felith across their laps. Sidney immediately started trying to determine what was wrong with Felith, as the car pulled out and started winding its way through the streets. Nobody spoke, each had only one thought on their mind, saving Felith.

"She is so cold. Cover as much of her body as you can, Fred. Honey, put the heater on up there. General, drive faster, we have to get her some place warm and get some fluids in her," Sidney ordered as if he was back in the Marines.

"Make us a hole," barked General Richards. No sooner were the words out of his mouth than two black cars zoomed pass them flashing lights at the traffic in front of them. Fred, for once, didn't care about wasting the taxpayer's money on an escort. He laid his body over as much of Felith as he could, giving her his warmth, whispering over and over to her, "Come back, dearest, come back to me." He was careful not to kiss her or touch her in any manner that might send her deeper into whatever place she had gone to escape that dark room, just surrounding her with his own body warmth.

The car became so heated inside that Sidney took off his suit coat and still sweat dampened his shirt. Fred didn't care, he'd burn in Hell if it would warm Felith up. He could feel her heartbeat and thought it was getting stronger. Come on, baby, he thought, fight your way back. The car was slowing, it turned and entered what felt like a covered garage. Car doors opened and slammed around them, then Sidney was getting out and reaching for Felith. Fred shook his head at Sidney, and held Felith to him as he scooted out of the car. Then they were surrounded by men in dark suits with guns in holsters, and shuffled off to an elevator.

"Do they have some fluids for her, Sidney?" Fred was asking when the elevator stopped moving and the doors opened. There stood his mother and father, mom twisting her hands nervously and his father looking as if it was an every day event taking in people like them.

"We got them, sir. No problems. Girl's ill though," General Richards barked. He went over and parked himself in a plush chair as if the whole thing had taken the wind out of his sails. The dark suits had taken up positions around the room their eyes watchful, their mouths shut tight.

It was Fred's mother who broke the tension of the suddenly still room. "Bring her in here. There is a bed set up for you. You can put her there," she said, well aware that Fred's face held a dark angry scowl. As they walked to the room his mother constantly twisted her hands as if she wanted to say or do something but didn't know if Fred would allow it. Rushing ahead she turned down the bed so Fred could lay Felith down.

As gently as he could, Fred laid Felith down on the bed. He carefully removed her shoes and pulled the covers up to her chin. And despite his resolve not to kiss her he had to just kiss her forehead, just to touch her in some way that spoke of how he felt. Finally he turned to his mother. "She needs fluids, liquid nourishment."

"I'm certain your father has already called for a doctor. She'd be more comfortable if we removed those jeans and maybe her blouse. I have a nightgown she can use," his mother said in that I'm taking charge voice she always had when he was a little boy.

"No. You leave her clothing alone. In fact nobody touches her but Sidney or myself. You let anyone else touch her and I'll pick her up and leave this place. Understand?" Fred said, letting his mother read the determination on his face. He had nothing in common with her or his father any longer. His only concern was his family.

"Fredrick, despite what you think, your father and I love you. He pulled this whole rescue off in a matter of hours. Anything you want we will get for you, just know we love you. And your wife is welcome to stay here for as long as you both want. You don't have to be rude. We know you have no reason to love us. But try to remember, we do love you," his mother said with a slight tremble in her voice.

She could feel the lights were on, that touch on the eyelids which spoke of light. Along with that touch there was the thought that something was on her forehead. Slowly she reached up and touched her forehead finding a slight hint of something. What she didn't know, just that something had touched her there. She was certain of it. The lingering feel of the touch somehow soothed her. Felith heard a door open and let herself wake the rest of the way up. She struggled to sit up feeling weakness sweep over her, sapping what little strength she had. A woman stood watching her from the doorway. Not a monster, Felith thought as she started to swing her legs off the bed she lay upon.

"Oh, dear. Let me help you up. I have a few dresses that might fit you once you have had a shower. Do you need help in the shower?" the woman asked.

Felith took a moment to let the words play over her mind, as she tried to reason where she was, and what had happened after the monster locked her in the dark room. Fred must have gotten her out. But who was this woman? "No, I do not need any help. Where is Fred?" Felith countered.

"He is getting dressed, after his own shower. Believe me he didn't want to leave you even for a moment, but that man, Sidney, talked him into washing up."

"Sidney is here? Where? Is Rags here too? And the kids, where are my kids?" Felith swung questions left and right at the woman while struggling to her feet. She managed a wobbly stand, holding up her hand to ward off the woman, who had started crossing the room towards her. A door on the other side of the room opened and Fred stood there. Felith breathed a sigh of relief.

Looking from Felith to his mother, Fred's mouth hardened into a straight line. The woman never gave up. He looked back to Felith and drank in her essence. Striding across the room he stopped in front of her. "Are you up to taking a bath? I'll stay right outside the bathroom so nobody disturbs you. Rags went to buy you some new jeans and a top. She should be here any moment. Lean on my arm, honey, and I'll see you to the tub. I'll have Rags bring those clothes to you when she arrives. Just take a nice long soaking in hot water. Okay?" he said, as much to prevent his mother from interfering as anything else.

"Sidney first. And the kids if they are here," Felith said and sank back down on the bed.

"Food," he added to her list of firsts. Fred looked over to where his mother was standing, disapproval plain on her face. "Tell Sidney we need him and have some breakfast brought for Fel. Eggs, bacon and pancakes with some juice," he told her.

"I do have some dresses that should come close to fitting her, Fredrick. There is no reason to put her in those jean things," she argued.

"Yes, there is a reason. My wife prefers jeans and that is enough reason for me to keep her supplied in jeans for as long as she wants them. He said, clearly up for any argument she might put forth. "And have them hurry that food along," he added in a dismissive manner.

While they waited for the food and Sidney to arrive, Fred called the kids and handed the phone to Felith. He smiled listening to how her voice changed when she was talking to the kids. She was a great mom. Rags arrived with Sidney and several shopping bags. They took turns talking to the kids, and then to Rosemary and Emily, who only listened, and lastly Robert. A table was brought with chairs for all of them to be seated upon, along with a huge breakfast for everyone. Fred's mother came in to take a seat and eat with them. Finally Felith came up for a breath from stuffing food into her mouth. Fred's mother had watched Fel as if fascinated as she daintily ate her own grapefruit.

"Are the monsters going to come after us?" Felith asked Sidney.

Sidney's expression turned fierce as he remembered her being locked up in that dark room. "No. They have orders to erase us from their records and forget about us. They won't bother us again," he told her, hoping that assurance would be enough to keep her from retreating again into whatever safe place her mind took her to. Then she surprised him.

"Tell me about antibodies. What do they do?" Felith asked. Fred looked worried beside her. He knew that she was thinking of all the people who might get ill without a vaccine for the virus which had devastated the world.

For a moment Sidney gathered his thoughts, worrying because he knew that for Felith to ask about antibodies she was looking for a solution. "The simple answer is that the body has a defense system. Antibodies are used by the body to fight off threats to the body. Antibodies are recruited by the body to identify and fight off things like bacteria and viruses. They rush in and attach themselves to whatever is causing the sickness and destroy it. When a new sickness comes along the body has to find the right way to fight it, and thus needs to create something that will work. That is, if it can fight off the disease before the patient becomes too ill to recover. It is more complicated than that, but that gives you the idea."

"So instead of killing all the things attacking Rags, I should have worked creating antibodies? If I had then they could have made a vaccine to help others?" Felith asked Sidney.

"It wasn't your fault," Sidney, Rags, and Fred said at the same time. It was Fred who continued. "You didn't have time to think on such things, and neither did we. Rags would have died. What we need to do is practice, like we did on controlling how much you heal at a given time," he said trying to send her reassurances. "We will figure it out, honey." He could see the subject was still on her mind as she got up and leaned on him to the bathroom. Going to just outside the bathroom door he looked to where the others sat at the table. "You know she will have to find a way now that the idea has been planted in her mind. We need to find a way to help her. How can she make the body produce antibodies for that damn virus or anything else, Sidney?" he asked.

"We don't even know how she heals. I think we need to understand how she does that to get any idea on how she can do the other," Sidney said. His face was lined in worry.

"What sort of voodoo is this you are talking about? Who are these people you have gotten yourself mixed up with, Fredrick? You need to start thinking sane thoughts, not let this cult, or whatever it is, think for you," his mother tore into Fred, a mother out to protect her baby. Three shocked faces looked at her and suddenly she felt maybe she should have approached this some other way. The look on Fred's face made her fear she would lose him entirely.

"Once again you have judged me without knowing the facts. The people you are talking about are my family. That girl in the bathroom almost died using her power to keep me from dying, but you don't know that, having never bothered to find out about my life, or try to understand who I am. We will be leaving here as soon as my wife is ready. Thank you for letting us stay over night," Fred said, grinding his teeth and scowling so darkly that his mother took a deep breath, then turned leaving the room.

"Son, she just is afraid of losing you again. And remember it took all of us a while to come to terms with what Felith can do. Rags and I will support you in whatever you do, but don't part from your parents without trying to make them understand," Sidney said. "They may never understand, but you will know you tried at least."

Fred's shoulders drooped, he didn't want to disappoint Sidney, for the man had stood by him and been honest with him. Finally he nodded his head. "I'll give it a try before we leave. I promise," he said.

That promise found Fred in a room with his parents an hour later. He didn't know what he was going to say, really not even wanting to talk to them, but he had promised Sidney he would talk to them. He had just stepped into the room and was about to tell them he was going to be leaving when Felith came up and stood by him. The relief he felt was so strong it swept over him giving him strength he hadn't realized he needed. "You haven't formally met my wife. This is Felith. We have three children named Middy, Eric and Susan. At the present moment we are living with Felith's parents, whom you have met. I suggest you learn who we are before we speak again. Thank you again for the help."

"One moment, Fredrick," Stanley Whiting barked. "Your mother tells me you almost died. How did that happen?"

Anger sparked in Fred, but he pushed it down. They couldn't learn about him if he didn't answer their questions. "There was a confrontation between Felith's brother and a rather nasty fellow over Robert's girlfriend, now wife. The guy caught me unawares when I bent down to see if Robert was okay. He pretty much beat me to death," Fred took Felith's hand for support. "Fel…," he turned to Felith, "You scared the shit out of me healing me like that. I was so afraid you'd kill yourself, and you almost did." Then back to his parents. "Felith almost died while helping me live. I was never so scared as when I saw the life going out of her eyes. Now we have a plane to catch. This is our home phone number and address. Goodbye."

Felith too extended a slip of paper to them. "My cell phone," she said, then turned and left the room with Fred.

There was something about riding up that long dusty road to the house that brought the feeling of arriving home to Fred. His body finally relaxed from the tense battle-ready state it had been in ever since the General had first arrived on the farm to take Rags. He looked over at Felith and realized that her face was glowing. She too must feel that sense of coming home. He smiled, a real smile, that bloomed on his face and spread through his body like a light seeking out darkness. She didn't flinch any more when he touched her hand, or when he kissed her cheek. He was making progress. One day he would be able to fully make her his. "Their here!" The shrill shout from Middy penetrated Fred's musing. They were truly home.

The car door was flung open and two small bodies launched themselves into the car and latched onto Fred and Felith. "Emily made ice cream and cake and so much stuff. Hurry, hurry! We have a feast for you," Middy's babble was so fast that Felith could barely understand her.

Eric had finally let go of Fred and was shyly watching Middy bounce up and down on Felith. It was Fred that brought the kids into order in his usual calming manner. "I believe that you want us to hurry into the house. So how about you let Felith get out of the car, Middy. And you, Eric, may help carry in the luggage." He watched Eric's face take on a look of importance at having been giving a task. It was great how Felith had implanted such a sense of purpose in the kids. They didn't look at being given something to do as a chore, but more as a reward. With that outlook they would never end up dissatisfied and grumpy over anything they had to tackle in life.

Baby Susan was crawling across the floor when the others walked into the living room. The baby gave a happy screech and crawled to Felith. Fel picked the baby up and gave her hugs and kisses then sat her down. To her surprise Susan got up and toddled two steps in Fred's direction before sitting down with a heavy thump. "She walked," Fred and Felith said at the same time. They looked at each other and smiled. Fred's eyes soften. "I want to kiss you so much it hurts," he confessed. Shaking his head at his own foolishness he picked up Susan and headed to the dining room, wondering if he had just blown all the progress he had made with Felith.

Dinner was a joyous event with even Julian behaving herself. They had been gone only a few days, but it seemed so much longer to Felith. She had not liked the bustle of the big city, or the constant feeling that people were in a struggle with each other over things that it made no sense to be tugging over. And then there was Fred. What had he meant by it hurt him? She wanted to touch him and see if she had missed something in healing him at that monster's place. Felith watched him carefully, ready to lean across the table and heal should he show any pain.

Julian fidgeted at the table wanting the dinner to be over. Somehow she had to get that girl, Felith, alone. The baby had started kicking and seemed active, only she was gaining so much weight, it didn't seem normal. As much as she had fought the idea of having a baby, that little fluttering movement inside her had her already loving this baby. It had to be okay, it just had to be healthy. She waited until that girl was done helping with clean up in the kitchen, and the others were outside playing with the children before approaching her. She found that girl in Middy's room straightening the bed for bedtime. Stopping on the opposite side of the bed she crossed her arms and waited for that girl to look at her.

Only when she was satisfied that the bed would be comfortable for Middy did Felith look up at Julian. It was clear Julian wanted something. To try to make her feel bad, to feel superior, or some favor, something was there in her eyes. "What is it?" Fel asked going directly to the question as usual. She was surprised that Julian hesitated and almost looked embarrassed.

For a moment Julian thought she should just leave, after all, she had never shown anything but her contempt for this filthy creature. Only she wasn't a filthy creature, was she? So Julian swallowed her pride and spoke. "I'm worried about my baby. I think I'm gaining too much weight. Can you tell if something is wrong?" she asked.

"I must touch you," Felith stated and reached out placing her hand on Julian's bulging belly. She closed her eyes to concentrate better on following the path to the baby. She could feel the blood rushing through Julian as her blood pressure went up. That wasn't good. Carefully Felith sought out the baby, and paused, eyes opening in surprise. There was the reason for the weight gain, but what was the cause of the blood pressure going up. She explored, uncertain as to what she should do. Ever since she found out she had messed up in how she healed Rags she had questioned herself, her ability to heal. Was she doing more harm than good? Julian shifted as if wanting to draw away from Fel's touch, and Fel knew it was time to stop exploring. She withdrew her hand, rocking back so there was some distance between her and Julian before she spoke. "The babies are doing well, but there is something going on with you that does not seem right. I think you should consult a medical doctor?"

Julian just stared at her, not speaking, not moving for a long moment. Finally she found her voice. "Babies?"

"Yes, two. I think you should either see a medical doctor, or let me read up on things before I try to heal the other thing.

"Babies," Julian mumbled to herself as she walked away, leaving Felith wondering if she was to read up on Julian's condition or not. Read up she would anyway as she needed to know what else might be wrong.

It was late by the time Felith had researched the problem she felt inside Julian over the internet. Clearly she would have to tell Julian to see a medical doctor, as there was no way she would endanger the babies Julian carried by trying to treat her, and doing it wrong. Tissue she could make heal back, but this was something she just didn't know how to fix. It was becoming more and more clear that she needed to study medicine to understand what needed to be done for people. The injuries she could heal. Even the virus she could heal, but was she doing it the way it needed to be done, the way it was needed done to help everyone?

Her eyes were tired from reading the many articles on the internet. What she needed was sleep. Entering the bedroom she saw Fred already asleep laying on top of the covers, his face a study in pain. His words 'it hurts me' flashed through her mind. Why? Why did it hurt him? As Fel watched Fred he began to toss about as if fighting off demons, or monsters. The monsters couldn't have him, she wouldn't let them. Carefully she laid down and placed a hand upon Fred's out stretched hand, she sought out the pain he was feeling, only something strange happened….

He was with a girl walking through what looked like a gate into a huge yard behind a house that looked closed down. They were laughing, Fred gazing at the girl taking in her beauty as if it was all he needed in life. "I think this place would be beautiful once it is fixed up. The garden is something to see, Fredrick. Come on," the girl said grabbing Fred by the hand and tugging him around the house into the secluded yard. Four boys of Fred's age were standing as if waiting for the girl and Fred. The girl left Fred and went to the boys. "I told you I could get him to come here," the girl said.

*Felith saw the boys surrounding Fred grabbing
him as he looked in silence at the girl he had trusted,
his young heart breaking at her betrayal. The boys
twisted his arms behind him tying him up. "Fag" one
of them spat out the word as if spitting on Fred with it.*

"NO!" Felith shouted the word in her mind
and suddenly she was back on the bed with her arms
wrapped protectively around Fred. His body relaxed,
softly his breath swished out as if on a sigh, and he
slept quietly. I'll protect you, Felith thought, from
the monsters.

The light penetrated Fred's eyelids alerting him
to the early dawn. He felt someone wrapped around
him and shoved the person off him with enough
force to send them off the bed. It was an automatic
reaction, and by time his brain caught up with where
he was, he heard the thud of Felith hitting the floor.
Fred rolled and looked over the bed, almost afraid to
see her reaction considering how hard it was for her
to let others touch her. She was rubbing her shoulder
and looking up at him. He felt like a heel. "Are you
okay?" he asked, his voice graveled with regret.

Fel nodded and, instead of looking at Fred
as if he was one of the monsters she had grown up
among, she lifted her hand to be pulled up. "I want
to study medicine," she said, completely throwing
Fred's mind sideways.

"Okay," Fred said carefully, unsure what his
reaction should be as his mind was still on having
thrown her out of bed. Still he managed to make the
shift to what she was saying. Already he could see
obstacles in the way. She would need a high school

diploma to apply to a medical college. And how was he to get her accepted without a 4.0 average? "Medical school is hard to get into. You'll need a 4.0 average to stand a chance of being accepted. You were being home schooled, right?" Felith looked at him as if it had not occurred to her that it would be a problem.

"Then I will just study from home. Surely there is information on how the body works, like on antibodies. Those are the things I want to know," Fel said.

The antibody thing again. She's lost faith in her abilities, Fred thought. Her abilities were too precious to be wasted because of one miscalculation, so he nodded. "We'll start today. I'm going to order two high tech computers for us. You will study on one of them, I'll look up information for you to study on the other one. We will have you so full of knowledge even the best scholars will pale before you," he assured Fel. She nodded in that way she did when having decided the course was set. Inside he smiled, this was something he could do for her. He was so relieved she hadn't gone away in her mind from him throwing her off the bed.

They settled into family life, laughing at the children when they were playing, the others joking and yakking at the dinner table. Fred even threw in a joke once in a while to everyone's surprise. He seemed less angry as the days and weeks passed, even content in helping Felith study through all the science of how the body works. The nightmares seemed to have eased off for Fred. They had only been triggered back in full force at having the lack of control when he had been locked up at that laboratory. The hard knots that were so often a part of Fred's life began to unravel. The only thing that was keeping his life from being complete was his desire to make love to his wife, to Felith, and that was an ever throbbing pain in his groin. Yet, despite the constant desire for his wife to love him and want him, Fred was happy. He smiled more, and was kinder to Rosemary and Julian. Part of him thought he was finally working through the anger he felt at having been betrayed by those he knew and had thought were his friends, but another part of him still held that anger tight in it's fist, ready to distrust, to scorn. Only that weird girl, his wife, made him want to open that fist and let the anger go.

It was the day before Easter, and Julian was gathering eggs from the hen house for the egg hunt they would have on Easter after breakfast, when she saw dust clouding the dirt road from the highway to the farm. She shaded her eyes trying to make out who was driving to the farm. Black cars all in a line were getting closer and closer. Julian rubbed her belly where one of the twins moved around. "It is okay my little one. Mommy is here." She had found herself talking to the babies more and more as they grew and took on personalities even in the womb. She smiled at herself remembering how she had sworn never to have children. How these two little lives inside her had changed her over the months. Who was coming? And what could they want here in this haven built by that weird girl?

Black cars full of powerful engines and

powerful people lined the drive in front of the farmhouse by the time Felith made it back from the field where she had been tending the plants that would bear them vegetables in a few weeks. She slapped the dust from her hands and braced to catch the small boy running all out towards her. Eric had changed from the little boy afraid of any and everything into a child that ran about taking in life with deep joy. She caught him as he leaped into her arms. "It is the grandparents, Mom. They have come to visit," he said, almost beside himself with pleasure.

"Then let us not keep them waiting, honey. Come on," Felith said, taking Eric's hand and swinging it back and forth between them as they walked to the waiting black cars. She looked around to see if Fred was back from his chores, and was relieved to see him trudging in the distance in her direction. These were his family waiting at the farmhouse for them. As he caught up with her and Eric Felith could see the worry on Fred's face. "What is it?" she asked, looking to where the black cars sat in a row.

Fred glanced at her, his mouth seemed to want to shut tight and not speak, but he knew it was better to tell her the truth, "There are too many cars. This isn't a simple visit." He saw her nod of understanding, and that scared him. She was so protective of everyone that he feared she would do something which would bring her harm. Why couldn't he have just lied to her? Because he couldn't, not to her, not ever. So Fred slipped his hand into her free hand, looking at her, his eyes trying to communicate how much he wanted her, he said,

"Let's see what they want."

Suited men had spread out and were searching the outbuildings, their faces grim and determined. Fred's expression was one of worry mixed with anger. His parents were invading his home with the crap he had grown up having to accept as an everyday part of his life. More than his irritation at what was going on was his worry over what Felith thought, and he watched her closely for any sign of withdrawal. His father saw him walking towards him. There was a wary look upon his father's face that Fred had never seen before. And that as much as anything else worried him. His father was not an indecisive man. If he was having cautious thoughts then something serious was up.

"Fredrick, sorry to show up like this, but if we could talk in private for a moment," Stanley said, watching his son's interaction with the little boy by his side. It was clear the boy adored Fredrick. When the little black baby toddled over and wrapped her arms around his son's leg, Stanley's mind went blank for a moment. Three children, two of them too old to have been fathered by his son and the other black. What in the world was his son thinking taking on this bunch of riffraff? That girl must have something on his son, be blackmailing him or threatening him in some way. Then Stanley saw his son look over at Felith and the wind went out of his sails. No, Fredrick was smarter than that and he adored that girl. So he kept his mouth shut and let his son take him off to the side after the meet and greet bit was over.

Felith saw Fred motion for her to follow as

he walked off with his father. Yes, it was time they learned what was going on, so she told the children to show their rooms to the grandmother, and went to join Fred and his father. She nodded to Fred as she stepped up beside him, then turned to his father. "You may tell us now why you are here," she said in her usual blunt manner. The older man's face held an annoyed expression as he glanced at Fred.

"Really, Fredrick, this is best handled by us men," Stanley protested.

Holding up a hand to stop any protest that his father might be ready to spit out, Fred said, "We are a family and anything that happens is both our concerns. So just spit it out, Father."

The two men seemed locked into some staring contest for several seconds before Stanley gave in and spoke. "There has been a threat on her," he said motioning with his head towards Felith. "Some babble came through one of our sources mentioning her, just her. Seems she has pissed off a low life who was having trouble getting back into the country. Unfortunately this guy was allowed in before the babble reached the right ears. We are going to leave a team here for your protection, or you can come back with us to D.C.."

"To protect my wife you mean. She is the one being threatened, and they will extend that protection to the rest of our family, especially the children. Or, you can leave now taking your men with you," Fred said, his voice soft and dangerous. He reached over and took Felith's hand to make his point.

God he is hardheaded, Stanley thought. "I

will talk with them and see what we can arrange. But you are my concern, you will always be a target because of my work," he said, not even looking at Felith. So it was, he didn't see the slight turn of her head as if to check on the children, or the way her expression became smooth, a non-expression. Fred saw it, and it scared him. This was Felith prepared to do whatever it took to protect those she loved. He'd have to watch her close to be sure she didn't go sacrifice herself to protect them.

Middy and Eric practically vibrated with excited energy, but unlike the children Virginia, Fred's mother, had experienced in her life, this pair sat with serious expression upon their faces taking in ever word the adults spoke. The black toddler, Susan, she corrected herself, was the only child that moved, toddling from person to person offering up toys, or reaching up her arms to be picked up. They were all well behaved children a credit to Fredrick no doubt. This place was so... low class. Virginia smiled and nodded at all the right moments in the conversation that floated around the room, for she hadn't become First Lady without putting on a good face when around the voters. It was just that this was her son, her Fredrick, and he appeared to want to live this way. She could feel a headache coming on, as she took the toy from Susan and then gave it back to her. It was a relief when dinner was announced.

Dinner was a shock to the visitors. Everyone was included, a line of tables had been set up with what looked like every available chair in the house. It looked like something from a comical movie. Then Fredrick was calling to the guards to come in and eat. Servants at the table, how crude. Only the expressions on the faces of the people who lived here seemed to say this was the way meals should be served, so Stanley and Virginia took the offered seats beside Fredrick and nodded at the men serving them to come on and join them. The second surprise was holding hands while the blessing was said. But what shocked Stanley the most was when the meal was winding down and they were on dessert. It was then that Fredrick's wife spoke to these people, her family.

"We have been told there is a threat directed, so they say, at me. Robert and Julian you should go to town to be certain you are safe. Emily and Rosemary you will take the children to town for the same reason," Felith said, then looked over at Sidney and Rags. "I do not wish for you to stay here in harms way, but the decision will be yours. However, I'd like to know you are with the children to take care of them if needed," Felith paused and turned to Fred. "They need one parent alive," she said, in that straight forward way of hers.

"I'm not going to leave you. We're family," Middy said standing and stamping her foot.

"I stay too," Piped up Eric, his bottom lip sticking out in determination. It was the first time he had taken a stand on anything. Felith wanted to hug him.

"I'm your sister now, you can't just send me off like that. And like she said, we are family," Rosemary said, her face pale as if afraid of being sent away anyway.

"I'll take Julian to town but then come back to help," Robert said, his lips drawn tight as if just saying that was scaring him.

A hand slapped the table and Emily, her face crimson in anger, pointed at herself then at the floor, her meaning clear.

Sidney stood up. "It looks like we have decided to stay with you. That is what families do, stay and help each other."

"Um, I'm not leaving either," Julian said, to everyone's surprise. "You are my doctor and I want to be nearby, besides…" she lowered her gaze as if embarrassed, "We are family."

They were all looking at Felith, watching as she looked from one of them to the other, waiting for her to give the final verdict on what they may do. She finally nodded. Inside she was unsure what had happened just then, but outside she couldn't show a weakness.

Fred watched Fel as her mind raced with thoughts of how to protect all of those she loved. She was still and silent. That did not bode well. It was then that Dog decided to make an appearance. Perhaps he sensed the tension in the house. Whatever the reason, he bound in and skidded to a halt with his lips drawn back and slobber dripping from his jaws. Ten men stood up and drew guns on Dog.

"You will not shoot my dog," Felith said. "He is here to protect, and must approve of anyone who is to stay here. Put your guns away while Dog looks you over."

Not one man looked away from the huge beast facing them, or put away their weapon. To their credit they didn't flinch when Dog came up and sniffed each of them. All but one. When the man broke and ran screaming at the top of his voice Dog sat down with his tongue hanging out one side of his mouth as if laughing. Then he went over and licked Middy and then Eric on the face. The tension in the room broke into a sparkle of laughter.

The effect of everyone speaking up saying they would stay was like a shock-wave flowing over Felith. She had to protect them. No matter what, this monster was not going to harm anyone here. And in order to protect them, she needed information about who the threat might be. With this in mind, she turned to Stanley Whiting. "I would like to ask you, just who it is that is threatening me?" she said.

One of the security team stood up, he put his hands behind his back and took a stance, legs set wide, shoulders back and head held level looking Felith in the eyes. "We have verified the man making the statements is your step-father. He evidently had fled the country after his attack on you. Although he seems to claim he was abducted by someone and transported to Africa while sedated. He blames you, as ridiculous as that claim is knowing that you were unconscious yourself at the time of the so called incident. Believe me we have investigated the ravings of this man thoroughly. When we realized that the ravings about killing a girl was actually pointed towards the wife of the President's son we tried to intercept the man making the threats, however, the team sent failed in that attempt," he held up his hand to stop any interruptions. "He was seen on a security cam exiting a transporter which docked a week ago in Louisiana. That sighting placed him too close for comfort. We will be watching over you until he is apprehended."

Felith's face had been draining of color as the man talked. For a moment her knees threatened to give out on her. Then she saw Fred stand, and resolve stiffened her knees. She was the one holding up her hand to stay Fred now. He didn't stay. Instead he came to place an arm around Felith taking her weight, offering his warmth to stave off the chill that seemed to be seeping into her bones, freezing the bit of happy she had found. "Sometimes," Fred whispered into her ear, "you need to step back and let someone else take the lead, let them take care of you."

Chapter Fifteen

PANIC AND PUZZLES

Everyone was exhausted after the emotional meeting where it was revealed that Felith's stepfather was coming to do harm to her. The feeling of family was running high. Where Fred's parents fit into this rag-tag bunch was yet to be decided. Felith, as ever, did not expect anything from them. She would go by what they did or didn't do while staying with them. So it was when morning came and the family gathered for morning orders. The first thing that she became aware of was the absence of Fred's parents. The security team was around, watching, searching for hidden threats. All the family were assembled in the living room with two of the silent security men standing at each of the doorways. Just as Felith was about to issue work orders for the day Stanley and Virginia entered from the room provided them for the duration of their stay. Felith nodded and began. "Emma, you and Rosemary will have meals today, you are excused to start breakfast. Robert, you and Julian will gather eggs this morning and feed the animals, after which you are free. Middy and Eric have laundry collection, I want the two of you to stay close to the house and report any strangers you may see immediately. Fred, you and I will have the side field today. Rags, I want you on guard duty. Sidney, we need some extra supplies with this many to feed, so you figure out what we need and go into town to get it. Virginia and Stanley you may do some dusting and straightening around the house today, and be with the children. I want most of the others to guard the house and family, three of you will take turns in the front field hoeing weeds. That is all for now," she said, giving one of her dismissing nods.

All the family stood and were about to go to wash up for breakfast. It was then Virginia stood up and protested. "I'm not some maid. For God's sake I'm the First Lady! And these men are not your servants, they work for the government of the United States. You can't order them around," she said, her voice gradually rising in tone, while her chin trembled.

Stanley took his wife's hand. "We actually came here to take you all back to the D.C., where you will be safe. Playing house is not part of the game plan. There is a country to run. I can't just drop everything and stay here," he said looking over at the head of the security team whose face was so red it was only a matter of time before the veins in his forehead ruptured.

Felith looked around at them all, these strangers she had accepted, perhaps mistakenly, into her circle. "Then all of you are excused from chores. You may leave."

"Fredrick, do something, don't just stand there," Virginia said, throwing her most commanding look at her son.

Standing, Fred looked at his mother, the woman who had had such grand plans for his life. "You are welcome to stay and visit with the others while the rest of us begin our chores. Emma and Rosemary will have breakfast ready shortly, so I suggest you wash up before our morning meal. This is a working family, you can't expect us to stop and let the farm go to ruin over some threat. I know the children and everyone else would like to get to know you better, so at least stay for breakfast." He couldn't help but notice the glances between the security team. There was a glint in their eyes as if this whole thing was totally amusing to them.

It was the head of security that broke the stare down between mother and son. "If you will instruct us in the hoeing I'll see to it three men take care of that field. Am I right in assuming the field in question runs along the track into the farm?" he asked. The family, as if one, turned eyes from him to Felith. He couldn't help but suppress a grin, clearly it was the girl who held the power in this family group. He too looked to her, his face holding the expression of respect he gave heads of countries and the President himself. He had to give the girl points for not blinking an eye during this whole struggle for power.

"Yes, we have some young plants there which are just now starting to mature and produce.

Normally Fred, Robert, and I would take turns on
it, and the side field. Julian is becoming heavy with
child so I want Robert with her as much as possible.
We alternate days between weeding and other chores
to produce the food we eat and sell. You may start
after breakfast," she said, turning she walked off,
clearly finished with everyone in the room. Off to
the side, Virginia's mouth was clamped shut. The
look she shot Felith would have burned anyone else.

Seated around the table Virginia found herself
next to the boy child her son had adopted, Eric. The
little boy gave her sideway looks then reached out
and patted her arm as if comforting her. She didn't
know what to do with such a gesture, so she moved
her hand into her lap. She tried to keep quiet and
watch this mismatch bunch of people her son had
become involved with. Truly she could not see the
appeal, well Middy was very forward and charming,
and she supposed the little boy could be endearing,
but that black baby, how in the world had it come
into Fredrick's life? It was time she brought up
something that Fredrick just had to do, he had to.
"Fredrick, I want to hold a proper wedding for you
and your wife. Call it a renewal of vows if you want.
It will be the talk on everyone's lips. I know you
couldn't have afforded much of a wedding, certainly
nothing as spectacular as what I'll have done for
you and your wife," she waited for some sign the girl
approved. What she saw on the faces around the
table puzzled her. They looked at her as if she were
demented. "Well someone say something," Virginia
urged.

Of all the people in the room it was Julian

who spoke up. "I don't believe anything can top the wedding they had, Mrs. Whiting. Haven't you seen it?"

"No, dear, You have it on digital then? We'll watch it after breakfast. Only I'm certain it can not be as grand as you assume. The wedding I'll put on for them will be the talk of the entire town," Virginia countered.

Julian gave a scoffing laugh. "Talk of the town? Their wedding is the talk of the world. Look it up, millions of sites have it on the internet. Last time I looked there wasn't a country in the world that wasn't showing it." In typical Julian manner she gave a, like you'd know, look to the First Lady. "Look up The Butterfly Wedding." Several cell phones appeared in the hands of the security team sitting at breakfast. A soft 'wow' escaped from someone. Julian looked pleased with herself and turned to Robert with a smile raising an eyebrow in that, am I good, way she had.

What struck Stanley more than anything was the way this group of people worked together. There was no bickering over who was to do what, his son's wife just told them what was to be done and they did it. The kids even appeared to look forward to having a chore to do. As strange as the group was, they functioned like a well oiled machine. Maybe he should take a lesson from them. All too soon breakfast was over, Stanley sat watching as even the little boy, who looked so frail, carried his dishes to the kitchen. Fred had it all here, a family that anyone would be proud to have, and certainly that girl loved Fred. This is their life, we are the intruders, Stanley thought, as he picked up his own plate and took it to the kitchen. Virginia still sat at the table, her expression unreadable. She was in diplomatic mode. It wasn't until little Eric came and started picking up her plate that she finally unbent enough to rise and carry her own dishes into the kitchen. Good for you, Eric, Stanley thought, giving the boy a pat on the head when he walked by him. There was a difference in the security team which Stanley noticed right away. They seemed to look differently at the girl, that Felith. It was as if she had been raised in their eyes to a new level of importance. He had to see this wedding film for himself, it must be really something to change hardened men that quickly.

Despite her resistance to having been told to help, Virginia found herself helping little Eric carry laundry to the washing machine. Middy, her lips drawn tight as if in disapproval, watched every move Virginia made. When Virginia and Eric reached the washing machine Middy held out her arms for the clothes basket. Together Middy and Eric sorted the clothing and filled the washing machine with the first load of clothes. Then Middy pulled a step stool up to the washing machine, and climbed up it to set the timer and water temperature. Virginia was remembering Fredrick at that age, all knobby knees and eagerness. He had been into everything, asking endless questions, chasing butterflies around the lawn. She couldn't remember him ever taking a plate to the kitchen, or sorting a load of laundry. That was what servants were put on earth to do. She heard Stanley calling her, so she left the children to their chores and sought him out.

"Virginia, come look at this," Stanley said poking his head out of the room they had taken over. He watched his wife coming, her face had softened since breakfast, taking on a look of longing, almost pensive. "Sit down here. I found that wedding video. The girl was right, the thing is all over the place. I typed the name in and over a million sites popped up. Let's watch it together," he said.

The photographers were being lazy, taking shots here and there of the first two weddings on the video. And when Felith appeared ready to be walked down the aisle to Fredrick, the photographer certainly wasn't holding the cam recorder steady. Suddenly something caught his attention and the camera swung away from the bride where she was standing ready to walk down to where Fredrick stood on a small bridge. The camera picked up hundreds of things fluttering over the people having a day's outing. The camera followed the butterflies as they flew straight to Felith and became her train as she walked to Fredrick. The lovely colorful butterflies settled during the service, until Fredrick raised a necklace to place on Felith instead of placing a ring on her finger. Suddenly the air was filled with butterflies again, circling the couple flying down and up over the necklace, enclosing Felith and Fredrick in a cloud of pure beauty. And when their son kissed Felith the butterflies formed a whirlwind over the couples heads bursting apart when the couples lips ceased to touch like a fireworks display on the Fourth of July. Over and over again forming up, and bursting into a million bright colors. Then they were gone. There were no words Virginia could say. The girl Julian was right, nothing could top this wedding.

For three days the grandparents stayed.
Felith ignored them when she was giving out the
instructions for the day at breakfast. Virginia would
notice Middy looking sideways at her, as if each time
Felith passed over her in giving instructions for the
day's chores, it meant something. Just what it could
mean Virginia didn't know. Yet, certainly something
was troubling the child, perhaps she resented having
to do chores. Even little Eric occasionally came up
and patted Virginia on the arm as if giving comfort.
It was odd to Virginia to feel as if she, the First
Lady, was in the dark on what was going on in the
household. She wasn't use to feeling that someone
knew more than she did. Thinking she would sit the
little girl down and ask her what was wrong, Virginia
walked outside to where Middy was feeding the
chickens. Careful, so as not to step on chicken waste,
Virginia called to Middy. "Middy come, we will have
some cookies, and talk a while," she said.

Middy bit on her lip as if undecided upon
what to do. Finally she spoke in a voice way too shy
to have come from her. "Go and rest, Grandmother.
I can come in after I feed Bouncing Billy. Mother
says Billy is really a girl goat and will give us milk one
day," she said, while continuing to feed the chickens.

"I'm certain Billy won't mind if you wait until
after you have some cookies to feed her," Virginia
said. The look Middy gave her spoke of pity and
sadness more than anything else Virginia could
compare it to. "Okay, after you feed Billy then come
in and have some cookies with me, please," she said,

wondering how it was a little girl got the better of her when she had faced down the leaders of countries, as Middy ran off to feed Billy.

"Something is troubling you, Middy. Tell me what is wrong, child," Virginia said when Middy returned. She sat down and took a small cookie off the plate of cookies she placed in front of Middy.

Middy's face scrunched up for a moment then went smooth all over. She glanced sideways at Virginia, then squared her little shoulders. "You hate my mother like Julian does. I don't want you to hate my mother, grandmother," she said in a serious tone.

It gave Virginia pause. Why did the child think she hated anyone. "Darling, I don't hate your mother. I love my son, and I'm just worried she is taking advantage of him, that is all. I don't know her well enough to hate her."

"Then get to know her," Fred said from the doorway. "Middy please take one of those cookies to Eric and Susan, but only one for each of you, Emily is making cake."

The little girl's face seemed to glow at the idea of cake. She carefully selected a cookie for each of her siblings and took off like a rocket. Fred, on the other hand stood fast. "You will not grill my children on my life with Felith. Do you understand?" he said to Virginia, his voice cold, deadly.

"Frederick! I would never do something like that to a child," Virginia said, her look of horror almost convincing Fred. "I do worry though, son. She seems to have latched on to you. I am concerned that she may just be with you for your money, darling, that is all it is, a mother's concern for her child."

"You are wrong about Felith. I count myself fortunate that she accepted marriage to me," Fred growled. "She, unlike you, believes in me and takes me for the person I am," he paused before he said words more hurtful than those to his mother, walking over to confront her. "If you weren't grilling Middy, what is it you were doing?"

Glancing down at the floor, his mother took a breath as if girthing herself. "The child has been looking troubled when around me. I just wanted to know what was upsetting her. I don't hate her mother, dear. I just wanted to help the child," she said, finally looking up at Fred so he could see she was sincere. "Why would she think such a thing about her mother and myself?" Virginia asked.

It was a long moment before Fred spoke. He thought of the life they had here, the balance between people, and it occurred to him that his parents were not part of the daily life here. They behaved as outsiders, not accepting the manner of life his family lived. "I think it is because you behave like you are not part of the family. You made it very clear you would not stoop to doing daily chores, which is something all of us do to maintain the family. Felith does not give you chores, not because she doesn't like you or judges you, but because you have shown you can't be trusted to think of the whole instead of yourself. Julian was like that for the longest time. A primping girl feeling she was entitled to others serving her. And it is true, you do feel entitled to being served. Do you know that, for Middy, the worst punishment given is to tell her she is free from chores? You are free from chores, so there must be something wrong with you in her eyes."

"I never... I never thought of it that way, son. So if I'm not sick Middy expects me to do something around the house too?" she mused.

"Don't try to convince her you are sick, mother. She knows Felith would heal you if you had the slightest thing wrong with you. She'd make herself sick doing it, but she would be there for you," Fred snapped, leaving unsaid the words, unlike you and father deserting me, then turned to leave before he let his anger take over and ruin the small peace he had made with his mother. He was trying. Trying was harder work than plowing a field.

Virginia stared at Frederick's back, she just couldn't believe in witch healing, voodoo, or whatever Fred thought the girl did to heal people. "Dear, can we keep it quiet, that voodoo thing? The election is coming up so soon on us, and we don't need bad publicity. Please, son," she said.

He started to turn around, only barely able to stop himself from losing control of his temper and swinging around to shout at his mother. He knew his voice was cold, cynical. "You should both be very happy. I've handed you a dream for the campaign haven't I? Your only child married what people consider a nothing girl, adopting three orphans, one of them black. Hell, your husband should win on that alone," he said, then realized Felith was standing at the door. It felt like his heart stopped beating. She didn't change expression the tiniest bit, but she did one slow blink of her eyes and walked on out of the house. "Oh, God," Fred said, his voice filled with the pain he knew he had caused her. "If I lose her my life is over," a hand on his shoulder surprised him.

"I'll go talk to her. I'm going to make this right son," Virginia said softly, passing him up in a flurry of perfume.

Panic, pure panic seized Fred's heart. He must have sounded like an opportunist trying to take advantage of Felith to her. Should he run after her, tell her that he was trying to make his mother see how ridiculous her and his father were to always think of the campaign and never the family? He had only just began to feel Felith was trusting him a little. Now, now he may have killed anything she felt for him. Sidney had made it clear that all her life Felith had been used by men in the most despicable ways, and now he had made it sound as if he was using her too. Why, why did his mother have to always push for the glamour instead of having feelings for others? Suddenly Fred stopped as if frozen. What he saw on the porch wasn't Fel, she was not in sight, which didn't surprise him knowing how fast she could move at times. No, there was his father bent over, with one hand clutching his chest and gasping. In the other hand he held one of his work satellite phones. "Father, what is wrong?" Fred asked, reaching out and guiding his father to a seat.

"White House, bomb," his father gasped, his pallor pasty and lips grimacing. "Heart, think heart, son, get help."

Fel, he had to find Fel. Off near the goat pen

Fred saw his mother's skirt swish around a corner. His mother had gone after Fel too. Not even pausing he ran at full speed to where he thought his mother and Felith were standing. Relief flooded over him when he saw his mother talking to Felith's back. He didn't think of all the hurt he must have put on Fel earlier. The only thing in his mind at the moment was getting Felith to his father. "Fel, come quickly. You are needed, right now," he said barely waiting to see if she heard him before dashing back to his father. He was relieved when it registered that she was running beside him. She hadn't stopped to question why she was needed, she just ran with him. Maybe he hadn't completely lost her. Behind them Fred heard his mother's huffing and puffing after them. When the porch came in view, Fred heard his mother cry out "Stanley!" Then they were there.

"Do just enough, honey. I don't want you to die for him. Like we practiced, find the worst and heal it. Please, darling," Fred said, knowing that Fel could be stubborn when it came to healing.

Behind Fred and Felith Virginia was frantically pushing the panic button on her phone. It would immediately call all the security guards to her location. She pushed it over and over again, not stopping even when she heard the snicker of guns being pulled out by the guards as they rushed in from everywhere. Then she saw what was going on in front of her. That girl, that weird girl was touching her Stanley. The girl paled, all color draining from her face, then her lips moved. "Bad, so much damage," Felith whispered.

"Let go of him, Fel," Fred said, more afraid

now of losing her than his father. "Let go of him. Don't you go killing yourself for him. I won't forgive you if you do. Just do enough that he can make it to the hospital." He kept on trying to talk her out of the healing mode, trying with everything inside him to not grab her and move her body away from his father. All the while he warred with himself. One-half wanting her to do enough to save his father's life, the other half wanting to protect Felith. The guards didn't help as they tried to push him away to get to their President. He was having none of that, his job was to protect Felith, to be there to catch her when she passed out. "All of you step the hell back!" he finally yelled at them. "Call a frigging chopper to take him to the hospital. Don't ANY OF YOU touch my wife while she is healing. Or ever," he growled. It was then that Fel collapsed, her body just started sliding down to the porch. Like a viper striking, Fred was there, stopping her fall, holding her to him. "Tell the medics coming I need IVs with glucose in them," Fred said, turning with Felith in his arms, he saw his mother standing there staring at him, her mouth set in a grimace. Fred couldn't bring himself to speak to his mother. Not now, not while Felith's life may hang in the balance. Let her go on not approving of Felith. It was enough that he knew his wife's worth.

He pressed his ear to Fel's chest checking for her heartbeat. "No!" The word came out of him in a gasp of anguish. Immediately he laid her down upon the hard planks of the porch and started CPR. "You damn well better not die on me, Fel. Breathe, damn you, breath you stupid, stupid girl," he ranted as he pumped on her chest over and over. A shadow fell across Fel's face as a black suited figure knelt down on the opposite side of Felith. "I'll do the breathing part, keep pumping, kid," the guys rough voice growled. It seemed like time froze. There was just Fel, the guy helping, and Fred. Nothing mattered, nothing in the world mattered but saving Fel. What the hell was he to do if she died. She was the glue that held this bunch of ragamuffins together. She was a miracle worker, a healer. A gift to a world that didn't deserve her. A million thoughts pounded at Fred, but only one screamed so loud inside him that he didn't even hear the sound of a chopper coming in. Breathe! Then she did, and Fred's heart started beating again. His head dropped to his chest.

Fred allowed himself one sob before gathering Felith in his arms and rushing into the house with her. She needed warmth and glucose. There was a small amount left in the IV bag Sidney had used last time on Felith. Middy streaked ahead of Fred to their bedroom and had the covers pulled back on the bed by time Fred got there. Tears had left tracks down the little girl's face, and it was only then that Fred realized she must have witnessed Felith dying. She was so much like Felith, already poker faced doing what was needed, thinking only of others. "Middy, I need that bag of stuff we used before. And see if you can find one of those needle things so we can get the stuff in Fel's vein," Fred told Middy as he piled blankets on top of Felith, knowing that keeping Middy busy would be best. Eric's pale face peeped around the bedroom door, and Fred motioned him to come in. The boy ran and clutched Fred's leg for a moment before letting go and looking at Felith on the bed. "Get up there next to her, son, and hold her. You'll be giving her your body warmth and that will help her. Go, on," Fred no sooner said the words than Eric was laying clutching Felith to him. "Not too tight, son, she needs to breath too." The little boy loosened his grasp and looked to Fred for approval. Fred nodded.

Middy came pounding into the room with the used IV bag in one hand. She practically ran into Fred before she stopped. Hands shaking, not knowing if he could even get the needle into Felith's arm, Fred took a deep breath and knelt down beside the bed. There was the sound of footsteps coming up behind Fred. "Move out of my way, young man. I was told this woman needs medical attention," a high pitch voice said. Fred whirled around prepared to do battle to keep Fel safe with this newcomer. "Whatcha trying to do to her?" asked a tall skinny man in green scrubs. Looking haggard, with his hair messy from the chopper ride the man rushed over and dropped his kit on the night table.

"Glucose. She needs it right away. She died again. We have to get her warm and get some sugar in her. Sidney says protein is better, but it doesn't come in IV form," Fred said, bringing the medic up to date.

The medic didn't bat an eye at Fred's words, just knelt down and began to prep a vein for the catheter he took from his kit. "You can rig some hot water bottles from old two liter coke bottles, or any bottle with a tight lid really. Run the water as hot as you can get it, then fill the bottles. You can place them around her body under the covers. They will warm her up. Oh, and wrap them in a kitchen towel to keep them from burning her skin," the man said calling over his shoulder as the little girl in the room dashed off, full speed, and the young boy/man followed her. Andy examined the girl once he had a steady drip going. She was cold, the guy hadn't been wrong on that at least. Next he pricked her skin and checked her blood sugar level. It was so low he couldn't get a reading. His adrenalin spiked as he opened a sealed syringe of huge volume. Quickly he drew up what he needed and pushed it through the IV. He'd have to monitor her sugar to be sure it didn't spike high now, but he suspected that there would be need of another dose of glucose before the night was over. Diabetics were the worse to treat. You did one thing to save their life, and it caused the opposite bad situation to manifest. You silly girl, he thought, surely you know to eat.

A member of the President's security team came into the room. "Chopper is about to leave, sir. Do I tell them we are taking her too?" he asked.

"No, I think we have this under control. I'll stay the night here. Doc has things under control on the chopper. You can send a car for me tomorrow," Andy said. With a curt nod, the security man left. Andy settled in, checking the girl's vitals, checking the drip flow, working around the little boy clinging to the girl's side. "This your sister?" he asked the little boy. Eric shook his head, all the while watching every move Andy made. "Your aunt?" inquired Andy. Again Eric shook his head. "My mother," the little boy said. Andy shook his head, this kid was mistaken, she was too young to have a child his age.

"You related to Mr. Whiting then?" Andy asked, he was only trying to distract the child, put him at ease.

"Eric is Fel and mine, as is Middy here, and baby Susan," Fred said, coming into the room with a tray filled with bottles of hot water. "Son, you can get up now and help me put these bottles under the cover next to your mother," he told, Eric. "Pull back the covers for me. You too, Middy. We'll get her nicely snuggled in warmth."

Andy watched as the young man managed to include the children in taking care of their mother. This was good, the girl had a supportive family. Now as to the why of a diabetic, known by her family, ending up in this condition. "Did she forget to eat today?" Andy asked. There was such a silence then that Andy looked up at the young man. He looked as if he had been caught in a lie of some sort. What the hell had gone on here? "She takes insulin, right?" Andy said, and noticed a look of relief flash for a moment on the guys face.

"No, Fel isn't diabetic. But she over did it today," Fred hesitated. "We know what to do for her, you can go with the others. We have her now. And thank you for the help," Fred said, hoping this medic would leave. He wasn't ready for Fel to be put under a microscope and torn apart by scientist. Ever since the time she was rushed off to that lab, Fred had been afraid she would be taken again. How was he to protect her from ignorant people who needed to tear things apart to see how they worked. If he knew nothing else, he knew that you just had to take Felith's power to heal on faith. It wouldn't be found in her blood or organs. His heart started pounding as adrenaline rushed through his body again. He was prepared to fight anyone who might try to take Felith away.

"Then you don't know that she is diabetic, or… she could have hypoglycemia. It is the opposite of being diabetic. With hypoglycemia the person produces too much insulin naturally so their body is constantly burning the sugar their body needs to function. Eventually such people become diabetic," Andy said, watching Fred closely. This young man looked to be trying to think of some excuse to get rid of Andy. Something was going on here.

"You might be right on that last part. She has been weak a lot. And she certainly is an active person. It is hard to get her to rest and relax. I think all that scare with Dad's heart sent her over the edge. We'll make certain she eats and takes care of herself. Thank you, doctor, for all the help," Fred said, sitting down beside Felith's still form, clearly indicating Andy could leave.

"I'll be staying over night. There is no way I can leave a patient in crisis, so I either stay, or we take her in with the President," Andy said, prepared to do battle for his patient. This wasn't his first time facing down a patient's spouse.

Fred flicked his gaze to Felith, so pale and still laying there upon the bed. He didn't need a doctor to tell she was in poor shape. She had died. How much worse could she get? "We have a couch you may sleep upon," he stated, still he felt the fear inside him, panic at the thought of losing Fel. Fred didn't know if he could survive losing her to death, or science.

News came back through security that the

President was doing very well, and would be tending to the country. In other words, Fred thought, he was gone from their life. Typical, real typical. And Fred's mother would be at her husband's side putting on the airs of the rich and famous people. Had they given even one thought to Fel, who lay in the bedroom once again in some coma like state? Fred doubted they had, but he was taking a page from Felith's book, and dismissing those who didn't care from his mind. This Andy guy, however, now he might be a threat to Fel. Why was he staying? What did he want?

Andy watched the girl Emily making up the sofa bed for him. He had taken an immediate liking for the girl. She was very quiet, in fact he hadn't heard her say a word during the evening meal, or afterward. Dinner, now that had been an experience. The family group was like a well oiled machine, each with their chore to do, each seeming to do it with no need of prodding. Such well behaved children. And the teens, who didn't have at least one rebellious teen in the family. But these kids…. He had never seen a family work together the way this bunch did. Andy saw Emily glance sideways at him, maybe she liked him too. "Are you worried about your sister?" he asked, thinking that it was up to him to start a conversation. Emily nodded. "I'm willing to stay for a few days and make certain she knows how to monitor and treat her low blood sugar. Would you like that?"

Emily looked at the tall skinny man. Was he stupid? Did he think for one moment Felith didn't know that healing someone so near death wasn't likely to kill her? She pulled out her tablet and wrote on it, then handed it to him.

A puzzled look upon his face, Andy took the tablet from Emily and read the two words written there, "She knows." A mute? Emily was mute? But how? What was the cause? A million questions raced through Andy's mind, none of them did he ask. "So this has happened before? I see, and Felith knows how to prevent it. Well it wouldn't hurt to go over things with her again. I may have some new ideas for her to try out since she was last to the doctor with her condition. At any rate I would not feel right leaving until I know she is stable again," he said. And this girl, this mute girl with the most amazing eyes just looked at him as if he didn't have a clue. How strange was that? He watched as she scribbled again on her tablet and handed the note to him, "You know nothing. Please don't hurt her." He looked back up, ready to give a pledge not to harm anyone, but Emily was gone. There was nothing left to do but get some rest.

Twice during the night Andy woke up and went to check on his patient. Each time Fred was there keeping a watch over Felith. Andy would prick Felith's finger, checking her blood sugar levels, and adjusted her IV drip each time. Felith lay unmoved never seeming aware of anything going on around her. Andy worried if he had done right by not taking her to the hospital. At the time it had seemed like a sugar low, but usually the person affected came back rapidly once the blood sugar levels came up. This, this was something else, something he hadn't experienced during his time in medical training. Near dawn, Andy finally fell into a deep sleep.

The quiet bustle jogged Andy's consciousness first, then someone tapping his shoulder brought him fully awake. For a moment he thought he was back doing endless shifts with little to no sleep. That is, until he opened one eye and saw the little girl standing by him with her arms crossed and a scowl upon her face. "You are going to make us late for breakfast," she stated in a no nonsense manner. He faked a yawn to keep from laughing at her as he sat up. It all came back to him, the frantic call that the President and another person needed immediate medical help. He remembered the rush, as the medical team assigned to the President gathered and were hurried to the chopper. He was brought as the extra, for the other person in need of attention. He couldn't be so lucky as to be assigned to the President himself, nope not him. That was the story of his life. Not that Andy was upset. The young woman was a patient and needed his help, that was all that counted. It was just that they always seemed to over look him when it came to the famous people.

Middy began to tap her foot, clearly this man was slow witted. "You are making us late, do you need help getting up?" she asked, remembering to be polite, well as polite as she could be to someone keeping her from breakfast. "My mother needs to eat you know. It is import-ant."

"She is up?" Andy asked, as he scrambled to his feet.

One of Middy's eyebrows shot up, the other scowling down. Her mouth scrunched to the side. "You might put on some pants, cause we don't go to breakfast like that," she said, then ran off towards the dining room.

Looking down Andy realized he was just in his underwear, having undressed for sleeping as he hadn't brought a change of clothing, and figured what he slept in wasn't a look he needed to show off around the President's family. Rubbing his forehead wondering what the little girl had thought of his undressed state, Andy scrambled into his clothes. After visiting the bathroom he went to see his patient only to find the room empty. He blinked, not use to patients just leaving without him checking them out first. Where the hell was his patient?

It was in the dining room that he found her. She was looking so pale and weak, yet doggedly pouring milk into glasses around the dining table. There were several others setting the table for breakfast. Andy wondered why they didn't make Felith sit down, then he noticed the worried sidelong looks that were being taken of Felith. Clearly they were worried about Felith, yet something held them in restraint from making her sit down and rest. By then the table was set and Middy was again at his side. She looked him up and down, as if making sure he had dressed, then motioned to a seat in the middle of the table. Andy watched with interest as the two older children positioned themselves to either side of Felith. The President's son sat directly across from her. Clearly she was the head of the table, which was interesting as there were two people in the room more mature and experienced than this young woman. Each of the others settled into what Andy assumed were their regular seats. The hierarchy was apparent to a good observer, Felith and the President's son at the top, next the two adults, then everyone else in various steps down the tier. Andy glanced up at Felith. "I will need to give you an examination after breakfast and test your blood before you eat," he said. Oddly, everyone in the room seemed to still as if waiting for something to happen.

It was Fred who broke the sudden silence. "There is one important rule in this house you must abide by, you never touch Felith, not without asking Sidney or myself first."

Andy looked around the table and saw the truth of Fred's words in the other's eyes. How odd. He had touched her last night. But nobody was saying he is just joking, or don't be a bully, or anything to suggest Fred wasn't deadly serious about this no touching. Okay, he'd make Fred explain that later, right now he wanted his patient to eat, Middy was right she needed to eat, but he wanted to check her blood sugar levels. "I need to monitor her blood sugar levels so we can determine how to treat her to prevent future episodes. If I check her now before we eat then for a couple times over the next two hours, that will give me and idea of what is going on. May I check her? It is a simple prick of the finger and a bit of blood put on a test strip," Andy argued.

Felith spoke up. "I can do the test myself. You may watch," she said. The wonder of it was that her words seemed to be the final decision on the argument. So Andy placed the test kit on the table and explained which end of the test strip to put into the machine and where to prick her finger, and place the blood on the end of the strip. He was slightly amused to see everyone flinch when Felith pricked her finger. Then it was done and she showed to be in the middle of normal with her blood sugar level.

Breakfast was so different from what Andy was use to having. The cup of coffee and microwave breakfast sandwich he usually managed couldn't begin to compare to the feast set out on the table. Hot biscuits with gravy, a platter of hotcakes, eggs, milk, and fruit filled the middle of the table. Andy could barely contain the growing hunger that such a sight brought out in him. He felt a bit self conscious as he heaped food upon his plate, that is until he saw Felith's plate. Her entire plate was loaded down with some of everything on the table, and just when Andy thought the plate couldn't hold anything more, Fred leaned over the table to place more eggs on Felith's plate. Felith looked at Fred and began to eat. Andy watched in fascination as Felith shoveled food into her mouth. Mentally he gave a shake of his head and started eating.

Several hours later Andy studied the results of the blood test he had run on Felith. They didn't make sense. There should have been a rise in her blood sugar. Admittedly the amount of the rise would depend on how much insulin she put out after a meal. But these tests looked more as if the food she had eaten had been sucked into a black hole with only a nominal amount being released into her blood. He'd have to send the results off to a specialist. This family warranted study, their social interaction, the influence this one young person held over the others was just not something you saw every day. Then there was Emily, a mute, how fascinating.

Pulling out his phone Andy punched one number and listened to the phone on the other end ringing. This might mean the end of his blooming career, but he had to know more. The drive was in him to learn what was happening in this family. "I'll be staying here for now, sir. I think it is called for." He heard the 'Very well' at the other end of the line and the call ended. How odd, not one word of disagreement, what did that mean? Was he already fired and blacklisted from any work with the government? He rubbed his face feeling weary, and confused, but mostly he burned with curiosity. He had a puzzle to solve.

A knock on the door brought Andy from his musings. He walked over and opened the door to find Fred about to knock again. "Come in. Are you going to explain the no touching to me now?" he asked Fred.

Fred closed his eyes briefly, as if he had been dreading this moment, but he nodded and entered to sit down in one of the chairs in the room where Andy had been going over the result of the blood test on Felith. He nodded to the test results. "I take it you found nothing unusual about Felith's blood."

It was a statement and not a question. Andy nodded, then sat down across from Fred and waited for him to explain.

Fred sighed, then began to speak, "The reason you didn't find anything is because Felith only goes low when she uses her healing power." He held up his hand to stop any protest Andy might think to raise. "Let me finish. Felith is a natural healer. She heals by touch, not as a faith healer, which is where everyone's mind usually shoots to when they think of a healer, other than a medical doctor. To understand you need to know how she was raised. Felith is an extremely intelligent person. She was kept locked up inside a house, for the most part in a darkened cellar, taken out only when the monster who held her wanted to torture her. She taught herself how to read. And in the books she read there were Magi who did wonderful things. They could transport from one place to another, use magic to heal, and so on. She didn't have anyone to tell her these were just stories. In her mind, they were written about real people. One day, after she had been rescued and brought to Haven, she saw Robert do some magic tricks for the younger children. You know the sort, pull flowers out of your sleeve, make it appear you magically made a rope grow back together, things like that. It was the rope trick which made her wonder if even she could heal, heal people. So she practiced, healing a bird, then Rags, then me. But, she pays a price for each heal. You see in order to heal she has to send her own strength to the other person. It saps her, draining her system to the point of even death. She died the first time curing a guy who was having seizures so bad that his temperature was spiking so high he was dying. I..." Fred's voice cracked, "did CPR. I've found that if she eats beforehand it helps her. It is only if she is saving someone from death that takes her to the edge. Father's was that sort. I'm afraid that even a casual touch when she is so drained will do her harm. I won't risk it. I won't have you or anyone endangering her more than she does on her own. If you can't live with this rule then I'm going to ask you to leave. Understand?"

Andy could see Fred was dead serious, it was just so hard to believe such a wild tale. He needed to see this so call healing. There was no way he was going to leave until he understood what was going on. Healing, or just hysterical fainting after believing that she healed. Whatever it was, he was going to find out. He nodded to Fred. "Agreed," he said. "But when she is well, not in recovery, will it be okay if I examine her? And I'd like to witness her healing someone, so as to maybe find a way she can heal without such a strain on her system," he almost held his breath as he waited for Fred to reply. Relief filled him as Fred nodded consent, but held up a hand saying, "Just get approval first." With that, Fred stood and left the room.

The second day of observation Andy watched closely at breakfast as the meal was placed upon the table. The same pattern followed with the exception that Felith contributed a great deal more, placing the larger portion of the workload on herself. It was clear she was still feeling the affects of her illness, yet her strength, what little, which had returned, was focused on taking the workload upon herself. She wasn't selfish about it, just saw to it that Julian didn't have to carry anything other than the napkins, relieving Emily from any activity so she could sit down after cooking the food and enjoy the meal. He realized everything she did was in consideration of the others.

The rest of the family, except for Julian, stayed

out of her way and let her do whatever she wanted. Concern etched some of their faces, with admiration shining in Middy's eye, love on Fred's face mixed with what appeared to be a constant anger. Julian appeared to be in a bad mood. She sniped at Eric telling him to get out of her way. This brought an immediate reaction from Middy who placed herself in front of Eric, arms crossed as if to dare Julian to say more to him. To Andy's surprise Julian backed off seeming to calm down. How interesting.

After the meal Felith handed out assignments again, and to Andy's shock she gave him the task of helping Eric with the laundry. He carefully nodded as if this happened to him everyday. Inside he was in a panic. He had never done laundry in his life. Little Eric took over, motioning Andy to follow him. They went from room to room taking the laundry baskets set just to the side of each room's door. That part was easy, it was the washing bit that had Andy in a panic. In his mind, he kept remembering a pink lab coat he had had to wear in one of his classes because… as the class professor stated as he held up a bright pink lab coat, "This is what happens when you wash clothing altogether. Now can anyone tell me exactly what happened?" Half the class had raised their hands, Andy was one of the people who had not. His half of the class had to wear those pink lab coats all week as a sign of their ignorance. So Andy had learned how the dyes could bleed when placed in water. The colors were more set in todays age, but that was not an excuse for not understanding what could happen in his professor's eyes.

The little boy stood in front of Andy, hands on

his hips very much an imitation of the girl Middy. "You have to sort the clothes. All the real dark ones go here, the reddish ones here and the white ones here," he paused in his lecture to Andy. "You don't want Middy to get mad at you for doing it wrong," Eric finally stated, as if he didn't want to speak poorly of Middy. Andy nodded as the two of them began to sort the clothes. Once a pile had quite a few clothes in it, Eric stopped and started to put that pile into the washing machine. The little boy began to lift the detergent bottle up to pour some in a measuring cup. It was clear the bottle was too heavy for the boy, but he surprised Andy by setting the bottle on the edge of a short stool then tipping it just enough to let some pour into the cup. Andy smiled wondering if he would have thought of doing that when at that age. Soon a load was slushing away in the washing machine, and all the other clothes were sorted. Eric turned to Andy then and almost cracked a smile. "Now we can have some free time. I like to go help Middy feed Billy. You want to come?" Andy smiled and nodded. The day was going well.

Chapter Sixteen

PATHS WE TAKE

Eric woke with a sense of urgency, something was wrong. He closed his eyes for a moment, trying to shut any bad that may be going on out of his mind, only... instead of dark peace, an image of Billy swam in his mind. Billy's leg was caught in some wire, the goat was bleating, calling for help. Eric scrambled out of bed and ran fast as he could to his mother. Like a rocket he zoomed into the room his father and mother slept in and dove on the bed. "Billy, you have to help Billy," he cried shaking his mother.

Felith woke instantly, her own childhood had made her stay vigilant when sleeping. Seeing Eric's face in front of her kept her calm. No reason to fight off an attacker, and her instincts kicked in, someone was in trouble. She didn't question how Eric knew Billy needed help, just nodded and slipped on her shoes. As always she was dressed in her jeans with the nightgown over it, so there was no need to put on clothing. Taking Eric by the hand, she hurried out of the room. Behind her Fred got up and followed. Another shadow slipped into step with the trio, Dog.

Dew soon had their feet and clothing feeling damp against the skin, but they hadn't gone far before the sound of Billy bleating in panic reached their ears. Eric ran ahead with Fred hot on his heels. There was no way he was going to let Eric face an injured goat alone. Felith hurried after the pair, while Dog bound ahead of them all. Everyone came to a stop at the sight of Billy thrashing about kicking wildly, trying to leap away from the wire wrapped tightly around one of her forelegs. Blood was running down Billy's leg where the wire had cut the skin and the flesh beneath with all the jumping round Billy was doing. The little goat was making matters worse in her panic to get away from the thing painfully holding her leg.

"Go back to the house, Eric, a pair of wire-cutters will be in a tool box inside the hall closet. Bring those as fast as you can," Fred said, wanting to get Eric away and knowing that the next few minutes would be very painful for the little goat. As Eric dashed off, Fred looked at Fel. She nodded and reached out a hand to touch Billy.

The little goat knocked her hand causing pain to shoot up her arm. Felith held her hand steady letting the goats panic seep into herself, feeling the pain. She mentally caressed away the panic trying to ease the pain the goat was feeling. It was difficult as she couldn't heal Billy until the wire was removed. Billy stopped jumping though and stood, shaking, panting hard. Her eyes wide with fear.

Andy heard someone making a lot of noise in the hallway. Then he heard a sob, that was enough to shake him fully awake. Getting up he slipped on some pants and went to see who was in distress. Little Eric was sobbing while digging through a tool box. "Eric, what's wrong?" Eric looked up at him, his face streaked with tear tracks. Something about Billy and wire cutters came out of the boy in gasps. At least, that is what Andy thought the boy said. "Step back let me find them," Andy said. It didn't take long before Andy had the wire cutters in hand, and Eric was tugging at his hand urging Andy to run all out across the yard.

Eric skidded to a stop beside his father. It was then that Andy saw the frightened goat with Felith's hand on Billy's head. It was the goats leg, however, that had Andy slipping into doctor mode. The leg was a mess, the muscles so mangled by some sort of wire tangled around her leg that Andy knew the leg would have to be amputated, or the the goat put down. "I'll help hold her down," Andy said to Fred handing him the wire cutters.

Fred shook his head and motioned Andy to stand back. "Don't touch Fel," he said in that soft deadly way he had, and Andy took a step back in reaction. Fred knelt down in a pool of goat blood, and began to cut Billy loose. The little goat stood still as a statue, her eyes full of fear, as Fred snipped the wire away. Then Fred felt Felith kneel down beside him. He glance over his shoulder to be certain Andy was staying his distance and prepared to catch his wife once she was done doing what she could for Billy. "Don't you dare kill yourself doing this,

dearest. I need you, the children need you. Stop
once the worst is done. Andy will treat the rest.
Listen to me, my love, listen and remember to stop,"
he kept on talking, telling her how much they needed
her, as he watch the bleeding stop and the muscles
start repairing on the goat's damaged leg. He so
seldom allowed himself to actually watch the healing
taking place. Always his eyes had been on Felith.
This time he was watching, ready to pull Felith away
the moment he sensed the worst of the damage was
repaired. He put a hand on her back and willed
his strength into her to give her aid healing. For a
moment he though he could feel some of his strength
ebbing away, then Felith pulled back and fainted.
Fred caught Fel, cradling her to him. "Eric carry the
cutters. Andy you have to carry Billy, take her to
the kitchen. I have to see to Fel." Having issued the
orders Fred stood, Felith in his arms. He kissed her
forehead, saying in a mumbled whisper, "You did
good, darling."

Looking stricken, Andy approached the
injured goat. He didn't know if it would go nuts
when he tried to carry it or not. More than that he
didn't know if he could believe his own eyes. What
had he seen tonight? Before he could sort out what
he had seen happen, Eric was pushing in front of
him. "No, let me," Andy said, fearing the goat would
harm the child. Bracing himself with a deep breath,
he reached both arms under the goat's belly and
picked it up. Eric dashing in front of him pointing
out where to walk to Andy as he carried a very still
goat back to the house and into the kitchen. All the
while Andy's mind was circling around to and from

what he had witnessed Felith do. No way, he had seen it actually happening. Just no way it was true, still…. Around and round.

Once in the kitchen Andy placed the goat upon the table. The goat suddenly came to herself and started trying to jump off the table.

Eric was immediately at Billy's head. "No, Billy, be still. Dr. Andy will help. Please, Billy, please," Eric sobbed into the goat's neck. The amazing thing was it seemed to work. The little goat stood, her head down as if giving up. Andy didn't stop to wonder at the change in the goat. For all he knew it could be shock, and that meant he needed to clean and dress the wound as quickly as possible, then warm the goat and let it relax so it could heal. As he cleaned the leg he marveled at signs of the skin pulling and growing back together. It was as if time had sped forward and the tissue had healed naturally, only better. He couldn't spare time to think on the implications of what this meant. He had a patient, make that patients, to tend. "Okay, Eric, lets pin a couple of those big bath towels around Billy. Then we need to keep him somewhere warm and quiet."

Once Billy was settled, Andy went to see about his other patient. The girl had passed out, Andy wanted to get a blood sample and make certain she was out of danger. From what he had learned during his stay at the small farm, Fred was quite capable of taking care of his wife. It was the mystery of it all that intrigued Andy. He wanted to know the why and how behind this strange girl being able to seemingly heal others. Once he learned those things perhaps others could learn how to do the same, to heal the critically ill, to save those who didn't stand a chance of being saved. Take tonight, that little goat would have lost a leg, if not its life. If, and it was a big IF, that ability could be learned, could be spread to every doctor on earth… the possibilities were mind boggling. Then he saw them, Fred and Felith. Fred was curled around Felith holding her, and both were sleeping soundly. Fred looked as pale and drawn as the the girl, and Andy thought the boy had too large a burden on himself with a wife like Felith. It wasn't until he started to turn away that he remembered the way Fred had pressed his hands upon Felith, as if, as if connecting to her, helping her in some way. Was that possible? Was Fred like a battery giving Felith a charge to help her heal? Now that was an interesting thought. One thing was certain, there was no way he could leave this family now.

Middy was worried about her brother Eric. Ever since the goat, Billy, had been hurt Eric had been quieter than usual, which was saying a lot since Eric seldom spoke. The day after Billy's accident, Eric spent most of his time caring for the little goat, making sure she had fresh water and food. At breakfast he had cast wary glances at mother and father, as if worried they would think less of him, or the possibility it occurred to Middy that he was keeping something from their parents. If that was the case, it was bad. Mother did not like for people to lie to her. So it was that Middy became determine to find out what was wrong with Eric.

For the hundredth time Eric brushed Billy's

coat. The little goat's coat was already shining, but it was something that kept Eric's hands occupied as his mind mulled over the question of should he tell his mother and father that he hadn't heard Billy bleating last night when she was hurt. The problem was he wasn't certain that he hadn't heard the cries of Billy for help. Had that been why he thought he was dreaming of Billy caught in the wire, or had he really had a dream where he saw Billy in need of help? Middy's head peeped around the door of the make-shift stall Billy being kept in to recover, breaking Eric from his musing. He knew that look on Middy's face. She was up to some mischief. She crooked a finger at him, and Eric shook his head. He wasn't in the mood for whatever Middy had planned. Reluctantly he gave in. More because Middy was a force that you didn't want to fool around with than anything else.

With a mischievous glint in her eyes, Middy led Eric to a corner of the house. Just beyond was a tree which spread its arms out, and shaded the sitting area beneath it. There on a lounge chair sat Julian with one of her fashion magazines on her ample lap. The twins were nearing full term thanks to mother constantly doing little heals on Julian. Middy crouched down and motioned Eric to do the same. She stared at Julian as the woman slowly turned a page of the magazine. Then, Middy flicked her finger, just a slight flick of the very tip of her finger, towards Julian. The pages of the magazine fluttered in a breeze losing Julian's place. Brushing a curl that dared to stray across her face back into place, Julian found the page she had been looking at again. Once more Middy flicked the tip of her finger, gently this time, forward then backward. One page flipped in one direction then back again. She flicked her finger tip again and again until Julian slammed the magazine closed, and struggled to her feet. Suddenly she gripped her stomach as if in pain. Middy's reaction was immediate. The little girl looked stricken, turning she started to run into the house to fetch her mother, before she remembered her mother was still recovering from healing Billy.

Eric was just as upset as Middy, perhaps more so as he had a kind heart and never wanted anyone or anything to be harmed. He looked at Middy then marched out to where Julian was standing as if she were glued to the spot she stood. "Lean on me, I'll get you into the house. Just put your weight on my shoulder, Miss Julian," he said in a quivering voice. Middy was suddenly on the other side of Julian offering her own shoulder for Julian to lean on. Between them they moved in slow start and stop motions into the house, with Julian stopping to gasp in pain ever few steps.

The moment they entered the house a full bellow came from Julian. "Felith, I need you!" Beside Julian, with her face a mask of concentration, Middy refused to cry. She felt so guilty for having caused Julian to come to harm. If nothing else she had learned from her mother that other people are allowed to live their lives, no matter how grumpy and irritable they may be. You didn't have to be part of their life. The choice was up to you. Become part of that irritation, or dismiss them and be the person you wanted yourself to become. She still remembered her mother's words to Julian when Julian had sworn she wanted to be part of the group again. "It is a matter of trust," she, Middy, had to stop thinking up ways to torment Julian and get on with her own life. She had to prove to, if nobody else herself, that she deserved being trusted. Her feeling of guilt tripled when her father and mother came out of their bedroom looking bleary-eyed and far from rested. She had done that, caused them to have to get up and deal with Julian when her mother needed the rest to recover from healing Billy. She had to do better, be better. She was the protector, the one who stood between evil and her family. There could be no room in her life for her own failings.

Dread filled Fred when he saw Julian. Her face was pale, fear apparent upon it. Not now, he thought. Not while Fel is still weak. Yet it was clear Julian was in labor. Even without Felith going into healer mode he knew, and it felt as if the whole thing was out of his control. How could he protect his wife and still let her do what she must do? It was the expressions on Eric and Middy's faces that gave him the strength needed to take charge of yet another crisis. They looked so scared. "Lets get you to the sofa, Julian. Eric, you go get Andy. Middy, go find Sidney and Rags. Fel, diagnose only for now. This is a natural thing, Julian, your babies are ready to be born. Your job is to bring them into the world so they can finally see their mother, and you can hold them. So quit acting like a child and be the woman that you are." With a sense of satisfaction he watched each person go about the tasks he had assigned, not that he had any idea of what to do. Julian sucked in a breath and looked at Felith as if her life depended on her. Felith, paler the usual, which worried Fred to no end, was doing her thing. Eric and Middy had already raced off to their assigned task. Finally Fred could breath. He was back in control.

It was hard doing what Fred told her to do, still Felith held off the urge to take away Julian's pain. She reached the babies and knew they were still healthy. There was little she could do for them. She could stop the labor, shore up what was needed to stop the babies from coming, but as Fred had said, this was a natural occurrence. All the medical data she had gone through said that babies needed to be born. Unable to continue, knowing that Julian was in pain, Fel muted some of that pain. Julian immediately relaxed. "Fel," Fred warned beside her, causing her to nod her head to let him know she understood. "The babies are okay," she assured Julian noting the relief on Julian's face at her words. Then Andy was there, and Felith moved aside to allow him to examine Julian. She watched what he was doing, attempting to understand what it was he might be understanding that she couldn't. When she had realized the mistake she had made during healing Rags, Felith knew, that just healing wasn't enough, it had to be done right. One of her greatest worries now was healing someone the wrong way. She could have stopped the epidemic if only she had understood about making the bodies defenses natural.

"Eric, go get your mother some food, anything that is sweet, or bacon and eggs, just hurry and get it," Fred told the boy next to him. He had no idea if

Fel would be needed again to help Julian. Now was the time to shore up her energy. Soon Eric returned with Emily in tow. Each carried a tray, Emily's laden heavy with food and glasses of milk, Eric's held just a single plate of food. "For you, Daddy. Emily has Mom's," the boy said. Yes, he needed to eat too so if the time came he could give Felith some of his strength. He smiled at Eric to let him know what a good job he had done. Then pulled the reluctant Felith over to a place to sit and eat. Never once did her eyes leave Julian and Andy as she stuffed her food in her mouth, not even noticing what she was eating. Fred for his part watched Fel as he ate, making certain she continued to eat.

Stuffing the last bit of food into her mouth Fel stood while still chewing. Julian was screaming at Andy, actually cursing him, evere time she had a contraction. "Give me something, you useless bit of scum! Now!" She had Robert's hand in a death grip and his face was so pale Felith was certain he was going to pass out at any moment.

Not hesitating for even the amount of time it took her to swallow that last bite of food, Fel was at Julian's side. She looked to Andy. "What do you want me to do to help," she asked.

It was Julian who made the decision for all of them, as she heard Fel's question. Julian reached out and grabbed Felith's hand holding on as if her life depended upon it. "Take the damn pain away, now, do it now," she moaned as another contraction hit her.

Felith sought out the pain and started absorbing it, standing stead-fast with Julian crushing her hand. She took away the pain being careful not to stop the contractions needed for birthing the babies. She could take the pain. It crashed into her over and over. Still she stood and let it. As a tiny child she had learned not to cry, not to let on that the monster could cause her pain. No tears, no out cries, nothing to let him see and have satisfaction. Even when he had broken her other arm with the first one still in a cast she hadn't cried. So she stood and took the pain Julian couldn't bare. Somewhere in her awareness she felt a warm touch on her shoulder as Fred stepped up and sent supportive energy to her, and a smile almost came to her face.

Through the deliveries of the twins the four of them helped Julian. Andy delivered the babies, Robert soothed his wife, while Fel took away the pain with Fred's help. Night was upon them by the time Julian was asleep and the babies were tucked away warm and safe. Fred was so relieved the whole thing had gone so well that he couldn't help kissing Felith. He was careful not to prolong it and force her into going off in her mind. Still the joy filled him at what they had accomplished, all of them.

It wasn't until the middle of dinner that Fred noticed something was bothering Eric. The little boy was fidgeting more than usual and a fear was in his eyes which Fred hadn't seen since they had all become a family.

Eric didn't know what to do. Everyone was so happy with the babies having been born, so how was he going to tell them the bad man was coming?

In the end, Eric turned to Middy for advice.

He hadn't intended to talk with her about the vision he had while the twins were being born, but then again, he hadn't figured on Middy noticing he was hiding something. Dinner clean up was finishing when Middy hopped down off the step stool she used when helping in the kitchen to announce that she was going to help Eric with Billy. It was enough to make Eric feel guilty for not having thought about the little goat's needs, with the vision hanging so darkly over his head. He stuffed his pockets with treats for Billy before following Middy outside.

That crease was between Middy's eyes, Eric thought, and her eyebrows were peaked. She was either after something, or up to mischief. Either one he didn't want any part of being involved. "I'm not going to do any more bad stuff, Mids. Whatever you want me to do, I'm not," Eric said before she could spring whatever she was up to on him.

For a moment Middy's mind went blank wondering what Eric was talking about. He wasn't getting off that easy, confusing her like that, no sir. She was getting to the bottom of what was bothering her brother. "Just tell me what is wrong with you. I'm not letting you out of here until you tell me, so tell me," she demanded, then felt a twinge of guilt as the righteous color that was flushing Eric's face drained to leave him pale and trembling. He was so weak. "Just tell me. You know I'm going to help. Tell me," Middy begged in one last attempt to get out of Eric what was bothering him. Finally Eric nodded and sank down onto the floor near Billy. Biting her lip Middy sat beside him, and waited for her brother to gather his courage and talk to her. When tears started rolling down Eric's cheek Middy wanted to be anywhere but there, still she had started this and their mother would never have turned away from anyone feeling the pain that Eric seemed to be feeling. Slowly Middy took Eric's hand, leaned her head against his, and waited.

His voice quivering Eric explained as best he could what was wrong. "I've had these things come into my head, Mids. I don't know what to do. When Billy was hurt, I didn't hear her crying, like they said I did. It was one of the things coming into my head. I saw Billy, in my head, Middy, really saw her. It scared me so much," Eric hiccuped before going on. "Then the babies were born and they are all happy, really happy. I can't tell them, Mids, I can't tell them the bad man is coming," he sobbed burying his face into Middy's shoulder.

The bad man was coming, that was all Middy had to hear to spring into action. She was the self-appointed protector of the family. It was up to her to keep Eric safe, to keep them all safe. "We won't tell them tonight. Do you still have the thing grandpa's men gave you?" she asked Eric. He nodded, wiping his face with the back of his hand. "They said push the button if we needed them. We need them, right?" Middy waited for Eric to nod at her. "Then push it now."

"But they will call to see what is wrong, Mids," Eric said, his voice full of worry.

Middy nodded. "I'm going to answer the phone, don't worry, Eric, this will work, I promise. Now wash your face, kiss mom and dad good night, then push the button. Okay?"

Reluctantly Eric nodded and went to wash his face. Trouble was that he didn't feel right lying to their parents, and it was lying to not tell them what was going on. Daddy had always been good to him, always known what was right to do, what to say to make him feel better. Mother was, well she was magical sure, but... she just didn't tolerate people being bad. Worse of all he felt he would be letting her and daddy down. Would they still want him?

By the time he reached the living room to say good night to his parents, Eric was certain his parents wouldn't want him anymore if he lied to them. He trembled as he climbed into his mother's lap and kissed her cheek good night. When his father held out his arms for him, Eric broke. Tears rolled down his cheeks as he buried his face into Fred's shoulder. "Talk to me," Fred said, his voice both soothing and commanding.

"The bad man is coming. He wants to hurt mama. He is almost here. Don't hate me, daddy," Eric mumbled between hiccups, certain that this would be the last time he'd be hugged by anyone in the whole world.

"Eric, listen to me. I love you. Nothing you tell me will ever cause me to stop loving you. By warning us of the bad man you are, to us, a hero, son. If anything I love you more," Fred soothed, as a line of concern began to form on his forehead between his eyes. "Go get Middy. We need to tell the others and get ready."

Even though night was falling outside the sun came out for Eric. His doubts were forgotten in the praise given him. "Okay, dad," he said, so thrilled that he could still call Fred dad.

What happened next was an organized chaos. From without the house it seemed that an emergency had occurred, with Julian and her babies. Andy was seen following beside a litter to the van with Julian on it, her babies tucked protectively in Robert's arms. Emily and Rosemary hurried with little Susan and the kids to the van, while Rags and Sidney directed them all to hurry along. Andy kept checking Julian's pulse looking concerned. As they drove away Felith could be seen clearly upon the porch under the light waving to them. Fred was no where to be seen.

The children remained rebellious even as they were herded into the van. Middy had put her foot down determined to stay and help protect her family. No amount of reasoning with her, telling her that they would have less to worry about with her and Eric safe, swayed her. On the other hand Eric had shown such fear of being separated from Fel and Fred that he had to promise the boy he would come and get him once the bad man was under arrest. The whole idea did not sit well with Middy or Eric. Thus, while strapped into the backward facing trunk-seats, as the seats that folded down in the very back of the van were called by Middy, watching the farmhouse getting smaller and smaller, the two plotted how to get back to their parents. The rest of the passengers in the van whispered among themselves hoping to keep their concerns away from the children.

They had only made it a couple of miles when the twins began to scream in ear hurting screeches. Frantically Julian, Emily and Robert searched the hastily packed bags for the prepared bottles of breast milk pumped for the trip into town. "It has to be in the back. Middy look back there and hand up the small purple bag, please," Rags commanded.

Only Middy was not in a mood to help anyone but herself and Eric in getting back to Fel and Fred. The impish child ducked her head and twisted her body about as if looking everywhere around her for the said bag, all the while she was kicking the bag up farther up under the seat she sat on. "I don't see it, Grandma Rags," she finally called back, clamping a hand to Eric's mouth to keep him from telling on her. She gave a knowing look at Eric as the van pulled to the side of the road, and a car door open and closed. It was Rosemary who came back to search for the missing bag of baby bottles. She jerked the back doors of the van open and rummaged around impatiently. When she spied the bag up under Middy's seat she mumbled something under her breath and yanked the bag out, barely closing the doors back in her rush to get back up front and shut the babies up.

Quickly Middy unsnapped her seat belt, and Eric's belt too. Holding a finger to her lips for quiet she barely opened one side of the double back doors and slid to the ground while tugging on Eric to follow her. Once Eric was out Middy softly closed the back doors and motioned to the ditch along the side of the road they were traveling. Eric was gasping and shaking his head no, even as he tumbled into the ditch along with Middy. Eric's face was so pale that in the moonlight he looked like a ghost to Middy, so she pulled him up against her and whispered into his ear. "We are close enough to walk back home and help mom and dad. Don't be scared." She felt Eric nod against her. They stayed still barely breathing as the van pulled out and headed on down the road.

The night seemed to close in around Eric and Middy as the taillights of the van disappeared into the distance. "I'm scared Mids," Eric admitted. "The bad man has a gun." He knew that had her attention as one eyebrow shot up and her mouth did that sideways scrunching.

"Why didn't you tell mom and dad that?" she said scrambling out of the ditch and walking fast in the direction that would take them back to the farm road home. Eric hurried to catch up to her, afraid of being left alone, afraid of going on. Scared to death that he was going to lose his family... again.

Fred watched through a window as Felith waved bye to the others. He wasn't certain he had done the right thing by allowing her to stay as bait for this monster who had abused and held her captive throughout her childhood. At the time, his father's men had seemed reasonable over the phone, assuring Fred they would be there well before this filthy monster showed up. Felith had agreed, but then of course she would. Now, as he thought about things, the truth was seeping into his mind. If they had taken this threat seriously wouldn't there still be guards on the farm? Certainly the country was still in crisis, but wasn't it always in crisis? When had there been a time in his childhood that one crisis or another hadn't taken up more time than what his father gave to his family? Or believed in his son? Not as other rich father's sons had..., no he wasn't

going there. He couldn't let his thoughts distract
him from protecting Fel. He thought about Eric and
how much courage it had taken for him to tell them
he was having visions. Not for one moment did
he doubt Eric. He wasn't his own father and never
would be. Never would he treat the kids as if they
were stupid or strange.

He saw Fel give a final wave and start back
inside the house, relief of her coming in lifted a
heavy yoke off his neck. Moving carefully so as
not to attract attention as a moving object, he went
to the side of the door and waited. As soon as the
door closed behind Felith he swept her into his
arms. "Remember, you promised not to take any
chances. Say it again, promise me," he whispered
into her ear. She pulled back slightly to look him in
the eyes. Those eyes of hers all seeing, all knowing
eyes, that saw right through him. Did they see how
much he cared about her? He heard her whispered
reply, "I promise." For a moment he thought he
saw butterflies fluttering outside, knowing that
they shouldn't be out in the night. It felt as if
their fluttering wings were inside him. Had she
summoned them from the air? He didn't care, so
long as they were here to keep her safe. He led her to
the sofa where they sat down and began the long wait
for something to happen, for it all to end.

Along the road Middy was walking so fast that
Eric had trouble keeping up. The night was getting
colder and his thin frame began to shiver, only it
wasn't the cold that caused his body to tremble the
way it was shaking. He threw up his hands as if

warding off a threat just managing a weak, "Wait!", before falling to his knees. It was clearer this time, the man, the gun, him shooting at Eric's mother, daddy, blood, a sound like an explosion, then it all went black and he was there on the road crouching, crying out. "Don't hurt my mother, don't kill my daddy! No!"

Middy turned to see what was holding Eric up, didn't he know they had to hurry? When she saw Eric on his knees with his arms up in a defensive manner she started to rush back to defend him from whatever was hurting him, only he sprang up in the next blink of an eye and started running towards her, then passed her and kept on running.

Eric ran past Middy, not really even seeing her. He was in a panic mode that over took him when danger threatened, and he fled to safety. Except this time he wasn't running away from danger. He was running all out towards it. He had to save them, save his family, save his mother and father. Middy yelling "Wait!" behind him hadn't registered on his mind. He had one thought, get to mom and dad.

With a look of determination Middy took off after Eric. She was not one to be ignored. It took a bit of effort before she was able to catch Eric. He was very fast when he was in a panic. She didn't try to stop him, instead she asked him, "What did you see?"

It took two more tries before Middy was able to penetrate the mist of panic surrounding Eric. He slowed, but only a fraction, making it easier for Middy to keep pace with him. His eyes blinked as if he was waking up from a nap. "He shot at mother and daddy jumped in front of her. They were on the

floor and there was blood. The world blew up and
I couldn't see anything more," Eric gasped in a huge
breath picking up speed, his thin legs pushing him
forward towards all that blood.

The idea was to continue the day as if they
didn't know the monster was coming. Somewhere,
out there, the men who were to protect her were set
up and watching all approaches to the farm. Only,
Felith didn't feel as if anyone was watching, except
Fred. He was watching, and getting bossy, telling
her where and what to do, instructing her on staying
only in certain areas so he could see her at all times.
She had come to realize this was hard on him too.
He didn't feel secure in having to stay out of sight.
There had been little they could do once darkness
fell. The animals had all been given food, and they
had taken their meal out of sight of the windows in
the farmhouse, so Fred wouldn't be seen. It had been
almost two hours since the rest of the family had left
for safety, and already it seemed an eternity.

Out on the road, Middy and Eric crouched
in the ditch just before the turn off onto the road
leading to the farmhouse. An old truck skidded
around the turn-off, only to slowed down and turn
off the headlights, then crept up the road and coasted
to a stop a short distance before reaching the farm
yard. "It's the monster, Mids. He is here," Eric
whispered into Middy's ear. She looked at Eric and
nodded once, as if they had decided on something,
what that was Eric didn't know. Still, he followed
Middy as she started sneaking along the road to the
farmhouse. The quiet and darkness was eerie. Every

whisper of the grass, the rattle of a stone beneath the foot sent a chill up Eric's spine. He ran until he was up with Middy and grabbed her hand holding on as if for dear life. The things in his mind started hitting him in quick flashes. The gun going off, the world seeming to explode, dog crawling across the floor, dad and mom on the floor covered in blood. He stumbled blindly, letting Middy pull him along the road, all the while the flashes exploding in his head over and over.

Within the house Felith sat before the computer trying to concentrate on a biological book she had found online. Fred had moved the computer so that she could barely be seen sitting there from outside. He kept out of sight of the windows. Fel could tell the waiting was wearing on him heavy. Still, he didn't lose patience, or rant, or do any of the things the monster had done in her young life. He was, she thought, the guy in the books she had read who was steadfast and true, someone she never believed was real.

Dog got up from where he had been laying beneath Fel's feet going to the door with a look of purpose about him. Fel got up and let him out. He hadn't growled so she didn't think it was the monster he was wanting out to get. Still she was uneasy, wanting the whole thing to be over with and done. She felt helpless depending on others to protect her, letting go of the small amount of independence she had acquired. She sat back down listening for the slightest sound which might indicate Dog had returned, but it was quiet and the night seemed to be closing in on her, putting her back in that dark room, alone, with the rats. She shook the feeling off, or tried to, and went back to studying the computer screen.

Eric stumbled falling to his knees, he braced his loose hand on the road and gasped as the bad images flickered through his mind once more. "Middy, how are we going to stop him from killing mom and dad?" he whimpered.

Middy stopped and squatted down to look Eric in the face. "I'll use the wind somehow. If I can make it strong it may blow him away from the farm even. You've seen those torn-aid-does things, what if I try to do one?"

"It might hurt mom and dad, Mids," Eric said, his face showing horror at the thought of hurting them. He saw the defeat in Middy's eyes as she realized that the tornado was a bad idea. "We will think of something, Mids. I know we will," Eric soothed. It was strange to be the one offering comfort, but it felt good to do it. Suddenly Dog appeared out of the night placing his huge body in front of the two children staring ahead into the darkness. His statement was clear, they were not to go on. There would be no budging the huge beast, not unless they could reason with him.

"Dog, mom and dad need you to protect them. The bad man is going to hurt them. Go, help them," Middy said in her best commanding voice. Dog turned his head and licked her face then swung his head back to stare down the night, his ears twitching at ever sound, and there was a deep rumbling in his throat. "Please, Dog, please help them. I'll protect Eric," she reasoned. Still Dog stood fast, his lips drew back into a savage grin as his chest rumbled deep, but quiet threats at the unseen danger ahead.

Eric knew it was up to him, he had discovered that he had a touch of what their mother had in calming Billy when the little goat had been hurt, although he had never tried to use it to influence Billy. Putting his arms around Dog's neck Eric buried his face in Dog's fur. He let the terrifying vision take over thinking them to Dog, showing the horrible scenes covered in blood. Next thing Eric knew he was on his butt. Dog had ripped free of Eric's arms and loped off towards the farmhouse. Relief eased Eric's breathing for a moment, Dog was going to protect them, he had to. Middy grabbed Eric's hand and started off again towards the farm.

Fel shut down the computer. She just couldn't concentrate on the monitor. Her mind kept having flashbacks to that dark house, being tortured and molested, and the monster was coming. The waiting, anticipation, was wearing on her. She was afraid, not for herself, it was Fred and the kids that haunted her with fear of their being touched by a monster. She was nothing, but they were everything to her. "Fred, I want you to call and see where the security team is, then go wait with them," she said softly.

"I won't leave you," Fred said in that soft yet deadly voice. "But I will call and see where security is located." With that he left to go make the call.

There hadn't been a sound to alert anyone, still Felith knew, the monster had arrived. She had always known when he came in, had always felt the evil inside him, known that pain was coming for her. After being free for a couple years she still knew he had arrived. She heard a snick as the window unlatched, as if on its own, and was raised. He came through the window, huffing as he pulled his beer-belly over the window frame. Fel could have run over and knocked him in the head as he was dragging himself into the room, but that was not the person she ever wanted to be, nor did it occur to her that she could do that, hit a monster, a person, over the head. Then, she was staring at the barrel of a gun pointed at her. It was fitting, she thought, she had had a couple years of happy. It was time for the monster to kill her, maybe bury her body in a dark basement where she would be in the dark forever, cold, alone.

"Where is that young fellow? He owes me a bunch of cash for doing you while I was gone. Nobody touches my trash without paying up," the monster said, his lips in something between a snarl and a grin.

"No," Felith said keeping her eyes glued to his so as not to give away where Fred had gone.

"What do you mean you've been delayed?" Fred whispered into the phone in the kitchen. "You were suppose to be here before dark, what is the hold up?" he listened to the woeful story about choppers malfunctioning, cars brought in and eighteen-wheelers over turned on the highway. The whole thing was unreal to Fred. He had only agreed to this plan because security was coming to take down the scum. While the voice on the phone was swearing they were breaking every speed record getting there, Fred heard voices in the house. "Damn you, you won't be in time, he is here!" He spat into the phone. Such terror hit him in the chest that he almost doubled over as his breath swooshed out of his lung. He didn't wait for a reply just dropped the phone and silently worked his way toward the sound of the voices. He heard a sharp 'No' from Felith and stopped, thinking she was telling him to not go into the room.

"No?" the monster snarled. "You don't ever tell me no."

"No, Fred doesn't owe you anything. You don't have any claim or hold over anyone here. You must leave here and never come back," Felith stated in that way of certainty she had. Fred trusted her completely, still he knew she had no sense of self-preservation, and aggravating this guy didn't seem the smart move to him. He prepared himself to rush and beat the guy to death if needed, damning the people who were sworn to protect her for not being there for them.

Middy and Eric had followed the monster and watched him crawl into the house through a window. Eric was shaking so much his teeth chattered, all his nightmares of his family being killed seemed to be smothering him with freezing cold. There would be no warmth left in the world if another family were taken from him. It was then that his teeth stopped chattering, his thin shoulders squared and his head came up. He and Middy would have to save them, he wasn't going to hide in a cabinet again and listen to his family dying. Reaching into his pocket Eric pushed the emergency button on the pager given him to carry at all times by grandfather's men three times. "Middy, make a strong tiny wind," he said, while looking around from something to hit the bad man.

"You have no say in what I do or who owes me what, you are nothing, a speck of dust is worth more than you are, so shut up before I bury you like I did that whore mother," the monster raised his gun and pointed at her heart with it.

Felith squared her shoulders, put on her nothing face, "Yes, I know I am nothing, but my family are worth more than you can even know. They are worth dying for, so go on shoot me, be done with it," she said.

What? How could she say that? Fred's whole body felt as if the bottom of a deep well had just slammed up side his head. His mind seemed to go blank and all he could see, all he knew, was that gun was pointed at Felith and she was willing to die, again. Time slowed and at the same time sped up, it was as if there was no time to think, to plan, and all the time in the world was frozen in this moment. He charged into the room placing himself between that gun, which was going off and the one person who meant life to him, his wife. Just as he mentally braced for the impact of that bullet he heard a swish sound like the wind blowing through the trees, then felt a burning in his arm just as the world seemed to explode and air was sucked out of his lungs. Fred's ears popped when the explosion happened. He kept thinking he hadn't seen a bomb. That this was death, the world blowing up around you, the air leaving your body, and you going to hell where the fire bit you in the arm. And had that been dog he heard growl? He was happy though, he had stopped the bullet. It had to have hit him in his chest. He saved

Fel. He could hear crying, it sounded like the kids. Was he at his funeral and the kids crying over his casket? Something was crushing him, something was on top of him. Had they buried him without a casket, just dumped dirt on him? No, the something had hair that tickled him and smelled like Fel. With that realization his mind came back to him, and he sat up.

She had been ready when the gun went off, prepared to use the one power she thought she had but hadn't explored. Fel wanted him firing the gun so that everyone knew he was a monster, and her plan was working, except she hadn't counted on the speed of the bullet, Fred, or Dog. Horror seized her when Fred jumped in front of her to take the bullet intended for her. If the wind hadn't kicked up through the window and diverted the trajectory of the bullet so it went through the soft tissue of Fred's arm and into her he'd be dead. It was enough to power that other talent. Fear, then anger poured through her body and mind as the world imploded and the monster went far away again. Another shot popped off as the house shook and air rushed into the spot where the monster had stood, Fel was knocked down falling to the side taking Fred with her as Dog took the brunt of the second bullet. She heard her friend yelp in pain and looked around frantically for him. The faithful dog was crawling pulling himself forward to her with one leg. His eyes were those of worry as he pushed and pulled his big body the few feet to Fel and Fred. Fel's hand couldn't quite reach Dog when his head sank to the floor and his eyes closed. She felt the tears rolling down her check and her heart began to ache with terrible pain.

It was then Fred sat up making it possible to touch Dog. Her fingers caressed Dog's huge head as automatically her power reached out hunting for some way to help him. She found the faint flutter of his heart, the place where blood was rushing out making a pool on the floor. It was there she began by making the bleeding cease and the area heal itself rapidly, enough so the blood could go the way it was suppose to go, reaching the heart and circulating through the body. The heart flutter strengthened, but dog didn't wake. Carefully she explored until she found the worst of the damage to Dog. Each spot she started the healing process, being careful not to go to the extreme and empty her body of its own resources, for in the back of her mind she knew Fred needed healing too. These two were a special part of her heart. Even as Felith thought of Fred, she felt his hands go to her shoulders and strength flow from him to her. He was feeding her, giving her of himself, just like he had jumped in front of that bullet. When the worst of Dog's damage was healed and Felith knew he would live she turned to face Fred.

Fred knew that he had to support Felith's efforts to save Dog. He was the battery for her engine. That was how he thought of it, the feeling that flowed when he touched her as she healed. He monitored her while she healed, watched the tissue on Dog for signs she was healing too much and draining herself. When Middy and Eric each entered the room and placed a hand on him. He should have been shocked they were here, but something told him this was a family thing, and it was right they were part of it. They quietly gave their support to him as he fed Felith his strength. All of a sudden Felith whirled around to face him, then hit him, actually hit him. It shocked him so much all he could do was stare at her.

"Why? Why did you jump in front of that bullet? You know the kids need you. We can't both die," Felith said, her face tear-streaked and eyes red.

That too shocked Fred for he had never seen Felith cry but that one single tear, which had dropped on his leg in what seemed like a lifetime ago. All of a sudden he wanted to laugh. She cared. She must care. Why would she cry if she didn't care. His insides went all mushy and he strained not to smile. Instead, he rubbed at the tears on her face with his thumb. "You stupid, stupid girl. Don't you know that I love you? You and the kids are my everything, what keeps me going, gives me life, makes me want to live. I love you," he said, all the tenderness he felt, the love was glowing in his eyes as he watched her for a reaction. She stared at him for a long moment as if he had lost his mind.

Finally Felith found her voice. "I love you too, but you can't love me, I'm nothing, nothing at all," she mumbled.

"Wrong, you are everything that anyone should ever be. Now shut up and fix my arm," he said, the last being more a tease than anything. Still, he saw her eyes go to his arm and the healer was back as she reached a hand out to touch him. How he loved her touch.

The silence which had fallen over them ended as Eric dropped the brick he was holding in one hand. The brick he had intended to hit the bad man with. Middy drooped as if all the energy in her body was drained. Then all hell broke loose as security finally arrive in a crashing of doors and windows with guns drawn, blood in their eyes, ready to shoot whatever threatened Fred and his family. Dog, waking with the loud noise raised his head and growled.

Fred knew he had to take charge immediately before these men ended up killing each other in the madness going on. First, he needed to know what had happened to the man who had shot them. He had seen Felith do things there was no explanation for, as his mind raced over what had happened. He went over those last moments, the feeling of air being sucked out his lungs, the loud boom like a sonic boom. He leaned close to Felith and whispered into her ear. "Where did you send him?"

"That cage in Maryland," she said, as if this was an everyday occurrence.

Of course it was the only place logical to send a monster. Fred should have known, well he would have if he had known Felith could transport someone through space. "Stand down," he said managing to get to his feet and face the team of men surrounding them. "I have a call to make, then you will all be recalled," he said. "Oh, and get a medic here to treat these wounds, and a veterinarian to treat our dog. He took one for us, so make sure he has the best care."

Much later the rest of the family came back home. Dog had been treated, stitched and given antibiotics. Fred and Felith patched up, the kids fed and put to bed. It was confirmed that the monster had appeared in Maryland. From what was said he tried to shoot again when he appeared, but the same team which had wrestled Fred to the floor managed with ease to take the monster down. He was stood on quite a lot, stripped and search, bound in cuffs, at one point gagged. All in all he was having a fine time of it from what Fred heard. His gun was tested and proved to be the same one which had shot Fred, Felith, and Dog. His fingerprints were found on the window where he had entered the house, and in the vehicle he had driven to the farm. The case against him was solid, as was the bit about the murder of Felith's mother. After all, they had found her body and knew he was the last one to see her alive. What it boiled down to was, he was never going to see the light of day again. The only sticky point was, well, how did he get to Maryland? None of that seemed to matter to Felith and Fred. The family was safe, and Dog was recovering. Felith and Fred had found each other, and finally Fred made love to his wife.

Eric crawled into Middy's bed needing the contact, the sense of protection she provided. "You did good, Mids," he whispered as he fell into a sound sleep with no dreams, no visions of bad men. He never heard her whisper back "You too."

The End